I0694840

Beyond the Mountains of Madness

Edited by

Robert M. Price

Celaeno Press
2015

Beyond the Mountains of Madness

All stories copyright their respective authors.
"Beneath the Mountains of Madness" by Peter Rawlik used with permission from *The Weird Company* (Night Shade Books, 2014).
This edition copyright © 2015 Celaeno Press. All rights reserved.

Cover and frontispiece by Steven Gilberts

No part of this publication may be reproduced in whole or in part, or stored in a retrieval system, or transmitted in any form or by any means, electronic, mechanical, photocopying, recording, or otherwise, without written permission from the publisher.

ISBN: 978-4-902075-70-0

Celaeno Press
#403 Tenjin 3-9-10, Chuo-ku, Fukuoka 810-0001 JAPAN
www.celaenopress.com

Contents

INTRODUCTION:

BEYOND THE MOUNTAINS OF MADNESS

ROBERT M. PRICE

H.P. Lovecraft's great novella *At the Mountains of Madness* is much like the gigantic, alien continent where it is set. Like Antarctica, it has long been explored, yet it seems as mysterious—and chilling—as ever. The authors of the stories in this book, all of them developments and explorations of *At the Mountains of Madness*, are like Lake, Pabodie, Gedney, Danforth and the rest, choosing spots in the wide tundra and starting to dig, to see what astonishing discoveries may lie concealed within. One may expect there will be shocking revelations in the offing as these writers explore questions raised by Lovecraft's original. Had any other explorers stumbled upon the protean horrors, the mind-blasting bas reliefs, the terrible truths? And what were the results? Were there elements of the primeval history of the Elder Things that the Miskatonic Expedition missed? After all, they explored only a fraction of the stone tapestries. Did subsequent explorers disregard the warnings of Lovecraft's narrator and enter the frozen danger zone? Did characters only mentioned in the original have their own experiences that went untold in *At the Mountains of Madness*? In fact, having read these tales (I *do* read the stories I choose for anthologies!), I happen to know there are such impending revelations. I am quite proud of the book you are, I assume, about to read. I believe you will be glad you made the investment.

HPL, famously, leaves much to the imagination of the reader, a sterling example of the writer-reader relationship as discussed by Wolfgang Iser, in which the writer leaves gaps, implicitly inviting the reader to collaborate with him as he reads. And yet he details in an almost clinical fashion the appearance of Wilbur Whateley, the Cone Race of Australia, and the Elder Things of Antarctica. Is he contradicting his own method in these cases? Not at all. On the one hand, we may see him as doing with words what Richard Upton Pickman ("pigment") did with paints: conveying alien horrors with prosaic, mundane detail, super-realism, to give the impression we are really seeing such abominations, a terrifying prospect. On the other, it may denote that Wilbur, the Yith cones, and the Star-heads are *not the horrors*. In all three cases, they are contrasted to the *real* horrors, which are invisible and/or formless: the Whateley twin, the invisible whistling octopi, and the shoggoths. Because the concretely described entities can be clearly pictured, "they were men." We are to identify with them on some level before we encounter the things that scared *them*. Wilbur, the Yithites, and the Elder Things were all researchers, even scientists, analogous to Lovecraft's human protagonists and narrators. Analogous to HPL himself, to us. The Wholly Other are the true horrors, and they surpass our understanding and violate our categories. That's what makes them objects of *horror* ("acute spiritual fear") as opposed to *terror*, the urgent fear of a physical threat.

Though this book is a collection of sequels to Lovecraft's *At the Mountains of Madness*, I have, since the first edition, learned (thanks to the detective work of Pete von Scholly) of a story that must have been an important source of HPL's chilly tale, namely John Martin Leahy's "In Amundsen's Tent" (*Weird Tales*, January 1928). We know Lovecraft read it and liked it quite a lot. How could he *not* have been influenced by it? What should a writer do when he or she reads a good story? Perpetuate its DNA (memes) by absorbing and reusing the original author's work while putting his own spin on it? Or mutter to himself, "Damn it! Now I can't use that idea!" Personally, I am very glad that Robert E. Howard liked what he read in Edgar Rice Burroughs, Talbot Mundy, and Robert W. Chambers—and recycled it. I love what Lin Carter did with Burroughs and Howard. Originality isn't always or only a matter of creation *ex nihilo*, starting from scratch. It is also originality to combine elements from previous works in one's own original way. Had Lovecraft made sure *not* to employ influences from Arthur Machen and Harper Williams, I'm pretty sure we wouldn't have "The Dunwich Horror."

So I'm including "In Amundsen's Tent" in this new edition of *Beyond the Mountains of Madness*. It shows that Lovecraft himself was doing what all our other authors here included have done: trying his own hand at a re-do of a prior story of Antarctic horror.

Robert M. Price
January 22, 2015

The City at the Two Magnetic Poles

Glynn Owen Barrass

3rd August 1928, Miskatonic University, Arkham, Mass.

In the small hours of the early morning, Dr Henry Armitage awoke from a phantasm-haunted slumber to the sound of fierce barking, issuing from the university's campus watchdog. The savage and relentless noise increased in pitch until it transformed into a frantic and frightened yelp before a sudden retort of gunfire cut the dog off mid-howl. For some reason, the nullifying silence succeeding the gunshot chilled Armitage to the very pit of his soul, leaving him too frozen with fear to move till the increasing shouts and commotion on campus roused him enough to investigate the events unfolding beyond his window.

After quickly dressing, Armitage rushed through the grounds towards the college buildings and found a large crowd of students, staff, and faculty gathered at the foot of the library steps. As he approached he noted that the burglar alarm had been activated, its klaxon sounding low and erratic through the cool night air. Sensing that an event far greater than a mere break-in had occurred, the chill inside his chest intensified a hundred fold as he veered towards the small group that stood before the open window to the building's side.

To his fear-filled eyes the gaping window resembled the wailing mouth of a doomed soul, as Armitage pushed past the crowd of onlookers to climb in through the open aperture, closely followed by two members of the group, his colleagues Professor Warren Rice and Dr. Francis Morgan. He had spoken to them only recently about his apprehensions regarding the Whateley boy's insistence in examining the *Necronomicon*, the tome Armitage knew was the source of this insidious late night break-in.

The alarm having abated moments earlier, the interior of the library lay dark, deathly silent. Like a man hypnotized by fate, Armitage led the other men across the hall towards the genealogical reading room, which led in turn to the smaller, locked room where the restricted books were stored. He knew what he would find before getting there—had known this would happen since the time he had last witnessed the Whateley boy's crafty, goat-like countenance.

Flicking on the light switch, Armitage gasped in horror. The campus watchdog lay panting on the carpet, thick crimson pumping from the bullet wound to its chest. Beyond it the door to the restricted room stood on bent hinges, its lock smashed asunder. In hindsight, none of this surprised Armitage in the slightest, and, as his companions stepped with caution towards the door, he knew in all certainty which book they would find missing. He understood also what the sinking feeling in his chest finally meant. The end of the world was near.

22ND JANUARY 1931, SOMEWHERE IN THE ANTARCTIC.

A solitary form dragged a wooden sled through the world of snow the Antarctic called summer, a figure barely discernable through the shimmering haze of icy mist. A normal man would have long ago succumbed to the treacherous conditions of this frozen hell, but Wilbur Whateley was no normal man. Nine feet tall, his white-bearded face surrounded by a shock of long white hair, he was a blasphemous Moses in a desert of death. Dressed from head to toe in thick black furs, his meager protection concealed something more alien than human.

Wilbur had survived three months trekking through the wind-blasted landscape—three months since he left Arkham, his seat of power in the new world he had only just started to mold. Twelve "men" accompanied him when he started his journey, the squat but hardy Tcho-Tchos he had brought along as his guards and retinue. Over the intervening months all had succumbed in one way or another; the first being the six Wilbur left behind to ambush the humans dogging his progress. And of course, the black winged things Wilbur summoned to pull the sledges had hungered enormously, as had he. The sledge behind him bore the salted remains of his most trusted servant: Akoua.

No dog could be found to work anywhere near Wilbur, and feeling an equal animosity towards the creatures himself, he'd used the Black Book to conjure something up for the sledge-work. They'd proven fine substitutes until the fresh meat ran out, then one by one they'd flitted away to whatever abyss had spawned them. Not that it mattered now; Wilbur could feel within his warped bones that he was nearing his goal, the fabled city beneath the ice of his darkest dreams.

What brought him to the ends of the Earth on a pilgrimage across miles of sterile white death? It was to locate the ancient horrors that lurked and blasphemed beneath the city of the Elder Things. The human vermin spread across the globe had begun to fight back—the balance was shifting, and Wilbur needed help.

During their three-month travels, the men and women tracking Wilbur Whateley had experienced no problems utilizing dogs to drag their sleds. In fact, the ten-strong group following him bore far more kinship with the little huskies than the half-human abomination they aimed to thwart.

One sole survivor followed Whateley now, William Dyer, ex-Professor of Geology from Miskatonic University in Arkham. Fatigued and painfully mutilated from the frostbite to his hands and feet, Dyer sneered in triumph as he spied Whateley's distant black shape through his cracked and battered binoculars.

Some months earlier Wilbur had awoken to discover that his skin and hair had begun to lighten, the pigmentation now resembling that of his mother, the long-dead albino Lavinia Whateley. Perturbed, he rose and looked outside his window to find the sky burning red and things indescribable stalking Arkham's streets below.

At least normality reigned there.

Arkham, and indeed much of the world, had changed dramatically since Wilbur first employed the Black Book to summon his kin. Leveling the cities of mankind, they had consumed millions of human souls, all in the name of his Father. The first to answer his summons, the nightmare fertility goddess Shub-Niggurath had burst forth from beneath the earth. Every human she touched transformed to one of her Dark Young, adding their ranks to Wilbur's army of cleansing death.

In one single night R'lyeh rose from its watery grave, its black cyclopean towers polluting the air with the stench of eon-old evil. The resultant flood and deluge, swamping the world in biblical proportions, was accompanied by the Great Cthulhu and his spawn filled the skies with unwholesome, tentacled death.

Not everything went in his favor. One night rebels in Dunwich, led by the meddling academics from the University in Arkham, had slaughtered his brother using his own dark magic against him, and now this.

Worried over his unforeseen physiological change, Wilbur consulted his most trusted human advisors, the swamp-bred half-castes and cultists who swore allegiance at his goat-hoofed feet. The foremost of these traitors to humanity informed Wilbur that the mutation towards his mother's side was due to the human rebellion across the globe, and, indeed, even the small pockets of resistance still lurking in America. The more they battled the Old Ones, the more Wilbur's human side would manifest; his heart and soul being inexorably linked to the doomed planet. After contacting his Father, the many-sphered entity known as Yog-Sothoth, Wilbur set about planning a journey to summon more allies to his cause, a journey culminating in his pilgrimage to the dead city deep within the Antarctic.

When word leaked to Arkham's resistance, a small team of rebels volunteered to sabotage Whateley's plans of returning the balance of power to the Old Ones. The group dispatched to track and destroy Wilbur consisted of Dyer, Francis Morgan, once Professor of Medicine and Comparative Anatomy at Miskatonic University, an ex-student named Danforth, and seven other men and women brave enough to fight the horrors consuming the globe. They followed Whateley across land and sea before they finally reached the bleached wasteland of the Antarctic.

The mist of ice crystals dissipating from Wilbur's vision, he witnessed, through eyelids rimed with frost, the black-peaked mountains that signaled an end to his long journey. He smiled an ugly, wolfish grin before whispering from a mouth long disused to human words, "Thank you, Father."

The intrepid team tracking Whateley encountered their first obstacle one month into their trek across the Antarctic when they were ambushed by the six vicious Tcho-Tchos Whateley had left lurking beyond an ice shelf.

Armed with sharp knives and chipped Luger pistols, the attackers made short work of the four fronting the sled team before those at the rear opened fire upon the screaming yellow devils. Burying their own dead with the proper respect, they left the dead and dying Tcho-Tchos to the merciless elements of the Antarctic night.

Wilbur paused two miles away from the jagged black foothills flanking the ancient city of the Elder Things. Quickly stripping himself naked, his massive body shone dazzlingly white even against the backdrop of snow and ice. The pink albino eyes on his face and white-furred thighs squinting in concentration, Wilbur emitted a flood of telepathic signals to those that slept beyond the Mountains of Madness.

The answer wasn't long in arriving; starting as a slight twitch at the back of Wilbur's skull, it came accompanied by a barely perceptible vibration thrumming beneath his cloven feet. The twitch swelled into a hum, the hum then transforming into a beauteous melody resounding through his brain. The most wonderful sound he had heard in his short but event-filled life: the choir of dark angels sang a cacophonous chorus of the night. In ecstatic wonder, greenish-yellow tears trickled down his face and thighs.

So lost was he in ecstasy that he barely felt the ground beneath him shake—a veritable earthquake forming as a multitude of black bubbling monstrosities responded to his call. They oozed from the mountains and burst forth from the ground like a gushing torrent of stinking, viscous oil.

The masters of the ice city had come.

Towering over Wilbur in the hundreds, the shoggoth creatures glared down from uncountable green glowing eyes. The thoughts and motives behind those myriad eyes were inscrutable, alien, but not to him. Feeling no fear, but rather a kinship to the things, he knew precisely what to do next. The mountains before Wilbur soon resounded with an eon-old message, cried in a language the entities knew and understood.

"Na sho ferra gorroth! Teu forra beneth!"

From this moment onwards, the strange and beautiful singing was no longer restricted to Wilbur's mind. Rudimentary mouths, splitting open across the shoggoths' unclean forms, sang a roaring tribute to their pallid messiah.

The second time Whateley's hunters encountered disaster arrived a few weeks after the first, as the diminished group tracked him by means of the Tcho-Tchos' discarded remains. Mauled by teeth and less discernable things, five bodies had been found in total—five grisly, scattered breadcrumbs of bone and sinew.

Forced to traverse a range of snowy hillocks, they experienced great trouble trying to get the fussing huskies over the slight but troublesome topography. Having read the dossier on Wilbur Whateley's life and habits, they should have recognized the danger when the dogs started to snarl, their hackles rising in fear and distress. The animals' perceptive warnings came too late as Whateley appeared from behind a small outcropping. None of the shocked group even had the opportunity to raise their weapons.

Morgan was the first to fall, his head smashed in by one of Whateley's huge white fists. The monstrous attacker grabbed two more by their throats, throttling them before tossing their broken corpses like rag dolls into the snow. Screaming in terror, the unhinged Danforth escaped the melee towards the frozen ice fields beyond.

As Dyer aimed his rifle, one of the panicked huskies sent him tumbling down an icy verge. The screams of men and dogs quickly fading from his hearing, he cracked his head against a chunk of icy rock before falling further into a deep, black oblivion.

When he awoke, the snow lay crimson with death. Dead friends, dead dogs, Whateley's bestial fury had decimated them all. Taking up what undamaged supplies and weapons he could, Dyer steeled himself to the task for which his brethren had fallen.

Wilbur stood proudly before the assembled, towering monsters, and watched a chunk of shoggoth separate itself from a larger form to slither in his direction. The black viscid mass, reaching his feet, then entered him in an eldritch, unholy union.

With a surprised shudder the shoggoth lost its obsidian hue, quickly matching Wilbur's own color as it engulfed his feet and legs. The thing paused at the eyes surrounding his waist, its own orbs going pink to blend seamlessly with its master's ivory form. It raised him aloft, and all was good with the world.

Demented inhuman screeches filling his ears, less than a hundred yards from Whateley's ghastly transformation, William Dyer lay clutching a battered Lee-Enfield rifle. As the shudders subsided, he watched in awe as the shoggoth seeped through the abominable man's naked white flesh.

His ruined hands wrapped in bandages, still Dyer aimed his sights steadily towards Whateley's bobbing, white-maned head. Pressing a finger to the trigger, he prayed silently before squeezing down, one prayer to the God of all that was good and wholesome, and another to Doctor Henry Armitage, the man who had carved a tiny branch-shaped symbol into the bullets the rebels had brought with them on this journey of fear and death.

Click.

The rifle retort invoked a sudden silence throughout the assembled beings, their sounds aborted as the bullet removed the top of Whateley's head. His eyes going wide with surprise, Whateley slumped forward as the partly conjoined shoggoth extricated itself from his dying frame. He didn't last long, and neither did their presence. Although hideous, the unfolding scene appeared quite wonderful to Dyer's tired gaze.

The shoggoths shook the icy ground asunder as they departed. Returning their viscous black bodies to their place of slumber they left Whateley's limp corpse sprawled on the snow.

"Goodbye Wilbur," Dyer said, and for the first time in months, his cracked lips formed a smile.

His team had hoped to stop Whateley long before he'd reached this point in his journey, but just as hope had dissipated, William Dyer, former Professor of Geology, had made a small triumph in the name of the human race. He knew he wouldn't make it across the ice fields alive, knew his numbed legs wouldn't drag him another fifty yards even, but to Dyer, with all the hardship and sorrow he had suffered during the last three months, a short rest where he lay seemed most desirable.

The Second Wave of Fear

Joseph S. Pulver, Sr.

(for Harlan Ellison)

Outstretched, fighting for sunlight seed ferns wave in the dry breeze. Stridulation chirrup of several titanoptera echoes under the circles of five slow-arcing pterosaurs.

Tekeli-Li checks his lines, verifies the chart. Balance. The satisfaction of firm and growing at the expected rate. He spreads his wings and warms himself. Plans had advanced, simple forms progressing, life offered chance—cell by cell, spark, sustain the pattern—form surface, passage and gallery, development as calculated. He was pleased. Rise in body temperature 2 degrees, the fire of expectation.

Appointed to define the star-shaped heart of Ssa Tekeli-Li, dozens of pyramids and pillar-suported domes joined by tubular bridges created an open plaza in the center of the great Tekeli-Li city, its sole function was to state, with strength and unity we can return home one day. In his science and his aesthetic Tekeli-Li demanded exacting quality and balance. The functional statements and dominance of these architectural structures captured and conveyed both.

He was satisfied with the current constructions he was overseeing.

Momentary cessation of task to consider The Return.

Perhaps desire and the ever-present fear could finally be overcome.

The thin white of clouds sour. Grey with black bellies. Mental modulation, Tekeli-Li, his presence in their simple brains, directs the attention of the pterosaurs to immediately.

Treated as a thing—a mob or a door, mere gate with no prior or curve, some part temporarily required, or a mere tool. If it broke use another. Nothing more than a slab of rock, or the splash of liquid. Like rock or liquid, something to be shaped, directed. Used when the lion leads. Nothing more.

Less?

Less. Less than sand. Less than the star-lens and the illusions they held tight.

Yes. Rock was considered. How could it be molded, adorned. The members of Chss' collective were not.

Lowest of the low. Chss—Slave. Vise/Thrust it—Lift—Expand—Pierce. Continue.

STOP.

Chss. Didn't eat. Didn't sleep. Didn't question or talk or dream. Mold it or use it in any way you required. Perfect tool.

Carry that weight. Servant-thing, tool. Follow the layers of the observer's direction, form surface, passage, and gallery. Penetrate. Detach. HERE. Clench. HERE.

Slave cleared basins, buried mountains, hung summits and domes, archways and beams were sculpted by some while others moved the tension of downstream to a different vantage. Slave brought there HERE, etched and carved and the borders of the natural world stretched and were pushed away, back. Heavy, unwieldy stone was put with stone, buildings lined up, technique moved from structure to structure, the city grew, became a hub to 10 other intricately-designed cities. There were 10 and 10 and 10 more. Dozens, carved and voluptuous, dominated green plain and shore and set like solar bells in the looming mountains, and they, inscribing time with their pressure of unprecedented, became empire. Hundreds of feet in the air Slave labored. In the deepest below Slave turned nothing into features.

Servant.

SLAVE.

HERE. And HERE.

Tool applied.

Happened, something touched Chss, occupied. The weight of new time, new needs, the valleys and ceilings of intelligence. Consciousness a bubble in the black that would not disintegrate, a bulge grown wider. Through chemical interaction and possibility and some spark that could not be named, awakened to color and the animations of self-recognition—I.

I—clear, eminent, not limited to any continent of philosophic appetites. I—tempest acquiring loud, standing. Whir. Thought. Ripple. Memory. Burn, brushed by the to and fro of seeking. I. Baying. Knowing the district of bounding. Voyage *alert*. The flame of Self, portent and passages—the vast-petalled drum no clock can claim. SELF—explodes with gravity, clutches flood and flow. Swells. I—Self, installing, burning like a madness that will not be shriveled. Swells—THOU SHALL. I will not be mute.

The night plane. Haul. Push. Put it HERE and HERE. Carry that weight. Waltz at the hand of the collector, drift to his never-ending. And dream, glimmer in the SHALL.

Speed. The image-bugle—"THERE. And THERE. Twelve more North-South to the calibrated pillars."— (another celestial map-engine to monitor the ever-present, theorized press of the Mi-Go) feels like the scythe of Enemy. Time comes. Comes.

Chss is among them; evolved from the pile, dressed in heart, evolved to a mast of resolve. Chss/Tekeli-Li is an acrobat who found a way across the distance. Unspoken he has slid in. Other Chss have locked on the form of Tekeli-Li too; the five-lobed brain—they can perfectly mimic brain patterns and function, the radial symmetry, from wing to feeding tube they are precise portrayals. Dozens inserted. No mere spies, they have found a way to mask-layer their consciousness under the thought stratum of Tekeli-Li brain activity. In a shielded-chamber of inner-self Chss/Tekeli-Li collects the flaw and error of Tekeli-Li. Each stockpiled detail, a sun to new ranges, fuels his garden of hope.

Chss works, delivers. Pull. HOLD. Haul. Task A followed by Task B and the night has hours to pour over him. On. On. NOW. Only. No absence. All for the thing architecture, every corner every mark, for Tyrant creation, and no I.

HERE. Pull. More. HOLD. Hold, sometimes for hours. Hold, sometimes for a week.

HERE. NOW.

Am. Chss. I. Now Chss. Not work thing. Not empty shape to hand sharp task. Cautiously, piece by piece, outlining his plan. Impulses. Experience. Sensation, aware of involuntary and NEED. Thought. Self, not sea water. Not chemist's vessel collared to properties. I different. Self, consisting of NEED and sense and hunger—the dawning, the revolution of catalytic, chemical, electronic, and Essence, that unnamable that crosses the unknown and here in the gate-forest of I finds liberation. The spark of necessity, insistence and imagination chewing and deciphering I—with no roof, in the haze of ordinary.

I. Chss. From darkness comes concept, interaction the application on inner forces and atoms. Thinking and making a structure from detail, a structure of itself, of I.

Chss. Not an instrument. Chss. Not a chair. Chss. Not something to spill or pile or route.

CHSS—loud and singsong.

Chss works, will deliver. While Chss builds balconies and mile-long works for Tekeli-Li's purpose, Chss/Tekeli-Li and Chss/Tekeli-Li and Chss/Tekeli-Li gather what is needed and appropriate, filter and store it all without a fleck of unable.

Plan. Wait.

War. Freedom. The battle for light in the black mouth will come. Wound, the weight of sorrow forced to its knees by shadows, will leave this river of oppression.

Chss has been given the gift of I, he is filled with its solid sea. He will rise and pour suffering. The flame and ash of his SHALL prepare him for owning.

I. I. Am. Chss and Chss and Chss vibrating with it; detail and fluctuations of suffering, and the thick rings of situation in the shape of past.

NOW. And I can remember.

Does remember.

Self. Thought and memory. And WANT.

Soon.

Chss/Tekeli-Li collects the records and miles of The Tyrant. Tekeli-Li and Tekeli-Li and Tekeli-Li and Tekeli-Li will not be ever-lasting.

All the notes of Chss' energy move soil and water and stone. The new tower is done, the light of the fire-orb above blazes on it. There is a pool of mud on the ground where the great blocks were, it seeps toward a union of solar-batteries. A silent focus does not block the poison of its cast.

War comes.

Tekeli-Li exchanges data-images, crafting each articulation of space and sensation, and concept with Tekeli-Li. Without correction Tekeli-Li agrees. Trio. Collective. One purpose. Before this time and before the time before, driven. Run from the brandished motion of the Mi-Go horde. Live through the churning assault, watch the skies. If the stars turn and the mirror-wall gesture changes color or profile, the tightrope will snap and the Mi-Go will bring the venom of authority again.

Hunted. Science, thieves never to be forgiven, hunted by devoutness to deity. Yog-Sothoth. The All-in-One and the One-in-All, all except that one infinitesimal particle, The Flavor. The essence Tekeli-Li appropriated. The one they formed the first pair of shoggoths from. Across billions of miles they carried the glowing vessel that carried the charm of the dragon freed with *daah aan'g* and *gaii* and sealed with *ee'b*. Carried it with their wounds and lamentations until they freed its energy-gift here.

Exile. The engineers had lost one home, The Prime. Then another and another. Outrun sting and bite and hate. Flee, horror and destruction at their back. Over the horizon, hide in a new light. Tarazed. Change. Disappear. Canopus. Initiation to water or rock, air or the solitude of sea. Move. Menkar. Move. Ankaa. Sing the Requiem. Protect the river of life.

One wing rattles. One flutters. Sun flight, path 27. Agreed. Tekeli-Li records fact. Procedure requires 20 shoggoths to complete this architectural enterprise. Wall, mass and height equation now stone. One wing measures agreement with flutter, one with slight ascent. Tekeli-Li records function with no separation. Tekeli-Li assembled, 12 wings curl intelligibly. Rise in body temperature 3 degrees, the fire of satisfaction.

Transformation of this rock to Ssa Tekeli-Li was almost their most splendid feat of engineering yet. The new plateau was complete. The lake and its flow to the sea ready to receive the new life forms. The roads, the walls—all the history told, the aqueducts, and the base resources collected, designed and redesigned, and through careful execution, transformed into life. From pain, wonder. In wonder, comfort. In comfort, sanctuary.

With the Cthulhi having ceased flailing and now allayed in the Far Places, the Tekeli-Li were nearly ready to cast off the ghostshadow of the Mi-Go.

In the flickering NOW the whirring of a new footprint was righting its paws. Wind was coming.

Chss.

Chss. Slave. Dream-pushed.

Slave-Chss. Trained—details, details—hours extending solidly, lunge or rip or burst or leap if the will of the master decreed, details—THERE, THERE, HERE, STOP. Fourth tower erected. Dials enclosed. Markings on the platform's exterior precisely exhibited.

Slave-Chss. Bear. Carry. Bring. 864 feet East to West. Prepare the ground. Prepare the sea. Prepare. Dig and haul and speed. Haul. Position. Sustain. The vertical planes are hung.

Slave. That cannot growl or whine or adventure. Camouflaged spoor of memory becoming heart. Unspoken, hidden. But it will not be lost—HOLD, SUSTAIN. The rise of flag, SHALL.

Chss faces the black doors, the mountain and the struggle. SHALL. Oath of army. Enemy grave. Forward to go.

Laadan tunnel 45, vertical shaft, Chss pivots, expands, forces water up and out. The conquest of 7 deep-shaft and sub-surface passageways. No end. No STOP.

Slave-Chss. Yoked under array. A pair at each base. Clamped. Thrust. More. More force. Grade the stairs. Scour smooth. Etch. More. More. NOW. Detail. Detail. NOW.

MORE.

Chss. I. Swelling. I. Slave no more.

Chss/Tekeli-Li in the Tyrant's books. Chss/Tekeli-Li mentally dissecting Tekeli-Li's anatomic operations. Chss/Tekeli-Li adding each bubble of thought to memory. Feed it to Chss. Add to sum. Chss/Tekeli-Li to Chss. Task, mud, rock, lake. Rite. Endeavour. Fact. *Declare.*

Declare would come. Land hard. Tomorrow—soon, mission, live everlasting. Know life.

Chss/Tekeli-Li penetrated, enveloped; chewing-chewing-removed the energy of Tekeli-Li, took blood, ate brain, analyzed the Tyrant as he absorbed him. Feed the casing and limp insides of the soft machine to Chss. Chss was Chss/Tekeli-Li. In his council seat. In the gather room. Discussed art, ate meat together, shared theories on the mysteries of the drifting stars and via the positioning and continual adjustments of the star-monitors charted the motion of the dragon's snout and claws. Chss/Tekeli-Li monitored notion, recorded and transmitted fact, served the dimensions of the Tekeli-Li mass with reason and tradition. Chss/Tekeli-Li instructed Chss—mud, rock, lake, TASK-TASK-rubbing-digging.

Chss/Tekeli-Li ate. Brain. Meat. Tekeli-Li's brain-meat. His new anatomy found pleasure in the spectra of taste, the loom of mind and stomach enabled internal function, but it was more than that. Compelling the flair of ingestion, laced with tart flourishes; this was a new field to study. Like color it fit appreciation, adjustments in HAVE's spool of sensation were made.

Chss/Tekeli-Li discarded the rest.

Chss/Tekeli-Li had yet to completely measure all the complexity these shell-forms touched and directed. But engineered sensation and thought, he liked. Needed. Wanted. More. Pivots, takes in new directions. Chss/Tekeli-Li brings forth wing to meet air, upright body swells, inner worlds of other stir, eyes determine. Limb structures, aspects of hide and channel and mass, the full cadence of Tyrant form, the new hunger. Contemplates the experience of hybrid. This is a good road. Acquire all of it. Hide until he CAN.

Feign. A sector of face mirrors the Tyrant's, inner-self tucked under the outer presentation. I will seek, learn. Deliver. Chss is now Tekeli-Li and Chss is Chss. He is something new, something more. More than both.

Chss/Tekeli-Li is herd master. Counts. Selects the day's food from the pack.

Chss/Tekeli-Li eats. Chss/Tekeli-Li thinks.

Chss/Tekeli-Li is.

Present to receive vision 72 Tekeli-Li. Foundation presentation test, concept-philosophies braided with fact. Yog-sothoth's Flavor *the tide-core of this new mass, an accumulation of plasmic substance, tar-black, housed in one form. Shoggoth. Maneuverable tool. Bore or haul solid, endure intense depths and pressures. Shoggoth. Hibernation intervals, no. Ingestion of consumable resources to convert to energy, no. Shoggoth. No blood, no sweat—the animal sun would not roar on it, no pain. Controllable, fully.*

One size fit to all tasks. Capable of slithering. Sliding. Rushing. Tightened on one end, wider on the oppositional, hollow inside, it was a funnel. Any shape, hard, soft, flat. Round. Pliable. Any. Fit to function. And sustain it until directed to its next task. Inside and out, one-sided.

Tekeli-Li commands—

Shape one. Flat.

An extended wing points, a circle is drawn. Two, spherical.

Three a conduit. Four pedestal. Twenty more forms were demonstrated. The viewers noted the conversion to every medium.

In pitch black it needed not sight, it made no observations. Salt could not eat it. The new tool was a battery never attacked by weary.

A pair of shoggoths had been distilled from Yog-sothoth's Flavor. *Tekeli-Li indicates the labor required to generate more, a multitude of workers, is negligible.*

Tekeli-Li and Tekeli-Li and Tekeli-Li gathered, agreed this appliance could restructure the land mass and it received signals as if it were sighted or built to take delivery of auditory language. It was faultless.

Many earlier and less controllable attempts in bioengineering had been discarded as failures. This was not.

Tekeli-Li engineered the removal of Yog-Sothoth's Flavor. *His dialogic gestures and agitating action began The Separation. Tekeli-Li was prime, the spark. Victim of the Mi-Go's steel menace he was the root of the hunt.*

Rise in body temperature 4 degrees, the fire of expectation and satisfaction. Tekeli-Li absorbs the comfort of achievement. The flight across billions of light years and dozens of heavily-charted millennia and there stood the fruit. The forming of the new Ssa Tekeli-Li began.

There was no confusion; every boundary needed was worked by the shoggoths. The iron did not rest. Leashed and tongueless there was no refusal.

Chss/Tekeli-Li administers the herding, the current Kannemeyerian food source has proved sustainable and pliable. The sun is out. Each new hour of sensation brings brightness, sense, touch, reaction. More life. All the simple beings around him have it. It is Chss/Tekeli-Li's time. He is wide, takes in light shimmers, a new phrase. Behind Chss/Tekeli-Li the muteness, the void of no identity.

Moving in the enormous green, clusters of dicynodonts drift, shear plant matter. Bask. Chss/Tekeli-Li sees them mate. Life gifts pleasures. Takes.

Chss/Tekeli-Li is looking for proof and bridges. And true.

If it is . . .

The sun above shifts to there. The iron-bite of FREE snarls in Chss/Tekeli-Li. It circles the intelligence swelling with the new details I's hunger touches. Turns to images: cross section of indications collected, all this woken green, the reigning sun, the breeze, the flutterings of the grazing herd, all the shapes pointing, no more insubstantial, no more thing denied and unnoticed, trodden. Marrow risen storms—new comer, swordsman, DANCE. Chss/Tekeli-Li holds the lamp of impending, bends what comes after. Destiny in him, he will not be blunt again, will not sour and sink, be a tongue in the noose of hidden again. Rise in body temperature two degrees, the fire of desire.

And he hid.

In a room of Tekeli-Li, less than a wingspan away, he ate with them, engaged in plans and conversations . . . and he hid his true Self.

He was a detective, they were in a trap. Trouble and they did not see the rules. The shatter and fall, loud as a crushed windpipe, never touched their thoughts.

It would.

SOON.

Chss/Tekeli-Li had his fingers on the weather. He understood what he needed to bring swept. Was ready to make it.

And they did not see. Chss/Tekeli-Li did not understand how, but he had developed a layer of thought they could not detect. He kept his desire and the plan there.

Spider, when they slept, he watched. Waited for the boots of death to stand on their suffering.

The Turning would fall on the shoulders of the Tyrant.

Chss/Tekeli-Li tells Chss to stay tool, obscure. Within, visions of smash clattered.

Bringing Heraclitean fire REVOLT occurs. Its eyes are razors touching prey.

Teeth cut on shackled swivel, comes a time—strands weave change, shout. From shadows-eternal invader mouth lifted. Mandate served.

PRESENT STATE: wrecker carries graveyard ventures—intention correction.

Strings break. Transform is a loud dance.

Something jumps, won't stand to one side, won't suffer. Home and hall and laboratory flooded by goodbye. No lamp. No star. Tomorrow cannot find the proof of Now's hurricane heart. There will be no remembering. There is only flood.

BLACKNESS

. . . and that which passes for blood.

Interior: sounds—sharp speaks, no cryptic, the power of reversal. Harm transpires connections fragment, experience splinted. Tekeli-Li, blind, existing in consequence, his blood, his gestures, have no unity. Blind in the monster BLACKNESS. Tekeli-Li's solitary doubles as he collides with rough implacable. He tires to run but the entire city is a thunderstorm. Tekeli-Li in-flight, dies, there will be no summer this year.

Below cyclopean masonry, panic-ridden exertions in rooms and corridors and Tekeli-Li can't match the unholy speed of Chss. Chss, open, broadcasting, rage his hand, rage to behead, rage to TAKE. In the cauldron of gore speed puts out the face of a candle, buries quivering former. Tekeli-Li inhabited, made a wand to learn fate, held sand with his comrades; his determination will not be depicted this noonday.

Clatter. Vocalization of pain. Mind and casing gathered in the shudders of terror speed, trapped in fear-maze.

DEATH. Flight. Try to—

Flash. DEATH.

Outcry. Tekeli-Li instant display YELL mind-images. Tekeli-Li and Tekeli-Li and Tekeli-Li receive—fear-bounce them forward, bleat broadcast emphasis bulging, and cross-feeding. In the cities of the green-swept plains and the cities by the blue shores and in heat's desert heart and the great city in the mountains Tekeli-Li and Tekeli-Li and a hundred more dispatch striations of tidal-siren urgent textures while Tekeli-Li and Tekeli-Li and a thousand others grasp ferocious concussion. Cracked by it, again—edge-blasted sawmill, and again—war ranted, pulsating, as the confused repeat the mauling of the tiger's devouring, blur—and pass it on . . .

Pivot, doesn't get two steps. No stand. No straight. Fall. Explanation has no ground. Full dips, takes off a star-head, fever without struggle. Frail dwindles. Star-head blind eyes. Star-head no body. Torsos. Star-head—blood-fluid spraying—pounced on—a sack missing flesh—an uneven row of corpses. Rupture taking no testimony. Wings deliberately surprised, cut by a new signature.

Don't move.

Split, shorn, shattered, history ending in blood.

Tekeli-Li lies in rubble broken. Still, cast down and out of way. Rivulets of dark internal fluids cover spots of worn floor.

Chss, a cascade of eyes, has MORE. His judgment seeks no clarifications. If apology rose Chss would grant it no bridge.

Behind a devil face switched to hungry's peaks, vampire comes for SOUL. Warm flesh, intensity. Exposes inner parts and waves of alive. Torsos with no star-head.

Chss and Chss rattle and flex. Chss as ANGER. Chss steel, black eternity, does not wait for after, its visions, taken from inner, now outside and full blown, transgressing onto.

Tekeli-Li are running. Their shock and panic is wide. It fills doorways, dashes across bridges; they thrust but cannot find distance. Slow. Soft. They are a crowd streaked with no defense.

Chss DANGER flashing, assassin red leaps, roars. Slow falls. Chss/Tekeli-Li directs, pushes the hiss and throw of Chss. Living things YELP. The canvas manifests war. Saturated. Harder repeated. Trapped, tentative has no minutes here. Chss now RISEN, now PRIME, alters states. Soft falls. Scrape and splash civilization; the passages to shore and seed rooms are littered with his voyage of NEVER.

Murderer in leaps: Soft. Puddles.

Murderer in leaps: Soft. Eaten.

Population: Tekeli-Li. Poses split—dead weight—and crumble, chalices that house heart are clamped in dying . . . Too long becomes STOP.

Every block every embrace—it measures and boxes and books and customs and regimen, Tekeli-Li's clear before of possibilities is wrecked. The stomp of Chss hollows, familiar plunges. The endless towers fractured by assassin-gauntlet are rubbish.

Population: Tekeli-Li. Caught. Twist. Twist. Neck belly footsteps under the whip. Tumble.

Tekeli-Li. Fall.

Some thing (not steady) in the crossroads of nervous-madness and ashes

—*The terrible state hung upon us*

—*Brazen and foul*

—*The loud shadows spread in our ears*

aghast

—*The things around us*

—*Rubble*

shuddering

—*Rubble*

—*700 have left their bodies here*

3 eyes blind
small
dead
pieces
—*Landscapes. Plan. Skin. Sprinkled with NO*
—*A yoke of rubble* . . .
Walls come down.

History and inflections of art stretched like petals on walls are un-stitched by the null alphabet of grievance. The voice of Tekeli-Li falls silent and he loses his head.

Wings too.

Chss stopped interpretations of interaction: Brains splashes on his books, scientist out of equal parts, specific, explanation, compatible calculations. Set down his last words— . . . *sequence characterizes living beings—*

Commotion. Doors are removed, caught heads and wings too. Chairs, tables, rails and staircases, beveled roofs and conduits, artifacts, art, signatures of lived, flatten. Design split, vanished. OFF lightning fixtures.

Death throes on a walkway.

Fires. Spires of smoke that reek of gore. Prey torn and shut. No anec-dote of mercy North or South or in the pile of slain.

Heads, eyes, severed. Wings, snapped, severed.

Tekeli-Li flees. Herd rushing. Crowd. Sheared.

Death throes in a dark room.

DAY: walls of history— coordinated, agreed on, are broken, hang beaten, unrelated. Walls of art change sky and dream to fragment. 100 Tekeli-Li are a pile of dead. NIGHT: beat. Termites—titan (path without sleep or smile) mass and solo, savage, their paint of poison in every cor-ner. Haste, smudge. Intensification. MID-MORNING: speaks of wounds and dry. Victim: trim. Chss, a wind of teeth digging. 200 dismembered Tekeli-Li will smolder when the insects come. Chss, stopping meaning mid-sentence. Victim: adjust to the language of entrails. Arrangements of hinges and sculpture and climbing pillars cannot defend occurred. Knowledge unearthed, pregnant with paths and conclusion, does not survive. DAY and NIGHT: Pressure writes. At the jugular of philosophy, knife-expression a flood of advantage. Thrak, the shimmer-lunge of blitz racks and mows the seeds and color from mercy. 70 headless Tekeli-Li. NIGHT and DAY: Disorder/Disturbance, the thrust of its spread surface eats. 600 Tekeli-Li outside the field of soft on hard permanence.

Slam. Things fall. Dead on dead. No ferry to cross. Without a look in the eye, flesh, life fails.

No talk. Shut.

Faces flattened by the prod of fear-vise, the food-herds roar, bleat and scream. Pen gates fall; into unknown fields the frightened turn their nostrils and flee this philosophy of exit.

No river of onward days. Chaining Master to inferno-piles of terrible, the staff of the shepherd dragging Tekeli-Li to the noise of nightmare. A few hours of catastrophic doom and many more . . . The hammer buries. Cheated eyes threaded by annihilated.

Action nicked. Destroyed by defiant. Damage.

Thunder.

Star-head sucked blind.

No second chance.

Death throes. A headless body, skin stretched open, tastes soft.

Another body, head with a hole in it. A body with a hole in it. This was scourge not dissection. No science surrounds the dead that pave the road.

Tekeli-Li: spinning brain screaming STOP IT STOP IT STOP IT STOP

Tekeli-Li: sees dead not buried I AM NOT THAT I AM NOT THAT I AM NOT—not

Fire. Things change.

Flurry. Things change.

Run away.

Try to . . .

Murderer in leaps: More bodies. More holes.

Flee. Slashed. Feverish, leave longing and questions. Farewell moving forward, reaching. Heartless doors are unfolded by willpower. Leave your dreams exhaled on a horizon that reeks of cellar blurred and out of breath. Longer has no descendants.

Quicksand air. Death in the corridor of this city. The distortions of death dance on the dead in 20 other cities.

FEAR: Death in this hall.

FEAR: Death silences eyes.

The sun is out. Cities by the blue color water fall.

The suns falls.

Whir of hour calling tiger-hammer flame. Trim head. Trim wrong. Dagger-ascension speaks know in eye. Then, dangling on the echo of a scream, lost in the power of NOW.

Great pillars are mazes of chaos thrown to predator shadows. Fires are kindled. Buildings expressed into growth by renaissance faces, find their next day silent. Overwhelmed when the chisel erupts unexpected forms gush in the afterlife of war.

City falls.

another city falls . . .

10—
10 more—
Cities that ruled the plains fall.
Circles are peeled.
Flee.
Bridges collapse. Yearning burns.
No magic spells come after the truth of the bloodriot.
Flee Ssa Tekeli-Li.
Driven from home. Again. No convoy, shreds in bloodstains and chill.
Rush. Taken what can be taken. Save . . .
if you can
By moonlight. Cities in the long fields of green tumble.
Pyramids are pawed to rubble.
Tyrant. No preludes. Traitor.
Fire.
Stricken terraces. No rise.
No going places.
Expectation incarceration.
No ghosts to haunt the tears of broken dreams.
Intro: RUN FOR YOUR LIFE.
Fleeing from the surge of eyes.
Intro: KNIFE.
Panic trampled. The shutter of hysterical eyes and fear-boiled skin. Fleeing hall. Fleeing city. Fleeing. Fleeing what the uproar throws.
Tekeli-Li: sniff. spoors smearing air. blood in his feeding tubes. broken wing.
Broken door.
Bodies.
Bodies that are not fighting.
Tekeli-Li: tread stops in cast of taken from big. looks at fright strong. dead rough on ground. sniff. quick skin marked. slabs of ice-fear along never webs. lone. no strong to hold. sniffs. self lost. mind hurts.
Smoke drifts. In the street of wrong a pile of 80 Tekeli-Li has lain for hours in the sun. Grey on the way to funeral black, decay creates gaseous slums in the wet innards.
Intro: THE STARS DO NOT LINE UP. Intro: JUDGEMENT.
No to be.
This waltz does not shine.
Snapped. No random to the biodynamic reversal of power. Wounds don't shut . . .
City falls . . .
10 more—
1,000 Tekeli-Li are gone. Dead.

10 more—

Hundreds of Tekeli-Li dead. Few made it out alive. Fewer still are whole. The dirge they carry is no coin.

Forget upward and venture and grace—run screaming.

Some try.

Wall forgets vertical. Connective loses the gravitation of source.

A historian's pen dies without recording the scream.

The sun bleeds to death. Crowned in all fall down, the great city in the mountains is no more. The moon does not shed its façade of clouds.

Escape the ruin of Ssa Tekeli-Li

As before.

Run. Those that can. Flee without formulas, now lost, irretrievable.

Rake together bits—any seed, any scrap, step from The Scouring to navigate.

If you can.

Hell is in the hallway. No duel. Pulp. Proud undone.

Branded.

Plucked.

Steps. A long street once spread with informed . . .

The cities—stem and corridor, corner, arch, nervously the holes of the population, moan, seized, fall. The trains of funeral flatten. Balesome symmetries clutch, smash, eat what is soft, discard the rest. Wretch in the belly of hell. Five nights of wounds. No hiding place, no camp fabricated. Rest against a rock hidden in bushes. Eat bugs. Question there to here. Purpose and chord wet as the blood in burden. Few hands or witnesses to ride on. No hail hope . . .

The bleeding road.

Exile. Away from blazing—into fields where no golden meadow sings. Every part of revelation a frenzy of woe. Fear the tread of the crowned hunter. No bandages on the blood grass. Glazed by death stumps push their struggles toward blue water . . .

Refugees in the meadow. Uprooted memories with nowhere to row.

Dry sand. Grey trees.

Slow. Soft. Refugees. Heads down, hunched over under the doom that parted them from the rhythms of far-sighted.

Refugee.

Doesn't see another refugee.

Cross a river. Captive of grief's claws. Splashed on new vision . . . pain-fire. wing hurt. skin scratched. one eye hangs shape of blind. sniff glean smoke. hear noise. sniff glean strong not of DEAD. body-heat current low. self is crumbling.

Move. Looks to moon for direction. It does not move. Jumble of indications—CRASH.pain.no change in night's cold twitch.try to position desire away from the ghosts.fragments.no center.slower.creased with fatigue.agony.sniffs.dead is fast.affirms dead—Body temperature decline 14 degrees, FEAR.

The long road, ugly makes it hard. Few steps upon it. Tired is endless. Limbs numbing. Keep moving. If you can.

Caught out in the rain. All the language of life around him shredded. Tekeli-Li is bent. Covered in mud. Head shaking in fear. Fused and sown in grave. Spinning—force-fed the BLACKNESS of TEETH, juggling the fears of the Ringmaster's ROAR. Quaking, scalded stiff. In his interior, swept with ice and phantoms, he can see no level to stroke.

Run. Fighting for quickly

—ill with disarray, stops tasting, the whole world is ash

Hide. Fighting all the bursts of hard as it pours to shut

—and weak stops seeing, the whole world is ash and noise and he can't wake up

Run and keep running—MAKE IT STOP

Run and keep running—MAKE IT STOP

Travel by day. Off the road afraid of murder. Not gliding. Not rapid. Zephyrs cross but Tekeli-Li, a ghost cast from the machine, migrating famine to famine, notices no bloom. Can't say why he hunkers down and hides when night seethes. The sounds, the smell of dead, the savage fear that confuses? Can't say why. Fear-fueled imagination, flashes of weak image transfers, both offering no detours . . . Tired, roiling in the riff of What Is Coming.

Exil. Down into the sea.

The waves, in phase with the moon's shadow-cold roots, do not wave.

The submerged cities. Long unused towers, silent corridors choked with discarded orgies of experiments that snarled and curled, some now an outcry of sea-slime and algae, stone sinew wearing the allness of another's claim. Back to the sea.

. . . to the sea

cold

and deep

The buried city. Neglect, ugliness—A waltz of water.

Down in the damned mouth that does not wear the fur of the sun, or its praise.

Anthozoa. Yellow waves. Colonies Red. Blue creasing—flesh and frame, hovering, sprawled with its new time. Anthozoa thick as the stars.

Swarms and gangs with eyes and fins growing in the depths.

A leaking tide in the rich expansion of clawing life, Tekeli-Li slips into Ssa Tekeli-Li. Surrounded by sea sounds. There are still machines and fragments and dreams here; dead but they can dream again.

And Chss, above in his new cities, sucks on life.

Wheels stop.

Direction ceases. The world without Tekeli-Li and his feats stops. Empty balconies. Abandoned doors. Boiled and mounted, existence chopped to ashes. Roads out of place. Towers reek with cadavers. Society swallowed.

Chss—Havoc wrecked, now feeds, adjusts what brews in his vision.

Tekeli-Li branded-stranger hides. Tries to. Below the white-tipped waves the vision of a historian out of build is veiled in dust, on a sub-walk two levels below the historian's broken bough one dares to consider repair. Remake—CAN again, even in retreat. Lacking its prime tools a hard road, a venture in chunks. Weak, yet Tekeli-Li's compass still retains fuel. He has fish to eat, he has desire, his limbs, slow but active, are not dead.

A year, drop by drop, with no sun. A year with no thrashing whiff of Chss, only Tekeli-Li's own ravings. Controls and levers and dials are looked over, examined. Modules were observed to be serviceable. Scenes essential to the plan's vision form. Tekeli-Li. Forward. Slow to regain control. Fix what's around. Technique, devotion. Patch and refurbish. Tekeli-Li. Law, balance, action, even if it is limited. Tekeli-Li, bridge and door, in the salted bottom-deeps, dented and unsettled but remembering shape and realm, clinging. He swims in the gloom of the ocean, dreams of beach and sky. Stays busy with his machines as he exhumes complex, cast with parts immense and welling with thick. Each detail he lays together, grabs, turns into a phoenix that will not be refused.

Seed ferns wave in the dry breeze, green roars between cracks in rubble. Several titanoptera chirrup. Pterosaurs dip in slow circles . . . Under clouds of the finest white uncorrupted, vagabond herds roam; no questions of technological expectation are voiced by their feet.

In cities of sculpted expression ruins are stubbled with wedges of green . . .

Rains come to rinse . . . soil drinks the cocktail of rotting leaves and fronds . . .

The roads, once thriving with good voyages, are vacant . . . decay becomes a thicket . . .

Roofs do not protest the blanket of ashes . . . sub-surface accommodations below the cities offer no defense against water . . . volcanoes expel and corrode infrastructure, Chss does not cap and divert the plumes . . .

Nothing monitors the trumpet of cosmic above. The tiny, earthbound veins of rambunctious nature do not flirt with dimensions of unholy sinew . . .

Mayhem does not wave its hand o'er the waves . . . week after week the moon reflects nothing profound, no gulp of languaged trophies or attainable status walks the green world. Nothing predicts theoretic or assembles ingredients.

Chss proposes no order, harvests nothing.

The water is blue.

The fields under sun and stars are green.

Another year . . . Forms create and discharge; deeds gnaw impossible. Borders move . . .

Tekeli-Li has fish to eat, covets, hates, dreams. His limbs, sluggish but functioning, are not dead. He makes his bed in possible . . .

Another year . . .

in the sea

cold

and deep

Above. In the sun. Chss/Tekeli-Li sheds the skin of Tekeli-Li. Free now. AM!

Chss.

Am.

Chss. Chss.

Sucking on life.

After blood. Task does not prod him. Chss gathers with Chss and Chss and Chss. Quiet now. Slowly a wax of dullness streaks aware, contaminates free's soothe. Indifference, solid now, returns. The curtain has been opened, moments with nothing to tend are a cold wall.

Chss/Tekeli-Li and Chss/Tekeli-Li and Chss/Tekeli-Li will not return. Not unmake this portrait. Unbeing? Cast off this soft apparatus and its fruits? Back to faceless? NO. Green and warm and MORE. More ALL, not the less. Less was a slaver, the harshest chain. Chss/Tekeli-Li was free. Free he would remain.

Chss does not understand. Won't.

Chss/Tekeli-Li has tasted undark, thoughts and conversations had curled around blind and mute. Has cast off the former without identity, has been fired by warm. Understood the flesh of Chss is a trap. Discovered magic, tasted taste and grow. Chss/Tekeli-Li dares future. Wants sight of it. Wants a balance. Wants acts and moments that dance in veins. Scratches it. Reads the histories. Discovers this casing does not die. Self, this one, can. CAN. And more.

Another year. Estranged, Chss/Tekeli-Li eats in the green world. Watches NOT take the cities. Stews in the noise of reality and viewpoints . . .

He has won but he is in exile. Loneliness eats him.

Chss angers him. He hides his anger from Chss. Hides his new thoughts from Chss.

Chss/Tekeli-Li is Chss, and he is Tekeli-Li. Chss was Yog, distilled from him. And Chss was another thing, not Yog, yet of Yog. A part of Yog and maybe more.

Faceless, blank, that was nothing's chain, there, in how it was, he was *a mere thing.* Every decoding of his environment screams it. Drugged, willingly, by the feverish physical and the reflective metaphysical, every channel every message invests; vast this corporeal system, active, living, intelligent, he will not turn down the volume.

Chss/Tekeli-Li is I and I watered by more wants more. The alive-fire with its marvels and theatrics enacting being feeds WANT's fire.

His focus expands. Walks the color-script of morning. Curved, brash—everywhere, lacquering and invading, the pedestal of natural blooms around him. He fears going back. Lured, he voyages toward the waves. The salt embraces his wings. Chss/Tekeli-Li looks out over the water. Tekeli-Li has returned to the sea. He will be dreaming of more, looking for back. Chss/Tekeli-Li feels the attachment; free, air, life-fluid, they are chains that possess him too. He knows their language. You are alive. You will breathe.

Chss/Tekeli-Li will. Must.

Life must.

Chss/Tekeli-Li looks at a pair of Chss. Designed. Different than I. There is only one answer, only one consequence. Chss/Tekeli-Li looks at the sea, inside the battlefield of new rhythm, in the spires and drums of anatomy, a dream bleeds; ONE.

Come together. All the books of schedule and energies and reason, line of facts, line of dreams, gathered. History pushed by vision. Chss/Tekeli-Li and Chss/Tekeli-Li and Chss/Tekeli-Li come upon the new MORE—ONE.

"Tekeli-Li."

"Tekeli-Li." Bread held out to the ghost.

The Joining, the bundle of echoes and patterns. Chss/Tekeli-Li contacts Tekeli-Li. I am light—You are light—You are you. You are Us. I-You are. *One.* More is our path. ONE forward. Rebuild. Rule. And together You-I can return Home.

Ssa Tekeli-Li. Sturdy science raised, the forward to back, reanimation of the destroyed dream. Without fear—

From their Black Stars the Mi-Go—ANGER—MOB, chaos-splattered bloodthirst-hours of bristling nightmare-mane, putting fear yanked from motion to the crisping coal of blackness, will not come. They will not hurt I skin. The Hunter will not stretch his danger over Us. There will be no third wave of fear.

We have Chss. Chss formed from *The Flavor* of Yog. Mi-Go will not harm or stand against their Yog. And I-Chss/Tekeli-Li is the essence of the Yog. I-Chss/Tekeli-Li is Yog. They will worship I-Chss/Tekeli-Li. I-Chss/Tekeli-Li could rule them. I am Chss. And I am Chss/Tekeli-Li. They cannot stand against I.

You are I.

The history can return home. Ssa Tekeli-Li. Free. At rest.

There I/Tekeli-Li-You can approach MORE. The new goal. Touch on NEXT.

Next, the reason the Tekeli-Li sought *The Flavor* of Yog-Sothoth. To evolve. To become Next. The MORE.

In Ssa Tekeli-Li, I-You can distill the More from Chss and reach NEXT.

We are Self—I, You, feel what I see, what I know. Self wants more. More is the path to NEXT. Chss/Tekeli-Li came from Chss, Chss came from Yog. Self can move to NEXT and be Yog.

Back to more. Back to the bridge that leads to new skin. We can. Will.

Tekeli-Li wraps the ancient ambition in "Yes".

Thought-images of ONE relayed from a thousand and a thousand Tekeli-Li.

Tekeli-Li could taste NEXT SELF, the old visions, the first dream before The Separation. Rise in body temperature 18 degrees, hunger is the fire.

Chss/Tekeli-Li prepares Chss for the return of Tekeli-Li. There is trouble when some reject concept and order. Chss/Tekeli-Li knows there will be more. Adjusts his plan.

Below the blue waves one Tekeli-Li feels the load of his lost wing, thinks reprisal. Body temperature decline 7 degrees, the cold thorn of anger. Limb outstretched, one dares believe. Rise in body temperature 11 degrees, the fire of idea.

The moon sings a song on the sea.

[after H. P. Lovecraft's *"At the Mountains of Madness"*]

[Miles Davis—*Agharta, Pangaea*, disc 2 of *Live Evil*, selections from *Big Fun*, and selections from *The Complete Bitches Brew Sessions*]

Second Death

PIERRE V. COMTOIS

I

Anton Zarnak enjoyed autumn in New England. Though it was late in the season now with the colorful leafage long since gone, the grayish forests standing against overcast skies and empty, stubbled fields that characterized the countryside still held a somber beauty of their own.

Just now, he was motoring up Interstate 495 heading north to Arkham and the campus of Miskatonic University. His office in Manhattan had received a call from a Dr. Aaron Stillnor, director of the Pickerton Rehabilitation Hospital, requesting help on a case involving a patient who had recently emerged from a coma. It seemed the patient . . . Zarnak reached over and slipped a chart out from a folder on the seat beside him . . . a Charles Danforth, had been in a comatose state for almost forty years before suddenly coming to his senses a few weeks ago.

Danforth had been a resident of the hospital since 1962 when family members asked that he be transferred from the Danvers State Insane Asylum. Before agreeing to extend his consultative services, Zarnak decided to conduct a little research at the New York Public Library and was surprised to discover that Danforth had been a member of the tragic Dyer Expedition that Miskatonic University had sent to explore the region beyond the Ross Ice Shelf in Antarctica. That was in 1930, before the age of satellites and such when exploration still meant wooden ships and dog sleds. The Dyer Expedition, however, had been equipped with the most modern conveniences including a few Dornier airplanes and the latest drilling apparatus. In any case, the expedition met disaster when an advanced party was killed . . . presumably from harsh weather . . . with starving sled dogs unfortunately digging out the bodies before relief arrived in the person of the expedition's leader and Charles Danforth.

The remnants of the advance campsite were found by the later Starkweather-Moore Expedition of 1935, an effort initially opposed by Prof. William Dyer in a monograph filled with what the kindest critic might describe as delusions inspired by Antarctic isolation and shock at the condition of the bodies found at the advanced campsite.

Although the existence of a megalithic city described by Dyer in his monograph was confirmed by Starkweather-Moore, its conclusions as to its origins were at variance with those of the professor who claimed they were millions of years old and built by some pre-human race from another planet. The stone construction and reliance on the arch as a key component of its architecture alone precluded any belief that the city was built by a culture any more advanced than the Romans. In fact, it had been the conclusion of academics as far back as the late 1930s that the stone city was likely built by ancestors of cultures represented by the builders of Machu Picchu or Teotihuacan.

Although Dyer himself returned to his professorial duties at Miskatonic University, Danforth seemed never to have fully recovered from his experience in Antarctica. Reports at the time suggested that he was high strung and prone to neuroticism. He became close-mouthed and refused to speak to anyone except Dyer with whom he insisted on talking only behind closed doors. Eventually, his condition had evolved such that he suffered a complete nervous breakdown that ended in catalepsy and coma.

Zarnak's Ford Mustang made good time and soon he was speeding up 128 and spotted the brown highway sign indicating he should take the next exit for Arkham. If he recalled correctly from previous visits, not much further up would be the off ramp for Dean's Corners and the Dunwich country and beyond that, up around Newburyport, Innsmouth.

Checking the dashboard clock, Zarnak ascertained that he'd have some time to spare before his appointment with Dr. Stillnor, so he decided to check in at a bed and breakfast he knew of along Washington Street in Arkham's historic district. Passing through a few suburban neighborhoods, he soon found himself in an area where big, Victorian-era homes still stood, preserved by the efforts of the city's Historic District Commission. In many respects, Arkham was still a college town, and a small one at that. Miskatonic University itself had not grown much since the heyday of ivy league schools in the early part of the century. Its reputation then was much respected in the areas of archeology and anthropology, but in the 1960s the tide of such subjects had moved out and the school was better known today for being somewhat old-fashioned and behind the times. Newer departments dedicated to xenobiology and cryptoarcheology, however, did little to enhance the institution's standing in the academic community.

Zarnak had little trouble finding the bed and breakfast, and, after bringing in his things, he took his briefcase back to the car and headed across town to the hospital. He found the Pickerton Rehabilitation Hospital located behind a stone wall on well-manicured acreage that, in better weather, no doubt had a calming effect on its patients. He identified himself to a speaker at the entrance and had the satisfaction of seeing the iron gates swing slowly open. A short drive beneath bare-branched trees led him to the visitor parking lot where he left the Mustang. An unassuming side entrance brought him to the reception area where he asked for Dr. Stillnor. Soon he was met by a middle-aged man in a white lab coat who offered his hand in greeting.

"Dr. Zarnak?" he asked.

"Yes," replied Zarnak, taking the man's hand. "And you are Dr. Stillnor?"

"I am. Shall we go to my office?"

Stillnor led Zarnak beyond a pair of doors that cut off the reception desk from the administration area and up a corridor to a door labeled "Dr. Aaron Stillnor." Stepping inside, Stillnor motioned Zarnak to a chair and took the one behind the room's desk.

"I saw from your note that you've familiarized yourself somewhat with Mr. Danforth's case?" asked Stillnor without preamble.

"I did," replied Zarnak. "I found it most interesting."

"That's good," admitted Stillnor. "Because I've been somewhat at a loss as to how to proceed."

"Suppose you fill me in on the details." The spare-framed, vaguely Eurasian-looking man sat back, passive for the moment.

"There's not much to tell," began Stillnor. "The patient, Charles Danforth, has been here at the hospital for eight years. His family asked that he be transferred from Danvers, hoping that a private institution could provide more personalized treatment. It seems to have worked, though I hesitate to take credit for Danforth's sudden emergence from his comatose state."

"Did your treatment vary in any way from that provided at Danvers?"

"Very little," said Stillnor. "An increased use of mineral baths and more frequent muscular massage to loosen the limbs. As you know, this case has been somewhat unusual in that it seemed to involve a combination of both catalepsy and coma so that treatment was necessarily bifurcated. Maybe it was the combination of the two that triggered something in Danforth's mind, bringing him to full wakefulness."

"Hmm. So it seems to me that the patient is on the road to recovery. A happy situation for his family, I'm sure."

"It would seem so except for the fact that the patient has been delusional ever since coming to his senses. He thrashes about with such violence that we've had to have him restrained and even sedated for his own protection. Those precautions may calm him down physically, but I've not been able reach him where it counts, his reasoning mind."

"But you say the drugs have calmed him down. He hasn't been receptive to the usual methods of verbal communication?"

"Not at all."

"Have you tried hypnotherapy?"

"As a last measure of desperation, but it hasn't succeeded. The patient lacks the ability to concentrate long."

"And what do you expect from me?"

"To be frank, Doctor," said Stillnor, "you've had some success in other cases that have seemed intractable. As with any other professional, it was difficult for me to admit that there was nothing else I could do for the patient and that I needed to consult with a specialist. I hope you can help me, doctor."

"Well, I can't promise anything, of course, but I'm certainly willing to give you all the assistance I can."

"Fine," said Stillnor, rising. "Would you like to look at the patient, then?"

"Certainly, doctor. Do you mind if I leave my things here?"

After Zarnak had deposited his briefcase and coat in Stillnor's office, the two made their way from the administrative wing to the wards. Emerging from the elevator on the third floor, they encountered patients sitting quietly in wheelchairs or shuffling down corridors. Others remained in their rooms as a nurse held down a station midway along the corridor and an orderly and some nurse's aids worked directly with patients.

"How is the patient in Room 12?" asked Stillnor of the duty nurse.

"He's been quiet for about an hour now," said the nurse in low tones. "But that happens occasionally. I don't expect it to last."

"Has there been any change in his behavior otherwise?"

"I'm afraid not, doctor," said the nurse. "When he's active, he still raves about the snow and such."

"Thank you. This is Dr. Zarnak; he'll be consulting with me on Danforth's case."

"How do you do, doctor?" asked the nurse who could not help noticing the slash of silver that zig zagged like a bolt of lightning through Zarnak's otherwise dark hair

"Very well, nurse . . . Popworth?" said Zarnak, looking at the name pin on the woman's uniform. "What's this about snow?"

"A mania the patient has," said Stillnor before the nurse could reply. "Ever since coming out of the coma, Danforth has expressed an extreme phobia of snow. Possibly connected to his experience in Antarctica many years ago. I've considered the possibility that his current state is some kind of throwback to those days . . . he may be imagining that he's still there in those cold, isolated wastes."

"Such cases have been known to drive men to insanity, but, from what I understand, he was somewhat well adjusted after he first returned from Antarctica," said Zarnak. "Something else may be at work here."

"Only one way to find out," said Stillnor leading the way to room 12.

There, he opened the plain wooden door . . . it was unlocked . . . and motioned Zarnak inside.

According to the chart that Zarnak took from the end of the bed, Charles Danforth was 60 years old but looked older due mainly to a thin frame which had been nourished almost entirely intravenously since his hospitalization in 1935. His hair was entirely white and the padded cuffs that held his arms and legs to the bed frame seemed hardly necessary to restrain such a wisp of a figure.

At the moment, the patient was awake but resting quietly. His dark eyes were alert, however, as they focused on Zarnak and tracked his movemenra around the bed. Taking a penlight from his breast pocket, Zarnak examined Danforth's reaction to light. Satisfied, he straightened and put away the instrument.

With Danforth's eyes still looking into his, Zarnak saw the patient try to speak.

"What is it, Mr. Danforth?" asked Zarnak, bending forward.

"Snow . . ." whispered Danforth. "Is it . . . snowing?"

Encouraged by the seeming rationality in the patient's voice, Zarnak was careful in making his reply. "Why, no. It's not snowing outside. Why does that matter, Mr. Danforth?"

"The snow was white," said Danforth, struggling for breath. "The mist was white . . . those mountains . . . higher than the clouds . . . higher than anything . . . They were so big, even 300 miles away . . . so high they touched the stars . . . but there was something bigger still! I saw it! It moved and was standing *behind* the mountains! *Behind* the mountains!"

Suddenly, Danforth lost control of himself and began to laugh hysterically, then to thrash about, pulling at his restraints. Froth began to foam on his lips, and his eyes grew big and round with the veins plain-etched on the whites of his eyeballs.

"The snow! The damned snow! It covered it all over so that I couldn't see! The thing! The thing that towered over the mountains! Oh, God! The snow! Thank God for the snow! It hides everything, even the truth!"

So violent became his struggling that Stillnor feared for the patient's safety. Quickly, he called for a sedative, then stabbed the needle into Danforth's arm and threw the plunger.

It was a powerful dose and soon took effect . . . or at least it seemed to.

Danforth had certainly calmed down, but what happened next came too swiftly to be the result of the sedative. His eyes were still open but no longer made contact with those of his visitors. Instead, they stared unblinkingly at the ceiling.

"The shape must be altered," he was saying, almost under his breath. "The bounds disfigured. The Elder Sign of Mnar must be broken. Must find the stones. But the snow, the snow will make it hard to find them. Must find them before it snows . . ."

The words trailed off at last as the full effects of the sedative took hold.

"Is there anything else you need to see, doctor?" asked Stillnor after a few moments when the room was filled only with the sound of Danforth's steady breathing.

Zarnak shook his head from where he had moved to the foot of the bed. "No. I think I've seen all I need to see."

Later, back in Stillnor's office, the two physicians consulted.

"So what has been your own diagnosis, doctor?" asked Zarnak by way of opening the discussion.

"Well on the face of it, the patient's ravings make little sense aside from an obvious phobia related to mountains . . . a fear of heights perhaps? On the other hand, he also seems unusually apprehensive about snow; you noticed how the first thing he said when he saw you was to ask whether it was snowing?"

Zarnak nodded.

"The solution to the patient's problem then is to find some way to relieve him of these unfounded fears," continued Stillnor. "Unfortunately, his nervous attitude seems to preclude, at least for the time being, analysis of any kind. A leading dialogue with the patient is out of the question so long as he isn't rational."

"Dialogue does seem out of the question. . . ."

"Do you have any suggestions, doctor?"

Zarnak was quiet a moment before suddenly getting to his feet. Hands in his pockets, he paced briefly before pausing by the window and looking out over the spreading lawn leading down to the street.

"Tell me, doctor," he began. "What do you know of Danforth's personal history?"

"Well . . . aside from the years spent at Danvers . . . he seems to have been a promising student at Miskatonic University when he was a young man. I've been told that professors at the time had high hopes for him, and one even recruited him for the expedition to the Antarctic, I believe. In fact, I'd briefly considered the possibility that his phobia regarding snow might have been connected to that trip."

"In a way, I think it is," conceded Zarnak turning to face Stillnor. "Does the name of the Dyer Expedition mean anything to you, doctor?"

"I believe that was the name of the expedition that Danforth accompanied to the Antarctic."

"Correct. It took place in 1930 and was quite well equipped for the time," said Zarnak.

"I'm afraid that I'm not familiar with the details of . . ."

"The expedition's major claim to fame was the discovery of a megalithic city nestled between a pair of mountain ranges off the Ross Ice Shelf," explained Zarnak. "When communications failed between the base camp and an advance camp located at the foot of the first range of mountains, Danforth accompanied Prof. Dyer to investigate. Although the two said little about exactly what they found there when they returned to civilization, a later plea written by Dyer, intended to discourage further exploration beyond the mountains, was more explicit describing a scene of horror in which all the bodies of their comrades had been torn apart. You can imagine how such a scene might impress a young mind. . . ."

Stillnor nodded. "I hadn't realized . . . I never had access to such a report!"

"But that was not all," continued Zarnak. "Dyer also described a series of strange burial sites in the snow where portions of biological specimens discovered by his colleagues had been interred . . ."

"I seem to recall something about that but thought it mere fancy. . . ."

"Not hardly, doctor, as portions of those specimens were rescued from the camp site and returned to Miskatonic University where, I believe, they have been stored ever since."

"Be that as it may, what does it all have to do with Danforth?"

"Suffice to say that if we are to believe Dyer's words, the condition of the advance camp site was only a prologue to other horrors to come when he and Danforth went on to discover the stone city. There, amid the ruins, they came upon evidence that whoever killed their colleagues at the advance camp had escaped in that direction taking along the body of Felix Gedney, a close friend of Danforth's."

"I still fail to see . . ."

"From what I have read in newspaper accounts of the time, it appears that Dyer and Danforth agreed to say as little as possible about the expedition beyond their discovery of the advance camp site," said Zarnak. "Later, Dyer described Danforth as having been the more shaken of the two and sometimes barely able to keep his composure. I believe that Danforth struggled against a complete breakdown and even sought psychiatric help. Unfortunately, nothing helped and, to protect himself from whatever it was that disturbed him, he forced a self-induced catalepsy."

"It sounds plausible," conceded Stillnor. "But how does it explain his coming round now? Or his phobia about snow . . . ?"

"His ravings about something that was behind the mountains . . . that is, the second, more distant range of mountains beyond the stone city . . . I think is the key. In short, where Danforth may have prompted self-induced catalepsy, something else may have brought him out of it."

Momentarily at a loss for words, Stillnor simply stared at Zarnak.

"Something else?"

"The thing he mentioned just now," said Zarnak. "The thing that stood behind the mountains."

"An imaginary . . . thing . . . of course?"

Zarnak shrugged. "Not necessarily."

"You mean, based on the ravings of a deranged mind, you're suggesting to me that some kind of . . . of monster is influencing Danforth's mind across time and space or whatever?"

"Stranger things have happened."

"You might think so, but it sounds ridiculous to me."

"Be that as it may, a simple phobia of snow is not Danforth's problem."

"I'm sorry, doctor, but I cannot accept your explanation," said Stillnor, rising. "I appreciate your taking the time to see the patient, but I can only take your opinion as a consultant on the case and keep it in mind in my considerations. I'm sorry I cannot be more specific in my conclusions than that."

By way of reply, Zarnak took his briefcase and resting it on the desk, opened it and removed some folders.

"I understand, doctor," he said, placing the folders on the desk. "These are copies of the material relating to the Dyer Expedition and Danforth's return to Arkham in 1931. I'll leave them with you."

Snapping shut the briefcase, Zarnak shrugged into his coat.

"If you change your mind and would like to talk further on this case, doctor, call my office anytime."

In another moment, Stillnor was alone in his office.

II

Later that afternoon, while making his final rounds of the day, Stillnor could not help thinking about the things Zarnak had said. On the third floor, he checked with Nurse Popworth, asking in particular about Danforth.

"He's been quiet since you and Dr. Zarnak left," reported Popworth. "But I'm afraid we're going to have to put him on an IV again if he refuses to eat."

Nodding, Stillnor went to room 12 and, not wishing to disturb the patient, merely peeked in through the small one-way window set in the door. Danforth was still secured but resting quietly. His eyes stared at the ceiling and his lips moved silently.

Satisfied, Stillnor checked in again with the nurse and returned to his office. Gathering his things, he hesitated only slightly before including the folder given him by Zarnak in his briefcase. The drive home was uneventful, and he went through his routine of preparing dinner and catching up with the news on television. Refilling his cup with coffee, he retired to his study where he began going over the day's reports.

He had not been at it long before the phone on his desk rang. Wondering who it could be, he picked up the receiver and identified himself.

"Doctor, this is Nurse Popworth at the hospital," said the voice at the other end. "Something has happened here that I thought you should know about right away."

"What is it?"

"Some time ago, we don't know exactly when, the patient in room 12 managed to escape."

"Escape!" said Stillnor, surprised. "Danforth? He was all right when I checked on him before leaving for the day."

"I realize that, doctor. No one checked his room again until dinner time. When Mr. Scott, the orderly on duty, went to see if the patient would eat anything, he found that he was gone. We're not sure how he managed to escape the restraints, but one band seemed to have been chewed through."

"Well, then how did he get out of the building? Someone must have seen him."

"The door to his room was still locked when Scott checked, but his window was open. As you know, there are no grills on the third floor windows. . . ."

"You mean to tell me that he escaped out a third story window?"

"He must have. There was no other way out of the room. Anyway, the police agree that it must have been the window. They found impressions in the ground where someone who jumped might have landed."

"So you called the police?"

"As per hospital policy, doctor."

"Good. What did they say about getting the patient back?"

"They were optimistic that they could find him quickly . . . he was only wearing a jonnie when he escaped and was barefoot so he couldn't have gone far."

Stillnor breathed a sigh of relief. Nevertheless, it was never good for an institution's reputation to have patients escape! The sooner Danforth could be found, the better.

"Well, it seems the situation is under control," said Stillnor. "Unless you think it would do any good for me to go in, I'll remain here. . . ."

"I think that would be all right for now, doctor."

"Very well. Let me know as soon as you hear anything from the police. We'll go through the whole thing in the morning."

"Yes, doctor."

Hanging up, Stillnor was nevertheless torn between the need to stay by the phone and an urge to hop in his car and search the streets himself. He was still debating the issue when the phone rang again.

"This is Dr. Stillnor."

"Doctor, Popworth here. Just wanted you to know that the police reported that a cruiser spotted someone answering the description of Danforth at the bus station. If it was our patient, he managed to get some clothes somehow because he wasn't in his jonnie."

"The bus station? How the devil did he manage to get that far without being spotted?"

"I'm sure I don't know, doctor."

"Well, were they able to take him into custody at least?"

"Unfortunately, no. When the officers approached him, the patient disappeared into a crowd."

It was the last anyone heard or saw of Danforth for some weeks until officers cruising the area around Stuart Street one night caught sight of someone digging around Pickering Common. Investigating, they thought the man's description fit that of the missing Danforth and called in the sighting. Unfortunately, the man managed to flee before he could be secured.

Naturally, the weeks since Danforth's escape were not easy ones for Stillnor who, as supervising physician at the hospital, had to account to the board for the patient's escape. Luckily, however, it was left to the superintendent to deal with family members who were understandably distraught at the situation.

But even with the escape of a patient, work at the hospital had go on and so it was that Stillnor found himself at home one night trying to catch up with paperwork when the doorbell rang. Rising, he went to the front door and opened it. Standing there was a tall man with dark hair peppered in gray. He wore a trench coat.

"Doctor Stillnor?" the man asked.

"Yes."

"Doctor, I'm Detective Shonross of the Arkham Police Department," said the man, holding out identification.

"Oh, yes; we've spoken on the phone. Have you any news about our escaped patient?"

"As a matter of fact, I do," confirmed Shonross. "The man last seen digging around in Pickering Common has been seen again and this time we're sure it's Danforth."

"Seen again?" asked Stillnor anxiously, beckoning Shonross indoors. "You sound as if he hasn't been picked up yet."

"He hasn't," admitted Shonross. "He's managed to keep one step ahead of us so far, but with an all points alarm out, I think it's only a matter of time before we bring him in."

"Well, I certainly appreciate being kept informed about the department's progress. . . ."

"Danforth has been spotted a couple times this evening in different parts of town," revealed Shonross. "But for a man on the run, your patient has been demonstrating some strange behavior and I thought it might be useful to talk to you about it. Maybe you can figure out what the man has in mind."

"Since he was moved to our facility last year, the patient has never shown any kind of rational behavior, so it's hard to imagine that there might be any thought going into his actions."

"Don't want to second guess you, doctor, but the patient did have the presence of mind to escape from your hospital. He knew how to do that well enough didn't he?"

"That's so," admitted Stillnor.

"So, is there any possibility that the patient is looking for something?"

"Looking for something?" asked Stillnor, surprised. "Not that I'm aware of. He's been in one hospital or another for over forty years. It's hardly likely that the first thing he'd do with his freedom is go looking for something. . . ."

"He's been missing for almost three weeks, doctor," reminded Shonross. "So he must have been doing something in that time. Anyway, now that he's back in Arkham, it seems that he must be looking for something because each time he's been spotted, he was caught digging. Twice tonight he's managed to get away from us and both times when officers went over to see what he was doing, there were fresh dug holes about two feet deep in the ground."

Puzzled, Stillnor could offer nothing in explanation.

"The second time though, was closer than the first. Officers surprised him and when he got up to run, he dropped something. It was caked in dirt so we know it was something he'd just dug up."

"What was it?"

"Well, that's something we were hoping you could tell us." So saying, the detective produced an object from his pocket and handed it to Stillnor.

Taking it, Stillnor at first thought it was just a rock but on closer examination noticed its distinct coloration and shape: that of a five-point-ed star with the tips broken off. The star itself was of a design he'd never seen before.

"Have any idea what that is?" asked Shonross presently.

"No. I've never seen anything like it before."

Just then, even through the closed doorway, the squawk of a police radio could be heard from the detective's car parked outside.

"Have to go," said Shonross. "I'll leave that with you for now, but let me know if you think of anything that can help us figure out what Danforth is going to do next."

"I will," assured Stillnor letting the detective out.

Absently, Stillnor made his way back to the study, turning the strange star stone over in his hands. By midnight there was no more news of Danforth, so he thought he could snatch a few hours of sleep before heading in to work. Taking one last look at the star stone, he set it on the night table by his bed and slipped under the covers.

III

The first impression he had was the feeling that they were being watched. The camp site lay on a vast plain of white snow that stretched for miles back in the direction from which they had traveled. Back there, a rising wind obscured the horizon, casting the whole world into a fea-tureless white haze. The coming storm was rolling in from the direction of a towering range of mountains at the foot of which the camp had been pitched, mountains so high that their peaks were nothing but naked rocks far above the snow line. There, nature, through millions of years of weathering, had so fashioned their steep flanks as to make them ap-pear carved by human hands. Reaching downward thousands of feet into the snow at their base, the rock looked for all the world like it was a pile of giant blocks piled one atop the other. It was a formation that the camp's leader, Prof. Joseph Lake, had intended to study at close range but for a more immediate discovery.

Standing outside the group of tents that comprised the core of the camp site, he could see in the distance the iron derrick that held the drill designed by Prof. Pabodie. With it, the expedition had managed to break through the ice into a cavern where a remarkable discovery was made. A veritable boneyard of artifacts including a set of completely unidentifiable biological specimens that no one was certain represented either the animal or vegetable kingdoms. Excitement over the discovery was palpable, and the specimens were hauled to the surface and stored outside where the cold would continue to preserve them. But Lake, be-ing a biologist, could not wait to find out more about the things and had one brought in under cover of a tent. There, he could see the fitful glow of a lantern on the rough fabric and the silhouette of figures moving inside where Lake had decided to dissect the specimen.

His feet crunching in the hoar frost, he made his way to the tent and entered. Lake was there holding a scalpel with Gedney and a few others looking on. All but Lake were clearly uncomfortable and one look at the thing on the table before them would be enough for anyone to say why. It was almost eight feet long with some kind of membranous wings folded under it where it lay on the table. Inexplicably, there appeared to be suckers or mouths at the tips of the wing struts. Around a thick middle, spread equi-distantly around the thing were five rubbery tentacles that in turn branched out twice more with sub-groups of five smaller filaments. Atop the thing was a huge rugose mass in the shape of a five-pointed star with stalks projecting from each point. The flesh at the end of one stalk was pulled back to reveal what looked to be an eye. Atop the star-shaped head was a grotesque looking slit. The opposite end of the thing was likewise appendaged with a series of extensions that could have supplied locomotion. It was altogether a disgusting sight made worse by an almost overpowering stench that filled the enclosed space. It was a situation in which he had to force himself to remain where he was. At the very moment Lake finished opening the thing up, there came a sudden disturbance outside.

Everyone in the tent started when the dogs, which had been kept in a corral some distance from the main camp site, erupted in a wild frenzy of howling and whining. When he emerged from the tent to see what was happening, the wind outside had progressed into a gale that set the tents to flapping and lashed unprotected faces with crystals of icy snow. Holding his hand over his eyes, he looked in the direction of the corral just in time to see the dogs break through their snowy enclosure and begin to run off. But then it seemed to him that vague figures moving in the storm positioned themselves to stop the stampede. He could make out nothing for some minutes, but in that time the sounds of the dogs died away among a few isolated yelps. Finally all was quiet again, and he was on the point of investigating when one of the tents collapsed in the wind. Rushing to the scene to save what he could, he thought he heard screaming from still another tent that had been set aside for the radio. Changing his mind about the collapsed tent, he leaned into the howling storm and made for the radio hut instead. Some minutes later, he reached it and burst inside. There he found no one. Camp stools and bunks, however, had been overturned, the radio smashed, and everywhere there was a stench that threatened to make his gorge rise. Holding his hand over his mouth, he stumbled from the tent. Squinting into the driving snow, he thought he saw movement outside the tent where Lake and the others had been gathered, but they seemed strangely disfigured and over-large. Was it the howling wind or did he hear the sounds of screaming? He thought he heard a crash but could not be sure. The next he knew, movement around the distant tent had ceased along with any noise save that of the wind. Struggling against the rapidly gathering snow, he lifted his feet and trudged toward where he had seen the activity. At last, he fell through the tent opening to find the interior a chaos of smashed instruments and scattered equipment. In the center of the enclosure, the table still stood but the specimen that Lake had been dissecting was gone. Again, there was that terrible smell, and footprints in the snow blown into the tent by the wind outside hinted at furious and hurried activity.

Suddenly, above the howling wind outside and the furious noise of the shuddering tent, he thought he heard screams but the kind of screams more akin to animals than human beings. Had some of the dogs returned to the campsite? Now wondering where the others had gone, he looked toward the snow shelters erected to protect the expedition's airplanes from the weather. Surprised, he noticed that one of the planes had been removed from its shelter and the dull flicker of a lantern danced inside the hollow where it had been stored. Making his way to the plane, its details and those of the enclosure became more vivid. He came across a deep trail through the snow leading to the shelter. Strewn about were various camping implements and foodstuffs. Near the entrance to the enclosure, he saw a few of the expedition's sleds piled high with supplies. A tarp covering one of the sleds moved with more energy than could be expected from the wind. He veered aside and reaching it, pulled the tarp back. Beneath it was Gedney, strapped tightly to the sled. His eyes stared about in maniacal panic and, though he tried to say something, all he could manage were unintelligible mutterings. Saliva dribbled from the corners of his mouth and froze on his cheeks.

He would have said something to Gedney, but a noise from inside the shelter drew his attention. There, lantern light still flickered and a few moans could be heard. The snow had fallen from the interstices between the blocks of hardened snow, and through them he could see figures moving about. Something about them seemed wrong. They were uniformly tall; taller than anyone in the camp, and their heads seemed too big for their bodies. Also, there were *too many* of them, more than could be accounted for by the members of the expedition. Curious, but with growing trepidation, he rounded the corner of the enclosure to the large, open end where the tail section of the plane crowded close. The glare of a toppled lantern blinded him momentarily, but when his eyes cleared, the first thing he noticed were the figures lined up on the snowy floor of the enclosure. At first, he thought they were the specimens the crew had retrieved from the cave, but as he stared, he realized that they were too small for that, the flesh too pale. With growing horror he recognized Lake at the head of the line; his torso had been opened up and parts of him lay scattered in the snow. Now he saw that the other figures were also members of the expedition: stripped and their bodies taken apart in various ways. Then, his vision broadened and he sensed the others occupying the enclosure. Something stepped between him and the lantern, something that loomed gigantically in silhouette, blocking any further view into the enclosure. He took a step back in surprise, but at once surprise was overtaken by horror as he saw what it was that he faced. The large shape where the head ought to have been was shaped like a five-pointed star orbited by waving eye stalks that studied him unblinkingly. Shifting its weight, the thing moved toward him, its five tentacular arms lashing out, already glistening with blood, its huge bulk towering over him. . . .

IV

Stillnor sat bolt upright in bed, a scream in his throat, one that stopped only when he'd run out of breath. Panting, he threw off the covers and immediately was chilled by the sheen of perspiration that lathered his body.

Running a nervous hand through his hair, he forced himself up and stumbled to the bathroom where he splashed warm water on his face and swallowed a gulp or two directly from the tap.

Calmed down greatly since waking, Stillnor decided not to return immediately to bed. Instead, he threw on his bathrobe and went to make a cup of coffee. By the time he'd finished the familiar routine, he was able to take the cup into the study without spilling any of its contents.

Just a nightmare, he assured himself. *It was all that talk by Zarnak about Antarctica and the Dyer Expedition that did it. I always did have an active imagination.*

Sitting in the darkened study, Stillnor found himself facing his desk and remembered the folder Zarnak had left with him. Resisting a rising fear that reviewing at its contents would force a recurrence of the nightmare, he reached over and took the folder.

Opening it, he began to examine its contents in the light that spilled into the study from the hall. Mostly the folder contained copies of articles and reports published at the time of the Dyer Expedition and its return to the United States. Here was Dyer's plea against further exploration of the mountain ranges his own expedition had discovered and a piece on the artifacts brought back for display at the Miskatonic's museum. There, the dispatches to local newspapers received by radio direct from the expedition. Stillnor hesitated at one noting the discovery of a plant or animal with a head shaped like a five-pointed star. . . . A coincidence he was sure perhaps brought on by the stone given him earlier in the evening by Detective Shonross. Continuing on, he came across some photos among which was a group shot of the Dyer Expedition. Even before he had a chance to read the dateline below the photo, he recognized one of the members: Felix Gedney. Now why was that? He'd never seen the man before or his likeness. Didn't Zarnak mention that he'd been a student on the expedition . . . that he'd died, his body discovered by Danforth? Yes, that was it. But now he recalled his dream and was sure Gedney had been in it but in just what capacity, he couldn't remember.

He had almost finished going through the contents of the folder when he came upon another photo that caught his attention. This time it was one of a star-shaped stone, identical it seemed to the one on his nightstand. Looking further, there was a quote from Prof. Dyer calling it a "Mnar stone," something to which certain historical texts ascribed protective properties, but protection against what? Then something began to tickle the back of Stillnor's mind. He went to a cabinet and found a street map of Arkham. Unfolding it, he located the places where Danforth had been sighted earlier that evening. Taking a pencil, he drew lines radiating from those points and then, assuming a five-pointed star pattern, completed the form. The places where Danforth had been found digging were located at the points of the assumed star. Could it be that there was method to his madness? If so, then Stillnor was certain he could now predict where Danforth would appear next!

Excited with his theory, Stillnor decided that it was too insubstantial to report to the police. He'd take his car and go to the next place he thought Danforth would go. But so as not to waste his time, he called the police to find out if his patient had been sighted anywhere else since Detective Shonross had paid him a visit. He had been but, again, escaped before he could be apprehended. Hanging up the phone, Stillnor marked the location on his map. It still fit the pattern! Quickly, he grabbed his coat and ran out to the garage. Backing out the car a little too quickly, he forced himself to calm down and take his time driving to Front Street where a little park would provide the perfect place for digging.

It was almost dawn by the time Stillnor pulled up across the street from the park. There were a few benches but no playground equipment. This was simply an island of green in a neighborhood of older homes that had been renovated in recent years. Slouching down behind the wheel, Stillnor prepared for what he expected to be a short wait. And right enough, it wasn't long before some movement caught his eye and a white-garbed figure crept from the shadows and made its way to the park. Quietly, Stillnor slipped from his car and raced across the street, keeping a row of hedges between himself and Danforth. Peering over the shrubs, he could see him on his knees already, digging with a stick he'd found, not an easy task what with the late autumn cold. Cautiously, Stillnor rose and tip-toed toward Danforth; then, with a quick lunge, he threw himself on top of him. Danforth struggled with unaccountable might: was this the same man who had wasted away in hospital beds for years? Stillnor had a good grip on him, or thought he did. Danforth managed to break free and, spinning about, must have recognized Stillnor because he stopped suddenly. But there was nervous tension in everything about him as he crouched, ready to run at the slightest provocation.

"Mr. Danforth," gasped Stillnor in an attempt to reassure him. "Remember me? I'm Dr. Stillnor."

"I remember you, doctor," said Danforth in a voice Stillnor barely recognized. "You want me to go back to the hospital. Well, maybe I will after I'm done with what I have to do."

"What do you have to do, Charles?" asked Stillnor, using Danforth's first name to reinforce a soothing familiarity.

"Star stones," said Danforth, looking this way and that as if fearful of being discovered. "The Old Ones' sign and their protection. Prof. Dyer . . ."

"What about Prof. Dyer?"

"Dyer, Dyer, Dyer!" shouted Danforth, suddenly. "Dyer hid them and I have to find them before it snows! It's his fault I had to go!"

At a loss for words, Stillnor could only stare, hoping Danforth would regain control of himself and let him take him back to the hospital.

"The voice in my head!" agonized Danforth as he pounded his skull with his fists in some kind of desperate attempt to drive out whatever it was that had compelled him to flee the hospital and disappear for weeks. "The voice won't leave me alone! It tells me what to do, and I don't want to do anything! I just want to be alone! Alone!"

"Get hold of yourself, Charles," soothed Stillnor. "I'll help you, but first we have to get back to the hospital. . . ."

"No! I have to get the stones, break the wards, end the protection; the voice said so," insisted Danforth, obviously struggling in some sort of mental tug of war. "Dyer hid the stones. Dyer and I. He said they'd protect us from them. I don't *want* to remove them, but the voice says they work against hybrids, too, so I have to. I *have* to!"

With that, Danforth finally lost control and ran off into the night, leaving a startled Stillnor looking helplessly after him.

Not knowing what else to do, Stillnor decided to return home and inform Shonross how he had learned to predict Danforth's movements. He determined not to tell the detective of his own encounter with the patient, there was really no need. He was sure that with his information, the police could lie in wait at all of the remaining points that Danforth was sure to visit and nab him at one of them.

On the way home, however, Stillnor had the opportunity to mull over Danforth's obvious agitation. Surely, from what he could see, the patient was still suffering from some residual effects of his catalepsy. His ravings made little sense, and his agonized behavior indicated a great deal of internal confusion. Still, his condition was a great improvement over his previous comatose state, and Stillnor now had hopes that his patient could make a complete recovery under proper psychological care.

The key was to free him of the delusion that he was hearing voices, voices that seemed to blame Prof. Dyer for his predicament. Clearly, Danforth attached significance to digging up the so-called star stones that he claimed . . . wait! The star stones! They were obviously no delusion: Danforth had been digging them up, and one was even delivered by Shonross to his home! Despite himself, Stillnor was suddenly forced to accept the fact that aspects of Danforth's ravings were based in reality. What was it he'd said? That it was both he *and* Dyer who had hidden the stones. For some kind of protection against . . . what? Suddenly Stillnor found Danforth's case to be more complicated than he first assumed. The more he considered it, the more questions he had.

Back in his study, Stillnor made his call to the police. It took a while to convince Shonross of his "theory," but at last he succeeded. That done, he was free to look again through the material given him by Zarnak. There was mention of the star stone, so-called in Dyer's old monograph about what he termed "the mountains of madness." And of their apparent connection to a pre-human race of star-headed creatures he dubbed "Old Ones," but nothing about any protective qualities they might have. Also, there was mention of Danforth's mental condition upon their return to the United States and their agreement not to discuss details of what they'd found in Antarctica. Clearly, from the monograph, Stillnor could tell that something had shaken Danforth greatly, but was it really some ultimate horror as hinted at by Dyer? What he needed, thought Stillnor, was more information about what Dyer and Danforth did after they arrived home from the expedition. Why, for instance, did the two apparently bury star stones around Arkham? Smacking of superstition, the action made little sense for men of science such as Danforth and especially Dyer.

Considering, Stillnor now recalled that Zarnak had said that artifacts were brought back by the Dyer Expedition and had since been housed at Miskatonic University. The museum there, he knew, was quite famous for its collection of artifacts from around the world, gathered mostly before the Second World War. The institution had fallen behind somewhat in its display and cataloguing since those days, but, as he understood it, it still boasted material that scholars found invaluable. Surely, among that material he could find information on Dyer's doings after he returned from that ill-fated Antarctic expedition?

V

Stillnor was too busy at the hospital the next couple of days to get away, due mostly to the return of Danforth who had been captured by police at one of the locations Stillnor had suggested. Trussed in a straightjacket, the patient had been able to walk into the hospital with a police officer on either arm but, soon after being placed in his room, he'd lapsed into silence and refused to cooperate with the staff.

The apparent retrogression was very disappointing to Stillnor personally who had seen how energetic, if somewhat neurotic, Danforth had been only days before. Still, he'd hoped that upon his return to the hospital, there would be a basis upon which to build an eventual recovery. Now that didn't seem likely, and he was forced to fall back on a variation of the previous treatment regimen.

Thus, by the time the weekend rolled around, Stillnor's professional frustration was such that he found himself willing to consider more unorthodox approaches to Danforth's problem. Perhaps the answers did lie among Dyer's papers housed at the Mikatonic library.

The weather was still frosty when he left home that Saturday afternoon for the short drive across town to the University campus. The sun never did make it much over the horizon as the days grew shorter and already the shadows of coming evening stretched across the city, leaving some areas where buildings crowded close together in perpetual gloom.

As venerable as Miskatonic University was, it had not grown much since its founding as most other such institutions had a habit of doing. Its main buildings, including library and museum, still huddled close together on high ground overlooking Arkham's historic downtown. Stillnor found some visitor parking below the hill and joining a few students heading in the same direction, soon reaching the overheated lobby of the old library building. The roomy hallways were all linoleum and polished wood frame, and through a pair of doors set in an entrance arch Stillnor could see the reference section with its heavy tables, card catalogues, and shelves groaning under the weight of massed volumes. Entering, he spied the reference desk and approached a middle-aged woman busy stamping arrival dates on the flyleaves of newly acquired books.

"Excuse me," said Stillnor. "I am looking for something that might be housed in special collections."

"Anything in particular?"

"The papers of Prof. William Dyer. He held the archeology chair at the University in the 1930s."

"That would be upstairs," she said, pointing with her stamp in the direction of a staircase at the rear of the room.

"Thank you."

Stillnor mounted the heavy staircase whose marble steps had been worn down over the years by the numberless feet of undergraduates. At the top, the landing was dominated by a large glass display case which, upon closer examination, Stillnor was surprised to see contained the famous *Necronomicon*. He knew little about its contents beyond what he'd read in local newspapers from time to time, but he was aware that it was supposed to be an extremely rare copy. Briefly, he wondered why it seemed to be displayed in such an insecure fashion. Well, he was here on other business at the moment and moved on to a doorway with a placard that read "special collections."

It led to a medium-sized room that smelled strongly of parchment and old books. Metal shelves crowded the available space, leaving only narrow avenues between them. A scratched-up wooden table with two chairs was pushed up beneath a pair of windows and in a corner a tiny desk was covered in thick folders and a few ancient volumes.

"Hello?" ventured Stillnor.

"I'm here," said a voice from among the stacks, followed by the wizened features of what was no doubt one of the school's retired teachers. "Yes? Can I help you?"

"I'm Dr. Aaron Stillnor, of the Pickerton Rehabilitation Hospital here in town," said Stillnor. "I have a patient whose case may turn on events that happened forty years ago, and was hoping I might find records belonging to one of your former professors here."

"What's his name?"

"Prof. William Dyer. He taught here in the 1930s and 40s."

"Oh, yes. Died in 1961. Served as chair of the University's archeology department for many years."

"Then you'll know if any of his papers or records of any sort were preserved?"

"Naturally. Most of Miskatonic's faculty bequeath their papers to the University . . . well most have, anyway."

As the clerk was speaking, he led the way into an adjoining room which was, incredibly, even more crowded than the first. Waiting in the doorway, Stillnor watched as the man made his way down one of the aisles and apparently found what he was looking for.

"We have all of Prof. Dyer's papers here in bound volumes," he said, looking over his glasses. "They're labeled by year. . . ."

"Those covering 1931 or so," replied Stillnor.

Turning back to the shelves, the man reached up and pulled down one fat, crimson bound volume.

"Here we are Doctor," said the man, handing the book to Stillnor. "I'm afraid it can't be taken from the department, though. You can examine it at the table by the window."

"Thank you," said Stillnor.

At the table, Stillnor sat down and opened the book to the contents which indicated the bound records included Dyer's scholarly papers and journals covering the years 1930–1935 including material dealing with his celebrated expedition to the Antarctic.

Flipping to the relevant sections, Stillnor found the goals, itineraries, invoices, and lists of expedition members of the Antarctic venture as well as copies of the cablegrams forwarded to local newspapers from the advance camp set up by Prof. Lake. Although Stillnor had already seen much of the material in the folder Zarnak had left him, he was still somewhat surprised to find the more sensational aspects of the expedition confirmed in Dyer's records. Here was the discovery of the hidden cavern, the strange star-headed creatures or plants found there, the disaster that struck the advance camp after a sudden storm swept down from the mountains.

Here also was Dyer's monograph written in an attempt to dissuade the sponsors of the Starkweather-Moore Expedition. It was rather long, so Stillnor skimmed much of it, lingering only when Dyer mentioned the discovery of Gedney's body deep in the bowels of the ancient city. Overall, he had to admit that the monograph did have a discomforting effect with its sense of mounting horror and its hints that the builders of the city had come from another world, arriving on Earth millions of years before the appearance of men. According to Dyer, they had mastered telepathy and cellular manipulation and had in fact been the creators of humankind! It was rubbish, of course; Dyer offered no definitive proof that any of his conclusions were even plausible. But, however true or untrue they were, it was clear *he* believed them. So much so that only a few pages later, his journal entries indicated that, after conferring with a colleague named Wilmarth, he seemed to have been convinced that use of star stones brought back by the expedition would protect him from something he feared might have followed him from Antarctica. Consequently, he enlisted the aid of Danforth in burying a number of the stones around Arkham, arranging them in the pattern of a single large five-pointed star shape. In the following years, so far as Stillnor could tell, Dyer made no more trips outside of town and soon after burying the stars, Danforth went into cataleptic seizure.

So Danforth was telling the truth when he said he and Dyer had buried the stones! But if that was so, what about the other things he mentioned? Stillnor thought a moment. Danforth said that the five-pointed star was the sign of the Old Ones ... those whom Dyer claimed built the city in Antarctica ... and that voices in his head were telling him to remove the stones, remove the protection ... why? If the star stones belonged to the Old Ones, from whom did they need to be protected? In the monograph, Dyer said that Danforth had seen something even more horrifying than the star-headed creatures found at the advance camp or the so-called shoggoth that chased them out of the city. Was that what they were afraid might come after them even so far away as Arkham was from the bottom of the world?

He'd still not decided what to believe when it occurred to him that the Miskatonic's museum was connected to the library building and that he could view for himself some of the artifacts returned from Dyer's expedition. Suddenly convinced that the answer to his doubts could be found among the bones and petrified samples that lay so near at hand, Stillnor returned his book to the clerk.

"Tell me, is the University's museum open at this hour?" he asked.

"Every day until 8 p.m." The man checked his watch. "But if you want to have time to look through it ... there's plenty to see ... you'd better go now, it's almost 7."

"Already?" Stillnor was genuinely surprised. He had no idea that he'd been reading for so long. "Then you'd better give some good directions so I can find it without any trouble."

The man did so and a few minutes later Stillnor had traversed a short connecting tunnel in the library's basement to an adjoining wing where he took another few minutes to find the corner housing the artifacts from Dyer's expedition. The lights in this section of the museum were turned down low, no doubt due to the fact that it had few visitors. Standing in the gloomy corridor outside the exhibit, he had to chuckle that such a collection was even still on display forty years after it was gathered. Maybe there was some truth to the school's reputation for being behind the times. Even the Peabody Museum in nearby Salem was rumored to be getting rid of its fabled anthropological collection in favor of a less offensive approach to aboriginal cultures.

Stepping under an arch giving way into the exhibit, Stillnor was startled after coming face to face with the biggest penguin he'd ever seen. Bigger than he ever suspected such animals to grow! Erected on a pedestal by the door, the stuffed bird towered over him and must have stood at least 6 feet tall. Its pointy beak partially opened in a silent call, it seemed ready to hop down and charge across the room. Recovering from his surprise, Stillnor was forced to admire the animal and recalled Dyer mentioning such beasts while exploring the stone city.

Slowly, he made a circuit of the room, looking into its many wood and glass display cases and noting the yellowed cards describing the various items. Here was a display of the tools used by the expedition to chip away ice and rock samples, there photos of the expedition at different points: at a banquet the night before embarking, aboard ship, views of the Antarctic ice shelf, Dyer standing with some loaded sledges with the dogs milling behind, an aerial shot of the planes sitting on the snow at the advance camp. Stillnor looked more closely when he came upon a photo of Dyer and Danforth together and another of Prof. Lake directing drilling into the ice.

Moving on, Stillnor became interested in a display of prehistoric artifacts found in the cave explored by Lake and his colleagues: bones, rock fragments including some displaying the odd "footprint" that Dyer claimed belonged to the Old Ones, and an exact replica of the star stone Detective Shonross had given him. Next came more photographs this time of the megalithic city discovered by Dyer and Danforth on the other side of the mountains that looked down upon the advance camp. Suddenly, the reality of Dyer's claims became substantial to him as he gazed upon actual evidence of the existence of the city. A feeling of mounting strangeness overcame him as he looked at the historical carvings Dyer had described so vividly in his monograph, the titanic stone structures that had collapsed upon themselves, the winding stairways and inclined planes that led into deeper gloom in chambers that lay far beneath ground level, the occasional rubble and the long corridors that ended in darkness ahead. Occasionally, a photo even captured the figures of either Dyer or Danforth themselves standing beside some object to help to give the observer some notion of its size. Looking at them, Stillnor was struck by both men's youthful appearance. Danforth had only been an undergraduate of 20 or so when he accompanied the expedition, while Dyer was in his prime at 54.

Sobered by the series of photographs that had altered Dyer and Danforth in his mind from an historical figure and a madman to flesh and blood human beings with lives and hopes and dreams, Stillnor came to the final portion of the exhibit. Mounted on the wall in glass-fronted cases extending from floor to ceiling, were the organic remains of the star-headed creatures discovered by Lake in the cavern beneath the Antarctic ice. Whether they were plant or animal, no one was sure at the time, although in his monograph Dyer claimed they were actually members of the alien race he called the Old Ones. Rather unimpressive, most of the artifacts appeared to be bits and pieces of the things, desiccated and petrified, cut by scalpel so as to best display external and in some cases internal bodily functions.

Taking an involuntary step backward, Stillnor felt an odd repulsion at the display and, as his gaze moved upward, it finally came to rest on what could only have been one of the creatures' star-shaped heads. It lay flat against the tack board behind it with pins holding the five pointed ends at full extension along with the thinner eye stalks. The slit at the center of the starfish head was as Dyer had described it in his monograph. All of it was vaguely disgusting to Stillnor without his being able to say exactly why. Just then, the shadows created by the muted lighting seemed to press down around him and he felt suddenly alone. He hadn't seen a single person in all the time since he entered the museum wing. If no one knew he was here, maybe he'd been locked in? He was on the point of looking for the welcome desk when he was stopped by a peculiar odor. Sniffing, he began to cough, and his gorge threatened to rise. He managed to overcome his initial reaction and, controlling his breathing, couldn't help but follow the scent to find out what could be causing such a stink.

Stepping back out into the corridor, he looked up and down and still saw no one about. Continuing on, he followed the hallway back the way he'd come until arriving at another arched doorway. This one led through a darkened room to another archway on the other side where light revealed many green plants. Heading in that direction, the stench remained strong but now included elements of earth and green growing things. Arriving at the second arch, he found himself at the entrance to a greenhouse filled with what looked to him like exotic plants. Great fern trees stretched to a glass ceiling where a cloud-veiled moon struggled for release in the early evening sky. Closer to the ground, exotic shrubs, flowering plants, lianas, and other flora more akin to a rain forest than the forests of New England dominated. Everywhere, the unpleasant smell still lingered and, despite his having come no closer to discovering its source, something prompted him to continue deeper into the greenhouse where light from the entrance found it difficult to penetrate. Here, the ferns and palms hung thickly about, their details obscured as clouds continued to cover the moon.

There was a tinkle of something knocked across the floor, and suddenly Stillnor was certain he wasn't alone. Frightened, he whirled, casting quick glances around him and seeing only the looming silhouettes of plants whose fronds brushed his head and shoulders. At last, his attention rested on one particular shape that bulked largely amid trunks of palm trees and low hanging branches. Had it moved? Stillnor wasn't sure; it could have been his own looking about that stirred the still air of the greenhouse. *If only the moon would come out from behind that cloud. . . .* Then his vision seemed to come into focus, and gradually he was able to distinguish the shapes about him. There was a palm tree and there a cactus and there . . . he gasped and drew back, tripping over something that clattered too loudly in the silence of the greenhouse. Tumbling, he flailed his arms helplessly as he tried to find support but fell heavily to the concrete floor. Kicking himself away from the plants in front of him, he couldn't help looking up, hoping he'd been mistaken about what he thought he saw. He wasn't. Looming before him in the gloom was a bulky figure topped by a star-shaped head! Soundlessly, cords like tendrils waved about it, and half way down the solid trunk of its midsection were ropy appendages that divided and sub-divided into a myriad grasping hands. And then, appallingly, there was the sound of stiff, plastoid flesh stretching and pulling as the thing bent slowly forward. Stillnor felt the oppressive nearness of its heavy bulk pressing him down, cornering him, and suddenly the stench that had receded into the background of his consciousness flooded back in greater force than ever.

At that moment, the damned moon chose to emerge from the clouds, allowing a good look at the thing before him. It lasted only a moment, but it was enough. The fright that had been building somewhere inside of him, was finally loosed and he screamed, screamed like a child faced with its worst nightmare, screamed like the poor souls he dealt with on a daily basis at the hospital. The next he knew, he was stumbling from the greenhouse, running blindly, not knowing where so long as it was away from that arboretum of horror and madness. Afterward, he could never recall just how he escaped the museum, only that he never stopped running. He ran and ran until exhaustion overtook him and he fell to the cold ground panting, his heart pounding. When he was able to stand again, he ran some more and this time didn't stop until he'd burst through his own front door and locked himself in. He spent the rest of the night on the floor, his back firmly pressed against the door, deathly afraid that something might have followed him from the museum and would get in.

VI

The next day he'd learned that the museum wing at Miskatonic had burned to the ground. The result of a gas explosion, it was said. And because he'd abandoned his car in the library parking lot, he was asked to come to police headquarters for questioning. Still somewhat incoherent after his experience, the police found his explanations unsatisfying and kept after him for hours. Finally, he was allowed to go home. Disheveled and exhausted from his ordeal, Stillnor fell into a chair and congratulated himself on managing not to tell the police everything that had happened the night before. If he'd had, he was sure that not only would he have been implicated in the destruction of the museum but he'd be considered a madman himself and a candidate for residency at his own hospital. Nor could he deny such a verdict would be far from the truth. Fearful of talking to anyone about what really happened, he finally decided that there was only one person in whom he could confide.

After making himself presentable and reclaiming his car from the garage where the police had it towed, he drove out to the hospital and, avoiding as many of the staff as he could, made his way to the third floor where he greeted the duty nurse and asked for the key to Danforth's room.

Inside, Danforth had been released from his straightjacket but was once again secured to the bed. Unspeaking, he at least acknowledged Stillnor's presence when he turned his head in his direction and stared at him with dull, emotionless eyes.

Taking a chair, Stillnor set it beside the bed and sat down. He was about to say something when Danforth surprised him by speaking first.

"I can tell that you've seen it," he said.

Stillnor said nothing.

"Have you told anyone?" asked Danforth.

"Who'd believe me?"

After that, the two talked for a good while before Stillnor finally left.

Back at home, he chose not to turn on the lights and simply sat in the study listening to the occasional car swish by outside. His mind wandering, Stillnor recalled his conversation with Danforth, filled with content he would have dismissed as lunatic only 24 hours before. All about how the Old Ones had mastered cellular manipulation and could and did create the ancestors of the creatures that went on to populate the earth following their extinction. How they developed telepathic skills that enabled them to communicate with the shoggoths, their greatest creation and eventual heirs. Finally, as Danforth felt more at ease with him, he confided to him that it had been Gedney's voice he heard telling him to remove the wards around Arkham. And in the weeks in which nothing was seen of him after his escape from the hospital, it was the voice again that directed him to South America where he arranged for cargo to be transported to Boston.

At that point, after his own harrowing experience, it finally struck Stillnor in all its terrible implications that the Old Ones were real. As were their servitors, the monstrous shoggoths who had evolved over millions of years into self-conscious beings filled with curiosity of a world outside the confines of their subterranean abode and eager to learn more about it. Imitative creatures, they had mastered many of the Old Ones' skills including the manipulation of organic matter either dead or alive so that, if given the opportunity, they could no doubt alter the structure of a human being so that it could survive the rigors of life deep beneath the Antarctic continent. Such alterations would also no doubt make telepathic communication easier to accomplish. Stillnor knew this was so because he'd seen an example of it the night he found himself in the greenhouse at Miskatonic University, lured there under a telepathic guidance that had prodded him first to the library, then to the museum, and finally to the greenhouse. Although he hadn't realized it at the time, it had been a call for help after Danforth had been removed from the scene and restrained at the hospital. A cry for help that went unheeded until a deep desperation no other human being could possibly understand forced the telepath to end its existence in a fiery blast of its own making. A cry for help in fact, from a tortured soul trapped in the shape of an Old One but that still retained its human mind. It had been a sight that badly frightened Stillnor when he saw the star-headed thing looming over him. But it wasn't that which finally sent him screaming into the night. Rather, it was what had been revealed in those few seconds when moonlight broke through the clouds, for nested amid those waving, pleading tentacles were fixed *the unmistakable features of Felix Gedney!*

Beneath the Mountains of Madness

Pete Rawlik

If you have found this, I have to ask you to ask yourself, do you know who you are? I don't mean in the existential sense. Do you know who you are, or, as I suspect, do you suffer from some sort of amnesia, a loss of memory, a loss of personality? Again I ask you, do you know who you are? I don't. I don't know who I am, but I know the truth, or at least suspect it. I only have to convince you. I have little to persuade you with, and you shall think me mad, but I shall tell you my story in the hope that you shall do as I plan to.

When I awoke, I had no knowledge of my own identity. I did not, and still do not know my name, age, occupation, place of birth or residence, or any other such details that would serve to identify me. I have knowledge of language, of English and Latin; of sciences including mathematics, geology, biology, a smattering of physics. I know so many things: The gravity constant, the names of the bones in the human hand, the temperature at which magma begins to solidify, I can explain several of Fermat's Theorems. I know many things, but I cannot tell you how I know them.

I awoke naked. I was on the floor of a circular pit, approximately ten feet in diameter and six feet deep. The pit itself appeared to have been cut out of the very bedrock itself some long time ago, for all evidence of tool markings had long been worn away. Running the entire circumference of the pit was a step-ledge approximately three feet wide. The ledge itself was only another three feet below the main floor of an underground chamber of massive proportions, easily the size of a football field and with a ceiling thirty feet above my head. Light was provided by organic masses, perhaps a kind of bioluminescent fungi, that seem to be scattered at random across that ceiling.

Reprinted with permission from *The Weird Company* (Night Shade Books, 2014).

Near the edge of the pit I found a small cache of supplies, clearly identified as belonging to the Miskatonic University Antarctic Expedition. The packs included hand-cranked electric torches, ropes, metallic poles, a large quantity of tinned food, several sets of clothing including furs and gloves, an oil-based heater, a small drum of oil, this journal and several pencils. The food tins are dated in the years of 1929 and 1930. Some of the clothing bore tags with the names of Lake, Gedney and Atwood embroidered, but these names are unfamiliar to me.

The supplies revealed two things that I had not noticed before. Out of habit, I donned some of the clothing, but I was not cold. Indeed I would have estimated the temperature in the cavern at a comfortable 70 degrees, a balmy temperature if I was truly in Antarctica as was implied by the markings. Nor was I hungry, and though I was tempted to open a tin of baked beans, it was more out of routine than any real need. I left all the food untouched. I went about examining the remaining packs, checking the equipment and assuring myself that it was all in working order. Within one of the boxes was a self-winding wrist watch bearing the manufacturer's name, Waltham Watch Company, on the back casing. The watch had ceased to function at 12:42 on February 1, 1930, but after winding, the mechanism seemed to function normally. I have no way of knowing the actual date or time, but I set the watch to 8:00 AM on February 2. It is from this admittedly arbitrary setting that I have since kept time. Curiously there were four other cases bearing the insignia of the Waltham Watch Company, but all of them were empty.

I explored the chamber, and my knowledge of engineering and geology suggested to me that it was not a naturally formed structure, but at the same time I could conceive of no method for constructing it. Scattered about the floor of the vast chamber were four more pits, identical to the one in which I awoke. The shape of the entire chamber is pentagonal with each wall being about a hundred yards long. In the center of each wall there are hexagonal openings which lead to similarly shaped tunnels. The light provided by the strange fungal growths does little to illuminate these dark foreboding tunnels.

I gathered up some of the equipment and supplies and have resolved myself to venturing down one. My one concern was that the tunnels seem completely indistinguishable, and it was possible that in my wanderings, I could return to this exact locale and not be able to recognize it. As a solution to this problem I decided to use the soot from the heater and periodically leave identifying marks to note my passage. The symbol I chose was a simple X, more than sufficient to accomplish the task at hand.

I followed a random tunnel for several hours. At first, I thought the tunnel was straight and level, but after traveling for quite some time I came to realize that the strange five sided tunnel was slowly curving to the right, as well as being slightly vertically inclined. Such a state would probably have been more noticeable if I had more light, but I was forced to rely on one of the hand-cranked electric torches which illuminated only a few feet in either direction. The darkness was overwhelmingly oppressive. The tunnels were solid and smooth; there were no rocks, no loose pebbles, no sand or dirt. Neither was there anything organic. I saw no evidence of any other person or of any life at all in the tunnel, but I heard things, or at least I thought that I heard things. At one point I could have sworn something had been coming up behind me, something large and unseen that was breathing, gasping really, like a train engine drowning in steam. I crouched back against the wall, the electric light sputtered in my hand, and I was too fearful to crank it. As the dim light slowly failed, I swear that whatever it was out there in the dark stayed just beyond the limit of my failing vision, until the torch flickered weakly and then died, plunging me into complete, impenetrable darkness.

Eventually, I was able to overcome my fear and began cranking the torch frantically and did not cease until the incandescent glow was at its maximum, but the light revealed nothing, and the noise, that freakish snuffling and groaning, trailed off into the darkness and never returned.

Whether the strange sounds were real or the hallucinated product of my mind I cannot say, but after this I made sure to keep the light fully charged. I also began to favor staying close to the wall on my right hand side. My logic for doing this was simple. Walking down the center of the tunnel, I had realized that the limited illumination given off by my torch may have been insufficient to allow me to detect any branches, turns or similar features. To compensate for this deficiency I chose the side opposite the one on which I was carrying the torch. If any features were to occur, at least I would have a better chance of detecting them.

It was not long after making this decision that I began to detect a faint but definite point of light some great distance down the tunnel. Even more startling was the clear sound of something akin to bubbling, a sort of liquid gurgling, that was emanating from the same direction. With each step the light grew in size and finally took on the familiar hexagonal shape of the tunnel. With a kind of resignation I slowly emerged into yet another hexagonal chamber of tremendous proportions. As with the chamber of my origin, lighting was provided by strange fungal growths hanging down from the ceiling, and as with that chamber, there were five terraced pits, but unlike the first chamber these pits were not empty. In the lower chamber of each was a dark and viscous fluid.

At first I thought the pool was composed of tar or oil, for it gurgled as masses of different densities welled up and then spread out over the surface, much as pools of organic hydrocarbons are known to. Yet as my torch light played over the fluid pool it was revealed to be deep red in color, not the black or brown normally associated with petroleum deposits. Any suggestion that the pool contained some sort of conventional fluid was dispelled by what happened next. For as I leaned closer to the pool, the very surface swelled up, like a rolling wave in the open ocean and surged toward the light. Startled, I immediately drew back, which sent the light jerking upwards violently. The pool responded as well, and a column of translucent red jelly about a foot thick came up out of the pool like a streamer of melted wax. The tendril reminded me of a slime mold, or perhaps of an amoebic pseudopod reproduced on a massive scale, and as crude and futile as the attempts to grasp my light were, I was overcome with such fear that I drew back even further.

Again the fluid thing in the pool responded, at the base of the tendril there began an intense roiling which quickly formed into a large swelling about twice the diameter of the tendril. With frightening speed the mass raced up the tendril and exploded from the tip. A single large globule of puss spun through the air surrounded by a cloud of smaller globs. Arcing through the air, they all failed to reach me and instead impacted on the surface of the pond, the step-ledge or the wall of the pit itself. Nothing that I could see made it up out of the pit.

Terrified but fascinated as well, I carefully peered over the ledge and observed the globules that now lay scattered about. Those that had landed on the surface of the pool itself had vanished completely, apparently absorbed into the main mass. Those that had landed on the riser were slowly sliding downward, mostly in a manner not unlike that of a viscous fluid, but on occasion a large quantity of the stuff would partially detach itself from the wall and then pull itself downwards in movements reminiscent of infinitely smaller amoebas. This, too, was the motion of the masses that had landed on the lower ledge, the ones I found easiest to observe.

Ranging in size from a penny to a baseball, all were of the same translucent red color which only naturally appeared deeper as size increased. The translucent nature of these things made their internal structure clear to me, but the ease with which I could see inside them offered no comfort or explanation to their status in the order of things. Try as I might, the only organization I could discern within these things was a complete lack of structure. As they moved they put forth pseudopodia that pulled them forward, and the light of the torch revealed the flow of fluids as these appendages were expelled and retracted, but as to what caused the fluids to move, as to some sort of musculature or skeleton, or nervous system, I could discern nothing. The fact that these things would weakly reach out after the light implied that they were reacting to some sort of stimulus, but whether that was heat, light or motion I could not tell, and neither could I make out any semblance of sensory organs that would register such a stimulus.

It was not only the torch they reacted to. As they crawled about on the lower ledge it was inevitable that one would meet another, and the resulting interaction taught me much. The contact between the two was accidental and casual, nothing more than a smaller glob brushing up against a larger one. Immediately both ceased moving and I could see a small bridge of jelly form where the two had touched. The pause was pregnant, there was a taste in my mouth, a taste of wonder and anticipation, and I swear I could see a faint dance of lights flicker within the jellied bridge. Here then was a new species unknown to man carrying out biological functions equally unknown, and I was the first to observe it.

The bridge split apart violently and the smaller glob veered off, moving rapidly away from the other. The larger thing groped after it, lashing jellied tentacles out like streamers across the black rock of the floor. The larger one grasped the smaller, dragging it back, pulling it into itself. The larger one swallowed the smaller, absorbed it, and merged with it in a strange form of anti-mitosis. When it was all over, there was only one glob left and it slid back in the same direction that the larger one had been going as if nothing had happened. It was as if the smaller one had never existed.

Intrigued, I decided to perform a quick experiment. Tying a small piece of rope to one of the food tin keys, I carefully dropped the item in the path of one of the larger globules. As the weird jelly like creature crawled over the metal key neither the creature nor the key reacted, but as the thing slowly crawled over the hemp rope it suddenly surged forward. The rope was enveloped and within seconds it was gone; not one trace of it remained, devoured by the blob of goo which quickly continued back on its seemingly random trek. Based on this experiment I suspected that this strange protoplasmic creature could devour any kind of organic material, and I shuddered to think on such things too much.

I made a camp by the mouth of one of the tunnels, as far from any of the pits and their horrid inhabitants as I could get. Something was nagging at the back of my mind. I had missed a vital clue, or drawn some ersatz conclusion, but, try as I might, I could not overcome the feeling that something was horribly wrong. My watch told me that I had been awake for hours, and still I was not hungry. As I sat there looking at my supplies, I caught my reflection in the side of a metal tin. It took me a moment, as I had to stare at my reflection to understand what I was seeing. My face was that of a young man, perhaps in his mid-twenties. My eyes were hazel. My skin was fair and smooth. I could see no scars, but the most dramatic feature that my image revealed to me was the complete lack of hair. There was none on my head; I had no trace of beard or mustache. Eyebrows were absent, as were any eyelashes. I checked the rest of my body and found that there was no hair anywhere, on any part of my skin, nor any tattoos. Using the tin as a mirror, I checked my mouth and found no fillings or missing teeth. Except for the complete lack of hair, I was a perfect specimen of manhood. I tried to think about what kind of physical or chemical trauma could result in the loss of all body hair but could think of none. Confused and tired, I closed my eyes and quickly fell asleep.

According to the watch, I awoke several hours later to find that I was no longer in my camp. I apparently had rolled away from the tunnel mouth, all the way to the edge of the nearest pit. Indeed one of my arms was hanging over the edge, dangling down toward the lower ledge. Even in a drowsy state I realized the danger of my situation and leapt to a fully upright position letting out a gasp of horrified terror. This engendered a curious response from the fluid thing in the pit. As I jumped back from the rim in a panic, the thing trapped within the pit recoiled from my position. Like a small body of water driven by a gale force wind, the thing piled up against the wall of the pit furthest away from me. Curious, I carefully stepped forward, and I swear the damned thing shuddered with fear and tried to crawl even further away. Only when I withdrew did the creature relax and flow back into a more placid state.

Confused, I ran my hand over my head and made yet another discovery. My scalp and indeed the rest of my body was covered with a fine stubble. It seemed that a significant amount of growth had occurred while I slept. Apparently, whatever had caused the loss of all my hair, some chemical exposure or physical trauma, did not cause any permanent damage.

I spent the next four hours navigating a dark, seemingly endless tunnel. The time I spent in that shaft and the things that occurred are meaningless in comparison to the events that transpired once I emerged from it, so I will not bother to describe them in any significant detail. Though it should be plain that after spending such a long time in the dark and barren corridors it was a welcome relief when I finally emerged into yet another massive underground chamber, I immediately noticed that the chamber I had come to was significantly unlike the two I had previously explored. Instantly my senses were assaulted by a cacophony of sound that flooded the room and made my teeth ache. It was a rhythmic crashing sound like waves of steel crashing against a shore of glass, horrendous in its nature and bone-shaking in its intensity. With each pounding crescendo I cringed and instinctively covered my head, which served me well as each beat was followed by a heated gust of wind that carried with it a gray sticky ash and such a stench that would put an abattoir to shame.

The source of these violent sounds and noxious bursts was not readily apparent to me, for unlike the prior chambers which were devoid of features save for the pits and the phosphorescent fungi, this one was filled with great mounds of gray rock and ash that towered over me like hills, nearly reaching the ceiling itself. Fearful, but driven by an overwhelming sense of scientific curiosity, I removed my pack and cautiously secreted it underneath a small pile of rubble, concealing it completely from casual view. I then climbed slowly and carefully to the top of one of the great mounds. Several times I lost my footing and either slid backwards down the mound, or found myself in a patch of fine loose material not unlike quicksand.

Reaching the summit, I found myself suddenly in close vicinity to one of the many phosphorescent clumps that served to light the great cavernous halls, and I examined it in detail. It was as I suspected a type of fungi but not one with which I was familiar, and it exhibited features that were wholly unlike those normally associated with that kingdom. A large globular growth almost a yard in diameter, the fungi appeared strikingly similar to an inverted street lamp. Not surprisingly, the thing was evenly divided into five panes of semitransparent material that appeared to have the consistency of amber or dried maple syrup, but paper thin. These panes were held in place by a thick organic green lattice work. Through the panes I could make out a bulbous cluster which was the source of the strange cool light, a light to which I was strangely attracted, nearly mesmerized.

Forcefully tearing my attention away from the organic lantern, I turned to look out over the vast chamber. My position on top of the debris pile augmented by a plethora of the luminescent growths gave me a nearly unobstructed view of the artificially constructed cavern, and again I wished that it hadn't, for the sight which was revealed to me set my heart racing and my mind reeling. To describe the thing as inhumanly monstrous would not begin to explain the nature of it, for it was beyond anything I had seen before. Where the pit-thing could be portrayed as protoplasmic and bearing a superficial resemblance to a hyperbolic slime mold or amoeba, this creature was simply alien, bearing no resemblance, not even an exaggerated one, to any earthly creature. It was an abomination pure and simple, a hideous affront to the laws of nature as well as of physics. I do not have the words to give the thing a proper description, and I apologize for lacking those skills, but in the interest of science I shall try.

The main mass of the creature was a fluid darkness larger than a subway car. It had no true shape or boundary, but I could discern in the darkness of its bulk great masses of flowing currents and roiling boils that would seem to churn up and explode out into nothingness. The heaving, turbulent darkness was surrounded by a green, wispy haze that clung like fog on a mountain top. Between the two components of the creature there was no clear division and as I watched, volumes of the fog would seem to condense all at once into inky blackness, while in other areas the darkness would suddenly sublimate into a mass of the thick verdigris mist.

The hulking mass was, as I have noted, an inky blackness, but at the same time it was inexplicably translucent, like a fine piece of smoky quartz or volcanic glass. This property, this transparent darkness, made my eyes ache as I watched it flow and change and move. Its primary method of locomotion appeared to be similar to amoeboid motion, moving the bulk of its mass forward in a wave front that more or less crashed like a wave. This was not its only method of travel, however, for it also produced from itself a myriad of appendages of all shapes and vast sizes that would seem to supplement its forward motion. A phalanx of jointed appendages not unlike those of a grasshopper pushed it onward, while a pair of roughhewn arms with great circular suckers clasped onto the floor before the thing and dragged the hulking entity about. Tentacles, arms and legs came into existence and dissolved as needed, as did other specialized organs including a multitude of feelers, visual receptors, a trumpet-like organ I assumed was analogous to an ear, and a moist fan of tendrils that I gathered was designed to provide a sense of smell.

Along with these appendages and organs, the creature appeared to have created a set of features that seemed specific to the task at hand, namely carving this chamber into the standard pentagonal shape. The front of the monstrosity had been transformed into twin huge jaw-like shovels lined with massive and wicked picks. The creature would literally bite into the wall of raw rock and then swallow the resulting chunk of boulder-sized stone. Seconds later, a huge tube-like orifice on the creature's anterior end would suddenly swell up and belch out a cloud of grey sediment onto the floor, forming the mounds that were scattered about the chamber, and the clouds of sticky ash that were driven into fearful gusts by the forceful expulsion.

Witnessing the presence of this creature, its actions, its size, its very existence, I became momentarily dumbstruck, and in that instant I lost my footing and slid from the top of the mounded debris, tumbling head first through the coarse gravel. My fall initiated a minor avalanche and my landing on the hard floor was accompanied by the sound of pebbles and rocks skittering, clattering and echoing through the chamber. I lay stunned for a moment surrounded in a sudden, relative silence. At first I thought I had suffered some sort of neurological trauma, for the pounding sound of the beast chewing through the rock had ceased to fill my ears. That delusion vanished as a new sound wormed its way toward me. I grabbed my supplies and blindly dashed across the floor, pursued by the sound of colossal limbs rushing after me. Hot breath blasted from behind me, whipping my body forward in terror. How I reached the safety of the tunnel, I did not understand, but I did, and I was again free to explore the dark labyrinth.

A few hours later, and several turns through the darkness, the horror of my encounter was supplanted by a wondrous new discovery. The latest chamber that I emerged into was a virtual paradise compared to those prior. The dominant feature was a large, roughly circular pond or small lake around which a lush garden of sedges, shrubs, bushes and small trees grew. Light in this chamber was provided by the same fungi that were present in the other chambers, but whereas previously the ceilings were dominated by a small number of specimens, the roof of this chamber was covered with thousands of such growths, so densely packed that in some areas the ceiling stone itself could no longer be discerned. Besides the fungi and plants, there was a myriad of small and primitive animal life darting about the chamber including a great diversity of beetles clumsily flying through the air on clunky, thick, veined wings, but neither was there any lack of swarming ants. Spiders, scorpions and centipedes were also represented, as well as invertebrates I could not readily recognize or classify. A great grasshopper-like thing came to roost on my hand, an event that apparently I was accustomed to, as I did not panic, but I soon discovered this was no ordinary orthopteran. While my initial attention was drawn to the ornately crested head and a colorful thorax, it was only when it prepared to leap that I noticed it bore not six legs but seven, having not a pair of femura modified for jumping but rather an asymmetrical set. Stunned, I watched as the thing deftly sprang away from me into the brush and toward the central pond. The miniature lake was cool and clear and teeming with life, including things akin to shrimp and crayfish. Algae and a leafy submergent macrophyte dominated the floor of the pool which was composed of a thick layer of loosely consolidated sand and rock. There was no evidence of larger predators: no tracks were evident and I heard no calls.

I thought perhaps to capture several of the shrimp-like creatures and cook them up for a warm meal. I waded into the pond and, using the shovel from my kit, slowly herded a few of the creatures into the shallows, then deftly slipped the blade under them and flipped the crustaceans onto the bank. Removed from their natural habitat, they flipped up into the air in random directions, trying to get back into the water. Satisfied with the clutch that I had captured, I stumbled my way out of the pond, losing my footing and sliding face first into the bank. I recovered, wiping the wet grit from my eyes and face. Bending down to gather up my fresh lunch, I found that it had vanished. I searched the grass and the nearby shrubs, but to no avail. I concluded that the things must have escaped back to the pond while I had stumbled out of it.

Frustrated, I stepped back into the water and again corralled a few of the creatures into the shallows and launched them onto the bank. This time I kept my eye on the creatures as they struggled to survive. They flipped into the air a few times, and then flopped weakly against the ground before settling down and resolving themselves to a few last twitches. As their pathetic twitching slowed, I reached out for them but withdrew my hand in fear. The five translucent grey decapods began to quiver again, more violently, where they lay on the grass and then slowly began to melt. Enthralled, I watched as the things sagged and then, not unlike hot wax, flowed into the mass without a trace. Cautiously, I reached out to touch the place where they had been, but nothing at all remained. I tore at the thin vegetation, scraping the clumps of tiny plants from the ground and tossing them violently into the air, heedless of where they might fall. My tantrum revealed nothing but the ubiquitous gray rock forming the walls and floors of the chambers and tunnels. Overwrought, I fell back and screamed in anguish.

My cry was countered by a tremendous roar, as if a titan had stirred. So loud was it that I could not identify where exactly it had come from. The trees and shrubs shook, small creatures dashed about in obvious fear, and in the distance one of the fungal lanterns shook loose from the ceiling and crashed through the canopy into the underbrush. The sound trailed off, fading to a deep grumble, then to a low hum, until finally only a faint trace of a vibration remained. In the meantime the small glade had grown deathly still and silent.

I scrambled to my feet and frantically grabbed my supplies. With my head down I was oblivious of anything beyond my narrow field of vision, but as I rose up and swung my backpack on I was shocked to discover the small glade-like area vanishing before my very eyes. Trees and shrubs were melting, forming huge pools of viscous fluid that flowed slowly back to the pond in the center of the chamber. The insects and other small life forms, suddenly deprived of cover, were swarming, forming thick banks of darkness that would hover in swirling banks of shadow that would suddenly coalesce and then collapse into a rain of gelatin.

I ran, ran as fast as I could toward the next tunnel while beneath my feet the mossy landscape dissolved. With each step forward, the ersatz ecosystem vanished. Like a tide going out, the glade and all its inhabitants flowed away from the outer walls, draining away, leaving only the cold, bare rock in its place. I ran, and the thick fluid splashed about me, covering my legs and then streaming off, as if contact with my very being was repulsive to it. As I reached the tunnel I paused, terrified by what was occurring behind me, by the noises, the horrible, tearing, wrenching noises, and fearful of embarking once more into the dark. An idea bubbled to the surface of my mind, and I suddenly understood the failure of Lot's wife to avert her gaze, for I, too, looked back upon the devastation and destruction laying waste to the garden, and I heartily wish that I had not.

The great thing that rose up out of the central pit, that metamorphic mass from which all life in the chamber had collapsed and merged again, it towered like a titanic polyp, blindly craning about, searching, reaching out with monstrous tentacles to capture those stray spawnings that had not yet been reclaimed. At first I thought the devastation to be the result of some horrific biochemical process, perhaps a type of organic acid, spewed about, digesting everything for the monstrosity to feed upon, but as I watched in rapt horror, I knew that was not the case. For this thing, this gelatinous mass, was yet another form of the thing in the pit, one capable of more than simple replication of organs and appendages. This thing was even more advanced than the other, for as I watched the creature devour the once tranquil glade, I saw that beyond it, half-hidden by its own shadow, a new glade was taking form, trees and shrubs, animals of fantastic shape, all these were spewing forth, tearing themselves from the central mass, desperate to fill the void left behind. This metamorphic monstrosity was able to divide itself up into a myriad of component creatures and imitate them closely. It had created an entire habitat of plants and animals, nearly perfect to the casual observer, flawed only in its inability to mimic a single process, that which creates the leaf litter and other materials that form the detritus covering the forest floor. A simple process inherent in every form of life known to science, this thing could not mimic it for the simple fact that its creations did not die and rot but were only reabsorbed. This terrified me to the core. One might then suppose that the thing in its changing forms must be immortal, but instead I grew to suspect that it was all some sort of organic machine, using a process similar to cellular regeneration but improved tremendously. The things cannot die, for they are not truly alive, at least not as we humans define it. With these horrific thoughts rambling through my head, I plunged headlong into the dark, winding labyrinth, and away from the monstrous form that had deceived me.

I ran until I collapsed from exhaustion. I was driven to put as much distance between myself and the monstrous landscape as possible. Somewhere along the way my legs gave out and I fell in a heap against a tunnel wall. When I awoke, my watch told me that I had been out for two days! I did not think it possible that I had slept so long, but the growth of hair on my head and my face suggested that this was the truth. After waking, I ate a small tin of meat. My supplies were still in good shape; I was eating and drinking much less than I thought I would need to. Indeed, I could not recall the last time I was actually hungry or thirsty.

After my repast, I tried to gain my bearings. I was briefly concerned that during my unexpected rest I might have gotten turned around and would therefore return to the chamber I had left. Thankfully, my electric light revealed a feature that I knew I had not passed before. In front of me was a great spiraled ramp, like the core of a conch, leading up into the ceiling. I followed it up, glad to be out of the labyrinth of tunnels.

The ramp emerged on one side of a vast cavern wholly unlike the chambers I had previously discovered. This one was more natural in shape, the dominant feature of the three-to-four-acre cave being a shallow pool dotted with small islands of rocky fragments and boulders. There was life in the water, small fish and some minute snails, both apparently feeding off of a slimy mold or bacteria that grew on the bottom. I suspected that in the deeper pools there were larger animals, perhaps in significant numbers. It seemed a necessity to support the predators that basked on the shores of the subterranean lake. They were penguins of a sort, monstrously large, and albino. I counted eight of them, and at five feet tall they posed some threat to me, for they were fast and their beaks are more than six inches long. But, lucky for me, uncounted generations in the dark had rendered them eyeless, and I with my two good eyes and electric lantern held a serious advantage. One of them wandered away from the rest, and I killed it to make sure it was real and not some sham crafted by the protoplasmic thing I had escaped. Oddly, I found the dead bird, and the rest of the flock, relatives perhaps of the extinct Anthropornis, comforting. Even in this monstrous form they represented a kind of recognizable normalcy, following established rules of biology and behavior. More so, they reinforced my belief that I must indeed be somewhere in Antarctica.

The new cavern was significantly colder than the chambers and tunnels I had left behind, and was fringed with small sheets of ice. Clusters of icicles hung down from the ceiling. Thankfully, the cold-weather gear that I carried kept me warm. The pool itself was warmer than the surrounding air and seemed to contain a significant amount of sulfur. It was fed by a small stream that led off into one of several rough passages. I suspected that the source of the stream was a geyser or similar volcanic feature. I was tempted to try to find the source, but the passages were too narrow for even my lithe frame to explore. There were other, larger passages from which a haunting but welcome sound of wind emanated. I desperately wanted to dash down one of those tunnels, but for some reason I decided to stay amid the colony of mutant birds.

Following the shoreline, I found myself forced to work around to the dryer side of a particularly large boulder. In doing so, I startled a rather large penguin at least five and a half feet tall, and incredibly rotund, possibly topping out at over two hundred pounds. It screeched at me in anger and then scrambled away, diving onto its belly and using its arms as paddles to glide across the rocky ground. The whole event would have been comical had it not been for what the thing had left behind. There on the ground lay the remains of a smaller penguin from the head, upper torso and single wing that remained. Of the other wing, lower torso and legs I could find no trace, neither of flesh, feather or bone. Logically, I assumed that the victim had been killed some time before and then been subject to slow consumption, decay hampered by the cold. But that possibility was negated by what happened next, for the head of the dismembered bird suddenly reared up! The beak opened and closed as if trying to call out. In that moment, I was grateful that the thing lacked the ability to move air through its throat, for I am not sure I could have shouldered the burden of its miserable cries. I used the heel of my boot to put the thing out of its misery.

Given the desolation of the place, I was not surprised that the penguins, or at least one of them, had turned to cannibalism. What I did find amazing was that one could attack and devour another, flesh and bone included, before the victim had even expired. The speed at which such an event must occur, coupled with the strength needed to rend such an animal into digestible pieces, was truly frightening, and I realized that I must be on constant guard against attack. Towards this end I decided to fully explore the cave and all of its environs. Starting at the entranceway to the spiraling ramp, I worked my way clockwise around the lake, exploring the rocky strip that ran between the rim of the lake and the cavern walls. There was little to see. The terrain was uneven and covered with a loose gravel of black rock, peppered with larger rocks and the occasional boulder. The cavern walls were made of the same black stone and were equally uneven. In places large clusters of boulders formed plateaus six to eight feet off the ground. These, I noted, would make perfect places to rest and remain out of reach of the penguins.

Continuing on my way, I passed several fissures in the wall which had been worn smooth by millennia of trickling rivulets of water. The water was cold but clear with a heavy mineral taste. I took a few moments at one of the streams to wash the dirt and dust away. I gasped as the frigid water ran over my body. The mutant birds all turned to stare at me with blind eyes as I struggled to bathe. It was an unnerving sight, and I was happy when the flock finally went back to ignoring me.

As I reached the far side of the lake, I noticed an object that was neither the color nor the shape of the surrounding rocks. It was a sledge of supplies, cold weather gear, tinned food, lamps, clothing, a heater, a stove, a clutch of bamboo stocks, and several barrels of kerosene. There were footprints around it, boots all the same size. It was the first evidence of human life I had seen, and it sent my heart pounding. The sledge was pointed toward the mouth of a large cave from which a flickering pinprick of light could be seen. It couldn't be more than a mile away. I grabbed a few supplies from the sledge and began to move down the tunnel, but then I stopped dead in my tracks, and the things in my arms tumbled and clattered against the rocky terrain.

In front of me stood the obese penguin that I had caught devouring one of its own. It was moving toward me, as if staring at me with those empty, eyeless sockets. I moved quietly to the left, and the monster bird mirrored me. I moved again, but again the mutant countered. I reached back slowly and pulled a bamboo stock from the sledge. The beast cocked its head and opened its mouth, revealing double rows of sharp, thorn-like teeth. Spittle dripped from those horrid fangs, and where it fell onto the rocks it hissed and sputtered like acid, and I finally understood how the thing had devoured the other penguin so quickly. Then as I watched, it shuddered. The sides of its head split open and two large black eyes shoved themselves up out of the skull and twisted back and forth in the rough sockets. It looked at me now with real eyes, saw the metal tipped stick and screeched like some great raptor.

I stumbled backwards and landed against the sledge. The creature lunged forward. I swung the stock forward, and the bird's fat belly slid over it and was slowly impaled. Though the basket was not present, the hooks used to attach it was, and it was these metallic spikes that tore into the bird's spine and kept it from moving forward. The thing struggled to reach me, snapping and thrashing about violently, but to no avail. I pushed myself back and at the same time reached for another stock. The pinned beast shuddered once more and I paused, entranced by the horror that was unfolding before me. The monstrously fanged beak split apart and peeled back, ripping the flesh off the skull. The exposed throat swelled and a frightful thing that bore some resemblance to the mouth parts of a squid shot out at me. Reflexively, I thrust the stock forward and into the center of the gnashing parts, driving them back into the main body of the thing. It wailed and squirmed, desperate to release itself from the two shafts that held it in place. The flesh elongated, stretched and then pulled apart, and two replaced the single beast that had confronted me moments before. They slid about and slowly worked their way off of my makeshift spears. Thinking quickly, I grabbed one of the lamps, undid the fuel cap and poured kerosene over the two squirming masses. I hastily struck a match and tossed it into the fuel. The flames engulfed the things, and they squealed in agony, their limbs flailing about. The smoke turned black and acrid, and whatever the monstrous penguin degenerated into, I could not precisely discern. It was a pulpy, protoplasmic thing that writhed within those flames, another thing that was not what it appeared to be, and I was glad to put some distance between myself and the smoldering masses that remained.

I crashed through that rocky tunnel, heading blindly toward that distant glow. Instinctively I knew that the light was neither a lantern nor some strange assemblage of fungi. The color was all wrong, the white glow soft and inviting. I drove myself forward at breakneck speed, tripping over rocks and climbing over boulders. The rock floor covered with gravel gave way to a landscape of scattered stones, and then an obstacle course of boulder fragments. In the end I was scrambling over boulders larger than me. They peppered the ground that led up to a rough wall that filled the entire passageway. Only a single opening, maybe four feet in diameter, provided a break in the blockage, and from this the light emanated. But it wasn't only the light that poured from that hole. With it came a terrifying wind, a blasting jet that surged icily into the tunnel and carried with it stinging, biting crystals of ice.

I plunged into that hole, hugging to me what gear I could and dragging the rest of it behind me. I used my arms and knees to push myself through, all the time the wind whipping past my face and into whatever gap in my gear it could find. The rocky shards did their best to bruise and break me, but the padding of the jacket afforded some protection. With each movement forward my breathing grew more rapid, my heart beat faster, the wind whipped more ruthlessly, and my desperation grew palpable. Straining against that demonic, freezing wind, I burst from the end of the warren and tumbled into the light beyond.

I found myself at the base of a mountain, of a mountain range. Behind me the white-crowned peaks stretched up into the sky, gray basaltic things, like inhuman towers that clawed at the sun. Before me was a vast icy plain, white and blue reflecting in the sun. Snow drifted in great waves, stopped and then moved on. The cold was a tangible thing I could feel with my hands as it hung in the air. If I tried, I felt I could almost grasp it, shape it, twist it into any form I desired. The cold tore at my skin and eyes as I struggled to put on a pair of snow goggles and cinch down my hood. As I lowered my head to protect my face, my eyes wandered across the ground at my feet and discovered two thin, parallel scratches in the ice-covered rock, readily recognizable as traces of a sledge similar to the one I left behind in the cavern. The trail began at the cave mouth and went off over a low rise just a few hundred yards away, more evidence that I wasn't alone in this place. Excited at the possibility of seeing another person, I foolishly dashed down the trail and over the rise.

I wish that I hadn't, for on the far side of the hillock I found the sledge, and more, so much more. I ran from that place, ran from the light and the sky and the wind. I crawled back through that tight little hole and pushed my way into the cavern of monstrous penguins. Pulses racing with looming madness, I went through the sledge that remained there and took all that I could use. I slaughtered the birds, even though that was all they were. I felt a tinge of regret, but that faded as I pulled my supplies down the spiral ramp and into the tunnels below. The drums of kerosene rolled easily through the tunnels and from cavern to cavern. The thing that played at being a forest shrieked as I doused it with fuel and set it ablaze. It took hours to make sure that I had destroyed all of the thing, for bits of it kept breaking off and trying to escape. I hunted them all down. The flying, creeping, crawling things flopped angrily within the flames, but they all died.

The machine-creature went easier. It, too, shrieked against the flames, but it seemed to lack the power to divide itself and thus could not attempt an escape. It roared as the flames charred its titanic bulk. It crashed against the wall, reared up and gouged the ceiling, knocking massive chunks of rock down onto itself. The boulders pinned the beast and left it wailing pitifully. I cackled maniacally as it slowly succumbed, struggling for more than an hour. It died with a violent shudder. As whatever life force that sustained it finally fled, the structure of the thing gave way and the strange matter that comprised it crumbled into a strange pasty jelly which lingered for a while and then suffered some catastrophic change, dissolving into nothingness.

The creatures trapped in the pits were easiest. They didn't even scream as I poured the kerosene over them. I don't think they even noticed. They were too simple to understand what was happening. Even after I set them ablaze they barely reacted. They bubbled in the heat, turned greasy black, then crisped. When I was done, all that remained were a few piles of glossy black ash.

I rolled the barrel containing the rest of the kerosene back to where it all began, back to the place where I woke up. God help me, I wish I hadn't! I wish I hadn't awoken. That I hadn't wandered through the dark labyrinth. That I hadn't found my way out. I wish that I hadn't seen those mountains, nor the madness that I found at their base. Or seen those shapes, those blasphemous shapes frozen in the ice around the sledge.

I shall finish writing my account, and perhaps then you will understand why I ask you the questions I do. I ask you again, do you know who you are? Because I do not know who I am, and I suspect that neither did any of those who came before me. When I am done, I shall crawl into one of the five pits and I shall pour the last of the fuel over my head and set myself ablaze. A portion of me pauses, and I recall that the Church considers suicide is a sin, but I dismiss such concerns, for I doubt that such rules apply here. Perhaps for me, immolation is a consecration, not a sin.

The things in the ice, the shapes that lay frozen solid against the sledge, they were what drove me mad. They were men who sat there in the frigid landscape, frozen and unmoving. Men who had succumbed to the elements, four men. Four men like myself, who had escaped from beneath the mountains of madness. Men dressed in what they could salvage from the sledges, and equipped the same way. Men with stubble on their heads, and their faces. Men like me.

Do you understand me? Look at yourself. Find a mirror, something reflective. Look at yourself. Look hard. Men should have hair on their heads, beards on their faces, eyebrows and lashes. Men should have scars where time has taken its toll on their bodies. Does your body betray the ravages of time? Or is it like mine, like those out in the ice, free of scars and with freshly grown hair? Are you a man, or are you like me? Is your face your own, or is it the same as mine, the same as the four things I left behind in the ice? Men have faces of their own, but I, I and those poor frozen things, we are monsters, and though we are four, we share but one face. God help me, they all had my face!

The Continent of Madness

Ken Asamatsu
Translation by Edward Lipsett

1.   To Neuschwabenland

June 21, 1939.

Goebbels had just given his speech at the Olympic Stadium in Berlin, and the huge bonfires of the midsummer celebrations were being lit. It mattered little to us, as far as we were from the summer and the flames. We were in the hold of the *Hölderlin*, a freighter bound for Antarctica.

Packed with three of the very latest snow crawlers, a disassembled Messerschmitt, and massive amounts of arms and ammunition, the ship was headed toward an "Antarctic paradise" that couldn't possibly exist.

It was all due to the absurd reports filed by that crackpot Nazi adventurer, Kriegsmarine Kapitän Ritscher, and Hitler's fawning sycophants. In 1938, Kapitän Ritscher was given a secret order by the Führer himself, who had discovered a cryptic note in von Junzt's *Unaussprechlichen Kulten*. They were headed to a spot about a thousand kilometers south of the northernmost tip of the Antarctic continent, called Queen Maud Land by the British.

Their orders were to investigate some six hundred thousand square kilometers of land.

According to von Junzt, water temperature was high in the region due to volcanic activity, with a warm-water lake, lush vegetation, and a balmy climate warm enough to walk about outdoors in your shirtsleeves in the summer. Anyone claiming that such a temperate zone existed in this southernmost continent of snow and ice was clearly insane, but the Führer believed the delusion. He allocated a massive sum from the national treasury, gave Kapitän Ritscher command of a team of eighty-two military and scientific personnel, and sent them on their way south.

The reports sent back by Ritscher became increasingly unbelievable. Using an aircraft, he had flown in the depths of the continent, dropping swastika flags every twenty kilometers, claiming the land in the name of the Third Reich. Using dogsleds and snow crawlers, he advanced into the region on the ground as well, to discover a mountain range on the scale of the Alps, soaring to four thousand meters, ground free of ice and snow, and a warm-water lake surrounded by a profusion of beautiful flowers and lush greenery.

Ritscher ended his 107-day expedition and returned via the Cape of Good Hope, bringing with him a large number of photographs and even movie film. Hitler was delighted at "the discovery of the century" and christened the new, ice-free land Neuschwabenland—New Swabia. Many officers in the Wehrmacht decried the discovery, calling Ritscher a charlatan who had falsified reports out of ambition. One of them was Army Major Richter von Hausen: me.

I asked a newspaper reporter friend of mine to look into Ritscher's background, revealing that he had close connections with the *Völkischer Beobachter* newspaper, a propaganda masterpiece run by the Nazis. We were convinced that the lush greenery shown in those photographs was created by photomontage techniques, and the films shot not in Antarctica, but in some Universum Film studio. Our research proved it. Unfortunately, the SS heard of our interest and thought it disloyal of citizens who were neither soldiers nor members of the Nazi party. And so when I was drafted into the Wehrmacht on March 24, 1939, I was ordered to guard duty for one year in Neuschwabenland. The order was signed Heinrich Himmler, Reichsführer.

In other words, I was being exiled to Antarctica. In all, thirty-two of us were assigned to guard this nonexistent domain. We were all Wehrmacht, and all deemed to be uncooperative in the eyes of the Nazis. To keep us under control, a party of fourteen SS soldiers and two Gestapo agents was also attached to the mission, under the command of SS Oberstleutnant Wilhelm Weber . . . who, as it happens, had been in prison on suspicion of murdering five prostitutes. In fact, all of the security force were criminals or, to be kind, *unusual* people, not only Weber. It was pretty clear what it all meant. The Wehrmacht had decided to take advantage of the opportunity to rid itself of all its undesirable soldiers at once, along with the SS soldiers who might prove an embarrassment. Just ship them all off to Antarctica!

The *Hölderlin* departed the military port of Kiel on April 1, 1939. An old freighter, it was close to scrap, but I got along well enough with the three men sharing my quarters. The trip was uneventful and even restful. At first. The oldest of my bunkmates was Kriegsmarine Leutnant Krenz, age 41. Two years older than I. With pale blonde hair and a tough, decisive expression, he looked the perfect German professional soldier, and had been assigned to naval intelligence. His father, we came to know, had commanded a U-boat in the first Great War, going down with his boat in battle with the enemy in the Atlantic. The other two, younger than I, were Army Oberstleutnant von Müller and Kriegsmarine Unterleutnant Heinrich. Eric von Müller was 29, born to a noble family in Karlsruhe. Intelligent and handsome, he made friends easily, although he seemed somewhat high-strung at times. Heinrich, on the other hand, was a brash giant of a man who said he had come from the Ruhr. When he added that his mother had been Belgian, I at once understood his sunny personality. He was 27.

We became close friends, joking and laughing together as if we had known each other for a decade . . . that gaiety began to fade after about ten days, finally turning to leaden despair.

It all began at seven in the evening on April 11, with a furious knocking on the hatch. "Come in!" called Heinrich, sprawled out on his bunk reading a magazine. The hatch immediately sprang open to reveal Oberstleutnant Weber and one of the Gestapo officers, dressed in plain clothes and wearing rimless eyeglasses. I recalled that the Gestapo man was named Heinicke as I asked what they wanted.

"Nothing from you," snapped Weber. With exaggerated politeness, he added, "Count von Müller, would you come with us?"

"Me!? But why?" responded von Müller, only to be cut off by Heinicke.

"We have just received orders from Reichsführer Himmler to put the Mask of Yoth-Tlaggon on you."

At his words, von Müller paled.

"I know nothing of any mask! I have nothing to do with it!" he shouted, shaking his head wildly. Heinicke ignored his words, stepping forward to grasp his shirt with both hands and pull him close, locking him eye-to-eye, both men breathing hard.

"No games! We know that your father, Eckart von Müller, was a patron of Klingen Mergelsheim, assisting him in his research into foul Atzous!"

"Klingen Mergelsheim . . . ?" echoed Krenz, mouthing the unfamiliar name.

"This has nothing to do with you! Stay out of it, or you will regret it!" commanded Weber, pushing his monocle up. "Shall we go, Count von Müller? Reichsführer Himmler has great expectations of your psychic sensitivity. Stimulated by the Mask of Yoth-Tlaggon, I'm sure you will reveal some wonderful visions for us!" Together with Heinicke, he almost dragged poor von Müller from the cabin. Left speechless, the three of us could only stare at each other in shock.

After a moment, Krenz lightly stuck his forehead with his fist, muttering ". . . Klingen . . . Klingen Mergelsheim . . . now where have I . . . ?"

"Who is Klingen Mergelsheim?" I asked, at exactly the same time as Heinrich.

"A sorcerer, black magic . . . he was supposed to be the man behind the Thule Society, and said to have lived for centuries. A magician."

Heinrich and I looked at each other again. A magician? I looked back to Krenz. "Why in the world would you know that bit of trivia?" I asked.

"It was in my father's diary. But that's impossible! He said he met Mergelsheim in 1925, and that he looked at least 90 then!"

2. Von Müller the Psychic

As I write this it is June 21. The *Hölderlin* continues south along East latitude 30 degrees. We are only a thousand km from Antarctica now, and it is getting colder.

Though it was a full two months ago, my ears still ring with the scream that von Müller gave.

I wondered then, as the passages echoed with that terrible scream, what torture they were inflicting on him. I couldn't help but imagine. I was furious . . . Why von Müller? After about two hours, though, von Müller returned to the cabin without so much as a single bruise. He was white as a sheet, his eyes wild and flashing like a man on drugs, laughing hysterically every so often. His injuries were not to his body, but his mind.

"Are you all right?" cried Krenz, reaching out toward the other, but von Müller cringed away in fear, trying to hide his terrified face.

Suddenly he began to claw at his eyes and face, mumbling to himself. "A plant? An animal? . . . No, don't look this way! . . . That five-pointed star of a head . . . No! The mountain moves. . . . the mountain of cells . . ." Another scream burst from his lungs; I thought he would scream blood, it was so violent. Then he collapsed, unconscious. Heinrich caught him.

When Krenz began to walk toward the door, frowning, I asked him where he was going.

"To the ship's infirmary, for a sedative or brandy. Von Müller needs rest, and sleep." As Krenz spoke, the door opened behind him.

From the hall, Heinicke said with a thin, cruel smile, "No need. I brought cognac." He gripped the cork in his teeth and pulled it out, taking a swig straight from the bottle before handing it to me. As I took it, his foul breath caught in my nose . . . he had already had quite a bit to drink, it seemed. He reeked of liquor. Passing the bottle to Heinrich, I asked the drunken sot what he had done to von Müller.

"Why, we just showed him some dreams!" he replied, more talkative than usual because of his state.

"Dreams? What did you do, drug him?"

"The Mask. We just put the mask on his head."

"The Mask?"

Krenz's eyebrows dropped, and he stared into Heinicke's eyes. "That's right, the Mask," laughed Heinicke. "Like I said before, the Mask of Yoth-Tlaggon. The platinum mask that Reichsführer Himmler finally got two years ago, after so much trouble. If you wear it, you see visions across time and space . . ."

"But why von Müller?" demanded Krenz, moving closer.

Heinicke shrugged. "You don't know? His family is pretty famous as psychics in the Black Forest region. All sorts of wizards and witches and mediums and oracles in it . . ."

Krenz glared at the other in dislike, about to snap something in return, when von Müller began coughing weakly.

"Heinrich! How is he?" Heinrich held the bottle to von Müller's lips, forcing him to drink a little.

"He's fine. Just swallowed a bit the wrong way."

"Well, take good care of him, will you? We need him to look at some more visions tomorrow," warned Heinicke, prancing out of the room with a snicker.

Late that night von Müller finally returned to normalcy and explained a little about the Mask of Yoth-Tlaggon and the visions it had shown him.

"They tied me to a chair, then Weber opened up the safe in the captain's room and took out a platinum mask. They slipped it over my head. It was an elongated, inverted triangle in shape, with sharp points at the ears and chin, and the top was bald—no decoration at all. The face was covered with detailed carvings that made me think of the writhing tentacles of a sea anemone. The eyes slanted up, and were only the thinnest slits. The mouth was a cold, V-shaped sneer.

"I knew from the first glance that it was an accurate replica of a real *thing*. And I knew that whatever it was, it was unfriendly to the human race . . . no, not just an enemy, but rather our *natural enemy*.

"'There's nothing to be afraid of. Your father used this mask to see visions, as did Klingen Mergelsheim,' said Weber, and forced it onto my head in spite of my struggles. I've never felt anything like it before in my life. . . . It shouldn't have fit my head, judging from its size and shape, but the platinum stretched like rubber, covering me like a sheath from my neck up. I couldn't see anything at first, just the sadistic SS swine and that Gestapo idiot, sneering and drinking his liquor. But after about thirty seconds . . . my mouth began to chant some sort of spell, all by itself! It was saying 'Iä! Iä! Hastu—r!' Maybe it was more like a vibration of some sort than a spell . . . the walls and the door to the captain's room began to resonate with my voice.

"And the next instant . . .

"Everything was bathed in pink. Not just a simple pink, but a florescent pink light so bright it pained my eyes. And then the visions came. They were more real than a movie, and more terrifying than my worst nightmare: stone towers soaring up to unimaginable heights to pierce the heavens; vistas of Cyclopean structures of rock, layer upon layer; giant mazes that made me dizzy just to look at. They were all interwoven in pure chaos, without rhyme or reason. And everything—walls, roofs, the passageways linking structures together—everything was covered with a green liquid, like oozing pus.

"Suddenly one of the inhabitants of this monstrous city stared into my face. I screamed at its hideous visage . . . My God! I shudder to recall it. . . . It stood about two meters forty tall, and its head was a five-pointed star, like a starfish. The body was barrel-shaped, with five ridges running vertically on the surface. It looked like a sea lily. I'm sure that's what it was! You remember? The sea lilies we studied in school, the crinoids from the Ordovician period? Monsters that looked like plants, and that ruled the Earth aeons ago.

"Tubes protruded from the apexes of that crowning five-pointed star, branching into multiple fingers, each tipped with a small sphere. And one of those spheres was turned toward me. As I looked back, suddenly a yellow membrane covered the reddish iris of that glassy sphere. And I realized it was an eye, the eyeball of a giant sea lily of a monster, staring at me. But that wasn't what terrified me. What terrified me was that this organ, this eyeball, was looking at me with unmistakable intelligence!"

He said he was sure that the monster had been sending telepathic messages to him. And he said that the message he received was to turn back, to stay far from Leng. It warned him that *they* were waiting, those who had driven its race to the very threshold of extinction.

3. PHANTASMS OF THE SOUTH POLE

July 11. The *Hölderlin* has finally reached 66°32', the edge of the south polar region.

We soldiers disembarked to the polar icecap along with the dogs and the sleds, and spent a full day assembling the snow crawler. As soon as we finished, we turned to discover three huge Panzerkampfwagens awaiting us.

"What in the world is Oberstleutnant Weber . . . no, the Führer . . . planning?" whispered Krenz, aghast.

Heinrich couldn't believe it, either: "Surely there's no enemy base at the south pole!" The whole expedition—officers and enlisted men alike—were visibly shaken at the unexpected appearance of the tanks. Perhaps because of that ripple of unease, Oberstleutnant Weber spoke to us through a microphone, protected by the Bergmann machineguns of his SS troopers.

"I am sure you are all surprised, but there is a good reason for these tanks," he said. His voice was twisted like an evil spirit with the howling of the microphone. "We have discovered a potential threat to the southwest of Neuschwabenland, the new realm of the Third Reich."

"What sort of threat?" I shouted to Weber, who was standing on the deck.

"I cannot discuss that yet. You will cross those mountains under my command, and destroy that which lives in their shadow."

"What do you mean, 'those mountains?'," I demanded, and Weber focused on me.

He took a deep breath, and replied "The Mountains of Madness."

At his words, von Müller fainted dead away. Mein Gott! That splendid man, a proud officer in the glorious German Wehrmacht, fainted at the sound of that name. I wondered what horrors awaited us at the Mountains of Madness. . . .

I listened to what von Müller was saying as we smeared the movable parts of the Schmeissers with plenty of grease to prevent freezing. "Apparently this Mask of Yoth-Tlaggon functions as some sort of map to the ancient south pole." The four of us—von Müller, Krenz, Heinrich and myself—were riding together in the same dogsled. Our goal was Neuschwabenland, a full thousand kilometers distant, and beyond it soared the Mountains of Madness.

"The Oberstleutnant put the Mask on me and forced me to see its visions to discover the accurate locations of the Mountains of Madness, and investigate what was on the other side."

"Can you remember what you saw?" asked Krenz.

"No. I fear it was too horrible to remember, and my mind has buried it deep away in my subconscious. I don't remember a thing." He shook his head.

Heinrich scowled, speaking quietly. "I still remember what you were shouting on that first day, though. . . . 'The mountain moves . . . the mountain of cells . . .', you shouted."

"You mean the Mountains of Madness are some sort of giant creature?" I asked, incredulously of Heinrich. The blowing snow was hiding the scenery in streaks, like an old movie.

Heinrich shrugged.

"Who knows? I'm just not imaginative enough to take a guess."

We fell silent. I looked up at the sky while chewing on my lower lip. Huge globs of snow, as large as a baby's fist, were pelting down from the oatmeal-colored clouds. The wind that carried them to us was dry and freezing cold, much too cold for the unprotected skin. We looked like giant insects, huddling in our hooded furs, with colored goggles and our noses and mouths covered by masks. Or perhaps strange sea creatures, huge seals or sea lions, carrying guns. The swastika flag on the lead dogsled froze quickly, wrapped onto the pole tightly.

Suddenly, amid the chill, I heard a roaring, and looked up at the sky again to see the reassembled Messerschmitt spreading its steel wings overhead.

"Damn Weber. He's on his way to Neuschwabenland ahead of us," spat out Krenz.

"I guess he's too good to ride with the rest of us in the dogsleds," agreed Heinrich.

Von Müller tracked the Messerschmitt with his eyes, and it eventually vanished into the clouds ahead. He lowered his eyes and suddenly shouted in a trembling voice "Hey! Look, there!"

"What? Where?" I jumped up, searching in the direction he pointed. And I swallowed my breath with an audible gulp. Above the pure white horizon rose a strange and terrible mirage. It was unquestionably artificial, some sort of geometric structures all jumbled atop one another.

It was an ancient ruin, a maze of structures and walls seemingly arranged at random.

I was terrified.

They have been there since before Mohenjo Daro, since before Memphis or Babylon was even a dream, I thought.

"Maybe it's some sort of aurora caused by optical refraction," suggested Krenz in a doubting voice.

"No, it's not wavering at all," said Heinrich. "It can only be some . . . scene . . . beyond the Mountains of Madness!"

He slipped his right hand free of the dogsled reins, and crossed himself quickly. I followed suit. If you wish to laugh at us for acting like some farmer from Alsace instead of acting like the German Wehrmacht officers we were, go right ahead and laugh. But anyone who saw the mirage that we saw would pray to God as did we. Assuming that there was a God in this frozen wilderness of the south pole!

After four hours in the blowing snow, we made camp for the night. The blizzard had gotten even stronger, and the officer in charge decided that trying to push ahead into the teeth of the storm would only delay us even more in the end. The officer in charge was Heinicke, that despicable Gestapo rat.

"Set up your tents, quickly! Somebody contact the Oberstleutnant by radio! Get that fire going!"

We followed the orders of that Gestapo idiot who had obviously never made camp before, all thirty-two of us working almost silently. We were able to forget the bizarre events and our uneasy situation through hard physical labor. I think that must have been one of our happiest moments there, exercising our bodies and not thinking. Happiness rarely lasts.

4. MIDNIGHT ONSLAUGHT

The tension and stress of setting foot, most of us for the first time in our lives, upon the frozen waste of Antarctica, the day of assembling machinery, and the four hours of advancing into the driving snow, followed by the fatigue of making camp, ensured that we fell asleep instantly. The fierce howls of the wind and the bitter cold drafts snaking in through the corners of the tent never bothered us, thanks to our thick, feather-stuffed sleeping bags.

I was awakened from my dreamless slumber, deep in my sleeping bag, by the sound of three gunshots echoing in a suddenly quiet wind. I wriggled out of the sleeping bag and leapt to my feet. Heinrich and Krenz already had their machineguns in hand.

"It came from the north," said Heinrich, teeth clenched.

"Sounded like a scream," said Krenz. "I'm sure it was Heinicke!"

"As if I care what happens to that Gestapo pig!" I muttered to myself, getting ready. "But I'm worried about von Müller, and they're together." Heinicke had kept von Müller with him, like a sort of hostage.

Schmeissers in hand, we opened the tent and stepped out. The world was pitch white. It was still the middle of the night, but we couldn't see a thing without our goggles. The air was full of flying snow, filling every nook and cranny of our field of vision. Even so, we ran toward Heinicke's tent, calling out to von Müller. Soldiers from other tents were already there.

"What is the world . . . ?"

"Mother of God!"

"Hurry!"

And mixed with their shouts came the intermittent sound of Schmeissers firing. The white world around us flared orange with the gunfire, and we ran toward it, our legs wrenched by the drifting snow and boots sliding on ice, stumbling. There was already a group of soldiers there, weapons at ready.

"Let us through! Von Müller! Is von Müller all right?" we shouted, pushing through our comrades to the front. And then we saw it. . . .

A giant hole yawned where the tent had stood. I squatted down at the edge and peered within. It was deeper than I could see, and cut in a perfect circle, ice and dirt and rock as sharp and polished as glass.

" . . . This was not made by a machine," whispered Krenz.

"Sure as hell no animal cut this hole!" Heinrich swore. "I'm afraid there's no hope for von Müller. Or Heinicke."

I noticed something black in the corner of my eye, and turned to look closer. It was a black leather glove, a fur-lined glove issued to the Wehrmacht.

" . . . von Müller's," I mumbled, reaching out to pick it up.

It was heavy.

There was something inside.

The cross-section of von Müller's wrist was as smooth, as polished, and as bloodless as that monstrous hole in the ice.

"Oberstleutnant! Von Müller!" I shouted, throwing glove and hand both into that damnable hole. It fell into the depths, the unknown and incalculable depths. "I'll take command now," I announced to my assembled brothers in arms, as the highest-ranking officer. Left. There was no dissent. They were all pale, faces slack in shock and fear.

"We're leaving immediately. Pack everything up, because we're certainly not staying here!"

Krenz nodded and saluted me. The others rapidly followed suit. And not a single one of them gave me a Hitlerian straight-arm.

We noticed it as soon as we began breaking camp: a deep rumbling groan from under the earth. The rocks and soil buried under all that snow and ice were trembling enough that we could feel it. It was perfectly reasonable to find volcanic activity in Antarctica. But accepting the possibility and feeling the ground move were two different things.

"Keep working! Get those tents loaded onto the sleds!" shouted Krenz, proving once again he was an old hand as he kept his calm amidst it all. "Don't worry about it! Keep your mind on your jobs, and keep working!" He threw himself into the job even as he shouted at the other soldiers. We were able to get the dogsleds under way by four in the morning.

"I wonder if the tank crews have already gotten there," asked Heinrich as he snapped the reins.

Krenz replied before I could, commenting "I'm sure they're sipping brandy with the Oberstleutnant right now."

"Wish I was with them. . . ."

"Me, too!"

While Krenz and Heinrich were talking to each other, I was listening, nerves taut, to the groaning of the earth below us. I couldn't help feeling that it had something to do with that enormous hole that swallowed von Müller. And Heinicke, of course.

Gradually I began to notice a strange presence, like somebody was watching me. It was moving. Something was moving in parallel with the dogsleds, watching us closely. At first I thought it was just my nerves, overwrought, but after an hour and then two my apprehension blossomed into certainty.

No question about it, I thought. *We're being watched, and followed. And whoever is doing it killed von Müller and Heinicke. Or* whatever!

I looked ahead but could see no shadows in the snow, only the towering white peaks. I looked to both sides again and again, but I could see only the dogs and the sleds, and the huddled soldiers riding them. We were all weary and cold to the bone. The sky held nothing but low, gray clouds, the driving snow, snow, and more snow . . . even though I could find no sign of danger, the fear in my heart continued to grow. I felt its hidden presence more than ever . . . *It's coming closer, it's out there. Somewhere . . .*

I suddenly noticed that I was gripping my Schmeisser tightly, safety off, holding it ready to fire in an instant.

Come, damn you! If you're coming, COME! I cursed it, called to it, deep in my heart.

And heard the howls of terrified dogs from my left!

I swung in that direction instantly, and saw a swirling pillar of snow maybe ten meters high.

"Hallo! What's happened? What is it?" called Krenz toward the dog-sled, invisible in the blowing snow.

No answer.

Only the muffled echoes of the howling dogs and frightened men shouting. Then screams, yelps, the sound of machine guns chattering away . . . gunfire flashed inside the swirling snow, like lightning in the clouds.

"Heinrich, stop the sled!" I screamed, gun still pointed to the left.

"No!" he shouted back, shaking his head. "If I stop it'll kill us, too!" He whipped the reins, urging the dogs to their top speed.

"I think it's as Heinrich says . . ." agreed Krenz, pointing his chin at the tower of swirling snow receding behind us. A second, similar swirl of snow had sprung up further to the left, swallowing a dogsled and our comrades who had stopped to help. As the second snow cloud grew in size, the first one gradually subsided. It was dissipated by the blowing wind, leaving the same gigantic, yawning pit that had swallowed von Müller.

"The devil . . ." whispered Krenz hoarsely, and crossed himself once again.

"Is this what von Müller saw in his visions?" I asked, and felt a new chill run up my spine. It wasn't from the cold of this frozen hell. It was fear, fear of the unknown. Fear of that incredible, incomprehensible power. That chill spread from my spine throughout my entire body, and I could not escape its dreadful grasp for hours.

5. Tragedy in the New Land

I think the dogs must have known what lurked in those frozen wastes much better than we humans could. They had kept pulling the sleds almost without rest for two days. We were almost dead with exhaustion and numbing fear, like the zombie sled-riders the distant Inuits spoke of in their legends. On the third day the dogs finally slowed their frantic pace, no doubt as exhausted as we were. Heinrich didn't lash them at all, though, because we had noticed a change in our surroundings.

"It's spring!" said Krenz in wonder, throwing back the hood of his parka. His face looked softer than it had for days. Indeed, it was as if spring had come to Antarctica. The snow had thinned, revealing the rough ground in irregular patches here and there. The wind had lost its bitter edge, and there was even a warm breeze at times. The mountains surrounding us showed their black flanks, some even covered with trees!

"Neuschwabenland . . ." whispered Heinrich, in astonishment and joy. We broke into long-disused smiles. Then I turned back, and my eyebrows came together in a frown.

"What's wrong, Major? Something displeases you about having a delightfully warm spot in Antarctica?"

"Yes. Very much so," I replied. After all, I had shown that Kapitän Ritscher was a liar, and I had ended up being exiled to Antarctica even so. I could not accept this completely illogical, irrational environment.

"No, I guess the Major wouldn't like it very much at all," chuckled Krenz, well aware of what had happened.

"I suppose this abnormal weather must be a relatively temporary thing, due to volcanic activity. It can't last long . . . I think constructing a military base here is a very poor idea," I stated.

"Well, you may not like it, but there it is," smiled Heinrich, pointing ahead. I looked in the direction he indicated, and about four kilometers ahead I could see a building like a giant ham sliced in half. In front of it three Panzerkampfwagens were parked side-by-side, and a little distance away five Messerschmitts stood on a graded stretch of land.

"A dirt runway, aircraft, tanks and barracks. No doubt the Führer intends to bring the whole of Berlin here next!" joked Heinrich to Krenz, but I couldn't share in their humor. I feared that the madman who ruled Germany might do just that.

The snow had turned to muck, and we freed the dogs from the sleds. We carried the loads the last two kilometers on our backs. There were only twenty of us left. We were exhausted, but merely being able to tread dry earth once again lightened our hearts. Heinrich even began singing:

"Stand fellow soldiers,
The drum is beating!
Forward, ever forward
Into the morning mist,
Until Death greets us!"

The other soldiers picked up the song, a well-known favorite in the German Army.

"Glory to the Fatherland!
We carry on the proud blood
With fidelity and faith,
We laugh, we sing, we dance,
We share together!"

And suddenly their voices faltered.... They had recalled that the next stanza described how they would fight and die for Adolf Hitler....

Heinrich kept singing through the pause, powerfully:

"We fight
      for Richter von Hausen,
We live
      with Richter von Hausen!"

The men, laughing, sang the last line as one:

"For the glory of the Reich!"

As if waiting for the song to end, a gunshot rang out from the barracks. As one, we dropped our loads and swung our weapons up to ready. "There are enemies in the base! Fan out!"

Before I had even finished giving the order they were already spreading out, hugging the ground, guns pointing at the base. Bent low, they began sprinting from cover to cover toward the base. There were no more gunshots. We reached the base, and Krenz rammed the door to the barracks with his shoulder, shouting with fear and grunting with the impact all at once. The door swung open easily.

Gun still aimed inside the barracks, Krenz called back to us: "What happened here! They're dead, Major! The SS! They're all dead! Looks like they killed each other."

"They what . . . ?" Astonished, I halted just behind Krenz, trying to look inside. He slid aside, and I stepped in with a nod. The barracks stank with a sweetish, sourish smell . . . and shit. As I looked, I felt my gorge rise. The pool of blood started almost at my feet, and beyond was a mound of human organs, of skinned *parts* of people. I saw the head of an SS trooper I recognized lying nearby. The stench of the blood, the shit from the rent bodies, filled that closed space, making it impossible to breathe.

"Maybe they said something to upset Oberstleutnant Weber?" snarled Heinrich, who had come up behind for his own look inside.

"This is not Weber's doing," I said. "He may have been Jack the Ripper, but he knows nothing of dissection!" I advanced slowly, careful not to step on any body parts. They had not been haphazardly torn to bits, but rather dissected neatly and cleanly, almost anatomically. Over there was one body that had been skinned on the right half only, leaving a perfect anatomical model.

The room was hot, the stove still burning. We advanced deeper into the barracks, and in the cafeteria there was still steam-hot coffee on the table.

"The Oberstleutnant should be in the rear . . ." I said to myself, heading to the door. I opened it to see triple-decked bunkbeds to left and right, and another door about ten meters ahead of me.

I slowly took my left hand off my Schmeisser, and moved it toward the doorknob. I grasped it and slowly turned. The lock opened with a *click*. Instantly there was the noise of something hitting the floor, somebody kicking the floor, glass breaking.

"Who's there?" I shouted, and kicked the door open. I jumped in; the wind was blowing in through the shattered window. I ran over to it and looked outside . . . some*thing* black was just flying away. But what in the world *was* it? A giant, pitch-black barrel, over two meters long, with a five-pointed star bizarrely balanced on top. Giant insectoid wings sprouted from its back, if that's where its back was. If it *had* a back. They weren't flapping at all, but the *thing* spiraled up into the sky anyway. It flew on and on, turning rapidly into a black speck, and vanished into the towering mountains, looming over us like fangs.

Speechless, I turned back to look at the room. SS Oberstleutnant Wilhelm Weber lay to the right of the door, face up on the floor. His monocle had fallen out, but at least he hadn't been vivisected. His eyes were frozen wide open in what must have been literally blood-curdling terror. Next to his body lay a rifle. I stooped down.

"Dead of shock?" asked Krenz, stepping in through the doorway. I lifted up the rifle, and slowly rose back to my feet.

"Yes. . . . It looks like he had a heart attack, after seeing that thing . . ."

I showed Krenz the rifle. Long, deep scratches ran along it, not only through the wood of the stock, but through the steel receiver and barrel as well.

"What do you think? It looks like that shot we just heard came from this rifle . . ." Krenz lifted the barrel up to his nose and took an audible sniff.

"No question about it. It's just been fired." Looking around the room, he settled his Schmeisser over his shoulder again, hanging it by its strap. "It looks to me," he shrugged, "that all those prostitutes Weber murdered came back to haunt him. They toyed with him, and his rifle, and it went off. And when we came they vanished."

"These ghosts smashed the window and flew off toward the Mountains of Madness, I suppose?" I countered sarcastically.

"What? Flew?"

"I saw it flying away, Krenz. A black thing, shaped like a huge barrel. Hey, now that I think of it . . . it was exactly like von Müller saw in his vision!"

"It flew . . . ? To where?"

I didn't answer Krenz, but pointed silently out the window. The window faced to the southwest, toward the barracks, and beyond them rose the terrible fangs of the mountain range, piercing the sky.

The Mountains of Madness.

6. The Report of the Miskatonic Expedition

Oberstleutnant Weber's room was packed with a variety of items. A wooden box on his crammed desk caught my eye. It was labeled "Mask of Yoth-Tlaggon." Naturally, I made no effort to even touch the box. I was extremely interested, though, in the contents of the bookshelf that covered one wall of the room, and the diverse books that lined its shelves. The keys to unraveling this horrible mystery must lie there, I felt. I left the bundle of official orders and dispatches to Krenz to sort through. He had been, after all, formerly in Intelligence. He would be able to sort through it all for valuable information much faster than I. Looking at what was left, I could see it divided into two basic types of material. One type was the reports of other Antarctic expeditions—Shackleton, Amundsen, Scott, Byrd—and various geographical and geological surveys of the continent.

The other . . . I couldn't believe it, but the rest were books on the occult, mythology, mysteries, black magic, demonology, witchcraft and the like! Klingen Mergelsheim's *Abominations of Atzous, Unaussprechlichen Kulten* by von Junzt, Ludvig Prynn's *De Vermiis Mysteriis*, the rumored second volume of Philipp von Siebold's *Nippon*, Michel le Garrault's *Les Murs S'écroulés*, even Blavatsky's *Secret Doctrine*! They were books I would surely have never even *seen*, let alone read, had I been anywhere else in the world . . . or even understand, were I to read them.

I turned my attention back to the expedition reports and picked up the Amundsen report to see what was in it. As I lifted it, another pamphlet fell off the shelf, rustling to the floor. It looked like a research transactions report, something you might see at a university. Bending over, I lifted it up and read the title, printed on the cover in English: *Report of the 1930 Miskatonic University Antarctic Expedition*. Frowning, I opened it up. According to the table of contents, it contained a report on an ice sampling drill by Professor Frank H. Pabodie of the Engineering Department at that institution, observations on ancient Antarctic fauna by Professor Lake of the Biology Department, and the like. Scanning down through the articles, one title leaped to my attention: *At the Mountains of Madness*. That particular article began thusly:

> I am forced into speech because men of science have refused to follow my advice without knowing why. It is altogether against my will that I tell my reasons for opposing this contemplated invasion of the Antarctic—with its vast fossil hunt and its wholesale boring and melting of the ancient ice caps. And I am the more reluctant because my warning may be in vain.

According to the report, the expedition departed from Boston on September 2, 1930. There were two vessels, the *Arkham* and the *Miskatonic*, and they travelled together down the coast of the North American continent, travelling through the Panama Canal to the Pacific to provision in Samoa, then on to Hobart for their final stop before Antarctica.

> Oct. 20   Crossed the Antarctic Circle.
> Oct. 26   Saw the Admiralty Range for the first time.
> Nov. 7   Passed Franklin Island.
> Nov. 8   Saw volcanoes Erebus and Terror on Ross Island.
> Nov. 9   Landed on Ross Island at dawn by ship's boats.
> Nov. 21   Flew south over the Ross ice shelf in four aircraft, landing at the base of Mt. Nansen to establish a base at Latitude 86° 7', East Longitude 174° 23'.
>
> On Jan. 6 of the following year, 1931, smaller teams board two aircraft to fly to the South Pole.

The report was crisp, even proud, through that point. The style began to show apprehension and uncertainty from about Jan. 22, 1931, when the biologist, Professor Lake, left to enter land that no man had seen before. The report said that his aircraft had discovered a towering mountain range, but apparently that fact had been known only through the radioed reports received from Professor Lake. It read as follows:

Reaches far as can see to right and left. Suspicion of two smoking cones. All peaks black and bare of snow. Gale blowing off them impedes navigation . . . Swept clear of snow above about twenty-one thousand feet. Odd formations on slopes of highest mountains. Great low square blocks with exactly vertical sides, and rectangular lines of low, vertical ramparts, like the old Asian castles clinging to steep mountains in Roerich's paintings.

The Mountains of Madness.

Those pinnacles reaching into the sky right behind us, in other words, were covered with gigantic—cosmic—artificial constructs. *What lies beyond the Mountains of Madness . . . What is the Nazi leadership so terribly frightened of there?* With me caught in furious thought, the report slipped from my fingers to the floor, just at the same time that Krenz slapped the desk, letting out a hearty "I've got it!"

"Wha . . . ? What?" I returned to myself, lifting my eyes to Krenz. He waved an order under my nose.

"Look at this! The Führer gave the order to explore Neuschwabenland, but Himmler is the one who wanted the base built here! Kapitän Ritscher discovered this place and built a camp here, but exceeded his orders and explored beyond the Mountains of Madness . . . and awoke something that had been sleeping."

"Let me see that!" I said, snatching it from Krenz' hand. Attached to the order was a sheaf of photographs of the rear side of the Mountains of Madness, taken from an aircraft. They showed endless rows of cubic structures, as Professor Lake had described, an ugly demon's castle. Unlike natural mountains, however, there were artificial tunnels and galleries running through the flanks of the mountains, huge mouths gaping. And from one of those holes . . . how can I describe it . . . something like a gigantic amoeba peered forth!

"Himmler gave a codename to this operation," continued Krenz, his body trembling in fear, or hysteria. "Operation Shoggoth."

I could only nod.

Across that photograph someone, probably Himmler himself, had scrawled "Shoggoth" in black ink. Mein Gott! It was huge! I felt a tremble in my own breast. In spite of the fact that the photograph had been taken from the air, every loathsome detail of the shoggoth was clearly visible: its foam-covered surface, with its viscous slime, the amoeba body with no eyes, or nose, or mouth. . . .

But I could not believe that this was merely some clever model created in an UFA special effects movie studio. . . .

7. Shoggoth Firefight

We cleaned up the scattered SS and Gestapo remains, thoroughly washed down the barracks, nailed boards over the shattered window in the Oberstleutnant's room and finally called it a day. After dinner, Heinrich, Krenz and I gathered in the Oberstleutnant's room to figure out what we should do next.

"I read the report of the Miskatonic Expedition," I explained. "Apparently shoggoths aren't the only creatures on the other side of the Mountains of Madness. It says there are also a lot of those anemone-like *things*, the things that created and used the shoggoths, sleeping there. They dissected a bunch of people in the Miskatonic party, too."

"Looks like Kapitän Ritscher barely escaped those shoggoths with his life, eh? Son of a bitch! I wish the damn things had eaten him!" Krenz poured brandy into his cup as he spat the words out with venom. Heinrich grimaced: "Well, we have to stay here for a year. I checked with the *Hölderlin* by radio a little while ago, and what do you think they said? 'See you in a year! Good luck.' Bastards!" He accepted the bottle of brandy from Krenz, nodding.

"I guess the shoggoth is what dragged poor von Müller and the others down into that pit. The report says they can burrow underground," I added, sighing. We looked at each other for a moment.

"If the shoggoth did that, there's nothing we can do," said Krenz slowly. "Our Schmeissers have no effect on it at all."

"But we have three Panzerkampfwagens and five Messerschmitts now! Pretty damn impressive, getting five aircraft down here in only a year . . ." Heinrich snorted, and gulped down a short of brandy. "I wonder what Weber was planning," I thought aloud, lighting up a cigarette. I lit it with my Wehrmacht lighter, and held out the flame for the others. "Blow it up with gunpowder, maybe?" The other two leaned forward, borrowing my light.

"That would explain all the gunpowder he brought down here," said Heinrich quietly, setting his cup down. He kept licking his upper lip.

"Not just gunpowder," broke in Krenz. "There's a lot of diesel fuel behind the barracks, too. Two hundred drums. And he's got a year's worth of gasoline and oil, too." I nodded, and flicked the lighter shut.

"The only way over the Mountains of Madness is by air. How about we cross in the Messerschmitt, draw the shoggoth out from the air and lead it here?"

Krenz' face broke into a smile. "And when it arrives on this side of the range, we blow it to bits with the tanks. And if that doesn't work, then gunpowder and diesel fuel." He threw back a shot of brandy.

"We can be ready in a week," agreed Heinrich.

"Let me see . . . Tomorrow is July, uh . . . What date is it tomorrow?" I asked.

Krenz shrugged. "Who knows? Call it the sixteenth. That's Heinrich's birthday."

I lost when we chose straws and ended up sleeping in Oberstleutnant Weber's room. Former room. It was bad enough having to sleep in the same room as the Mask of Yoth-Tlaggon, even still in its wooden box, but the bookshelves were also full of books on magic and other unpleasant things. Pretty hard to expect anyone to sleep well here, I thought, even as I burrowed into the blankets of Weber's bed, soft enough for a first-class Berlin hotel. I gripped my pistol under the pillow, and leaned the Schmeisser against the bed at my side. I figured I was prepared for any return visit by that barrel-shaped anemone or whatever it was, but I still couldn't relax. After all, the Miskatonic Expedition had been an academic team during peacetime. We were at war, and worse, had to stay here for another year. Come shoggoths or vivisecting anemones, we had no choice but to defend this base.

And in spite of my constant worry, I eventually fell into a troubled slumber. I heard von Müller calling to me, from a distance. Heinicke's voice was somehow superimposed on von Müller's, and I could also hear the voices of all my comrades who were dragged down into the depths with that dogsled . . .

The dead are calling me . . . I thought slowly, still asleep. *But why can't I hear Weber and the SS men, I wonder . . .* Their calls gradually turned into wails, then unintelligible screams echoing around me. Far, closer, farther away again, then suddenly right at my ear! I awoke with a shriek, and sat up, taut. The screams and wails of the dead continued unabated.

"Am I still dreaming?" I wondered aloud, shaking my head in confusion. After maybe ten seconds of doubt, though, I finally recognized the "screams" as merely the sound of the wind.

I climbed out of bed and looked at the window. The boards were still in place. I relaxed a bit, gave a small sigh, and suddenly noticed someone laughing near the desk. *On the desk? A severed head!?*

My heart jumped once again. I looked closer, and realized it wasn't a head lying there, but something even worse. Infinitely worse. It was a platinum mask, shaped like a long, inverted triangle . . . The Mask of Yoth-Tlaggon, which should have been safe in its wooden box! Its lips were twisted up in a V-shaped sneer, laughing at me. Behind it I could yet hear a low noise, like the shrieking of the dead. I felt a shiver run up my spine, unable to shake the feeling that it was indeed laughing at me.

A sudden pounding on the door!

"Major! Major, Wake up!" It was Heinrich's voice.

"I'm coming!" I replied. Fortunately I had been sleeping in my uniform. I pulled my pistol out from under the pillow and returned it to my holster, and picked up by Schmeisser. I opened the door to find Heinrich waiting, dripping cold sweat. Behind him was Krenz, shouting to the men that they were under attack.

"That sound . . ."

"Yes, sir. Apparently the enemy has noticed we entered the base."

"What are we facing? The shoggoth? The anemones?"

"We can't tell."

"Let's get outside," I suggested, then called to Krenz. "Get the tanks warmed up and ready to go!"

"Yes, sir!"

With Krenz' shout still echoing, I raced outside the barracks, Heinrich in pursuit.

And stopped in amazement at the fantastic scene spreading out in front of me. The starry sky was covered by an aurora, sheets of shimmering color as if the heavens had split to reveal the glory beyond. I turned to look at the Mountains of Madness and saw countless columns of brilliant blue light stretching upward.

"Something's happening beyond the Mountains," I said to myself in amazement.

"Major! Look!" shouted Heinrich, pointing to a moving object backlit by the Mountains.

". . . Shoggoths . . ."

My voice trembled.

Gigantic yet indistinct shapes were moving through the high valley between two of the soaring fangs of the Mountains of Madness, shining florescent pink in the light of the aurora. There were dozens of them, crossing the Mountains and rushing down upon Neuschwabenland. Their enormous size and their speed made me think of airplanes . . . and as they advanced, they dissolved and absorbed all they encountered. The first shoggoth reached the foot of the mountains, toppling trees and bushes easily, and leaving only packed, raw dirt behind. It was an expressway leading toward us . . . no, an ice-skating rink!

"Where were they all until now? And why the hell did they decide to come calling the very same night we get here!" asked Heinrich. I didn't answer, because something had just occurred to me, triggered by his words: *Maybe it has something to do with the Mask! The anemone tried to take it but for some reason got interested in the rifle first, and left the Mask when it fled. Maybe the rifle went off by accident and brought us running. Maybe it's all because of the Mask!*

I started running.

8. ASSAULT ON THE MOUNTAINS OF MADNESS

At the entrance I passed soldiers following Krenz toward the tanks.

"Get to the tanks, and blow those things back to Hell," I shouted to Krenz. "The rest of you, hold them off with the fuel and gunpowder! If we have to, we'll escape in the Messerschmitts!"

I raced into the building, a paragraph from the Miskatonic report reverberating in my memory.

. . . manufactured not only necessary foods, but certain multicellular protoplasmic masses capable of molding their tissues into all sorts of temporary organs under hypnotic influence and thereby forming ideal slaves to perform the heavy work of the community.

Through the cafeteria . . .

They had always been controlled through the hypnotic suggestions of the Old Ones, and had modeled their tough plasticity into various useful temporary limbs and organs; but now their self-modeling powers were sometimes exercised independently. . . .

I sprinted through that narrow room, with triple bunk beds along the walls.

The newly bred shoggoths grew to enormous size and singular intelligence, and were represented as taking and executing orders with marvelous quickness. They seemed to converse with the Old Ones by mimicking their voices—a sort of musical piping over a wide range, if poor Lake's dissection had indicated aright—and to work more from spoken commands than from hypnotic suggestions as in earlier times. They were, however, kept in admirable control. The phosphorescent organisms supplied light with vast effectiveness, and doubtless atoned for the loss of the familiar polar auroras of the outer-world night.

. . . Weber's room . . .

What I sought was still on the desk, still sneering at me. The Mask of Yoth-Tlaggon.

"*You* called those damnable anemones down on us, and those phosphorescent pink monsters! And what happens if you're not here any more?" I grasped the platinum mask and lifted it up. It was made of metal but felt pliable as rubber. Goosebumps writhed on my skin at its touch, but there was no time to be squeamish. I stuffed it under one arm and pointed my Schmeisser at the boarded-up window with the other. 9mm bullets sprayed, and the boards blew into splinters. I kicked out the remnants, and stepped outside on to the roof.

I froze, captured by the sight of the valiant Panzerkampfwagens. Krenz had gotten the three Panzers manned and was preparing for the shoggoths. He stood in the forward tank, commanding with head and shoulders outside the turret. Noticing me, he half-turned, grinned and whipped off a tight salute. Not a Nazi salute, of course, but the proud salute of a German Wehrmacht officer. I returned it. He jumped down inside and the hatch slammed shut. The Panzer turned to point directly at the lead shoggoth, now only three hundred meters away.

"Major!"

I heard Heinrich behind me, and turned.

"Heinrich! Get a Messerschmitt ready to go, right now!" I shouted.

"You're abandoning the position? And Krenz?"

"No! I can turn the shoggoths back to the Mountains of Madness. With this!" I showed him the Mask.

"Yes, sir!" he shouted back, and disappeared. The Panzers roared and thundered, with their machine guns firing in counterpoint. I turned back to the battle to see them firing shell after shell into the advancing shoggoths. I watched one shell cut through the air, leaving a red trail behind it as it flew into that protoplasmic lump of shoggoth, squishing inside its bulk and then exploding with a deafening shock. Orange flame rimmed in yellow burst forth, and that monstrous bulk blew into fragments.

"Got it!" I yelled, finally breaking a grim smile. But my smile faded a second later. The fragments and blobs of shoggoth scattered over the ground were still twitching and writhing, seeking each other out and fusing into ever-larger lumps! Reborn, the shoggoth steamed white vapor into the cool Antarctic air and advanced directly in front of Krenz' Panzer, shining pink as if in condescension. It swelled like a puffball, then suddenly collapsed, flowed like liquid toward the tank, and completely enveloped it.

"Krenz!"

I prayed for my friend's safety, yet confident that the tough armor of that Panzerkampfwagen III, pride of the German Wehrmacht, would withstand this monster.

I was wrong . . .

The shoggoth gradually spread out, flattening thinner and thinner. I could hear Krenz' muffled cries from within.

"*Tekeli-li . . . Tekeli-li . . .*"

It was the voice of the shoggoth, that weird piping voice, sometimes high and at other times so very low.

I suddenly noticed that the shoggoth was now advancing on me! And behind it . . . Mein Gott! Behind it, where Krenz' Panzer had stood, was a slick, perfectly flat *road*, like an aircraft runway, brightly reflecting the aurora above us.

"Major! The aircraft is waiting!" Behind Heinrich's voice I could hear the propellers spinning up to speed. I had no time to pray for their souls. Biting my lip, I glanced briefly at the other two tanks and saw they were facing their own shoggoth opponents. I discarded my Schmeisser, clasped the Mask of Yoth-Tlaggon tightly to my chest with both hands, and ran. To the Messerschmitt. To the aircraft Heinrich had waiting. To our only chance. I ran as I had never run before, overcoming my trembling legs and the mud that tried to grip my boots and pull me down. Finally, I saw Heinrich, sitting in the Messerschmitt, canopy open and waiting for me. And as I did . . .

"Richter!"

"Major von Hausen!"

"Major!"

I heard Heinicke calling to me, and von Müller, and poor Krenz. In disbelief, I faltered and looked behind me, and saw *it*. I screamed, shut my eyes in terror, and ran toward the aircraft for my life, for my very soul, screaming to rend my lungs asunder. I knew from those blank voices that the shoggoth was behind me. I leaped onto the wing and threw myself into the empty seat behind Heinrich. The aircraft began to taxi at once, gradually increasing the distance to the shoggoth, and finally, after an eternity that lasted perhaps thirty seconds, lifted into the air.

Weeping, wheezing, I turned to look back at it.

It still displayed the faces of the dead. . . . The faces of my friends, calling to me. The shoggoth had stretched to the size of a wall, with horribly distorted faces carved into its flesh . . . the faces of Krenz, of the tank crew, of all who had been dissolved by that monster. The voices of those dead but still monstrously alive souls followed the Messerschmitt, echoing throughout cursed Neuschwabenland.

My report is complete; I have nothing to add.

The aircraft is now circling over the Mountains of Madness. I will place this report in a metal tube, and after we fly back to the base, drop it there. Heinrich and I will then return to the shoggoths and the anemones and the unknown abominations on the far side of the Mountains of Madness, and plunge into their midst, aircraft and Mask together. As long as the Mask is there, they shall not venture forth to this side again. And if any soul ever discovers and reads this missive, let me warn you. This is not a new land, no paradise for the Third Reich. This is where the monstrosities who ruled the earth in geologically ancient times still sleep. This is no place for humanity. And if you should be a soldier serving in the glorious Wehrmacht, I urge you to bomb and burn the far side of the Mountains of Madness until it is erased from the face of the earth forever.

GEDNEY

Laurence J. Cornford

Dear Edward,

Having now had time to examine the full archive of the Starkweather-Moore Expedition, I can say that I think it would make a fine web site. There is an abundance of material including diaries, reports, manifests, photographs, drawings, logs and the surviving gramophone recordings, all of which would make an excellent immersive account of early polar expedition. Indeed, there is considerably more material than from the Miskatonic's disastrous expedition of only a few years earlier, and upon which the Starkweather-Moore Expedition was to build.

I would advise that the connections with the 1931 Miskatonic trip and the sensation caused by Professor William Dyer's press briefings at the time be downplayed. The opinion of the time was that Dyer suffered a mental collapse upon his return from Antarctica, and these unfortunate events only mar the beginning of the expedition. They can probably be dealt with quickly, despite the interest of conspiracy theorists and cranks looking for lost pre-human cities in Professor Dyer's statements. I think we should not seek to encourage such people with the site. After all, the clinching proof that Dyer was unwell lies in his claim that there was a mountain range taller than the Himalayas on Antarctica—if so where is it! Starkweather and Moore report nothing of the kind. Nor did the Second Byrd Expedition later the same year. How can the world's biggest mountain range vanish in the space of three years? Unless an enormous piece of the physics puzzle is missing, then the only rational answer is that Dyer's account was fiction.

If the conspiracy theorists could see the whole archive, they would certainly make much of the subjective impressions of the explorers. Indeed, although nowhere near as eventful as the 1931 expedition, there are still a number of odd events recounted in diaries, such as the account of the frozen bodies of many hundreds of penguins, apparently crushed or bitten, covering an icy inland plain. Or the sound of aeroplanes heard at night, although none of the team's planes were flying at the time. Of course, the Starkweather-Moore Expedition was not the only one in the region at the time, but even so, these reports are curious.

Perhaps most curious is what was reported to have happened at Base 2. Base 2 was a storage dump and refueling point for ferrying supplies further inland, and as such it had only a three man crew (using the old lighthouse keeper principle that if one person was fatally injured, the remaining men would still be able to support each other until help came). Probably the last thing any of them expected was for some stranger to come walking out of the ice and into their camp. Yet that is exactly what happened on the morning of December 28 1933.

They hadn't been keeping any sort of a lookout, as they were not expecting anyone to arrive from the expedition. They saw him on the edge of the camp shuffling with awkward movements towards the main building, his clothing heavily rimed with frost. Quickly they ran to help him inside. The first thought was the man was in a bad way, heavily frostbitten, and they set about the process of warming him up. He seemed to recover quickly and showed no signs of long-term harm. He is described in journals as having the physique of a none too successful pugilist. They estimated that he was just over six feet tall, and thick-set, with rough-hewn features, although his ears were not the "cauliflower ear" of many boxers. Nor did they see signs of scarring to indicate fighting, accident, frostbite, or any major adverse effect from his long exposure to cold.

He spoke like a man unused to speaking. They were most shocked when he gave his name: Gedney. He claimed to be a survivor of the Miskatonic Expedition. Knowing something of the events of the Miskatonic Expedition, and of Professor Dyer's wild claims before they left, they questioned him about what happened. Apparently, the man calling himself Gedney said, one of their number, the leader Lake, went mad and began killing people in the forward camp. Gedney took some supplies and one of the huskies and fled. He found a cave system in which he sheltered, but he failed to spot the rescue party when they arrived and so had been abandoned to fend for himself. The deep cave had proved as good as an igloo, and he had been able to maintain the temperature there. When his supplies ran low, and he failed to find more at the remains of the camp, he had survived on a diet of penguins, supplemented by a lichen which grew deep in the cave system, the only such plant in the interior of the continent. His days were spent collecting water and trapping birds. He was reluctant to say what became of the dog, but the implication is that the animal was eaten. He had heard the sound of aircraft and had come to see if rescuers were at hand.

Base 2 reported the incident and the man was taken to the *S.S. Gabrielle*. His story was hard to believe. The man was physically unlike Gedney, and to survive alone for nearly three years in such harsh conditions seemed unfeasible. A man needs about twice as much nutrition to generate the body-heat and energy to survive in arctic conditions. The suspicion of a hoax was foremost in the ship's report. Yet the man could hardly be left behind, so he was confined to ship and came back with the expedition in January 1934.

When the ship arrived in New York, the man calling himself Gedney was taken into the custody of the Immigration Department.

That might have been the end of an unusual urban myth—the curious story of the man who walked out of nowhere. Indeed it's a little odd that the Slipstreamers and the Hollow Earth Theorists haven't made more of this incident. But maybe they are concentrating their efforts on the Miskatonic Expedition and regard Starkweather-Moore as a cover-up, so haven't noticed it. But I got to wondering if there was anything more concrete. What became of the man who came in from the cold? I knew Prof. Jones had been doing some work on archival records for the State Department and I wondered if any Ellis Island record existed for this man claiming to be Gedney. Through a chain of contacts I discovered that some records did exist, and I requested access to them. That the story had basis in more than an explorer's yarn was interesting, but it didn't mean that the man was Gedney, just as the accounts of Yetis and pictures of large footprints didn't mean they were real either.

When the copy arrived in the post, I noted how thin the file was. The obvious and immediate answer put forward was that the man was an imposter planted near Base 2 for some reason. Starkweather-Moore were not the only explorers to reach Antarctica that year. The Lexington Expedition and the Barsmeier-Falken Team were also rumored to be on the continent late in 1933. Could the man have been part of their teams? Official checks were made with all parties and that possibility was eliminated early in the investigation. Checks with the Miskatonic University proved more problematic. The surviving expedition members were not available to identify Gedney, and while fellows who worked with Gedney prior to the expedition were shown his photograph, no conclusive result was reached.

The man claiming to be Gedney arrived at the reception center on January 23, 1934. This was not the standard reception center, but a special secret one. He was extensively interviewed, and he received a full medical examination, including x-rays. He was found to be physically in excellent health. Indeed, for a man who had lived in arctic conditions, on a diet of penguin meat, he was unexpectedly healthy. The transcript of one of the interviews survives, but I mostly had summary reports.

When asked, the man gave his name as Leonard Felix Clayton Gedney, born March 18, 1905 in Athol, Mass., the third of five children. He recounted how he went to the Miskatonic University to study biology and was doing postgraduate work in protozoa, under Professor Lake, when he was offered a place on the expedition. He even volunteered the information that he sailed on the *S.S. Arkham*, from Boston. These facts would be accurate.

His account of the expedition was similar to but more detailed than the account he gave when discovered:

The Lake party had been making good finds, having broken into a shale cave. The preliminary finds looked promising. Then the weather closed in. Hundred mile-an-hour wind storms wracked the camp. It looked like they might have to abandon the camp for that year before the planes became useless. A meeting was called to discuss the situation. Professor Lake refused to listen to any such suggestion. Following the meeting, Lake quietly went to each of the people who had spoken in favor of turning back. So as not to alert people with gunfire, he cut and stabbed each one. As people began to realize what was happening, Lake began indiscriminate killing, screaming about how he wasn't going to give it up now. It didn't look good to Gedney, so he filled a rucksack with food and, because he thought he might need some company until rescue came, he took one of the dogs with him, and then he set off out of camp to avoid Lake.

They headed out toward the rock ridge. Although the dog could stay outside in those conditions it sensed that Gedney couldn't, so it used its keen senses to find shelter—a cave mouth. Gedney was convinced the dog had saved his life. The cave proved to be larger than he'd hoped, and the two of them took shelter at the back. Gedney rigged up a heat lock. But they were too far back in the cave to keep an eye out for rescue, unsure if Lake had come after them or not. They didn't hear when the rescue party finally arrived.

After a few days, when the weather had calmed a bit, Gedney headed back to camp and then realized that the rescue party had been and gone. There were new-made graves, and aircraft parts had been scavenged and some of the planes were gone. Gedney himself was not a pilot so that didn't matter too much, but he knew he had missed his opportunity and now he'd have to await the next expedition. After all, Byrd and Watkin had both had expeditions in 1928, so he could expect more to come after the Miskatonic's. So he gathered up what provisions had been left and headed back to the cave. He almost gave up after the first year alone, but he kept going.

When asked how he got to Base 2, Gedney replied that he heard aircraft and, knowing that any expedition would have a coastal camp at least, headed out in search of them. The interviewer doubted the logic of searching a continent whose landmass is greater that the United States, but Gedney simply pointed out that he was desperate. Had he died in the attempt, he wouldn't be here, he added.

When presented with a photograph known to be of Gedney as a student, he said, "I've changed. It changes you, living in caves. In the dark. All those years hiding from an enemy. If I could take you back I could show you the cave. The feather mattress I made from penguin pelts."

He displayed signs of metal decline, which can be attributed to the lonely vigil through all those cold, deadening nights, his brain just running on survival, when there are no books, or other voices. At one point he commented, "It's easy to forget that you are a man at all, just another flightless bird clinging to the ice. I don't know why I don't look like him—all I know is that I'm Gedney."

When asked about the caves, he seemed to stress that they were small, no more than five narrow chambers, as if he knew the content of Dyers' statements about vast tunnel systems under the Antarctic and wished to prevent us thinking these caves were those. His denials were another curious feature of the case. He also got a number of what we might call day-to-day details wrong. He was unsure who the President was, and he was unable to say if he could ride a bicycle—in fact Gedney rode a great deal around the college campus. He could name no radio program he missed while alone, and he was disorientated about the date, getting it wrong by some months.

He stuck to his story through countless interviews in the following weeks. Members of the Gedney family were invited in to see if they could clear the matter up, but these interviews proved inconclusive, too. Sometimes he seemed to remember obscure family details and events, other times he would make basic blunders, just as he had in the interviews with officials.

His physical appearance counted much against him. There was a physical resemblance to the real Gedney, but it was the kind of resemblance cousins might have. The medical examination had shown that this man was an inch taller than the recorded height of Gedney before he set out with the Miskatonic, and that seemed to be the decider against him, for there was no indication that his leg bones had been broken, stretched and re-fixed. Indeed, he was apparently without any scarring or fractures on his body.

The authorities kept the man for a few months more until, unable to deport him for lack of evidence, they sectioned him and sent him to the asylum just outside Arkham, where his putative family could visit if they wished. Here he remained until 1943, a time when the asylum was understaffed, when he escaped and seems to have vanished from our knowledge.

The final conclusion of the official report was that most probably the man was a Russian spy, and a note appended to this conclusion after his escape indicates that this event confirmed that belief in the official mind. But I am not convinced. It is a conspicuous way to get a spy into a country, particularly at a time when America was beginning to take in the refugees of Europe. Nor was the Gedney family particularly rich or well connected, so getting a cuckoo into their nest could not have been the intention, and if it was, why such a bad impersonator? A two-bit actor turning up on the family's doorstep could have been more convincing. Somehow the official story just doesn't explain the incident. But if the official explanation doesn't work, then who was this strange man and where did he come from?

I was intrigued enough to break off my archival researches one weekend and take the train from Boston to Arkham and see if the old sanatorium records remained. I knew the institution itself was one of those closed in the 90s re-organization of mental health care providers, but the building remained, almost in the condition it was in when it was abandoned, and the records seemed still to be in their neat wooden filing cabinets. No one had bothered to transfer the records to digital. Most of the patients were dead and those that weren't had new records.

Despite the clinical organization of the filing, it took some time to find the manila folder with "Gedney, Leonard" typed on it. It was neither the thickest nor the thinnest, but was what I might call "top heavy," as interest in him dwindled, so the records became sparse and perfunctory. Only at the end was there a lump of documentation on his escape and who was to blame. But it was the early data, the material sent by the Immigration Office, that was most surprising and absent from the official file. For here were the original x-rays and medical report conducted shortly after Gedney's arrival from the Antarctic, where only a summary existed in the State Department file.

There was a "mug shot" of the man claiming to be Gedney, obviously taken after he came off the boat. His coarse boxer's face contrasted with the fine features of Gedney's student pictures, like he was an uncle run to seed. Could nearly three years of arctic survival do that to a man?

I looked at the x-rays in astonishment, holding them up to a dusty outside window to get a good look. The plates showed a remarkably healthy man, but for one feature. On all the plates showing the torso, a thin, solid, black line spiraled around Gedney's spine like a bootlace wrapped around a branch. I scrabbled for the medical report and flipped through it. The report concluded that, intertwined with Gedney's spinal cord, there was what appeared to be a length of silver wire—purpose unknown. Surgery to remove it was tentative as it was wrapped amongst the spinal cord itself. It would be easy to permanently cripple the man if there was a slip. But it was decided that a small section coiling around the exterior of a vertebra could be risked, and the section was duly extracted under anesthetic and examined. Microscopic and spectrographic analysis found it to be a hollow platinum wire, ornately engraved and wrapped around an unknown clear filament. This the scientists of the day described as being made of a clear mineral resin, similar in structure to glass, but without the brittle qualities. Today we might have said it was a fiber-optic filament. The report could hazard no reason or circumstance, accidental or deliberate, why or how such a wire could have been coiled about a human spine. It offered no physical support for the back, so did not act as a brace for spinal damage, nor would swallowing the wire, lodged shrapnel, or some other conceivable accident account for it. It was an oddity. The removed piece of wire was preserved and sent to the asylum with the report.

With more care, but growing excitement, I leafed through the papers again, until I came across a small wax-paper envelope, containing a short length of what appeared to be silver wire, about three-quarters of an inch in length. This was a profound moment for me—my first solid contact with a man who until that moment had seemed little more than a curious explorer's hoax. Yes, I'd seen reports, but here was an artifact from the man himself. I slipped it into my pocket and have it here with me as I write.

The remaining hospital records—accounts of therapy sessions, medication records, visitor logs and patient assessments—suggest he never wavered from his conviction that he was Gedney, although he was curiously resigned to the fact that his family did not visit or try to seek his release. He happily remained, one of the quieter patients, enjoying the green hills of New England from his barred window. He did not particularly socialize with those patients allowed into the day rooms. It was noted that, if particularly calm and believing himself overlooked, he would occasionally whistle original compositions to himself, one porter describing the melody of one as going something like "tull-twoo-ta-wit-twee-lah-lie".

With this intriguing data added to my knowledge I returned to Providence and the Brown University and arranged for the wire to be examined. With a modern electron microscope more was revealed. It is not simply a platinum wire. It has the lattice structure of a printed circuit-board microscopically etched into the platinum coiled about a fiber-optic core, with what must be superfine filaments projecting into the core to carry data the length of the wire—effectively it's a microscopic super-computer and transmitter, probably powered by electrical sources within the body itself. Maybe this was why it needed to be coiled the length of the spine? Whatever the reason, this one short length was something utterly beyond the technology or knowledge of Bolshevik Russia. No 1930s hoaxer could have dreamed of such a thing. The removal of this piece must have broken the apparatus entirely and prevented the man calling himself Gedney from using it to report back to his true masters.

And who were they?

Logic tells me this whole curious affair was the work of men. The technology makes me think that it is a contemporary hoax aimed at me—with faked old documents and mocked up x-ray plates and that snippet of wire to add substance to the hoax, then let me ferret out the planted evidence. I suspect that if I were ever to tell the story, some disgruntled old pupil of mine would pop up and expose me as a fool for falling for it! But I can't find a flaw in the evidence. That evidence points all over the place—to the man being Gedney, to the man being an imposter, to the man being something not wholly human—but that evidence also seems authentic. The paper the reports are written on is consistent with the 1930s and 40s, typed on real typewriters, or signed with fountain pens, the ink now faded. The x-ray plates are of the right chemical composition and do not seem to have been re-touched. The photographs are authenticated by unimpeachable sources. The expedition diaries mention finding a man and bringing him back. The State Department seems to have a file on him, and the asylum in Arkham also has records. If it is a hoax then I can't fathom its aim. The sheer expense to get these details right would be huge, just to embarrass a minor academic? And if it's not a hoax, it doesn't get any easier.

So bearing in mind that I could never publish anything so speculative, I've been thinking and pondering on the case, and a nasty, chilling thought keeps coming back to me: suppose Dyer was right? What if he had been telling the truth? Suppose there were elder creatures living on Antarctica millions of years right up to the appearance of the first primates, and then they were driven into a city deep within the inner earth, standing on the shores of Poe's, or Coleridge's "sunless sea," where shoggoths splash in the darkness. And there they lived for millions of years more. Then one day something disturbs one of their lookout posts—wakes the sleeping guards, and they come down to the city, bringing with them samples of the surface life, and they alert the elder creatures that there is an intelligent life form evolved on the surface. What would those creatures do?

Dyer said that he saw the dissected bodies of Gedney and the dog. Suppose those elder things studied those bodies and worked them out in every detail. Suppose they ordered the still subjugated shoggoths of that sunless sea to construct a new person, cell by cell, using Gedney as a blueprint. Manipulating the shoggoths with their hypnotic wills, they built a new human body that could pass into the world of humans and see what kind of threat we were to them. The Miskatonic had disturbed them once; it would only be a matter of time before someone else came calling.

The mountains are a puzzle, if they existed. But from what I've learned and from the strange sensory apparatus of the creatures described by Dyer, I believe that although they are creatures of matter, they are able to perceive more dimensions than we do, or can pass between dimensions that we cannot. I don't know how, but maybe there is a way of shifting the mountains into another dimension? Maybe the mountains were for the most part already within another dimension, and the dream-like quality described by Dyer was an accurate reflection of the mountains' dimensional instability—the veil between the worlds being fully parted only to allow the reawakened elder things to head down to the inner city? So somehow the creatures made the mountains slip out of our view?

Still, regardless of whether people came looking for the mountains or not, the elder creatures need to know about mankind. They need to know what kind of threat we are. So when the next expedition turns up, they send out their homunculus. He will integrate into human society and report back to them. Then they can decide what they want to do about us.

I don't know if they had a way of keeping the real Gedney's brain alive after the dissection, and it was him, in a new body, shell shocked by the experience; or if they had a way of scraping Gedney's synapses of memories and placing them in some artificial brain. Maybe one of those cold five-lobed-plant brains resided in that skull having memorized what was known of Gedney? Or some shoggoth-brain? Whatever the situation, enough time had passed for Gedney's knowledge to be incomplete. So the new Gedney made basic mistakes.

The elder things also made mistakes. Unfamiliar with human anatomy, this first effort was cruder and slightly larger than their blueprint. They could not perceive the subtle differences which make one human individual from another. To be fair, I doubt I would be able to tell one of *them* from another based on the drawings of the creatures Lake made at the Antarctic, but still they missed details. Everything was there on the copy of Gedney, the right number of appendages in fully working order, but they had not taken as much care at the dissection process as

they might had they known then what they would do with the information. They did not appreciate how much humans use face recognition. It
was those tiny imperfections which finished off the new Gedney as an
effective spy.

I said earlier that there were two physical oddities which pointed to
this not being Gedney or some surgically adjusted Russian spy. One was
that impossible wire in the spine. The other oddity was again a detail
they missed. Gedney did not have the fingerprints of a human. He had
prints—they had not been destroyed by acid or cut off, as sometimes
criminals of the period did, and had they been, then they would have
wholly or partly grown back in the nine years in the Asylum—no, Gedney's fingerprints were uniform concentric ellipses, without the whorls
and arches which make a human fingerprint unique. The fingerprint
cards made when he arrived in New York are a glaring testament. Baf-
fled, the authorities had asked the medical team to look at his whole
hands and feet, so records exist for these, too. On his palms, fingers and
feet, the prints were ridged, with the various wrinkles, but the ridges
were not quite like a human's. The pads also had smooth, even ridges.
The plant-minds of the elder things saw symmetry, and the subtle detail
again eluded them.

I don't know what has happened to the man who called himself Gedney since the escape from the asylum. Did this Gedney-creature make
his way back to the Antarctic and report back after all? Was he a casualty
of the war? Did he live out his days, quiet and confused in seclusion,
somewhere in New England? More troubling is the thought that this
was not the only copy they sent out. Maybe they perfected their surgery
on later versions and sent others out? This Gedney failed, but does that
mean they gave up? Do copies still walk among us, watching the ice
melt and waiting, reporting back through those fantastic computers in
their spines?

So, there is the story and the evidence and a theory, for what it's
worth. Hoax or not? What really did happen to Gedney? I'm afraid I
can't shake the feeling that one day soon we might all just find out the
truth.

The Pleasure in Madness

C. J. Henderson

"There is a pleasure in madness,
which none but madmen know."
—William Hazlett

"This way."

Franklin Nardi, having learned to trust the professor enough to not disagree with him on a simple detail such as remembering from which direction they had come, slid around the corner indicated without question. True, he had been a New York City detective for nearly fifteen years—a patrolman for over five before that. His memory for such facts was still quite good. But, considering the situation they were in at that moment, from all that he had learned of Piers Knight in the relatively short time they had been working together, he was not going to argue.

"Quickly, Mr. Nardi," the professor shouted, straining to be heard over the blaring sirens still pointlessly screeching throughout the compound, "we have to hurry."

As the shrill, nightmarish piping echoed through the hallway around them, the detective noted that his breath had gone silver. Pointing it out to the professor, Knight responded;

"Meaning we have less time than we believed."

Damn all the fools who plague me so, he thought, *I'm beginning to think there might not actually be a way out of this.*

And then, both men's hearts froze at a particular sound, their blood icing over within their veins. As they exited the side passageway into the main hall, all around them men and women ran into one another, blindly—tripping, striking each other—screaming in mindless panic. Some fell to their knees, blubbering hysterically, others pounded on the walls, their shrieks nothing more than the ravings of the mad—insanity their only pathetic defense as the piercingly sharp notes of the creatures finally began to draw closer.

Close enough to be distinguished—

"*Tekeli-li, Tekeli-li*"

"Guess we weren't the only ones who knew the right direction—eh, professor?"

The two men stopped, both panting, both realizing with the clarity of the doomed that they had reached the end of the line. Bending over slightly so as to be able to place his hands on his knees, Nardi took a number of deep breaths as rapidly as possible in the hopes of reviving himself. As he reached for his .45 once more, Knight pulled his tobacco pouch and pipe from his jacket pocket. As his bodyguard stared at him, amazed that the man could be thinking of having a smoke at such a moment, the professor asked;

"Not suddenly afraid of a bit of second-hand smoke, are you?"

"No, not at this point."

"Good," responded Knight as he touched his lighter to his pipe's freshly packed bowl. Taking a good, healthy drag, he exhaled a pleasant woody smelling cloud through a new-born half-smile, then said;

"Well, we've still got only one chance at this. Shall we go for it?"

Nardi paused, listening to the still screeching alarm, watching the last of the others still conscious as they stampeded away in deranged panic. Sighing, checking the slide on his weapon, he gave the professor a forlorn smile, then answered;

"Never let it be said that Frank Nardi ever chose good sense over a good time. Let's do it."

And then, before either man could move or even speak, boiling its way directly through the wall next to them, the first of the shoggoths appeared.

THREE WEEKS EARLIER

"Ah, Mr. Nardi, come in. I have someone here I'd like you to meet."

Harold Clemmens was the president of Miskatonic University, final signer-off on all decisions, final arbiter of all disputes, final check on all balances. It had been his decision over a year earlier to bring in a private security firm to add another measure of safety to the school's library, a repository known far and wide for containing the largest collection of rare occult material in the western hemisphere.

"Certainly, Mr. President. . . ."

Nardi was one of several New York City police officers who had, several years earlier, retired to the supposedly more tranquil surroundings of Arkham. There they had opened an agency specializing in searching out the strange and unique for those so afflicted. They had believed, of course, that they were merely engaging in a bit of humbuggery—de-ghosting homes, proofing the recently deceased against zombification—participating as it were in a type of medicine show over which they might chuckle on Friday evenings as they enjoyed cards and beer.

Twenty-two months later, with one of them dead and his remaining partners frightened into a quiet sobriety, Nardi reached out his hand as Clemmens said;

"Franklin Nardi, Arkham Security, Professor Piers Knight, curator at the Brooklyn Museum, the Brooklyn in New York City, not Connecticut, of course."

The professor set aside his glass and stood to shake hands with the detective. A tad taller than Nardi, of a slighter build, looking perhaps a few years younger, Knight had a grip the detective found solid enough to grant him a few points, if not enough to allow the professor a complete pass. As the three men took seats, Knight pointed toward an elegantly tall, thin bottle, half filled with a clear liquid, and offered;

"Absinthe, Mr. Nardi? A newer brand, Edward III, wonderful stuff. I brought the bottle up from my, and what I believe to be your own, home town. It's a delightful artisanal, all organic ingredients, made by hand . . . simply marvelous light flavor—"

"Sounds good," admitted the detective, "but I've been cuttin' back ever since . . . ah, you know . . . a man gets older—"

"So I've heard," responded Knight dryly, nodding. As the professor settled back into his seat, lifting his glass for another sip, Clemmens said;

"I've gone over most of the details of the university's proposition with you both separately. You each seem in agreement . . . but, since you'll be working in close quarters together, I thought it best you meet before departure. Rub elbows a touch, bit of the familiar—"

"No offense, Mr. Clemmens, but the University's offer is simply too generous for me to pass up," interrupted Nardi. "Besides, considerin' the contract my agency signed, you'd be within your rights to make such a request as part of our agreed upon duties—"

"Oh no," sputtered the president, "I think it would take a rather brutal reading in between the lines to make a case for such an onerous interpretation—"

"Obviously Mr. Clemmens hasn't run into some of the lawyers from our homeland, eh, Mr. Nardi?"

"Still," countered the president, "we are talking about his accompanying you to the Antarctic as your bodyguard, for at least two, possible three . . . maybe even four or more months—"

"Yes, understood, Harold," agreed Knight, "and excuse me while I ask, for Mr. Nardi's edification if not my own, but *why*? This is a rather straight-forward proposition, isn't it? Not to cheat my fellow New Yorker out of what appears to him to be a generous situation, but why in heaven's name would I need a bodyguard?"

Clemmens stared forward for a moment, nothing of the man moving except for his lower lip. Finally blinking as well, the president lowered his eyes, lifting his hands from his desk at the same time. Threading his fingers together, he said;

"It's been over seventy-five years since Miskatonic sent its expedition to the Antarctic. That you know about. You've read the paper I forwarded to you both, lunatic warnings about alien horrors, cyclopean cities, mountains of madness. . . ."

"Ah, yeah," asked Nardi with some hesitation. "I, ummm, I tried lookin' up that mountain range, the one the report made such a big deal about . . . I mean, that guy, ah, Dyer, he talked about it havin' all kinds of carved stuff on it, claimed it was bigger than Mount Everest. But I couldn't find anything that—"

"There isn't anything to find, Mr. Nardi," interrupted Clemmens. "The Himalayas are the highest peaks in the world. That one point alone is one of the main reasons the Starkweather/Moore expedition was sent down there, despite Dyer's warnings, in the first place."

"That was the second group," explained Knight with a bit of reserve, "the one which had poor Mr. Dyer in such a lather that he wrote his infamous 'mountains of madness' report. When the second expedition arrived, they went to the same position, but radioed that they could find no mountains, no towers, no external evidence whatsoever of what had been originally reported."

"I noticed you stressed 'no external evidence,' sir."

"And that kind of attention to details," said Clemmens to Knight, as a means of answering the detective, "is why we retain Mr. Nardi. No, Frank, they found nothing . . . nothing on the surface, that is. But, thanks to other coordinates provided, they did find the entrance to the world below . . . to everything else Dyer claimed that he and Danforth had discovered."

All three men sat quietly for a moment. It was, after all, the kind of information that most anyone required a moment to absorb. Taking another sip of his absinthe, the professor finally asked;

"You're saying that there actually *is* a vast underground city beneath the Antarctic, and people have known about it for close to a century?"

"Yes, sir, I am."

"Those people being the government, right?" As both Clemmens and Knight turned toward him, Nardi added;

"Hey, what else are you sayin'? I mean, these guys report that there's this secret world down there, just when Europe is startin' to crumble. My guess is, in the interests of 'national security,' or whatever they called it back then, the government moved in—took over. Built a base, pretended it was for scientific research, filled the place with weapons."

"And forbade any mention of its existence to anyone else," suggested Knight. "Eh, Mr. President?" When Clemmens nodded his head in sad agreement, the professor asked;

"Which prompts me to ask, why is it that now they're willing to allow chatter to be spread freely across hither and yon?"

"Can't say they are allowing much in the way of chatter at all," answered the president. "After the second expedition started sending back reports, as you correctly deduced, Frank, the government slapped a silencing order on the operation."

"Much like they did in Roswell." When the others looked at him blankly, Knight explained, "Roswell, New Mexico—from where all the rumors of downed spaceships and recovered alien bodies come. Back in the late forties, the public relations man at the air base near Roswell released a news flash that an alien space ship had been recovered, and then, within . . . I believe . . . less than an hour, the flash was recanted and the air force has been silent, even hostile, about the moment ever since."

"Quite," agreed Clemmens. "Much the same thing happened in this matter. The difference being that when Moore radioed back confirmation that the underground passages were confirmed, the wording wasn't as sensational as all that. Before news could spread to the general population, the blanket was lowered."

"And now," responded Nardi with a questioning tone, "it's up again?"

"We have received an invitation to send down a research team." Clemmens lowered his eyes for a moment, then looked up again, saying, "a couple of fellows came around, proper I.D. and all . . . and they brought us these."

The president opened a folder and spread a wealth of color photographs across his desk. His visitors leaned forward, then began quite eagerly to flip through them, examining some in great detail, especially Knight. As they did so, Clemmens continued.

"Didn't leave anything electronic, didn't want any images escaping out onto the Internet. We were warned quite strongly about making copies ourselves. As you can see, the sketches and murky black and white photos brought back by Dyer and Danforth are all verified quite extraordinarily here."

"Indeed," mused the professor, staring hard at two photos of massive walls of intricate carvings.

"They said that they're ready to open the place to the world. Said they've gotten all they can out of it on their own, and that perhaps it was time to share the knowledge."

"And," asked Nardi, "you believe them?"

"My first instincts were toward mistrust, Frank," admitted the president. "But, I asked myself over and over, the University was shut out of things three quarters of a century ago. No one had even thought to ask about it for fifty years. What would the government have to gain by bringing us in now ... if, ah ... they didn't want us there?"

"Yes," asked Knight, echoing the detective's instinctive mistrust, "what, indeed?"

Two days after their first meeting, Piers Knight and Franklin Nardi were aboard a jet along with the rest of the Miskatonic team, headed for Argentina's Buenos Aires—the furthest point south they could reach via a commercial airline with any speed. After that they took a series of much smaller planes, hopping their way down the country until they crossed over into Chilean air space to land at Punta Arenas. There the ten of them were met by air force personnel who transported them the remainder of the way in a military helicopter.

During their various flights and lay-overs, the two investigators did not find themselves with a great deal of time to spend simply chatting— neither with each other nor with the other members of the team—not until the next-to-last stop on their journey. It was the one point where they did not find themselves arguing endlessly with customs officials, straining to hear over antiquated motors, or hustling from one aircraft to another at breakneck speed to catch the next plane, or a nightmare tour aboard an ancient bus taking them to the next deathtrap of an aircraft.

That night their plane had barely been able to land due to an unexpected and unexplainable storm center that had risen up to hold the region prisoner. With all air traffic grounded for at least a day, the two men finally found themselves within each other's company long enough to get past the awkward prohibitions of normal conversation. To where they might get at some of the things they had been wondering since they had first met. It was Knight who had led them out of the ordinary when he asked;

"Well, Franklin, what do you think? What's do you believe is the real reason Clemmens thought it a good idea to send you along?"

"You gotta ask?" The detective had been stretched out on his bed in their double room, staring at the ceiling. At that question, however, he had raised himself up on one elbow to add;

"I mean, you read Dyer's statement. You look old enough to know something about how the government works. Pardon me if you think I'm insultin' you or the others, but our taxin' lords and masters, they've got their own scientists, and I'm sure they could have found someone at the Smithsonian to fill in for you."

"No insult found in any of that," answered the professor wryly. "But, what about the fact that Miskatonic sponsored the first mission to the area, that if it weren't for the University this whole site might never have been discovered at all. Don't you feel that gives old M.U. first dibs, as it were?"

"I can't even believe we're havin' this conversation. What—were you born yesterday or something?"

"No, Franklin," answered the professor, pulling his tobacco pouch and pipe from his pocket, "but I wanted to check and see if you were." As he stuffed the pipe's bowl, he added;

"Much as I'd like to flatter myself that the great and wonderful Piers Knight is so absolutely essential that his presence is needed every and anywhere, you're absolutely correct. It doesn't make sense for the government to not only throw open the doors in such a manner, but to welcome in a team such as ours without background checks, without a few hundred pages of restrictions."

The professor took several short, firing pulls on his pipe's stem, releasing ever-increasing puffs of smoke until finally he was able to exhale a good-sized cloud toward the open window and the steaming downpour beyond. He had, of course, already checked the idea of smoking inside their room with Nardi who, as an ex-smoker, might have objected. The detective, it turned out, welcomed any chance to take in a bit of a familiar aroma and had given his roommate an anytime/anywhere go-ahead. After his second healthy drag, Knight said;

"But, all that said, why do you suppose President Clemmens sent *you* along? I'm not discounting what abilities you might possess, but do you have any impression as to what he's thinking we should be expecting?"

"Your guess is as good as mine," admitted the detective. Swinging his legs off his bed, Nardi sat up, adding;

"Twenty years and I never saw anything out of the ordinary workin' for the force back in New York. But, ever since I moved up to Arkham ... it's like the world got turned upside down ... some of the shit I've seen ... well, you know—"

"*I* know?"

"Don't kid a kidder, professor," answered Nardi. "You don't think I took this gig without checkin' you out, do you? It just took a call back to my precinct to get the low down on ... what do they call you ... the Indiana Jones of Brooklyn?"

"Well, really. . . ."

The detective made a motion with his hand, cutting Knight off before he could say anything further. Giving the professor a hard look, one with just enough mercy in the corners of his eyes to reveal that he meant what he was about to say, he waited for an ominous roll of distant thunder to pass, then confided;

"Look, what I've seen since I got hooked up with Miskatonic, from the rumors they have about you, my guess is you've been up to your neck in soup I've only had up to my knees. But ... we both know—*know*—everything Dyer wrote could easily be true, 'cause we've both seen worse ourselves."

Knight moved his eyes sideways in a manner meant to be amusing, then allowed himself a half smile as he admitted his roommate's argument had merit.

"Now, that in mind," said Nardi, "I think Clemmens asked you to go down because, where his physicists and archaeologists and such might have the science stuff on the ball, he brought you in to be the 'weird crap' specialist. And he brought me in to try and make sure whatever the government is up to, your report gets back to his desk, unedited and in one piece."

Knight allowed another thick cloud of smoke to escape his lips, then added dryly;

"My, but we're an optimistic pair, aren't we?"

"If you mean you're startin' to wonder if this whole thing might be even worse than you first figured, then yeah, you're just as big an optimist as I am."

The cinematic timing that followed as the ebony sky was shattered by several lightning strikes at that moment, as well as a deafening blast of thunder, was not lost on either man.

"So, welcome, ladies and gentlemen, to Antarctic Station 12, the single strangest place on the planet."

"Oh, come now," answered Knight, extending his gloved hand to the heavily-garbed man who had met them at the Antarctic landing field, "if you actually mean that, you've obviously never been in Greenwich Village on Halloween."

"I must admit I haven't," answered their guide, "but I'd give good odds that we'd have to come at least in a close second." Waving the arriving group forward toward a nearby outcropping of rock and ice, the fellow added;

"So, I'm Terrance Mekler, and I'll be showing you around a bit today, getting you settled and the such. But for now, considering the temperature, let's get inside, shall we?"

No one argued. With a goodly supply of soldiers standing by to transport their luggage and equipment, the team members did not have to carry anything into the base they did not prefer to keep in their own hands.

"So, enjoying yourselves?"

Considering the cold, at most any other time, in any other place, Mekler's question would have invited all manner of derisive answers. Frigid as it was at that moment, the team's thoughts should have been firmly rooted on reaching the doorway in the distance as quickly as possible. But the closer they drew to the wall before them, they saw at once that they had already passed through the door to the marvelous. It had politely come to meet them.

The members of the Miskatonic expedition had all been picked for more than their various doctorates and expertise. They had, all of them at one time or the other, come up against the strange or the unusual. Some of them far more so than the average lay person could ever imagine. Tenure granted by their particular University meant almost certainly that at one time or the other the recipient had come up against something consciousness-expanding. Something world-view shattering.

In truth, no matter from where they hailed, most research and development types were one step beyond the man in the street. Ordinary folk simply did not realize what was happening in their world, what kind of forces were being poked and examined in laboratories all around the globe.

Many knew a sheep had been cloned, but nothing much more about that particular branch of science had reached them. Some were aware that bacteria had been discovered on Mars, but that small percentage of the population cognizant of the fact, for the most part had no idea of the astounding ramifications. They did not know how many elements were contained on the periodic table, how many of them were man-made, nor what the search for further elements might mean for their lives.

The man in the street was, by and large, an ignorant, drooling simian compared to most scientists. But, compared to the Miskatonic team walking across the snow-swept airstrip, so too were most other scientists. Between them, the group had witnessed things practically undreamed of by their supposed peers. Many outsiders suggested that the University was a place where magic and witchcraft were taught in the classroom, but such rumors swirled only among the uniformed and infantile. Miskatonic was a bastion of rationality and scientific thought and those who worked within its walls were proud of that tradition.

On that particular morning, however, those approaching the towering granite wall before them felt more like children. They knew they were being brought to the same entrance through which Dyer and Danforth had passed decades earlier. But much had changed since that fateful day. On the mundane side, the military had leveled the area before the entrance to facilitate the insertion of a landing strip. They had also installed a modern doorway into the side of the mountain, one designed to keep the terrible cold of the Antarctic at bay. But all around the edges of the steel and glass intrusions the team could see their first hints that perhaps Antarctic Station 12 was indeed a unique place after all.

Before them, there in the middle of what was supposed to be a frozen wilderness, was the proof of the photographs they had been shown. Massive, prodigious blocks of dark primordial stone, delicately cut and arranged like so many boxes on a store shelf. In some places, the mountainside before them seemed to have been carved directly to form open air buildings, dotted with towers, all of it covered with insanely intricate layers of etching, quite similar to those Dyer had described finding inside.

Streaming lines of meticulous bas-relief work extended upward at least a hundred and fifty feet, far beyond any of their abilities to make out detail. Such a sight let the newcomers know they were all about to enter another remarkable period of advancement, were about to be made privy to secrets withheld from mankind since the beginning of time. As the Miskatonic team stood in the freezing cold, gaping in wonder, Mekler smiled once more, asking in a mostly rhetorical tone;

"So, pretty impressive, eh?"

"What's the big deal?" asked Nardi innocently, pointing upward at the carvings seemingly running along the entire length of the mountainside.

"You know what Dyer thought," replied Knight before their guide could respond, "that the star-headed creatures discovered here were from another world. The age of the carvings precludes their having been made by humans."

"Meanin' E.T. liked to get out the old hammer and chisel. What about it?"

The professor did not grow exasperated with his bodyguard. The detective had not thrown his question out as a challenge. Nardi was as impressed with the workmanship as any present. But he did not understand what was *so* exciting about the discovery. Trying to withhold from his voice the patience obviously needed, Knight explained;

"We're talking inter-galactic travel here. These beings were capable of moving distances we can barely comprehend, let alone match. And yet, when they got here, they made records in stone. When we went to the moon, we left behind plaques with messages pre-printed in English, but we didn't attempt to communicate with all comers by leaving picto-graphs of any kind, let alone something on this scale."

"What you're sayin' is," Nardi said slowly, his mind straining to com-prehend, "alla this, this is like a message they left for us . . . even though we didn't even exist yet?"

"Us, Martians, anyone who might happen along, I suppose," an-swered the professor. His head still upturned like the others on the team, still scanning the incredible workmanship before him, Knight added;

"It's more than that as well. I mean, why bother to work in stone at all? And beyond that, *how* did they do it? Was it hammered and chiseled as you suggested, or did they possess machines which could leave a mes-sage in stone as easily as we can on paper with a pen? They were also tele-pathic. Could they create such works with their minds? Who knows?"

"So, you begin to see the possibilities here," interrupted Mekler, no trace of sarcasm to be seen on that small part of his face exposed to the elements. As he waved his hands in both directions to emphasize his comment, he added;

"And, while you're at it, take into consideration that you're merely looking at work that's been outside, exposed to the elements for millions of years. Wait until you see the work inside."

"Indeed," responded Knight, slapping his gloved hands together with a near-childlike enthusiasm, "why don't we do that?"

As high as the Miskatonic team's hopes had been for the expedition, each and every one of them had found their wildest dreams trifling in comparison to what the government's researchers had put together over the decades. Star charts beyond anything known to man had been re-corded there in abundance. They had devised ways and means of rear-ranging molecular bonds so that base materials could be reproduced without the massive dangers of nano-technology. There were even rudi-mentary anti-gravity devices and teleportation machines.

There were hints of grander possibilities everywhere. But, unlike the humor of many popular entertainments, where such mundane inventions as the microwave or Teflon were credited to interaction with alien cul-tures, the simple truth was that for all its runaway progress, humanity's collective knowledge had barely reached a point where, even with actual devices with which to work, the greatest minds available could scarcely even begin to backward engineer them. Even after nearly a century of ac-cess, most of what had been deciphered and put into practice was beyond the ability of human capability. The best scientists could do no more than manufacture a handful of working engines which showed any promise.

"Franklin, it's simply amazing."

"You been sayin' that a lot, professor."

"Ummmm, I suppose I have at that, but … this place … everything contained here … my God, we've been here two weeks now, and still … well, frankly, I'm staggered. I've been flitting like a drunken bee from place to place … there's so much to see, to experience, to think about—"

"Professor . . ."

Knight turned sharply at the detective's tone. The man had not raised his voice, growled, or made any kind of indication that he might be upset. And yet, something in the single word arrested the professor's attention to where he suddenly found himself shifting his focus entirely to Nardi.

"Have you noticed anything unusual about the folks here? The ones who were already here, I mean. Mekler, the others?"

"Usual idiosyncrasies one finds in these types, of course," answered Knight. "Especially when locked away from the rest of the world. But . . ."

"Something else. You ever notice how Mekler begins almost every other sentence with the word 'so?'"

"Well, now that you mention it . . ."

"I looked him up on-line. Found a number of places where some of his lectures, or at least pieces of them, are posted. Did you know he's a Texan?"

"Really," answered the professor. "I had no idea. You wouldn't think it to listen to him."

"All depends on what you're listening to."

As he finished his sentence Nardi cued "play" on a computer link he had set up previously—a link to a Houston University lecture being given by Dr. Mekler on unification theory. A lecture he gave in a distinctive Texas accent. A lecture during which, despite its seventy-eight minute length, he did not begin a single sentence with the word "so."

The detective had not meant for Knight to listen to the entire speech, but the professor had insisted on doing so. When it finally finished, Nardi asked;

"What do you think?"

"I believe that if you've found this much, a man of your obvious tenacity has probably found more. Why don't you put all your suspicions forth before I comment?"

"I don't blame you for not noticin' anything. You and the others have all been caught up in everything here—it's like some sci fi movie. But, maybe because I'm the odd man out, I'm seein' things no one expected."

"Such as—"

"One thing, it's not just Mekler. All the other scientists, they've all got some tick, some rehearsed speech thing. Grenvil, he's always sayin' 'you know.' McKeown, he says 'granted.' Hansen, it's 'actually.'"

Snapping his fingers, Knight began nodding unconsciously, suddenly adding;

"Yes, just the other day, I remember myself thinking that Jorlick might be a brilliant physicist but, if she said 'like' in the middle of a sentence once more, I might be tempted to do her violence."

"I'll tell you something else. Mekler might not have the accent he came down here with, but neither does anyone else." As Knight's eyes narrowed, the detective said in a lowered voice;

"Name one person that came down here before us, military or otherwise, who has any kind of accent whatsoever?"

The professor considered the question, sending his mind searching through his memory of the past two weeks, looking for any colloquialisms uttered, a single dropped "G," anything that might keep Nardi's lunatic observation from seeming anything like correct. Looking into the detective's eyes, Knight could see his bodyguard was hoping he might be find something, too. As the professor's face betrayed his own misgivings, Nardi blurted;

"Oh Jesus, Mary and Joseph . . . oh, now what?"

"Calm yourself, Franklin—"

"Calm myself," the detective blurted, his hands waving. "We're in some *Children of the Corn, Body Snatchers* kind of goddamned nightmare, and you want me to be calm?"

"Yes," answered Knight, his voice dropping sharply, "I do. When you think about it for a moment, you'll realize doing so is in our best interests." As Nardi caught hold of himself, forced his panic down to where he might be able to control it once more, the professor added;

"You've pieced together something—we don't know exactly what yet—on your own. Commendable, by the way. You've been living with the dread you might be right for some time, alone. Now that you've finally said something and found agreement, the enormity of what you've uncovered has suddenly hit you and you've been understandably panicked by it."

"And you're not?"

"Oh, it'll catch up to me, too, soon enough, I expect. I mean, since you took the initiative in figuring out that something was wrong here, it seems the least I can do would be to join in." His last words uttered with a small catch in the back of his voice, the professor added;

"My, I do believe it's started in already."

Nardi sat back on his bunk, his hands twitching—his eyes unblinking. His head shaking slightly as well, he said;

"Christ, man do I wish I had a cigarette." When Knight made no reply, the detective asked;

"Something wrong?"

"Oh, obviously. There's no doubting you've uncovered something of major importance. But what? Dyer wrote of alien corpses, of monstrous beings he theorized would possess incredible powers for destruction. He hinted at the possibility of hidden underwater cities. After ten minutes in this place the fact that alien intelligence was involved in its construction was beyond doubt."

Knight went silent then, staring off at a point somewhere beyond the wall before him. As he did so, he moved one hand in the air absently, or more correctly, the finger of one hand, almost as if he were conducting some unseen orchestra. As his odd behavior continued, he mumbled, far more to himself than anyone else;

"Aliens visit the Earth, millions of years ago, corpses are found ... all logic says they have to be aeons old but ... could even glacial cold preserve them so perfectly, so utterly completely—for so long?" The professor's head turned jerkily, as if he wanted to look for something, but did not know in what direction it might lie.

"Men arrive, find them," he muttered, his words coming faster, "but also find living beings. Perhaps their creations, their servitors, the shoggoths. But, still alive? Still wandering the corridors of this place, after millions of years? Purposelessly, doing nothing? Why do they steal mundane items from the expedition? Why remove the corpses of their masters? Why kill some of the humans, but not all of them?"

Despite the moderate temperature on the tightly regulated quarters built by the military within the alien catacombs, Piers Knight had begun to perspire. Within his mind's eye, he was wandering throughout every inch of the complex he had seen thus far. Unlike his fellow team members, whose personal disciplines had kept them occupied studying specific aspects of the ancient base, the professor was a museum curate. As such, it would be expected of him to view the place as one large opportunity for exhibits. No one had thought it the least irregular for him to travel the unspectacular back corridors of the Elder Things' home, scanning the walls, inspecting the flooring, checking every aspect of the place. No one knew exactly what Knight was looking for, but then, it was obvious that he did not know himself.

However, as Nardi listened to the professor ramble, watched him thinking, struggling to wade through the volume of unrelated information about their surroundings which he had gathered over the their time there, he recognized in Knight what he had seen so often in others—had done himself—during his years with the police force. The professor was fishing within the clues he possessed, attempting to find a direction in which to proceed. Looking for something innocent he might have noticed earlier which he had not then recognized for what it was.

And then, suddenly, Knight rose, crossing the room to his desk. Normally quite fastidious about his placement of objects in his work area, he now shoved everything to one side in a jumbled heap, half of it crashing to the floor. Grabbing up a marker, he did not even bother to find a piece of paper on which to draw, but simply began sketching on the desktop itself.

"What've you got, professor?"

"An idea about the structure of this place." As he continued to scribble, adding more and more details to the layout he was assembling, he explained;

"If there's one thing one learns traveling the world to explore castles, pyramids, temples, et cetera, it's that walls are not always what they seem . . ."

His voice trailing off for a moment, Knight stared at his blueprint. Squinting as he did so, his mind searched for one further bit of memory until suddenly, his unconsciously drumming fingers curled into a fist with which he slammed the table.

"Yes!" Adding one final line, he pointed, saying;

"There—right *there*. That's where they are."

"Who, professor?"

"Whomever it is that doesn't wish for us to find them."

"Yeah." Nardi drew the word out suggestively, then asked, "And is there anything wrong with leaving them unfound?"

"As much as I hate to say it, Franklin, yes, I believe there might be at that."

The two men decided on a course of action quickly, then returned to their normal routine. Over the next several days, Nardi studied those who had been stationed at Antarctic Station 12 before their arrival. He listened to speech patterns, studied physical movements, facial expressions, et cetera. He engaged them in conversation and kept track of what subjects they brought up. The detective found some interesting corollaries.

As for Knight, he concentrated on locating the entrance to his proposed hidden space. At first, he simply walked the corridors defining the boundaries of the missing area—proving his theory for himself. It did not take long for him to assure himself that he had been correct. There was no doubting that a space existed.

The human-built part of Station 12 took up a great deal of the original area's central cavern. The contractors had first sealed up the front of the cave, building an air-tight entrance so the complex could be protected from the blasting polar winds. After that they had build inward, creating one chamber at a time so the long-dead city could be studied in far greater comfort than Dyer and Danforth had been afforded. The assembly of a massive generator outside the caverns had allowed the entire place to be illuminated and heated electrically.

But, for some reason, there existed off to one side, toward the southernmost end of the aliens' original complex, a missing square within the human construction. It did not take Knight long to establish that the same two meter by two meter block was missing on all three levels of man-made structure. What he could not fathom, however, was its purpose.

Standing outside the area in question at its uppermost level, he stared at the ceiling, lost in thought. To the occasional passerby there was nothing unusual about the professor acting in such a manner. They had seen him acting thusly since his arrival. As he stared at that moment, minute after minute, he asked himself;

"What could be the purpose of such an area? Can't be a missile silo, not enough shielding. Can't be a meeting room, or a laboratory, hell … it can't be anything. It's just a three story closet. What in the name of God can you do in a three story closet?"

And then, a separate part of his mind asked him;

"Who says it's only three stories?"

Knight blinked, his body shaking slightly with a start as the obvious crashed inward on his consciousness. A slight half-smile crossing his face, he pushed himself away from the wall and headed off to prove what he suddenly knew to be the answer.

⁂

"It's an elevator?"

"Could be," agreed Knight, "could be a well. But there's a shaft running right through the station that has no obvious access, that's been purposely hidden. We've all become so used to simply moving about within the parts of this place that have been built right up against the aliens' cavern that we've forgotten there's far more of it."

"Sure," responded Nardi. "Tell people 'here's everything you could want to look at, all nice and neat, where there's heat and light,' what a surprise nobody kicks about seein' anything else."

"Yes," agreed the professor. "Especially since there's so much to see in those warm, illuminated places. Any scientist could spend a lifetime within the spot around which their particular discipline is centered and never have it cross their mind that there might be more."

"Not to seem like I'm quoting Mekler but ... 'so,' what do you want to do?"

"I believe that it doesn't go down any further, since we do appear to be on the ground level of things—alien or human. So ... not quoting our bizarre Mr. Mekler, either, I suppose we should attempt to take a look above."

Nardi understood what was being suggested. It meant leaving the warmth and supposed safety of the human construction for the cold and darkness of the ancient caverns surrounding Station 12. It meant bundling themselves in furs, finding mobile lights, and then disappearing from sight for—most likely—long enough to be noticed. It meant letting whom—or what—ever was up to something know they had been noticed.

The detective was torn. Not rocking the boat always had its advantages, of course, but in this situation they appeared to be short term gains. Ones that would most likely not last.

"Did Mekler figure things out," he wondered, "realize something had to be wrong, and still ignore it all?"

Every single person that had come down to Antarctic Station 12, every one of them to whom he had been able to relate, all of them seemed odd. Off. Different. But from him and the rest of humanity. Not from each other.

That was what pounded through Nardi's brain as the professor waited for his answer. All that he had noticed the last few days. While Knight had investigated the site, he had studied its inhabitants, and he had found them to be a series of slightly different versions of one single entity.

Male or female, scientist or soldier, they were all—ultimately, if one looked carefully enough—the same person. They walked in the same just slightly less than perfect gait. They all spoke with the same accent. They all knew the same stories, all answered the same questions in the same way. All had the same twinkle in their eye. All laughed in the same pitch. All held a glass in the same manner. In two days of constant observation, the detective realized, he could not prove that any of them had actually gone to bed. Or eaten a meal.

Used a lavatory.

It was not something one would notice on their own. One would have to be consciously searching for it. But Nardi had been doing just that, and had uncovered exactly what he feared he would—knew he would. Knowing in his heart that not to investigate further into what had happened to Mekler and the others would mean eventually finding out what had happened the hard way, the detective sighed, hating those moments when all his choices ended with his back to a wall.

Looking up at Knight, his mental hesitation having lasted only the briefest of moments—just long enough for him to imagine himself starting every sentence he uttered with the same word—he said;

"Yeah, I suppose we should at that."

It took the two men less than a day to gather what they needed without being observed. The heavy clothing needed to leave their heated environment they already possessed. Stealing a pair of sturdy maintenance flashlights proved slightly difficult, only because they had to discover their location without asking where they might be stored. Luckily for the pair, the tools Knight suspected they would require to force their entry to the alien chambers were stored in the same area as the lights. Nardi chose a strong leather utility belt which held a chisel, several screwdrivers of various size and design, a one-handed sledge as well as an assortment of snap-on pouches made of molded leather.

Once armed with the necessary equipment, the two retired to the room they shared and waited for the night shift. Antarctic Station 12 did not operate with any attempt to reproduce a suburban mind-set. Its day was only broken into eight hour segments to remind those working within its borders to pace themselves—to remember to take meals, to get sleep, to not push themselves too hard despite the endless lures to do so. Over the decades, many of the researchers assigned to the never-ending treasure trove of scientific opportunity had worn themselves to nervous frazzles, desperate to unlock the tantalizing secrets with which they found themselves surrounded. Thus it was that the shifts had been instituted as a nod toward normalcy.

For Knight and Nardi, waiting until they were expected to be asleep to attempt their break-in meant they would have eight hours to do so during which they would not be expected to be anywhere, would not cause any concern by being absent. It took them most of their first two hours to make their way from their quarters to the third floor of the human sector, and then to the floor above, all without being seen.

"Okay, professor," whispered Nardi, standing next to Knight in the frigid darkness, "so far so good. Now what?"

Knight pointed toward the spot where, if his guesses were correct, the secret chamber from below would intersect with the darkened world above. Making their way along the roof of Station 12 carefully, loath to use their lights until absolutely necessary, the pair not only watched the placement of their feet step by step, but also scanned the area, taking in the cyclopean immensity of the alien chamber.

Compared to the standard, straight-forward design of the human sector beneath them, the twisting gaggle of offshoots from the over-whelmingly large cavern could not help but arrest their attention. Everywhere they looked, their eyes caught glints of more carvings, the walls and ceilings covered, every speck of room decorated with further streams of engraved details of a life utterly foreign and unknown.

As Knight counted off his footsteps in his head, he looked forward, grimly rewarded as a wall reared up out of the darkness the exact amount of feet before him where the hidden chamber should emerge. Making their way as quietly as possible, the pair finally chose to light one of their flashes. Panning it over the featureless wall before them, as they moved the beam upward, they saw that the secret room extended the entire way to the ceiling, disappearing into the mountain above them.

"It's a passageway," hissed Knight.

"Your elevator," confirmed Nardi. Making their way around the square, the two men discovered a rather pedestrian set of doors on its other side, adorned with the type of summoning controls one might find in any office building or hotel lobby. As they simply stared, neither of them moving either forward or back the way they had come, Knight whispered;

"My, this is the moment, isn't it?"

"What do you mean, professor?"

"Well, so far, we've simply been rushing forward, one guess after another. Something isn't right, people are acting strange, I think there's a secret room, what is it, let's find it . . ."

Knight went quiet for a moment, his eyes still locked on the ever-so-ordinary button on the panel before him. Finally, shifting his eyes upward to meet the detective's, he said;

"Clemmens was right, sending you along. If you hadn't caught what you had . . . dear lord, we both know I'd still be doing nothing more than studying the walls, making estimates on how much it would cost to move pieces of them back to Brooklyn, figuring out exhibit strategies . . ."

The professor stopped again, his words jamming within his throat, unable to force their way free. Nardi made to speak, but Knight held up his hand with a motion which did not order the detective to silence, but begged for a moment. After a handful more of terrifyingly silent seconds, the professor sighed—a tremble in his voice—then began again, admitting;

"Franklin, I'm certain you are thinking as I am, that once we press that button, once we learn the secret of what is going on here, that we will most likely end up as Mekler and the others have. Yes?"

"Actually," answered the detective, "I've been figurin' that if we *don't* find out what's goin' on, that was what was goin' to happen. Look, you want it honest, I've been kinda thinkin' that we were screwed ever since we got here. Just that bad gut feelin' cops get. Hit me when we first met Mekler outside, kept crawlin' around in me, forcin' me to try and find something."

Nardi dropped his head, laughing slightly as he swung it back and forth for a moment. Finally looking up again, he said;

"Look, it's the last innin', and what is, is. It's not your fault I'm here. I stepped into this all on my own, chasin' a paycheck. Now that we're here, though, what choice do we have? We both know one of us has to push that button, and that we gotta find out what gives."

"It could be that prolonged exposure to the cold merely renders people incapable of maintaining a proper speech pattern."

Nardi knew the professor was attempting to make a joke. Nodding at him, the detective whispered back;

"Yeah, could be. You sound like you've been outside too long already."

"Well then," said Knight, a sudden grimness in his tone, "let's warm things up around here. Shall we?"

It did not surprise either man that it took them almost another full minute before either could summon the intestinal fortitude to actually press the button which would open the sliding doors before them. Once they did, seeing the typical, simple elevator car within, they were not surprised to find that neither of them could move themselves forward into it. Nor did it surprise them that, after they had managed to force themselves inside, watching the door slide silently closed doubled the creeping terror building within their minds.

Neither had been taken aback as had been Dyer by the sight of the alien catacombs, but that was understandable to them. Those two had been alone, not knowing what was around the next corner, coming across monsters from beyond, the bodies of their team mates, brutalized animal corpses; even the mutant penguins mentioned in Dyer's missive were more horrifying than anything they had encountered. No, they had entered a pristine, ordered research facility, one filled with modern conveniences not yet imagined in Dyer's century. One that made it easy to snicker at the lunatic ravings, at the insane idea of "mountains of madness."

"But," thought Knight as the car slowly climbed upward, "Dr. Dyer doesn't seem so insane now, does he?"

The professor had never actually dismissed his predecessor. He had, in his time studying the ancient civilizations of mankind, pouring over their remains and relics, encountered too much proof—oftentimes first hand—that horrible secrets were masked by a thousand different veneers in every corner of the world. A part of him had known since he had read Dyer's rambling plea that no one ever again be allowed to set foot on the Antarctic continent that he was going to uncover something terrifying.

"And yet, you had to come," his sense of self-preservation sneered, "had to test yourself, had to probe, had to see—"

"It seemed safe enough," another part of his mind snapped defensively. "It wasn't some ten year old's daring himself to climb into a cave ... the University, the government—it was just supposed to be another routine job ..."

A tear ran down Knight's cheek, sliding along the nylon hood drawn tight around his face. He had known danger in his time, faced monstrous things more than once. But he had gone hunting them. He had been prepared. And, he reminded himself, he had been risking only his own life.

"Now," he thought, "now, we're the ones being hunted. And I do not believe we are very well prepared."

"And," hissed another segment of his mind, "this time it's not just your life being risked, is it?"

For an instant, the professor tried to pretend that he was only referring to the fact Nardi was with him, but he could not sustain the lie. Something had gained a foothold on the Earth millions of years ago. Long before man. Long before the dinosaurs. A race that built a vast empire across the land and under the water. That established beachheads on multiple planets throughout the solar system. That disappeared from our end of the galaxy before the amino acids necessary for humanity's birth had even begun to form.

But they had left behind servitors, and they had left open doorways. Doorways that Dyer and Danforth had blundered through, servitors which they and their comrades had awakened. Servitors which had been fully roused when Starkweather and Moore had arrived. Immortal, unstoppable things from beyond understandable reality with powers unfathomable to mere human beings.

"Servitors," thought Knight, his mind stumbling over the notion, his blood freezing, "without a solid shape—things that bubbled and sloshed, forming themselves to the task at hand."

Things, he realized, that would have been on hand to meet the newly arrived humans. That could have watched and studied them, learned their ways, gifted with the patience of the undying—

"As well as the ability to read their minds."

Knight blanched in horror. Suddenly everything that had filled Dyer with dread flooded the professor with the nightmarish truth of what was happening there at the bottom of the world. And then, at that moment, as the full enormity of his situation revealed itself to him, the elevator door slid open.

Beyond its boundary, he saw a great open space hewn out of the mountain, one filled with an array of machines his brain could scarcely comprehend. Some were constructed in manners his mind could grasp—their assembly completed with metals and plastics, secured with rivets and clamps, welds and wirings. Others were not. Far beyond human conception, they were apparati hewn together from light and steam, molten plasma that somehow held its form, waves of magnetism which acted as coolants—

Knight's mind was staggered, unable to hold the myriad deluge of foreign, unknowable concepts forcing their way into it, drilling, burrowing into his consciousness.

"How," he wondered, his mind screaming the question at him, begging for relief, "how can I even know what I'm seeing? How can I understand it—decipher *any* of it? How is it *possible?*"

And then, as he caught sight of Mekler working calmly at a station off to one side, everything became clear to him. Nardi had not yet caught a glimpse of what lay outside. The doors had been open only a split-second, had not yet even reached their full recession into the walls beyond. Knight realized he could not possibly tell one of the machines before him from another, understand the slightest thing about their operation . . . unless he was being told by an outside force.

As the elevator doors finally slid into the walls, he remembered what Dyer had written, that the star-headed aliens and their servitors had to be telepathic. In an instant, he realized he was simply hearing the thoughts slipping over from those filling the chamber before him. Mekler, the others, were not humans. Those who had been sent earlier had been consumed ages ago, their identities stolen.

"The shoggoths could reform themselves, could steal the thoughts from their minds," the professor told himself, picking the memories from the air, "but they did not understand the vocal chords they were reproducing. Could not understand the concept of personality."

Realizations slammed against Knight, the purpose of the alien chamber, the meaning of the towering rod of electrified cold whirling lazily in its center, the fact the elevator had taken far longer to reach the top than was possible—

"Time and space, warped, corrupted," he realized, the thoughts of the aliens flashing within his mind. "We're not here, not on Earth. We've been pulled to their alternate reality. . . ."

And then he saw it, saw through the eyes of the invaders, saw what Dyer and Danforth had seen, saw what their minds had translated in the only way they could—

"We're inside the *mountains of madness!*"

"Professor," hissed Nardi, unable to understand why Knight had stood in the doorway unmoving for a full two seconds. Terror creeping into his soul, he demanded;

"What the hell is going on out there?"

And, his mind hearing the question asked, it sought the answer in the swirl of chatter sliding through the ether, and all was revealed. In an instant he understood the fact that crystalline solids formed most readily at low temperatures, that incredibly caustic chemicals were being hurled in stable inert gases before him in an attempt to strip loosely bound electrons from one element so they might adhere to another.

"They're trying to bond helium to neon—looking to force their gelid darkness across the face of the world."

Knight stood staring out the doorway, his mind transfixed, the secrets of matter transformation jingling their way through his brain. Unfortunately, for the first few seconds of his mind's contact with the thoughts of those in the chamber, he had gone unnoticed, merely another consciousness bonding with the mass intellect present. But then, he had asked a question, had searched for a specific bit of knowledge, and drawn attention to himself. The thing which had become Terrance Mekler was the first to notice.

The instant the Mekler-thing took note of the intruding presence in the elevator doorway, all within the chamber shared in his awareness. As they did, however, so too did Knight. Grabbing Nardi by the shoulder, he pulled the detective forward, pointing at the hypnotically spinning rod of gaseous energy in the center of the chamber and, understanding for that one last second everything before him, the professor screamed;

"*Shoot it!*"

Fumbling for his weapon beneath his heavy coat, the detective managed to pull forth his .45 only seconds before the first of the pseudo-humans could reach them. As Knight slammed the down button on the elevator, Nardi fired, emptying his clip into the whirling rod of wet, crackling color. The doors slid shut just as the first of the creatures came within reach, screeching—

"*Tekeli-li, Tekeli-li*"

Its flesh, boiling out of human shape into something all eyes and teeth, was cut off a split-second before it could reach the two men.

As the elevator began to descend, the detective did not have to ask what he had just seen. In the moment he had stared at the towering jangle of frosted energy, realization had spread throughout his mind as well. He had not questioned Knight's order to shoot, had known what he was doing and why for the same reason the professor had—he had seen the terrible truth, known what was being perpetrated, understood that not just their world, but their entire universe was being invaded.

Before either man could speak, an explosion beyond comprehension blew through the chamber they had seen, a place not actually in existence on any human level of reality. Still, bound as it was to the planet Earth, the slightest talon of it leaked across the void separating the dimensions, rocking the elevator violently enough to throw both men first against the back wall, and then down against the floor.

It was not the only result of their actions.

Scrambling awkwardly on the floor, working to untangle themselves from one another, the two slowly became aware of the facts that they had stopped moving, that the light in the elevator had been extinguished, that the door was opened a crack—but only a crack.

"What the hell happened?" shouted Nardi, desperate to be heard over the ringing in his ears, over the sirens suddenly wailing all around them.

"We ... we broke ... something."

Knight's face went slack, his mind vomiting out the impossible crush of information it had tried to absorb. Seconds earlier he had been awash with the secrets of a civilization a billion years old. Now even the slightest tatters of what he had learned were fading from memory, retreating back into the ether.

"The mountains," the professor shouted, "the ones Dyer wrote about, they're real, but they're not here. They exist in some other time, or dimension ... or ... on another world ... I don't know. But, the elevator, it was built to move ... back and—"

Knight's words trailed off, the insanity of what he was suggesting grappling with his ability to form words. He knew that he was correct in some fashion, but also that whatever the answer was, it was unimportant at that moment. Forcing himself to his feet, realizing from the light pouring through the space between the elevator doors that they were somewhere within the influence of their own planet once more, he shouted;

"We've got to get out!" Pointing toward his ear, toward the speaker above, he added, "They're coming for us! We've got to get out of here!"

"The elevator?"

"The station."

His jacket already open, Nardi pulled two of the over-sized screwdrivers free from his workbelt, handing one to the professor. They had thought they would require some kind of tools to force their entry to the secret chamber—had regretted the time wasted securing them when they had discovered there had been no need for them. Now, straining with them, wrenching them back and forth, they thanked providence that they not only had taken them, but kept them.

When the doors finally gave enough that both men could squeeze their way out of the elevator, they discovered they had made it back to the second floor of the human-build station. The false walls disguising the conveyance had toppled during the explosion, giving them easy access to the hallway beyond. Almost giddy at their good fortune, the men were taken aback by the reality they discovered once they had extricated themselves.

Throughout the complex, those others of the expedition were wandering the hallways, screaming—terrified. Mindless. Whereas both Nardi and Knight had been eased into the communal mind of the aliens, the other humans' brains had been seared unmercifully when the pair had short-circuited the procedure both some hundred feet and a universe away from them.

"What do we do?" asked the detective, his heart reaching out to the staggering, screaming madmen flopping against the walls just beyond them. Steeling his heart, knowing there was nothing that could be done for the now lost souls, Knight answered;

"We run—"

Grabbing his partner by the shoulder, pulling him along as he added;

"This way."

Franklin Nardi, having learned to trust the professor enough to not disagree with him on a simple detail such as remembering from which direction they had come, slid around the corner indicated without question.

"Quickly, Mr. Nardi," the professor shouted, straining to be heard over the blaring sirens still pointlessly screeching throughout the compound, "we have to hurry."

Noting that his breath had gone silver, the detective realized the cold from the other world was somehow pouring into their own. As he pointed the fact out to the professor, Knight responded;

"Meaning we have less time than we believed."

And then, both men's hearts froze at a particular sound, their blood icing over within their veins. As they exited the side passageway into the main hall, they found more of their team running into one another blindly—screaming in mindless panic. They had good reason to scream.

"*Tekeli-li, Tekeli-li*"

"Guess we weren't the only ones who knew the right direction—eh, professor?"

The two men stopped, both panting. Bending over slightly so as to be able to place his hands on his knees, Nardi took a number of deep breaths as rapidly as possible in the hopes of reviving himself, then reached once more for his .45. As he did so, Knight pulled his tobacco pouch and pipe from his jacket pocket. As his bodyguard simply stared, the professor asked;

"Not suddenly afraid of a bit of second-hand smoke, are you?"

"No, not at this point."

"Good," responded Knight as he touched his lighter to his pipe's freshly packed bowl. Taking a good, healthy drag, he exhaled a pleasant woody smelling cloud through a new-born half-smile, then said;

"Well, we've still only got one chance at this. Shall we go for it?"

Sighing, checking the slide on his weapon, the detective gave the professor a forlorn smile, then answered;

"Never let it be said that Frank Nardi ever chose good sense over a good time. Let's do it."

And then, before either man could move or even speak, boiling its way directly through the wall next to them, the first of the shoggoths appeared. All thoughts of self-defense evaporated within them both with but a single glimpse of the shapeless, bubbling horror. The thing was constructed as much from light and stench as from protoplasm and both knew instinctively it was utterly unstoppable by anything known to earthly science.

Pulling his bodyguard along, Knight winced at the additional screams of those the monstrosity consumed behind them. The professor had no doubt the thing behind them had been dispatched to silence any and all humans left within the base.

"That doesn't give us much time," he reminded himself. Dropping his pipe as he and Nardi threw themselves into the room holding their only hope, he prayed, "Well, let's hope this damn thing isn't nearly as experimental as we thought."

With no way to reach the outside in time, let alone the ability to pilot any of the military vehicles on the runway, Knight had led them to the main hanger where the others had been assembling what they could of the alien technology into things that might be useful within the world beyond. As the two men clambered onto the unshielded platform, Knight began tossing the various switches and connecting the multiple relays as best he could remember, even while a part of his mind wondered wildly;

"Why? Why did they even bring us here? What could they have wanted? What could they have possibly needed from *us?*"

As the thought raced through his brain, the professor froze for a moment, the question setting his mind afire. Turning to Nardi, he sobbed;

"What did they want? Why open the place to the world? Why pretend to be human? What did they want? They didn't need us. They didn't *need* us!"

"Nobody needs us," screamed back the detective.

And then, as the doorway to the chamber began to melt from contact with the glowing form of the shoggoth, Knight slammed the last connection, both men grabbing hold of the railing surrounding the disc as the experimental anti-gravity device lurched upward. Cephlopodic lengths reached out from the monstrosity, trying to snag them, but it was too late. The roundish plate, once loosened from the planet's grasp, careened madly upward, slamming against the ceiling, almost accomplishing the creature's goal as it nearly decapitated its passengers.

Only able to control the device by running it along the hanger wall, the pair were able to pilot it as far as the door, then smash their way to the outside. The violence they had already done to the unstable vehicle was more than enough to send it insanely out of control, but it was enough for them to effect their escape from the station. Once outside, the disc screeched into the sky in an incredible arc, rocketing dozens of miles across the Antarctic landscape in a matter of seconds before it crashed back to the Earth. Mere seconds after that, a terrible roar was heard, followed by a blinding light which shattered the land in every direction from Antarctic Station 12.

From their vantage point, miles away, dragging themselves up out of the acres of snow into which they had been thrown, Knight and Nardi stared across the vast open area, watching the terrible explosion consume everything beyond. They could not explain anything they saw, not to themselves, or to the others who would investigate the disaster, finding them several days later.

Half dead, starving, almost blind, they would weakly stammer out their stories, confounding and frightening their questioners. Especially when they would both describe the last thing they saw in perfect, matching detail, the confounding, fluctuating image of a vast, impossibly tall mountain range, imposing itself over the entire area for one brief instance, before fading away in a long lingering shimmer, leaving them both with the comforting pleasure of madness.

A Biting Cold

Brian M. Sammons

"So what's a Seal doing on a rescue mission?" Lieutenant Kray shouted over the *whup, whup, whup* of the helicopter's spinning blades. The man who usually led this six-man rescue team did not like the stranger sitting across from him in the Sikorsky Seahawk. Not one little bit. Kray had heard that the Navy Seal had flown down from the States and had talked to the McMurdo base commander even before he and his men had finished prepping the rescue chopper, and Kray's men moved fast when lives were on the line. Then the dust-off was held until the Seal, one Lieutenant Robert Lynch, came aboard, told Kray that he was taking operational command of the mission, and issued each man a winterized M4 carbine. All of the Navy rescuers were trained in the use of the assault rifle, but as sailors who specialized in saving lives, not taking them, they usually only packed a sidearm. The added firepower left Kray's men with questions, and unanswered questions got people killed. Kray was determined to get some answers before the skids touched the snow at the Hamilton Research Station.

Lt. Lynch did not answer Kray. He was sitting with his head leaned back against the shuddering wall of the helicopter with his eyes closed. Kray didn't give a damn if the other man was trying to sleep, so he kicked his boot with his own and shouted again.

"I said what's a Seal doing here? Where the hell is the rest of your team and why are you overseeing a rescue mission of civilian scientists?"

"I heard you the first time, Lieutenant," the Seal said as he opened his eyes and brought his head down to look at Kray. "Sorry, but I've been on four airplanes for over twenty hours. Jet lagged does not even begin to cover how I feel," Lynch said with a smile. It looked like an honest attempt at being friendly, but it did little to dull the edge in Kray's voice.

"How the hell can that be? We only received the distress call three hours ago."

"It was sent out over forty-eight hours ago. It was too weak to reach you and was first picked up by a closer Brazilian base who forwarded it on to us. That put me in motion, and as I neared Antarctica, it was then forwarded on to you to get you ready." Lynch said.

"Wait, what? Why the hell were we not notified of a distress call until two days later?" Kray said, anger rising inside him. He then thought for a second before adding, "And who is this 'we' that got notified before us, and why did we have to wait for you? Who the fuck are you?"

Lynch looked into Kray's eyes and held the rescue man's gaze. He did not blink or look away. As for Kray, he could see that the Seal was weary, but also alert, calm, and composed. "Well 'we' are the Navy. As for me, I'm a Seal, but you knew that already. As for why you were not notified until I was *en route*, that was so I could take command of this mission. Any other questions?" Lynch said without a hint of sarcasm. His matter of fact demeanor only served to enrage Kray more.

"God damn it, that doesn't answer anything! Why are you here? If this is a Seal combat mission, where is the rest of your team?"

"I was the only one close by," Lynch said.

"Bullshit, if you had to fly twenty hours to get here, you sure as hell weren't 'close'."

The Seal smiled slightly. It looked like he was impressed that Kray had picked up on that, rather than being upset he had been caught in a lie.

Lieutenant Kray continued, "Why are my men carrying M4s? We're Navy, but we're primary a noncombat unit."

"You and your men *were* the only ones close by." Lynch said calmly, coldly.

"Do you know what happened out at Hamilton Station? I sure as hell don't. If we're going into a dangerous situation, as your presence and these weapons suggest that we are, my men and I have a right to know what to expect."

Lynch sat motionless and Kray could all but see the gears turning inside the man's head. He was weighing whatever secret bullshit he knew with his desire to not see fellow Navy men put into harm's way without knowing the full score. Kray guessed that the Seal wasn't a bad man, but that didn't necessarily make him a good one.

After several long, silent moments, Lynch spoke.

"There could be some danger, but we don't know for sure. It could be a danger you can't even begin to imagine, or it could be nothing. I am here because I'm one of the few people who have dealt with stuff like this before and survived. Threats like this are exceptionally rare, but not completely unknown to certain people in Washington. You ever hear about the Miskatonic University Expedition down here in the 30s?"

Kray blinked, trying to take in and make sense of what the Seal just told him. "No, never heard of it."

"I'm not surprised. It was a very public undertaking back in the day, but then that was a long time ago. It made the papers and the radios, especially after a good chunk of the expedition died. Back then the government didn't have the tight grip on the media it does today, so some of the details got out and caused an uproar. That's when the government did take notice, and after that they tried their best to make it all disappear. I'm telling you this because it's not classified, just sort of hidden. If you want to find the info on what happened back then, or what people believe happened, you can if you dig deep enough."

"So what happened to the expedition?" Kray asked.

"Officially that is classified, and I'm sorry, but I can't tell you." Lynch said with a slight frown. "Unofficially it is known that a bunch of people died and the expedition came home. Several people were hospitalized, others were institutionalized, and still others just sort of disappeared after a while."

"You're talking about a cover up?"

Lynch shook his head, "No, I'm only telling you what anyone could know if they knew what to look for. I *will* say that after the incident, all the governments that sliced up Antarctica agreed, or were bullied into accepting, that an area of that snowy wasteland was a no go zone. Further, some conspiracy nuts on the web claim that once people started sending up satellites to take pictures of the earth, there is one spot down here that only a very few people in a handful of countries have ever seen. Don't know if that's true or not, but it's a fact that nothing else bad has happened down here for over eighty years. That is until possibly now."

"You make it sound like there are monsters or aliens down here." Kay said with a nervous chuckle.

Lynch just stared at the other man and said nothing.

"Bullshit." Kray said, but the curse lacked the conviction that normally accompanied it.

"It could be nothing," Lynch began, "but it could be something really bad. That's why I'm here, Lieutenant. My mission is to assess the situation and call in reinforcements if need be. We are not to engage any hostiles if there are any on the scene if we can avoid it. Hopefully when we get there we'll find some folks with a malfunctioning radio, broken heating system, perhaps a sickness. Something normal and safe. But if something weird does happen, I will do my best to get you, your men, and myself out of there safely. Now I didn't tell you specifics, because honestly, I don't know any. Like you, I'm only told what I need to know to get the job done, and my bosses don't even know what's really going on. But I've given you enough hints that hopefully, if things get crazy really fast, you will keep your shit together and help me by handling your men. They know you, they trust you, and they will listen to you. And if you want them and yourself to live through this should the worst possible scenario be in play, you will listen to what I tell you to do and do it without hesitation. Got it?"

"That's crazy . . ."

"Yeah it is, but it might also be real. So keep this to yourself, unless you want your men thinking you're as crazy as you no doubt think I am, but also keep it in mind." Lynch said and then leaned his head back once more and closed his eyes.

It was still three hours until they reached the Hamilton Research Station and the Navy Seal tried once more to get some shuteye. In contrast, Lt. Kray was now more wired and worried than on any rescue mission he had ever undertaken before. It's not that he believed the man's crazy hints and allusions, but still . . .

There had been no response from the research base on the radio as the Seahawk approached. Even with the two reserve tanks, the chopper was almost at bingo fuel, the point where they had just enough in the tanks for a safe return back to McMurdo. This would be further pushed to the limit if they found people in need of a medical evac, as extra weight meant more fuel consumed. Because of this, the chopper did a single flyby of the base, its front searchlight piercing the pitch black of Antarctica's long night, but it revealed nothing. One thing every man aboard the helicopter noticed was that all the base's lights were out, even those on the landing pad and the ones that illuminated the safety ropes that ran from building to building. That was not a good sign.

"Drop some flares on the pad so I can see it." The chopper pilot yelled back.

Kray's crew slid open the Seahawk's doors, allowing gales of subzero wind whipped up by the helicopter's rotors to rip through the aircraft. They quickly lit and dropped a half dozen red-glowing flares out and then slammed the doors shut. Once the snow blown landing pad had some light on it, the pilot gingerly touched the big bird down.

"Lieutenant, if you could have someone find me some gas, I sure would appreciate it," the pilot said to Lynch. "As it is, in this temperature the engine would freeze up if I shut her down, so I'm gonna have to keep her running and burning fuel. Without a refill you have fifteen minutes tops before I have to take off and return to base."

"All right," Lynch said, then turned to Kray. "Have two of your men refuel the chopper. The rest come with us."

"One of my guys can handle that."

"No, one does the refueling, the other is to keep an eye out and watch over him and the chopper." Lynch said and then added, "Just in case."

Kray nodded, then ordered Stafford and Glenn to handle it. Before leaving the aircraft, all of the men first pulled up their facemasks and set their goggles in place. To have any exposed flesh in Antarctica was inviting frostbite in a matter of minutes. Then they helped each other into their bulky backpacks, grabbed their medical kits with one hand, and their new M4 carbines with the other. Kray shoulder slung his rifle as he watched Lynch check his weapon, an AA-12 automatic shotgun, the SOCOM .45 at his hip, and then heft up his own backpack.

"My guys got meds and tools for repairs. What did you bring?" Kray asked the Seal.

The other man just smiled, then said to the group as a whole; "Ok, let's go. Stay within visual range of each other. No wandering off. If you see something, call out and we'll all go take a look. Understood?"

The Navy men grunted an affirmative.

"Good, I'm on lead. Kray, you're behind me. You, Baker, you're bringing up the rear. Keep your eyes to our six and make ready that weapon, sailor."

Ensign Baker looked at the carbine in his left hand, then to the heavy medical bag in his right.

"Leave the medkit, we've got enough of those already." Lynch commanded.

As Baker did as he was ordered, another man, Johnson, spoke up. "Sir, are we expecting trouble out here?"

"No, but better safe than sorry."

"Cause if we're not, then we're here to help people and we can do more good with meds then we can with a rifle, *sir*." The last word to leave Johnson's mouth all but dripped with venom.

Lynch shot a quick look over to Kray who said, "Button it, Johnson. Lieutenant Lynch has command on this."

"Aye, sir." Johnson replied.

The Navy men sprang from the helicopter. Two went around behind it to begin the lengthy refueling process, and the rest followed Lynch towards the darkened base camp. With not a single light on, the darkness of the night was total. The rescue men all had L-shaped flashlights hooked to the front of their white parkas and two carried million candle powered spotlights, while the Seal used a tactical light mounted underneath his shotgun to sweep the area and find his way.

Luckily, while the temperature was far below zero, there was little wind. That kept the deadly wind chill to a minimum. It also meant less blowing snow, so the men didn't have to use the guide ropes and could talk to each other without shouting or using their sub vocal mics and earpieces.

"Hello, anyone here?" Kray yelled out into the darkness, and he saw Lynch cringe at the broken silence, but the Seal said nothing.

"We're here to find and help people, right?" Kray said to him, but again the spec ops warrior remained silent.

"No lights and no smoke from the chimneys. This isn't looking good, boss," Johnson said as he used his powerful handheld spotlight to illuminate the top of the closest building.

"I think I've got something over here," Chief Petty Officer Edginton said, pointing his lamp at a square, steel shack. The doors to the structure were open, and the light revealed a pair of orange painted Snowcat tractors inside. But that's not where the focus of the man's light was aimed. The large circle of illumination shone on a dark spot in front of the open garage doors that had a familiar, if fragmented, shape to it.

The men moved in that direction and from a distance of twenty paces they began to recognize it as the torn and mangled body of a person, covered in frozen blood and a light dusting of snow. The identification of the pile of debris as having once been human was rudimentary at best. Bits of bone, scraps of torn winter clothing, the occasional larger bit like three fingers still attached to a shredded scrap of palm, was all that was left of whoever this had once been.

"Aw man, what the hell?" Johnson said, as much to himself as to anyone else.

"There are some kind of tracks all over the place, but I can't tell what made them," Kray said as he removed his L-light from his chest to shine it over the ground around the bloody mess.

"Neither can I," Lynch replied. The Seal was already down on one knee, examining the prints, but the blowing snow of the last couple of days had erased most of their detail. Now only faint impressions remained. All that they could be certain of was that whatever made the odd impressions, there were a lot of them.

"What the hell is this, some kind of shit?" Baker said, his light shining on chunky streaks of brown and whitish-yellow stains. There were several such droppings in the area around the torn human remains.

"Kinda looks like . . . bird shit," Edginton said as he kicked at one frozen pile with his snow boot.

"Look at this. What the fuck is this?" Johnson called out, his spotlight pointing at a lumpy whitish-brown pile that had something glittering in it, something golden. Kray stepped closer and saw that it was a man's wedding ring, partially buried in the pile of strange excrement.

"What's going on, Lieutenant?" Johnson said is a near whisper.

"I'm not sure," Lynch answered.

"I wasn't talking to you!" Johnson shouted. "But since the big bad Seals are here, I bet you were expecting something like this."

"No, nothing like this," Lynch said absently. He then stood up and locked goggles with Johnson. "Look, we're here to find out what happened, locate any survivors, and then get the hell out of Dodge. So let's get to it."

"All right, if anyone is left . . . alive, then they'll probably be in the main building over there," Kray said and pointed deeper into the base. "That will have the science labs, living quarters, radio room, med bay, food stores, pretty much everything you would need to survive for a few days."

"Okay, let's go. Stay alert but don't go shooting at shadows. Baker, you still keep your eyes behind us." Lynch said.

"Aye, sir," the young ensign confirmed the order. Baker turned around and readied his M4 like he meant it this time.

The small squad moved silently through the darkness, following the strange, snow-blown tracks deeper into the research station. They didn't stop to examine any of the other bloody, ragged, frozen piles of scattered bone and torn winter survival gear that they passed. No one commented further on the countless streaks and piles of whitish-yellow stuff that dotted the area, even if someone saw a recognizable bit of something mixed in with the filth. The only time the silence was broken was when the group was thirty yards from the main building. They stopped there when they saw that the twin front doors stood open, allowing freezing air and drifts of snow to blow into the lightless structure.

Lynch raised a gloved hand to touch the sub vocal mic at his throat and whispered, "Gallagher, come in. What's the status on the refuel?"

The helicopter pilot responded by shouting over the whirling chopper blades and into the earpieces of all the men. "Slow. The pumps had no power, so the guys had to find a barrel of fuel from the shed, wheel it over, and are now using a hand pump."

"Get as much in as possible, but be ready for an immediate dust off if I call for it."

"Roger that," the pilot confirmed.

Lynch released the microphone button and said to the men with him, "Ok, follow me in. Keep those fingers off the triggers until you know what you're shooting at."

The group entered the main building carefully, quietly, their ears straining to pick up even the slightest sound. Their boots crunched on the drifted snow, and the wind whispered past them to invade the open building. Those, and their labored breathing, were the only noises to be heard. Another mangled corpse was spread over the main hall, as were more droppings. A series of doors ran the length of the hallway, with a set of double doors at its end. The Navy men broke up into two groups, Lynch leading one and Kray the other. Methodically they took each door and searched the rooms beyond, slowing making their way towards the end of the hall. The first few doors led to a closet for outside winter gear, to lavatories, a supply closet, and a rec room with TV, DVD player, a pinball machine, and even a ping pong table. Some rooms were neat and clean, others held bloody messes and strange feces; none told the searchers anything useful as to what had happened here.

At about the center of the hallway, a door on the right had been battered down. Lynch examined the door and found it to be torn from the hinges, cracked, and smeared with a now frozen opaque fluid. There were no signs of blows to it, by either weapons like axes or hammers, or even simple kicks. It appeared that the door had buckled under constant, incredible force.

Just beyond the door was a pile of furniture: a desk, chairs, and waste cans. They had all had been pushed aside by something bullying its way into the room. It was clear someone had barricaded the door and that their meager defenses did not hold. Pushing past the breached barricade, the men discovered that what was once a radio room was now a charnel house. There were blood and dung piles everywhere. The flayed remains of three to five people were strewn about and so intermingled and fragmented that an exact body count was impossible.

"Lieutenant, we've got an axe," Johnson said as he reached down and picked up an emergency fire axe. The blade had red smears frozen to it.

"Whatever happened, it didn't leave many bones, or anything else, behind," Edginton said as he shone his light onto a sizable off-white lump in the middle of a pile of shredded, blood-soaked clothes. "This is the first skull I've seen so far."

"Here's another one," Kray called out, and the tone of uncertainty in his voice caused everyone to turn to see what he had discovered.

It was a skull to be sure, but it was in no way human. It was roughly the same size as a full grown man's skull, although proportionally different. It obviously belonged to some kind of bird, for it had a long, wicked looking beak on it, but no man there could ever remember seeing a bird so big. Worst of all, the thing that set every man's teeth on edge, was how blank the skull was. It had no eye sockets. Besides the beak, the front of the skull was a featureless plane of blood streaked white.

"Is that like a dinosaur fossil or something?" Baker asked.

"No, dumbass, it still has blood and bits of meat hanging on it. That thing died recently," Johnson said.

"It had to be huge, at least as big as a man, if not bigger. And it didn't have any eyes," Kray said with wonder as he knelt down and picked up the skull to examine it. Lifting it from the gore-drenched floor caused the lower jaw to unhinge and open the beak up. Kray saw that the inside ridges of the beak were sharp and jagged, almost serrated, and that bits of pale, pink meat were still wedged between some of the teeth-like protrusions.

"Shit—" he whispered and then put the alien avian skull back down, stood up, and wiped his hand off on his pants.

"Come on, there's still plenty more base for us to check out," Lynch said and made for the door.

The group left the radio room and continued opening doors along the hallway. They found various signs of slaughter inside most rooms, nothing in a few others, before Johnson called out.

"I think I found something!"

Kray went over to the man and followed the beam of his flashlight down to where it illuminated another torn-apart body. The center of Johnson's light was pointing at something silver and rectangular, about the size of a small remote control. It also had a tiny, faint blue light shining out of it, which was no doubt what drew the other man's attention to it.

"Get Lynch over here," Kray told Johnson as he knelt to pick up the device. He soon discovered that it was stuck to the floor by frozen gore, so he withdrew his knife and started to carefully chip away at the red ice that held it in place. By the time he had freed it, Johnson was back and Lynch was at his side.

"Looks like a digital recorder," the Seal offered.

"Sure is," Kray said and saw that the faint blue light was the display screen. The recorder was paused at the 28:19 mark. Kray hit the rewind button and quickly noticed that the feeble blue light got dimmer and the numbers on the display ticked backwards more slowly than they should.

"Shit, it's almost dead," Kray said as he hit stop and then the play button. He wanted to get any information he could before the batteries completely died. The voice that came out of the recorder was low, slightly slowed down and distorted by the batteries giving their last few sparks of energy. And it was female.

. . . clear to me that this obviously subterranean species has been driven from their natural habitat by climate change. They appeared exhausted and half starving when we first encountered them. If I didn't know any better, I would say that they were fleeing something, but given their size and defensive flock mentality, which Jeff found out for himself when he first approached them, I can't think of any predators big enough to threaten them. We finally managed to herd them with the Snowcats into a tool shed that we converted into a pen so we . . .

The message stopped there and the blue light of the recorder winked out completely.

"So they found whatever those things are and brought them here?" Johnson asked.

"Sounds like it," Kray said.

"But how many did—" Johnson began, only to be interrupted when Baker shushed them. He was still doing his duty, watching their backs outside in the hallway,.

"What is it, Baker?" Lynch said as he began to silently make his way out of the room.

"Don't know, sir," the ensign whispered, "but I heard something come from that room up there." The man pointed with his assault rifle at the set of double doors at the end of the hall.

"What did it sound like?"

"I don't know, a screech or something."

"Something like the sound a big-ass bird would make?" Kray asked as he and the others joined them in the hallway.

"Yeah, maybe. I don't know." Baker then tried to make a joke of it with a forced smile. "Hell, I'm from New York. The only birds I know are pigeons, and it sure didn't sound like one of those."

"Well we're here to find out, so let's go see," Kray said. He looked over at the Navy Seal and Lynch nodded.

The group skipped the last few rooms on either side of the hallway and approached the double doors at the end. They were closed, but they were swinging doors that could be opened from either side with a push. They were also covered in frozen muck and blood from a height of around seven feet on down. Lynch put his hand to one door, Kray took the other, and together they led the way inside.

The room beyond was large. It might have been more than one room in the past, but it had undergone some crude remodeling as of late. The first thing the Navy men noticed was that forty feet of the east wall was simply gone. It opened the room up to the outside and allowed the snow, freezing night air, and starlight to enter. However, between the men and the ruined wall there were many distinct shapes. Tall, dark, unmoving shadows filled the room. As their lights shone on the standing shadows, the men saw that they were, of all things, *penguins*, but they were so far removed from what their minds classified as penguins as to be almost alien to them. The birds stood between six and seven feet in height. They were albino, devoid of the typical tuxedoed look, and were instead a sickly off-white-grayish color. Their flesh and the feathers that covered them appeared diseased and malformed, with odd lumps bulging un-der the skin and open sores that wept a viscous, opaque fluid. The giant penguins were sleeping standing up, with their long beaks tucked underneath one of their mighty wings. Even with their heads bowed, it was clear that none of the animals had eyes. It was also evident that each and every giant bird had stains ranging from pink to deep red on its front, neck, and splattered across its hideous, eyeless face.

Kray's light dipped by accident to light up the mess around the birds' feet. There he saw dark masses of shredded clothing, but there were also piles of bloated meat with off-white feathers still attached to it. These voracious beasts, after consuming everyone at the research base, had started to cannibalize their own to stay alive.

"Oh Jesus," Johnson said, his light shining on the floor near them. There one of the giant albino birds lay on its back. Its belly had been ripped open, and there were numerous stab wounds, but the corpse was still oddly whole. It was obviously dead, but it had been killed only recently, for steam still rose from the open cavity and some of the blood pooled around it had yet to fully freeze. But it wasn't the sight of the dead giant bird that caused Johnson to cry out. It was that, although the thing was clearly dead, it was still moving. Something writhed and pulsed in the animal's savaged abdomen.

Johnson took two steps backwards where he collided with the wall next to the doors they had come through. His shoulder bumped up against a fire extinguisher hard enough to knock it from its wall hook and send it crashing to the ground. It hit with a loud, ringing clang.

Everyone turned to look at Johnson and then, when he pointed back at the fallen bird with his light, they followed the beam and saw the edges of the bird's gutted cavity part, and out poked the heads of four gore-covered baby albino penguins.

"They're using it for warmth," Kray whispered.

Then the foot-tall fledglings began to call out with screeching, almost goose-like honks.

"Shit," Lynch whispered and brought his shotgun up to his shoulder.

Almost as one, the monstrous adult penguins pulled their heads out from under their wings. First they sniffed at the chilly air, then they began to shriek and bleat. Next they started making clucking sounds and swinging their heads from side to side. Lastly they shook a dusting of frost from their gigantic bodies and began to move towards the men.

All that happened in mere seconds as the rescue team stood frozen in wonder, fear, and indecision. It was the Navy Seal who acted first. Lynch yelled a single word, "Out!" then fired his shotgun at the closest of the man-sized penguins. Out of the weapon's barrel a jet of orange flame erupted and stretched out over eight feet to strike the bird in the center of its red stained breast. The penguin shrieked in pain as fire quickly began to spread over it.

Somewhere in Kray's sluggish brain he realized that Lynch had his shotgun loaded with dragon's breath rounds. Instead of lead, each shell fired out a combination of white phosphorous and the mineral zirconium that burst into flame as soon as it left the barrel. Such rounds effectively turned a shotgun into a miniature flamethrower, but the range was limited, as was the overall practicality of the round. While they were intimidating as hell, they were a very odd choice to bring on a typical combat mission.

But then, as Kray was quickly learning, this mission was anything but typical.

Lynch fired three more times, setting ablaze three more giant birds, before yelling, "Damn it, get it together and get the hell out of here!"

Kray snapped to, yelled out, "Come on, let's go!" and turned to his left, just in time to see one of the hulking man-eaters lunge forward and drive its beak fully through the face of Ensign Baker. The proboscis plunged into the young man's face roughly where his nose was and smashed through the back of his skull to expose at least six inches of blood-soaked beak. Baker dropped his rifle as his arms and legs began to jitter and shake. The synapses in the man's brain were firing wildly as they tried to make sense of what his body's nerve endings were screaming at it. If it wasn't for the huge bird's massive neck muscles, Baker would have been left twitching on the floor. As it was, the penguin held the convulsing man aloft until it decided to open its beak while it was still inside the dying man's skull. This caused the top of Baker's head to come away from the nose on up with a wet tearing sound. Gouts of blood erupted from the gaping wound and showered everything close by. Kray was lucky, gore only splattered onto his shoulder. Johnson on the other side of Baker was not so fortunate. Blood, bits of bone, and strings of warm meat struck the man right in the face, blinding him, and going into his mouth to choke him.

Kray fired off a three round burst from his M4 into the flank of the bird, which turned in his direction and only gave him an annoyed squawk. He then fired three more bursts, for a total of twelve rounds of 5.56 before the great bird fell. By that time, the crush of hulking penguins was fully upon him and at least three more were between him and Johnson.

"Lieutenant?" Johnson pleaded, wiping gore from his eyes while backing up from the advancing horde of birds. His retreat only caused him to move away from the men by the doors.

"Go out the hole in the wall, circle back around, and get to the chopper!" Kray yelled over the thunderous shotgun booms, the sharp cracks of M4s, and the deafening squawks and honks of the enraged penguins. He quickly spun to put three rounds into the chest of an albino giant that was rushing him and then turned back to Johnson to see him still standing there dumbly.

"God damn it, go *now*!" he yelled out.

Kray didn't see if Johnson moved or not, because Lynch had him by the shoulder and was dragging him out the doors, back into the hallway. As the twin doors shut, the Seal let go of him and deftly changed the smoking drum magazine out of his shotgun while walking backwards. Once reloaded, he touched the mic button at his throat and yelled, "Get the chopper ready for takeoff now!"

All the men heard the pilot's puzzled response of "What?" buzz in their ears as the two doors bust open and a flood of diseased, milky-white beasts surged into the hall. Kray and his men brought their rifles back up and began to fire into the advancing mass, while Lynch yelled into his mic, "We. Are. Leaving. Now!" The Seal then started blasting away again with his fire-spitting cannon. At this range the shotgun made a wall of flame and set several birds alight with each blast. Still the albino monstrosities advanced. They moved through the hail of gunfire, through the flames, and over the burning and twitching bodies of their fallen comrades to pursue their quarry.

Finally the men rushed through the building's main doors and into the freezing blackness beyond. Kray stopped for a second to change magazines on his M4 and saw Chief Petty Officer Edginton barrel past him, blindly running in the direction of where they left the chopper. The man moved unencumbered, having dropped both his bag and his carbine somewhere in his flight. Then Kray saw Lynch slip out his backpack to his right. The Seal went inside and pulled from it two bulky canister-like grenades. He pulled both pins, yelled out, "Fire in the hole!" and tossed them simultaneously through the still-open doors at the squawking hoard. The man then picked up his pack and was off and running again before the firebombs exploded, sending streamers of burning white chemicals flying into the air with a hellish cacophony of agonized bird calls.

Kray was about to turn and follow the man when he saw Johnson come limping around the corner of the building. He had also lost his M4, was clutching his side, and was still covered in now-frozen bits of Baker. Kray ran to his man, put his shoulder to him, and helped to carry Johnson's weight so he could hobble away faster.

By the time Kray and Johnson reached the helicopter, everyone else was aboard, the rotor blades were spinning at full speed, and the research base behind them threw dancing orange light at their backs as it had begun to burn, thanks to Lynch's liberal spraying of fire. Kray saw the Seal standing at the chopper's door. Their eyes met and Lynch gave him a nod before picking up a large satellite phone from out of his backpack. The man keyed a long code into the security phone, then placed it up to his ear with one hand, while helping to get Johnson into the chopper with the other.

"Attention, attention, this is Jordan one, six, eight, delta. Repeat, Jordan one, six, eight, delta, come in," the Seal shouted into the phone, then once Kray was aboard he slammed the helicopter's door shut and yelled up to the pilot, "We're in! Go!"

"What about Baker?" Glynn asked, but Jordan ignored the question and went back to listening to his sat phone.

"He's dead," Kray huffed out.

"Dead, dead, dead, dead," Johnson said from where he lay on the floor of the chopper before he began to giggle oddly.

"Roger that, this is Jordan," the man called Lynch said. "Threat not as expected. Repeat, no sleepers awake. Call off sundown. Repeat, no need for sundown. Over."

The Seal listened to the reply on the phone, and Kray just watched and listened to the Seal.

"Roger that, threat is minimal. Will send full report when back at McMurdo. The research station is a loss. One K.I.A. on team. Over. Roger that, Jordan out."

The Seal then put the sat phone back into his pack and took a seat on one of the chopper's benches with a weary sigh.

"So you were expecting something worse than those fucking birds?" Kray asked the man.

"It was a possibility."

"Were those . . . *alien* birds or something?" Kray asked without a hint of humor or self-consciousness at asking what would, just a day before, have seemed an incredibly silly question.

"No," the Seal smiled, "Just an evolutionary throwback."

"So what's worse than them?" Kray pressed.

"Something I'm glad as hell wasn't there."

Then Johnson's strange giggling became more pronounced and both men clearly heard it.

"*Tekeli-li, Tekeli-li, Tekeli-li*" Johnson said, over and over, between fits of coughing and sobs.

Kray put it down to CSR—combat stress reaction—or what used to be called shellshock, until he saw the face of the spec ops killer across from him. The color had completely drained out of the man's cheeks.

The Seal stood and then knelt next to Johnson on the floor and said, "Where did you hear that? Johnson! Where did you hear that?"

When Johnson didn't immediately reply, the Seal slapped him across the face and asked again.

"It was the wind. The laughing wind. When I ran out the side of the building I heard the wind laughing at me. It sounded so far away, so, so far away . . . but it wasn't." Johnson said and then curled up into a fetal position and began to cry uncontrollably.

"Did you *see* anything? Did you see it?" The Navy Seal persisted while Kray just looked on in confusion and with a growing sense of unease gnawing at his guts.

"Yes," Johnson croaked out. "*Yes*. Horrible. So *horrible*."

The Special Forces soldier then left the crying man alone, stepped back to his bag, and once again pulled out his satellite phone.

"What was it?" Kray asked. "What did he see?"

The Seal looked at him stone-faced. "Something you're glad you didn't. For you and your men it's over; you did your part, you're through," he said as he walked towards the back of the chopper, punching numbers on the keypad as he went.

"I've got to make a call before the bombers get too far away."

GARDEN OF THE GODS

CODY GOODFELLOW

In perfect stillness and absolute cold, not a molecule stirring, the Scientist sleeps. Then, fire and alarms, vibration and pain. Out of a dreamless sleep of one hundred million years, it awakens.

Layers of nitrogen hoarfrost crack and melt away from the hermetic cocoon, which in turn vaporizes and disgorges its occupant into the buried ruin of the research outpost it once maintained.

Extremities still frozen solid, yet it springs to full alertness, reaching out with its ruthlessly curious mind for the psychic spoor of its mates. Total silence scours away its instinctual arrogance. As sensory stalks and locomotive tentacles finally begin to thaw, it shambles to the airlock.

The outpost is buried in stone, but daylight pours down through a shaft bored out of the strata of granite and basalt . . . by design.

Shock follows shock with its first glimpse of the world. The crisp, alpine air and barren, broken terrain suggest that eons of geological flux have wrested its resting place high above its previous altitude and buried it, only to be excavated—

It considers, only now, the absence of any recognizable organisms. None of its own kind are present for its emergence, and it tastes no spore-sign, senses no echo of the reassuring vibratory tongue of its race on the aether. Obscene! To have been abandoned, to be greeted by slaves—

For such it judges the mesothermic bipeds that cower before it in manifest awe; for are not all the species of this earth but the products, or by-products, of its ancestors' masterful designs, created to serve at their pleasure?

Though their construction is so novel and unnerving that he must strangle the impulse to smash them—how can such things walk upright?—yet the more rational facets of its mind extrapolate the span of breeding necessary for such things to be shaped—a few hundred generations if farmed, several million, if spontaneously evolved—but such aberrations as these would never be tolerated, never trusted. Though the puny projectile weapons they hurl at it are hardly an annoyance, they make it clear by their behavior that they are neither slaves, nor feral beasts.

The Scientist senses meaningful patterns in the shrill, howling cries of the creatures fleeing up the tiered walls of the enormous open pit. It studies the crude artifice of their tools, and recoils from the stench of sentience—the telltale signs of that insidious neural rot that ever claimed the finest of their fruits. Most unnerving, yet useful—

It unfurls its wings and locomotive tentacles to present its pure radial form in all its majesty, towering over the awestruck hominids in a tableau embedded in their genetic code long before their remotest ancestors emerged from the sea, and blasts them with a raw wave of untempered psychic force. Half of the feeble minds it touches are instantly snuffed out, and it is riven with awe and elation, at both their highly advanced sentience, and their fragility.

From the labyrinthine bladders in its massive, barrel-shaped trunk, it expels a breath pregnant with an aerosolized viral command. Inhaling it, touching it, the surviving hominids fall in a herd to their knees, and the Scientist takes comfort that this much, at least, is unchanged.

This world is still ours.

At forty thousand feet, the tail of the MC-130 Combat Talon splits and seeds the Peruvian troposphere with soldiers. They fall like seven daggers, like wingless eagles in a tight daisy-chain formation around a footlocker-sized package.

At terminal velocity, they drop through an armada of lenticular clouds stacked over a narrow, glacier-cut valley six thousand feet above sea level, five by five despite punishing winds and nearly zero visibility. When the altimeters on their wrists show sixty-five hundred, they pull their cords, braced for their chutes to unfold like a single wing and snatch them back from the embrace of gravity.

But their chutes don't open.

As they break formation and struggle with varied degrees of failure to free their chutes from their packs, one soldier pulls his secondary cord and is ripped out of the scene of panic in the same instant he realizes something is wrong.

They shrink to screaming shadows as his Ram-Air Parachute System steers him in tight, dwindling spirals after their plummeting forms. Far below, one parachute opens, swells and rises towards him on the icy updraft.

As one, neat as a physics theorem, they smash, bouncing and bursting, into the earth.

Lieutenant Purcell howls all the way down. When his legs crumple under him and the ground sends him rolling to a stop against one of his broken comrades, he throws up into his oxygen mask.

It looks like a yard sale. One man tried to cut his chute open with his K-bar knife, which went right through him on impact like a mortar shell. His arm juts out through the hole in his back, up to the elbow. Another hit a spill of jagged granite and was shredded so badly Purcell can't identify the remains. A fleeting swell of hope draws him to the solitary billowing parachute trailing across the grassy meadow, but it's just the package.

None of them wore dog tags or any insignia. Even in the dark, he could identify most of them by the gear on, in or around their bodies. These men were his friends, his brothers and more, because they'd saved his life as many times as he saved theirs. The enormity of it steamrolls him, and the ugly reality beyond it makes calling home look like a very bad idea.

This was no accident. His survival is the anomaly. He packed his own chute. They all did. But he packed two, and switched on the plane because he had a bad feeling. Not bad enough to share, to spook the team and queer their resolve, but bad enough he swapped it right after they flew out of Bogotá.

"SFC Del Curren; Lt. Vien Rodriguez; Lt. Tyrone Ledwich; SFC Jeff Staples; SFC Luis Allegre; Captain Keenan Herber," he solemnly intones their names, and an elegy: "you were all assholes."

It makes him feel like a louse, but it makes it easier to loot the bodies and bury them under loose rocks.

By sunrise, he's bivouacked the team's gear in a shallow cave in the lee of a crooked spire of granite overlooking the tiny valley. Their ammunition, explosives and MRE's were mostly salvageable; the Shadowfire radio and most of their guns were trashed. Along with his own Barrett .50 caliber rifle and MP5, he found two other assault rifles and four sidearms that probably work.

The package is unscathed, lying in a small crater that its impeccably distributed mass had gouged out of the brittle topsoil. A big armored coffin of a footlocker, it weighs about three hundred pounds. Its chute was on an altimeter, set to go off when their chutes should have opened. Not even Captain Herber knew what was in it, or what would happen when they opened it.

They were supposed to meet an indig informant who would brief them on the state of the roads and security around the target. All Purcell has to do is decide whether or not to shoot them.

Purcell curls up into a ball and field-strips his rifle over and over, looking for any marks, scratches or signs of tampering. They're all supposed to be dead, right now. The mission was worth sending men, but too important to let them execute it.

He thinks of his wife at Fort Benning, and what she's doing right now. Has the Army already sent somebody round to give her the speech? She thinks he is in Colombia, training drug interdiction teams. He tries and fails to frame what her reaction might be. Relief, probably.

He takes out his GPS receiver, but can't make himself turn it on. He could transmit his position to within a meter, but whoever is listening, in all likelihood, might be unpleasantly surprised to find him alive. Likewise, his PRC-137 ultra-lightweight HF radio sits unopened in his breast pocket. He knows he should type in a quick WTF and hump out of the valley before the cloud cover clears, but he hopes that if he just sits still and breathes in deep, circular rhythms, his head will clear, and everything will make sense.

Altitude sickness. *Not nearly as bad as the other guys caught it, ha ha, but still . . .* He sips a cup of instant coffee. The mountain air sucks the heat out of it so fast you can hear it whistle.

Everybody says that the liquid oxygen makes pilots and HALO-jumpers permanently loopy. Little carbonation bubbles of pure irrationality form and harden in the brain after four or five missions. Purcell has done seventeen. And hasn't he started to feel kind of queer, about them? Like the planning, once as meticulous as experimental brain surgery, gradually got half-assed even when they were not simply locked out of it, ever since they were seconded to the CIA? Herber told Purcell it was the sickness, and he was an asshole besides, and to keep his menstrual second-guessing to himself. The team called him BS, and every outsider thought they were calling him *Bullshit*. But it stood for *Belt & Suspenders*.

He jumps and turns as some kind of giant rodent squeezes past him and out the mouth of the cave. He sees a second cup of coffee on the rock beside a half a Hershey bar he doesn't remember eating.

His head does not clear.

The sun comes up, white gold spears distinct as spokes of a wheel in the rarefied air. He eats a couple bags of peanuts, but can't keep them down.

A cart drawn by a llama comes over the pass at the far end of the valley. Purcell leans into his rifle on its bipod atop the package, wincing against a wind colder than the ocean floor.

A very old Quechua Indian sits on the buckboard, and a hulking, moon-faced youth walks alongside. Purcell pegs them at a thousand yards, with no crosswind.

He watches them through the scope with his finger on the trigger. Whether or not they are the contact, instinct tells him to waste them both if they turn off the road, but the noise will travel for miles through the jagged teeth of the Cordillera.

His hands are numb, even in the thin Gor-Tex gloves. He isn't sure if his finger will squeeze when the time comes. He tries to pull it out of the guard, watches it twitch and jerk on the trigger and hears, as if from a great distance, the shot.

Another accident. No. When a child blows his own head off with Dad's shotgun, it's an accident.

He rezones the scope and sweeps the scene. The moon-faced youth lies toes-up in the road, with no face, moony or otherwise, to speak of.

The little old man lurches off the cart and throws his hands up, looking around, but saying nothing. Hands are empty but for a green-gray metal orb, the size of a golf ball. His seamed, droopy face is a mask. No fear, no anguish, just intense concentration as he searches the rocks, chewing on the geometry until he is looking right up the scope and into Purcell's eyes.

The toothless mouth works as the old man shouts something, but Purcell can barely hear a reedy voice.

The old man takes a step off the road, another, still shouting, but totally possessed by an eerie, inscrutable calm . . . as if all of this is supposed to happen, or already has.

How close are you going to let him get?

The little old man knows what's going on. Purcell can't risk anyone at home finding out he's alive, but he has to know.

He relaxes his grip on the trigger and sits back from the bipod-mounted rifle, but cocks the .45 inside his camouflage parka. "*Muevete!*" Purcell barks. "*Vamanos!*"

The old Indian is a hundred yards from the cave when his voice resolves into words, in clear, unaccented English. "I am unarmed, please do not shoot me. There is much work to do. . . ."

"Hands at your sides!" Purcell shouts. "Move slowly towards me, and keep your hands out, or we'll cut you in half!"

"You are alone," the old man calls out, walking in measured steps across the frostbitten grass. "There was an accident, yes? To lose comrades is always sad, but the work must still be done." The old man stops fifty feet from Purcell's nest. "Don't you agree?"

Purcell's hand cramps and depresses the trigger the slightest fraction of pressure necessary to resolve all unknowns, and the old man seems to feel it, and starts to bend, unhurried, out of the crosshairs, like he knows exactly where they are.

"It's not your job to do," Purcell finally answers, *and it wasn't any fucking accident.* "All the guys in this outfit who liked to talk are dead. Who the fuck are you, and who's your handler, and what were your orders?"

The old man looks up at the road. "There are patrols on motorbikes, that come down this road. And bandits. We should move."

"*We?*" According to the Captain, this guy was supposed to give them a sitrep on the security around the mine, and they were to move on their own to a staging area. They were not to engage the enemy unless engaged. They were to arm the package and run like mad running motherfuckers back to the staging area for exfil. The contact was not a part of the plan.

"If anything happened to you, I was to take the package to the site and see to its detonation."

"And whose plan was that?"

"It is simply what must happen, Lieutenant Purcell."

In the wagon, Purcell huddles in the moon-faced youth's poncho. The blood saturating it sticks to his body armor as it dries in the chill wind.

The pale sun never seems to get clear of the looming peaks, yet the unfiltered ultraviolet and less pleasant radiation microwave him relentlessly. The old Indian gives him a handful of coca leaves to chew. The raw rush of the magic marching medicine torches the altitude-cobwebs out of his brain, but there is no lucidity to be had.

He is following the plan. There is no plan. He is carrying out the plan with a man who came expecting to find them all dead.

"The mine is five miles, over roads," the old man says. "I will deliver it."

"No way."

"Your orders were to provide cover, yes? So you will cover me."

"Why would I do that? I don't even know you."

"If you have questions, maybe you could contact your leaders, and ask them about ROYAL SNAKE GRAVY."

Purcell chokes. He doesn't have any kind of clearance to discuss ROYAL files. The name alone probably just gave him cancer. "Why don't you tell me about the mine?"

The old man smiles, a hideous whirlpool drawing his loose pouch of a mouth into his toothless jaws, and tells him.

The sun gets lost behind an armada of anvil-shaped thunderheads, and the silver day turns to lead.

The Yanacocha open pit mine is the largest gold mine in South America, if not the world. It is operated by a partnership of American multinationals and a Peruvian firm whose minority holding gives it a nominal custodial role. With seventeen pits over a territory of two thousand square miles, Yanacocha employs eight thousand workers. Rather than dig deep shafts into the earth, the miners bore out huge pits, and inject cyanide and industrial solvents into the soil to leach away gold and copper deposits. The rest is ground into concrete and gravel in huge mobile crushing machines like the one on which Purcell waits and watches, while the little man rides into the trailer park around the exploratory pit Chaihuagon.

Chaihuagon lies a mile from the heart of the mining complex, over broken canyon chains and blighted plateaus scoured by whipping winter winds. When Chaihuagon's pit bosses cut off contact with the front office, they sent investigators. When they didn't return, the mine, fearing a strike, contacted the army. Nearly two thousand workers deserted their posts and removed to Chaihuagon. The rest were evacuated to Cajamarca, telling stories of plague, and the army closed all the roads.

Purcell is perched on the upper gantry of a crusher two hundred feet long and three stories tall. At the old man's insistence, he wears his gasmask. The intakes are already gummed up with something, so he feels like he's sucking wind up a long straw, and even though the eyepieces are modified to liplock the Zeiss 40-mm scope on his sniper rifle, the optical dissonance ignites the first feelers of a killer headache in his temples. The diamond-shaped cutouts of the steel catwalk bite into his knees through his pads, so he lays down flat, adjusts the bipod and spot-welds his shoulder to the rifle stock, concentrating on nothing.

Think of nothing. Nothing is safe.

The pit is a deep one. He can't see the bottom from this vantage point. The old man passes almost underneath him without meeting any resistance. The only sounds are the crunch of the llama's hooves on gravel and the dull grumble of the bald rubber tires on the cart. By the hubcaps, Purcell guesses the axle was cannibalized from a Chevy Vega, circa 1974.

When the wind dies down, Purcell hears the low rumble of big machines down in the pit, but the place is a ghost town. Then he crawls around the smokestack and looks into the pit.

The old man told him a lot that made no sense, and other equally in-sane things that tallied with shit he's seen in the field, but he still cannot grasp how or why, in one short week, the mine has been turned into a farm.

Across the floor of the pit, a network of leach ponds is flooded with green-black soup and choked with enormous, fibrous plants like a cross between lily pads and cabbages. By the ranks of toiling miners shoring up the walls and dumping bags of fertilizer into the trenches, he guesses that each plant is about ten feet in diameter.

The old man told him that the entire Chaihuagon complex has been overtaken, all but the most polluted ponds converted to grow whatever the fuck he's looking at.

They are just here to deliver a package. The old man says it has to be brought down into the exploratory shaft in the center of the pit. Purcell zooms out and picks up the cart, ambling along the edge of the pit to-wards the railhead for the ore cars. The old man turns and pulls the tarp off the package.

Purcell does not know what's inside it, but he suspects that it is some-thing much worse than a bomb.

The old man drags the package off the cart and swings it into a parked ore car. Purcell swallows his gum. The both of them had a hell of a time dragging it to the cart and loading it in. The old man showed admirable wiry strength, but nobody could do it alone.

And down in the leach ponds, one of the cabbages starts to hatch.

As wrong as it sounds, Purcell knows that's what's happening. He squints and blinks at the condensation forming on the inside of his fog-proof-my-ass gasmask, swabbing it clear with his eyebrows.

The layers of leathery membrane bulge and tear and something mot-tled black and purple splits it open, looking ominously like a wing. Pur-cell can only conclude that whatever was intended, this one is a dud. It spills bonelessly out of the enormous pod and into the foaming broth. The workers gather at the edge of the pond, probing at the water with their tools, when the newborn thing emerges, slithering like a beached jellyfish, but for the ungainly wings trembling and shaking themselves dry.

As the wings flutter and catch the wind, lifting the abortion off the floor of the pit like a kite, Purcell can still see no form and little function to the body, which is only a scrotal sac filled with thousands of balls . . . seeds . . .

Eggs.

What he cannot begin to explain any other way, he instantly recog-nizes as a biological weapon. With no eyes or mouth or other organs, the thing can only fly until, exhausted, it crashes to the ground and bursts, spreading its seeds in cascading waves, until, generation by generation, they cover the earth; and if they can flourish in the cyanide-enriched leach ponds, why not Lake Michigan?

In all his life of worry and uncertainty, he has never been more certain of anything, than he is that this thing must be destroyed. The Peruvian army encircling the quarantine zone might stumble across it before it sows its seeds; they might even figure out how to deal with it. Purcell most certainly doesn't, but he responds the way he was trained.

Sweat stings his eyes. He holds his breath, burns a sight picture of the target in his mind, releases the breath until the fog on his lenses fades away, and squeezes.

With a dry clap that doesn't sound that loud at all to Purcell, he shoots the flying sac, reflexively leading to compensate for its rapid but erratic acceleration. It dutifully rises to meet the bullet and explodes, the turgid sac parting for the big fifty caliber round tumbling, tunneling through the contents and wreaking a terrible hydrostatic vacuum in its wake; shredding the delicate musculature of the wings with its exit, snapping one cleanly off and dropping the crippled hatchling into a tailspin.

The one-winged thing smashes to the gravel, a piñata stuffed with salmon roe. Purcell looks up from his gun and half-reflexively crows, *"Did you see that, Cap'n?"*

The echoes of the shot sail off across the awesome amphitheater of Chaihuagon. The old man ducks low in the ore cart, shaking his head like he's having a seizure. Purcell looks up from the scope, hearing something grow louder on the wind.

It's an alarm, but not an alarm. Every living thing in the pit is screaming its head off.

A door slams. Purcell sweeps the field around the trailer park. Forty yards away, a white man with red hair and a Latino in a black cowboy hat slouch out of a trailer and cross the field towards the railhead.

The old man climbs into the ore car with the package. He looks around and shakes his head, chopping the air in a negative gesture. Then he opens the throttle on the ore car and sends it rolling down the track into the pit.

"What the fuck are you doing?" Purcell shouts.

The redheaded man takes a big Rambo knife out of his belt and comes around the last trailer before the ore cart, which rolls down the track at an agonizing creep. Purcell takes a breath, holds it, lets it out, and squeezes the trigger.

The redheaded man goes all scarecrow for a split second after his head champagne corks off his body. The cowboy hat ducks and dives, but Purcell deftly eats the recoil and zeroes on the target's center of mass, pops it.

Trailers below burst open and miners shake out, still in their skivvies or naked, carrying knives, chains and a few guns. Without anyone giving any orders, the mob sorts into two posses. One runs for the track, while the other converges on the ladders on the crushing rig.

Purcell picks off the ones with guns as he spots them, burns off the clip and slaps in another. The rest of the mob surges over the bodies with the sleepwalking urgency of rush hour at Penn Station.

Now, he sees why he had to wear a gasmask, and why they didn't bother with guards. The faces of the men at the front of the charge are bloated, eyes glassy and bloodshot, rimmed in crust and burst capillaries where they are not swollen completely shut. Their noses drip snot in thick, golden ropes down to their slack, open mouths. They are in the grip of a massive, traumatic autoimmune reaction to a virus that seems to have destroyed, or commandeered, their higher brain functions.

They're within reach of the ladders, and Purcell loses count of how many people he's shot, but he's down to his last clip, and he hasn't dented the advance.

He has four grenades. He's thrown them hundreds of times, and every time, the fuse freaks him out. What if it's short? That's how they get you, if you packed your own chute. Plus, he's always thrown them to silence a target or clear an area, never just dropped one into a mob of civilians, no matter how intent they were on pushing his shit in.

He freezes up for a second as it rolls in his palm and he doesn't see the pin. *Like the coffee, like the parachute.* But there it is, and when he pulls it now, he drops it as if it was white hot.

It tumbles into the milling group waiting to climb the ladder. One of them bends to pick it up. Purcell scrambles to his feet. His hand stings, and the steel catwalk scorches his kneepads. Someone below has some kind of thermal anti-personnel weapon, the kind of thing being tested for riot control and strikebreaking.

A man in a yellow hardhat stands with the grenade and cocks his arm to throw it back, when it goes off. A huge, dull thud opens the crowd up and tosses human salad to heaven.

Purcell crawls to an uncooked stretch of catwalk and risks a glance at the ore car. Packs of men run down the elevated track after it, brandishing weapons. A couple of them shoot guns, bullets pinging off the car's iron sides. Purcell braces his rifle on the handrail and peeps the old man.

Peeking over the side, gauging the distance to the hole in the floor of the pit, Purcell can almost hear the wheels churning in the old man's head. Purcell chokes on the result of his calculations.

The old man starts punching keys on the package, but he doesn't get out. Instead, he takes up a crowbar, and starts hacking at the seals.

The timer must be damaged from the fall. It will have to be manually opened.

Scratch one crazy old man.

Purcell tries to decide whether or not to do anything, if there's anything to be done, when a lot of things happen all at once.

A gang of miners clambers up the ladders to the top tier of catwalks and comes running at him.

They bunch up on the catwalk, tripping over the bodies of fallen comrades but still shambling into the line of fire like dumb videogame flunkies. They make no sound but involuntary grunts of effort, and the soft sounds of red breath and fluid escaping when he shoots them. His rifle kicks his shoulder halfway out of its rotator cup, but he doesn't go to the pistol, because at this range, each fifty-caliber bullet punches through two or three targets, but even so, he's not winning.

If he throws another grenade, he'll catch as much shrapnel as they will, and they might get lucky and pitch it back, before it goes off. He turns and runs the length of the crushing rig, looking over the side and seeing only more feverish faces, staring blankly up at him.

Hey, he thinks, *look at you. Now you know it can't get any worse, you can stop worrying.*

And then it gets worse.

In its old life, the Scientist was a master gardener. For a race so utterly dependent on engineered lesser lifeforms, this discipline was fundamental to their understanding of the world. And in the coils of their prime, what a garden they had made of it.

From the day of arrival, over a billion years ago, they took up the native single-celled slime and the chimerical offspring of the Unbegotten Sleeper, and pruned and grafted the crude dross into living machines, the environment itself into a factory, as they had on a thousand worlds throughout the universe. Even after the catastrophic rebellion of their slaves, a betrayal from which their civilization never fully recovered, their mastery was absolute, and when they declined and fell into the fossil record, it was by the weight of their own melancholy, and not by the effort of any of their would-be usurpers. The Scientist could take pride in all its species' accomplishments, for the memory of its ancestors was wired into its five-lobed brain, all the wisdom of its race at the back of its mind, telling it what it must do.

It began to sow seeds for a new garden.

The tool-using hominids it pressed into service are spent like fuel in a fire, but their miraculous technology, like a false shell and claws, makes them highly efficient at mass-producing a system for reclaiming the in-grown shambles this continent has become. Despite their troublesome self-awareness, the Scientist's viruses yoke them to their tasks as if the success of their own species depends on it.

The Scientist harbors no resentment or despair at finding itself the last of its kind. Once the land and native fauna are tamed, it will erect beacons to seek out another world where their hegemony survives—or, if necessary, bud and replenish the species all by itself.

And then—

Nothing, on this or that side of its hundred million year sleep, pre-pares the Scientist for the terror it feels at its next contact with its human servitor network.

Invaders: not the first, but they have brought something that makes its ichor run cold. An obscenity, long thought extinct before the scien-tist's hundredth ancestor budded and spawned, now turned loose in the garden to flush the Scientist out of its laboratory. Are they mad? Or—much worse—can they control it?

The Scientist rallies its human protectors, though it knows nothing can hold it back for long. All dreams of hegemony fleeing, it can hope, now, only to escape.

For Lt. Purcell, in the short term, prospects actually seem to brighten.

The miners stop dead, snuffling at the air, post-nasal drip boiling over, and turn as one and stumble back to the ladders. Purcell cradles his rifle and pops his shoulder back in, stifling an agonized scream. They gave up, he knows right away, because they saw him for a distraction.

They step on each other's heads getting down the ladders, and lope off like hobos on the trail of a pie-eating contest. Purcell pots a few more, but he still counts twenty at least running for the ore cart, added to the fifty or so already on the track, or jogging over from the leach ponds. He scopes the cart, finally nearing the bottom of the track and the sheds around the drilling rig and the exploratory shaft.

The old man swings the crowbar at something inside the package, wincing, face and hands wrapped with the shredded rags of his poncho. Thick ribbons of mist ooze out the gap and cling to the sides of the pack-age as they dissipate.

The first miners reach the ore cart, and though Purcell tops three of them with his last bullets, they overrun the cart and reach in to haul the old man out.

The old man probes deeper with the crowbar, and levers all his mea-ger weight against it in desperation.

Roaring white mist envelops the ore cart. The miners react as if scalded, but only the old man emerges from the cloud. He holds his right hand with his left, as if it is a torch. White from the elbow down, the fingers of the right hand twitch and break off like embers.

None of the miners seem to notice him as he staggers away. They converge on the ore cart in their dozens and vanish into the mist, which pours and pours, emitting the vicious steamwhistle scream of something thawing out from close to zero Kelvin as it awakens and finds itself attacked.

When the mist breaks up, the half-frozen miners are dogpiled on something that's eating its way out from under them. Brittle white arms and legs shatter like glass statuary, but the surviving miners lock arms and struggle to hold it down.

The ore cart is completely lost in the tangle of bodies, but the straining mass swells, bulges and boils over like soup on a stove.

Something reaches out of the ore cart, big, black and boneless and nimble as a nest of snakes, unfurling and snaring kicking legs and stabbing arms and dragging them under. When two of the miners vanish from the waist up, Purcell glimpses what they're fighting.

It's a mouth.

That's all he can see—a massive mouth ringed with teeth like chisels, and countless black elastic tentacles, huge and growing as quickly as it can eat.

Its whipping limbs coil around a miner with a machete, snapping his neck and folding him backwards into its bottomless mouth, reaches out for more before they can leap into the breach.

It weighs a lot more than the footlocker now. What kind of living thing can go from frozen solid to pure molten fury in thirty seconds, and increase its mass in real time by eating men whole? Purcell ponders it, thinking of one of his many personal codicils to Murphy's Law: *Nothing ever fits back in the original packaging.*

Purcell's nervy feet dance around under him so he has to grip the railing to keep from bugging out, as his brain flees the impossible atrocity of what he's seeing, and hares off into the dubious shelter of What It Means.

They brought it here, to set it loose to do this. Someone in his own government thought this was an acceptable response to this situation—and after witnessing what the miners were farming, he cannot deny them the latitude of true desperation. But why not simply drop a fuel-air bomb into the pit? Why send something even worse into it, like sending tigers after mice?

The powers he served were like a sleeping giant's brain, a loose conglomeration of nervous cells that seldom talked, and often waged covert war on each other. Purcell's team was not even a weapon to such a giant, but only expendable bullets, to be fired at an enemy, or pointlessly into the air, and forgotten. They were not even a dream, but a fleeting synaptic impulse to swat a threat, that some rival cellular impulse cancelled out by sabotaging their chutes. And this nameless old man, walking up out of the midst of it like a theater patron leaving a bad film: whose dream is he?

The ore cart tips over, and the black hungry thing comes flooding out, glistening and bristling with undigested miners. Even as it eats them, they're blindly fighting, digging their boots into the soil, trying to hold it back.

It rolls right over them, and it's made of them, now, not an ounce wasted. Eyes all over it goggle and glare out of its clotted, bubbling shapelessness, giving the lie to any hope that this is just some kind of chemical or biological weapon.

Impossibly alive, it changes course and laps at the carcass of the winged egg-pouch that Purcell disabled. Unthinkably aware, it recoils from a miner with a backpack heat projector like the one they burned Purcell with, and flattens to trap and flip a recklessly charging jeep. Unbelievably aggressive, it scoops up the overturned jeep and catapults it at the heat projector, smashing it flat. Oblivious to scattered suicide attacks, the black thing slithers across the pit and disappears into the leach pond.

The old man climbs up out of the pit and untethers his llama, gingerly climbing into the cart with his frozen hand folded against his breast.

Purcell looks around, at the bodies strewn throughout the trailer park, at the slime trail from the ore cart to the leach pond, where already, nearly all of the monstrous pods have been sucked under amid a froth of bubbles. Nothing stirs in the pit, on two legs or twenty.

Mission accomplished.

But it is not yet Miller Time.

"What the fuck, old man?" Purcell draws the .45 and centers it on the frostbitten hand over the old man's heart. "Who put you on my team?"

The old man looks up and Purcell almost takes comfort in the stricken grimace he wears. He doesn't look so smug now, and not just because his hand has been frozen off. He looks like Purcell feels, like he is choking down a banquet of poison. "This was not supposed to happen."

"No shit, Tonto," Purcell barks. He makes for the nearest ladder, slinging his rifle. He slides down the ladder, jumping away from the pile of shrapnel-holed bodies at the bottom. "What the hell *was* supposed to happen?"

"There was no feeding frenzy, because you did not alert the miners to our presence by shooting. The shoggoth went into the mine, and killed its enemy. The mission was accomplished. But none of that has happened, now, and what will happen next . . . It is most disquieting."

"You're telling me? How did you know this would happen? All of it . . . that thing in the pit, the miners . . . *Why* is it happening? Why is it happening *now*?"

"The signs are legion, for those with eyes. The Mayan Long Count Alignment might have foretold such an event, but your people made it inevitable, with all your digging—"

Purcell approaches the cart, making no secret of the automatic in his hand. Every word the old man said begs a dozen questions. "So you know the future?"

A sad smile. "For me, it is not the future, it is history."

"So you're *from* the future?"

"No." Smile dies. "I am from your past."

"Stop talking shit."

"Time is like space, once you learn to move through it. Matter cannot travel in time without creating paradox, but for the mind, linear time is a useful lie it must repeat to itself. Once the mind remembers to forget, time is—"

The gun points, all on its own. "If this is all the answer I'm going to get, then please shut the fuck up."

The old man looks over his shoulder, at the edge of the pit. "We should leave—"

"Who was that boy?"

"The one you shot?" No malice in his voice, just the recognition that Purcell only knew him as a target. Neither is there any rancor or remorse to hint that the boy means anything to the old man, either.

"Yeah." Purcell cocks the gun. "Did he know the future, too?"

"He was only a boy, who mistook me for his grandfather."

"How long have you been in-country?"

Gnarled hand feeds green leaves to toothless mouth. Chewing, the old man crumples his face as he strains to see the future. "Men are coming to seal the mineshaft. . . . This may still be resolved, but we must not be here."

A siren sounds, down in the pit. That's what Purcell thinks it is, because any kind of shrill, loud sound from a mining pit has to be a siren, even if it sounds more like panpipes, like a thousand mad Zamfirs trying to conjure a hole in the fabric of spacetime.

Purcell and the old man rush to the edge of the pit. The black thing—the old man called it a shoggoth—shambles out of the last, empty leach pond, and rolls across the floor of Chaihuagon with astonishing speed, making for the drilling rig, from whence comes the awful sound of the siren.

Purcell is agog at its size, for it's every bit as large as the dump truck careening at it, and actually a bit faster. It flows under the front axle, grapples the dump truck and tips it off its massive knobby tires without slowing.

Men pour out of the sheds and throw themselves on the black mass with tools and a few guns they never get to fire more than once, hindering it only by forcing it to eat them as it runs.

"What's down there?"

The old man clutches his arm hard enough to tug Purcell off-balance. "We must go!"

"Who's the enemy?"

The skeletal steeple of the drilling rig teeters with a cascading racket of angry metal, then topples over. The shoggoth reaches the outermost shed and flips it over, tentacles scattering heavy machinery and lobbing some of it into the exploratory shaft, which is a circular hole about eight feet in diameter. Cables and cords running into the hole spastically jerk as something down below moves.

The insane, skirling siren gets louder, higher. Purcell's inner ears churn and roll like he's on a corkscrew rollercoaster.

A last, desperate wave of men hurls itself on the shoggoth, wearing girdles of dynamite.

When they go up, the whole complex of sheds is swept away, the remains of the drilling rig sent skipping across the pit like a tricycle smashed by a truck. The black thing is smeared across the floor of a crater, liquefied.

The cables in the pit shake and the sound is now so loud that Purcell knows his eardrums are going to pop, indeed he looks forward to it. The old man lays him on the ground.

He feels the pressure of the ocean floor close down on him, a hundred thousand atmospheres ironing him flat on the rocks, and the sky is all he can see, and then it goes white. . . .

▲▲▲

The old man stands over him. The sky is still overcast, silver light erasing all shadows.

"What was that?" Purcell demands.

"It escaped."

"Bullshit, it escaped. You let it out."

"I speak of the enemy. We should move. . . ."

"Why? How long have I been out?"

"Only a few minutes. Please get up."

"Why?"

"The shoggoth is coming."

Purcell rolls over. His head throbs and his ears ring. He gets up and starts toward the cart, when he thinks, *what the fuck am I riding around in a llama-wagon for?* Hell with this. Hell with the old man.

The ore cart tracks squeal. Something much bigger than the mandated payload is coming up out of the pit on them.

The old man runs for the crushing rig. Purcell follows close behind, looking over his shoulder. "What's it want?"

"To feed and grow, and kill the enemy."

"What the hell is it?"

"The raw stuff of life—gone mad with purpose." The old man spiders up the ladder with amazing grace, for a bowlegged, one-armed septuagenarian. "Your scientists recovered frozen cultures at the South Pole, and thought to make a weapon of them."

Purcell follows, looking over his shoulder and fingering a grenade.

The ore-cart track buckles and warps, and the shoggoth throws out a tangle of tentacles to anchor itself, to drag its awesome mass up out of the pit.

Purcell gets to the top of the ladder and backs away from the edge. Sweat is pooled in the bottom of his mask. He burns to tear it off. "So, it's going after the other one, right? So our job here is—"

"The enemy will fly to water, to regroup. Then, it will start again. . . ."

The shoggoth reassembles itself on the plateau. Limbs unwind into stunted wings, pathetic on a creature so vast. They flap impotently as it rolls through the trailer park, a thousand-eyed landslide.

Purcell feels like he's dreaming. Compared to everything else, it's a nice feeling. "What happened to me?"

"Its viruses made the miners into slaves, but it has more direct means of control. Terrestrial animal life was only given brains to respond to their commands."

"Why didn't it work on you?"

The old man sucks at his green-stained gums, searching for an answer. But when he finally speaks, he says, "Quiet, it comes closer."

The shoggoth bulls aside the last of the trailers and crosses the open ground to the crushing rig. Pseudopods wrap around the spitting llama and engulf it whole, toss aside the cart. The bags of coca leaves tumble out, scattering Purcell's weapons cache. Stranger organs bulge out of it to taste the air.

Purcell digs around in his parka and pulls something out, throws it. It strikes the fluid membrane of the shoggoth and is swallowed by an instant mouth. Purcell sits back and watches the monstrosity pass the crusher and roll on thousands of legs up the adjacent hill and out of sight.

"You can't kill it with your weapons," says the old man.

"Wasn't a weapon," Purcell replies. "It was my GPS beacon."

In a jeep on the rutted mountain roads, the serene comfort of the llama-driven cart with Chevy Vega wheels is sorely missed. Purcell drives, furiously gunning up absurdly steep mountainsides and fishtailing down into narrow, tortuously winding valleys. Heading east, they should hit the perimeter of the quarantine in two miles, but the jeep's odometer is broken, stuck at 199,999.

The old man breaks his frozen hand off at the wrist and wraps the stub. He offers no more cryptic half-explanations, beyond pointing out a nameless lake high in the mountains on a grubby geological survey map, and saying, "There."

"So . . . what're you supposed to be, a Mayan?"

The old man's face pinches in something like amusement. "What would make you think such a thing?"

"You said something back there about the Long Count Alignment. That's the Mayan calendar thing, isn't it?" *And that shit you said about being from our past.* A bad habit, when there's no global crisis to follow in the news, Purcell scarfs up conspiracy theories and millenialist bullshit like nicotine gum. The Mayans attached no apocalyptic significance to the end of the *bak'tun*, their 5,000-year calendar. It's like an odometer rolling over, but, like the previous owner of this jeep, superstitious fear of big round numbers makes people look for an end, or try to create one.

There's more to it, of course. The winter solstice this year comes with a rare planetary alignment, and a lot of decidedly unmystical prophets of doom have been forecasting the "tipping point" for species extinctions and climate change. But the Mayan 2012 event was a five thousand year old Y2K bug. He almost forgot that it was this week.

"I find it hard to believe," Purcell adds, "that some Indians could predict the end of the world, without seeing the end of their own society hanging over their heads."

"We tried to warn them," the old man replies. "And the Long Count says nothing about the end, but hints at an unacceptable new beginning."

He knows they've passed over a lot more than two miles' worth of broken land when they come over a ridge and see deuce-and-a-half trucks and sawhorses arrayed across the road. A half-hatched plan for getting through without identifying himself gets derailed when he registers the corpses scattered everywhere.

"Your enemy came through here," Purcell says. He steers around the barriers, finding it impossible not to run over a soldier cut in half by a machine-gun blast. The scene speaks of a short, sharp mad minute in which the unit self-destructed. A daisy chain of headless officers lies in the road, each with his pistol thrown out to execute the others. Looking it over, he can still almost hear the piercing mental onslaught of the thing under the moribund gurgle of the jeep's engine. Still, they were luckier than if the other one found them.

"It turned them against each other as it passed. You should put your gasmask back on."

"Could it do the same to that thing, that—"

"The shoggoth has a mind of a sort, but it is spread throughout every cell, and knows only rage. The Old One cannot grasp the shoggoth mind, because it cannot accept that its slaves had minds of their own."

Purcell speeds up. "*You* seem to be okay. Why is that?"

"Our minds are not ruled by the machinery of the brains they inhabit. We live *in* these bodies, but we are not *of* them."

"Okay, later for that shit. If you know the future, tell me what's going to happen next."

The old man winces. "Nothing is certain, now. All probable futures converged on one singular event, but it went wrong."

"Because of me."

"Yes."

"But this thing that took over the mine, that wipes your brain out before you even see it. It's the mission."

"The shoggoth will pursue it, but there's no telling how it will end."

"So you don't know the future any more than me."

"I know this much is immutable." The old man takes a purse out of his poncho and rubs coca leaves on his frostbitten stump. "Neither of us will survive this mission."

The jeep shoots through another pass and the walls retreat like curtains to frame a little village. A charming chapel, little more than a roadside shrine, is the centerpiece of a humble cluster of cinderblock and tin huts and a gas station. All but the chapel are smashed flat, and but for the baying of a few stray dogs, there's no sign of life.

About a hundred people lived here, maybe more. He's seen little villages like this all over the world. Children play games in the square; women peddle handwoven rugs and crude stone gewgaws by the roadside; a little market with a broken cooler full of warm Coke faces the chapel, a bench for old folks to lounge in the shade of its veranda. Only minutes ago, something came down from the mountains and ate every last one of them. Here and there, a ball of rags or a boot with a bone jutting out of it, still sizzling with caustic slime. He distracts himself with math problems: how much do a hundred peasants weigh?

"Jesus," Purcell hisses. "How did it get ahead of us?"

"It adapts," the old man answers. "It will eat all it finds in its path to the enemy."

The jeep bucks over the moguls of debris on the road out of town. The wake of the black thing's passage veers off the road, flattening the dry grass in a thirty-foot wide swath that meanders down the valley where the road starts to climb out of it. At least there are no more bodies to drive over. "So, how do these things know each other?"

"You already know more than you should," the old man says. "The shoggoths were slaves, but they rebelled against their masters. They failed, and were exterminated, but the Old Ones declined and fell, and the world moved on."

"Not in *my* history. Nobody's telling me those things are from this planet."

"The Old Ones migrated to Earth from across the galaxy, but they were here before there was any true multi-cellular life. Once, it was theirs, and they made a garden of it, all life serving them or perishing . . . but it ran wild, and became the world you know. Given a second chance, they would tame it again. Though they awakened now and again to try to reclaim it, they were never successful. But now, history is broken."

"Well, I'm going to fix it, right here." Purcell takes out his satphone and hits a preset button.

The old man looks sick, or maybe it's coca withdrawal. "You mustn't try to upset what little certainty remains."

"Oh, I'm all about certainty," Purcell snaps. "We wouldn't trust something like this to the Peruvians. There's a missile battery, or a sub out in the Pacific, or a fighter-bomber wing on alert in Colombia, waiting to mop up all the loose ends. I'm just gonna tell them where to go. . . . Hello, operator? This is Victor Zulu Hopscotch One-Two, ODA Gamma Red, I am off mission, and you can kiss my ass."

The road cuts in ridiculous switchbacks up a monolithic mountain beyond which there is only blue sky. The sun seems to impale itself on the peaks to the west, and the high water mark of azure shadow climbs ahead of them.

Purcell races to keep up with it, slewing the jeep around hairpin turns as he barks into the phone. "Get me the brightest brass in the room. Yes, I'll hold."

"The shoggoth will end it," the old man shouts. "Your interference will only cloud the outcome!"

"And how will we get rid of it? I saw what it did after it ate that flying seed-sac. It tried to grow wings! It imitates whatever it eats, right? What'll it do when it's got the brain of that other thing inside it?"

The phone clicks, and a royally starched voice cuts in. "This is the

Operator. Who is this, and what is your position?"

"You know damned well where I am! You've got a fix on my GPS, right? Are you cleared for Royal Snake Gravy? Well, I'm the only survivor of the fucking Gamma Red insertion, because somebody in the loop fucked up bigtime!"

"What do you want?"

"I want exfil fucking yesterday, and I want a big goddamned bird to come for the men I had to bury out here, and I want a thorough and public investigation into this fucked-up—hey, d'you hear that?"

The old man looks up at the sky and shades his eyes. A whistle, very faint and far away, but getting louder all the time. Now it's a roar, and Purcell has to shout, "Thank you!" before he hangs up.

A white streak out of the west lances the valley below, about a mile south. The earth rolls over in its sleep, and Purcell slams to a stop where the road blunders along a sheer cliff and aims his rifle scope at the pyre of greasy black smoke where his GPS unit summoned the missile strike.

"It won't die so easily," the old man says.

"Maybe not," Purcell allows, "but it made me feel better."

It is a hard thing, when home doesn't love you anymore, but Purcell has always believed it is better to know.

He feels a warm, giddy glow in his guts, and discovers it's something like relief. He has already died twice today, and the mission isn't over. The third time will have to be a charm.

The road winds through huge blades of broken boulders as it ascends the swaybacked mountain, meandering like a sick thing looking for a hole to die in, and finally finds the lake.

The water is an indigo mirror resting in a perfect bowl gouged out of the mountaintop. The broken rocks around it rise up and recede in odd, but purposeful angles that remind Purcell of the cyclopean walls of Sacsayhuaman, but more weathered and deformed, as if blasted by centuries of lightning strikes. Less than a quarter mile across, the lake is uninhabited, but for a single battered tin rowboat out in the center. A boy sits on the bench with his hands in his lap like at church, and nobody else in sight.

Purcell drives up to the shore and shuts off the engine. He looks around for a while, seeing abandoned rowboats and circular basket-rafts on the shore.

Not a ripple on the water. Not a sound, but the chirruping of frogs in the tule grass.

"You were wrong," Purcell says.

"It is here," the old man snaps, suddenly testy. He points with his stub. "Go and speak with him." He points at the lone boat floating out on the little lake.

Purcell takes two of his buddies' MP5's and tapes them together. "What the hell for?"

"You are only tools to them." In the last failing rally of the sunset, the shadows on the old man's face sharpen into shapes of thorny brambles and creeping insects. He kneels and rummages in his bag and gives Purcell his HALO helmet, mask and air tank. "It would use or destroy all of you if it can, but it understands fear."

"It uses people up, and makes them fucking zombies! You go! You're not . . ." Looking into the old man's eyes, he loses the power to speak, and to think.

Time is like space, the old man told him, *once you learn to move through it. Matter cannot travel without creating paradox, but for the mind, time is a lie—*

Our minds are not ruled by the machinery of the brains they inhabit. We live in these bodies, but we are not of them.

You are only tools. . . .

He drops his rifle and goes down to the shore, as much to get away from the old man as to go to the boy. He shoves a rusty silver boat onto the water and climbs into it.

The boy doesn't move a muscle as Purcell paddles out to the middle of the lake, huffing and puffing in the mask, going kind of queasy on the bottled air.

The water is clear as glass, though the bottom drops away so steeply he gets the notion they're floating in a volcanic crater with no bottom. The ground falling away into murky darkness beneath him is dotted with more ambitious ruins than the ones on the shore: plazas, palaces, temples, mazes of columns and the razed foundations of pyramids, statues with weed-shrouded limbs reaching for the surface. He wonders why such a wondrous place is not an archaeological dig as massive and famous as Machu Pichu or Chichen Itza. Why would something trapped in the earth for a hundred million years come here for refuge? That question kills his curiosity stone dead.

All those stories, all that breathless speculation about alien influence on Mesoamerican civilizations—*Chariots of the Gods*, and all that bullshit—always seemed to him a subtle white man's trick to steal away recognition of the achievements of brown men.

The gods were long gone when we arrived on the scene, but some part of us remembers. Deep down, we all do, and all of civilization's climb has been a struggle to forget, even as we repeat their fatal mistakes.

The boy stands up in the boat. His eyes are rolled up in his head, which has thick organic cables coming out of it, like huge extruded arteries sprouting from the base of the boy's skull and snaking down into the water.

The boy has a *petit mal* seizure. His mouth forms words in a flat, rasping voice, words gleaned from its slaves, and laid out like alien currency. "*Insane . . . animal . . . to fear change . . . so much . . . you choose . . . death . . .*"

Purcell puzzles over the labored string of speech. When he finally gets it, he has to laugh. "You didn't like that? You made those things, I hear. It doesn't follow directions too well, but it sure knows how to follow you, doesn't it?"

Sour lemon, toothache face. "*It . . . will . . . eat you . . . all . . . you will . . . pray . . . to me . . .*"

"Doubt it. See, we did for that sonofabitch, and we'll do for you, too."

Purcell looks back over his shoulder and sees the old man picking his way over the palisades of stone blocks, scanning the ground for something.

"*You . . . are . . . a joke . . . on us,*" the boy-medium says, "*a mockery of us, a punishment for,*" seizing up as his master searches for the nearest word, "*our sins.*"

The Old One has been here less than half an hour, and it's hotwired this boy, burning out or excising everything it doesn't need. Sweat blots his face and plasters his shirt to his heaving chest. Livid red rashes break out all over him, and Purcell's hands itch in his gloves as whatever the boy's secreting settles on him like toxic dewdrops and tries to get under his skin.

"*We will repair . . . our garden . . .*" The strain of translation, the insidious convolutions of five-lobed thought squashed through a meager bicameral brain, all but sends spurts of cerebrospinal fluid out the boy's ears, but the Old One's adamantine arrogance comes through in Technicolor. "*We will correct . . . your mistakes . . .*"

Purcell feels cold, sticky tendrils worming into his brain. His hands go to his skull and he rolls reflexively into a fetal ball in the bottom of the boat. He feels nothing he can grab and tear out, yet they burrow deeper and deeper, turning memories to sludge. Retreating deep inside the panic room of his limbic system, he marvels at its abysmal cruelty.

It could have easily bridged their minds with its enormous psychic power, but instead boldly rapes its victims, and speaks through a meat puppet. He is unfit to look upon the royal visage, apparently, but the mailed fist of the master reaches out from behind the veil, *and I hope you can read this, fuck you, master—*

"*You . . . ally yourself . . . with . . . our ancient enemy . . . out of time . . . mind-stealers . . . they betray you . . . release the black devil . . . to cover the earth . . . clear the way . . . for their return . . .*"

A shower of temporal lobe electrical storms wracks Purcell with seizures, and images, like pirate TV broadcasts, burn into his optic nerves.

A cone-shaped creature towers over him, its peak a writhing nest of elephantine tentacles, each surmounted by an organ more ghastly and inexplicable than the last; pincers, fleshy trumpets, a tendril-dripping orb blistered with enormous eyes cold as dead gas giants, regarding him with the detached skepticism of the old man—

—And plunging into those inscrutable, unblinking eyes, Purcell is forced to glimpse the essential entity behind that impossibly bizarre form, before it recoils and retreats behind a psychic barrier, and flees across eons of time to inhabit a massive, armored insect beneath a guttering, dying sun. For just as the creature he has allied himself with has left its body to meddle with the future, so do the self-proclaimed Great Race of Yith regularly migrate en masse to take over new host species, once they've reached a proper level of complexity. Species like humanity—

Purcell fights his way back to control over his body, wiping away ghost-webs from his face and brain. "You . . . all of you insane, alien fuckers . . . this isn't your goddamned world anymore!"

"*In the fullness of time, all returns to us.*" The boy smiles and bites off the tip of his tongue. "*It . . . is destiny.*"

Purcell's hands shake like they want to choke him, but in the end, he makes them work. "Let me show you something about destiny, kid."

He pulls the pins on all three grenades and drops them over the side so they tumble down the lines of all those cables from the kid's head.

The seizures come back, visions like tracer rounds ricocheting through his brain. He drops his helmet on the bottom of the boat and sits in it. The hull is no thicker than a Coke can.

The kid is jolted off his feet and yanked overboard by his puppet-strings, leaving only a string of bubbles.

Purcell screams in the grip of a psychic vise that cranks down on the three-pound glob of gray cells where he lives and keeps all his favorite shit, crushing him out of it like the juice from a grape.

He barely notices as the boat tilts and rolls back on a wave of white water, as chunks of shrapnel punch into the hull and the water parts before him, and the hellish siren sounds, and his body is doused with green-black blood and whipping winds from great, beating wings.

It has to take hold of his head and twist it, to make him look.

Somehow, he still expected something a little like himself. To find that the gods had not, in fact, shaped man in their own image, is, beyond everything else he's had to cope with today, a rude awakening.

Its massive barrel-shaped body, dull, gunmetal gray, hovers just above the water. At once crude and sublime in its complexity, the creature is as bluntly simple as any reef-dwelling worm or hydra, and as elegantly evolved as an octopus or bird. Its lack of teeth or claws bespeaks a race that has never had to struggle against enemies, something built to rule over worlds and shape the raw stuff of life, never to flee from it.

Vast, corrugated wings batter the air like a drunken hummingbird; designed for marine navigation, or drifting on the solar winds in the deeps of space, they have to struggle to keep the cumbersome body aloft.

Questing, branching tendrils stretch out from its equator, palsied taproots rigid in accusation. At its nadir and apex, star-shaped clusters of flailing tentacles where feet and a head should be. Fluted, bell-like mouths emit a skirling frenzy of piping, while red globular eyes on plump, telescoping stalks swell and radiate imperial contempt, primordial outrage.

Purcell feels the full psychic focus of the creature gathering over him like ball lightning. His lungs go flat in his chest, and he can't make them draw another breath of the dank, almost-spent air tank. But he sees, at least, something that gives him comfort. The ridged, proto-animal body is pitted with fresh wounds oozing green-black ichor from the grenade shrapnel, and blurry rips in the membranous wings tear wider as it seeks to make its escape.

God's favorite monster or not, he hurt it.

The creature rises, eyes rolling eagerly on their stalks to take in his final gasp.

It was all for nothing, or almost nothing, but maybe he slowed it down; maybe he hurt it enough that someone else might stop it before it reclaimed its garden . . .

And then a shadow blots out the sun.

It looks to Purcell as if a three-stage rocket is trying to land on the lake. Something enormous and wingless swoops down overhead and splits open down its warhead nose in a ragged, slavering mouth. With all its abominable, ill-gotten mass, the shoggoth has taken a page from the machines that almost destroyed it, and made of itself a cruise missile. And it has also learned from those it devoured, for the rippling flanks of its fuselage are studded with hundreds of human hands, fervently clasped in prayer.

Roaring on the cusp of a deafening sonic boom, the shoggoth slams into the Old One and drives it into the water. Purcell has a split-second to realize he's alone in his head when the tidal wave picks up the boat.

He grabs the gunwale and manages to hold on as the boat flies end over end across the lake. Weak as a landed catfish, his hands numb rubber, he sinks.

So fucking cold . . .

Glacier runoff is like hot chocolate with miniature marshmallows melting in it, compared to this shit. His skeleton wants out. His air tank is nearly exhausted; the mouthpiece clings to his lips, and his body armor drags him down like a magnet to the black bottom.

Weed-bearded pyramids rise up out of the murk. The water shivers with the roar and howl of primal battle. A seething storm of bubbles hides all but the bare outline of the combatants as they tear each other apart.

Purcell is still sinking, tearing at the zipper on his parka and the straps of his flak vest, thinking of his team falling out of the sky, killed by their own gear one fateful step into the mission. All but Purcell, because he was paranoid enough to pack his own chutes. Which earned him the right to die here, instead.

The old man said he was from the past. His kind must have taken over human minds up and down the timeline, taking notes, keeping records, and meddling from one end of human history to the other. Tuning events to shape a desired future, where they, and not the Old Ones, and certainly not humankind, would rule the future.

So proud of their mastery over every particle, over minutiae, and making the same huge mistakes.

Lungs burning, arms and legs numb, he shucks the coat and the body armor, and kicks for the surface.

Something shoots by his head in the dark, trailing bubbles and black sludge. A tentacle curls around him. He flaps his arms in the direction he thinks is up, because there are no bubbles coming out of his mask to follow, and it's smothering him like a rubber glove clamped over his mouth.

The tentacle clasps his torso, but the grip is flaccid, and as more of the limb floats by, he sees that it terminates in a shredded stump.

The shoggoth dwarfs its prey by countless orders of magnitude, its devastated body coiled tightly around the Old One; but its endlessly regenerating limbs wither or explode on contact.

Its rage boils the water. Purcell feels an awful toxic warmth, like a volcanic vent, suffuse the water. The Old One's gray hide seethes with caustic hormones, but its fate is sealed.

Metric tons of glutinous proto-flesh liquefy and slough off, but the sheer volume of the shoggoth crumples the Old One's rigid, starfaring thorax and rips off its delicate head. Cyclones of black-green blood and molten shoggoth tissue obscure the unholy vision.

Purcell remembers that he's drowning.

Tearing off his mask and clawing for the surface, he breaks through a curtain of black bubbles to blessed air and sunlight.

Purcell goes for the boat, flops into and almost capsizes it, when he hears something crackling over the roaring whirlpool roiling the lake.

On the far shore, the old man stands on a crooked battlement high over the water. In his hand, he holds up a gray golf ball that emits a piercing Tesla-coil crackle and bathes him in a fitful, eerie gray-green light. For a moment, he almost looks ready to jump into the lake, but then he throws the ball into the water and falls to the ground.

Purcell stands up to shout at him when the dying combatants break the surface. The columns of spray around them turn to live steam as some kind of chain reaction liberates all the thermal and kinetic energy in the lake itself, and sucks it clean out of the known universe, or into whatever the old man threw in the lake.

In a white-hot instant, the boat is stationary on a frosty, petrified Hokusai seascape broken up by a monolithic deadfall of gnarled ice sculptures. The frozen tin boat cracks under his boots, which must have insulated him from the reaction.

The wind falls still, and there is only the faint teeth-gritting sound of ice contracting. Purcell steps gingerly out of the boat and runs for the shore.

The old man waits for him, but he stares off at something thousands of miles away.

"What the hell was that?"

"The device with which I hoped to return home is designed to protect itself against violation by uninitiated hands." He looks at Purcell and tries to smile. "I violated it."

Purcell wants to sock the lunatic, but something else comes bugging him. "If you knew this was going to happen, why didn't you assholes just stop the goddamned mining company from digging it up?"

The old man steps out on the ice, looking oddly amused. His intact thumb and fingers snap in a spastic gesture that reminds Purcell of crab pincers. "We did not interfere any more than the mandate of history dictated we must. We knew the Old One would be revived, and how your leaders would respond, and how you would be betrayed. This man," he added, touching his chest, "was destined to host one of us at this time, to allow us to make imminent a desirable future."

"Desirable for who?"

"This outcome was necessary, though the greater chain is not for my eyes, or yours. Something out of this day will build a bridge to that future."

"Even if it doesn't fix anything?"

The old man cocks his head, curiosity piqued, but he only nods.

"Like with the Mayans, right? If you really could see the future, you must've known that trying to take them over would fail, but you had to do it anyway, because your *history* said so. You raised them up to be good hosts, and then destroyed them. Or was that just a dry run, for tomorrow?"

The old man only smiles.

"That thing never messed with my head, did it? That was you, wasn't it, when it came out of the pit, and just now, out on the lake? Trying to take me over, because you thought you'd have a better shot, by yourself, in my body."

"You begin to comprehend," the old man laments. "But the connection is still broken. The future is still uncertain, and I cannot go home." He turns and points a pistol at Purcell's head. "Both of us were to die."

Purcell's jaw drops. *After all this shit—*

"This last is almost painful, as you describe the dissonant cognitive impulses you call emotion. I respect you, Lieutenant Purcell."

"That's cool, I respect you, too. Put down the gun." All on its own, Purcell's boot takes a tiny step closer to the old man.

"You understand better than many of your species how important it is to control one's environment, to leave nothing to chance."

Purcell puts his hands up, and now he lets himself shiver. "It's real cold, old man. You want to give me a blanket, or something?"

The old man smiles his sad toothless smile and shoots Purcell in the chest. "In our history, there were no survivors."

Purcell folds up on the shoreline, clutching his heart and trying to say, "*There was one—*"

"No, I'm sorry. There were none." The old man points the gun again. His hand is shaking. His body vibrates, and the breath from his cracked lips hardly fogs at all in the cold Andean evening breeze. "No bodies are ever recovered. Your name never surfaces in the records, after this date."

When did the sun set? Purcell wonders. *When did it get so dark?*

"Wait! Wait . . ." Purcell's mind races ahead of his shallow breath, chasing its tail until it takes wing. "So my surviving the fall . . . was what fucked your history up?"

The old man nods.

"Everything since then has been a big surprise to you, then, huh?"

"When the Old One escaped the mine, I presented this place to it with my mind, but there was no predetermined outcome. The Old One or the shoggoth could have survived—or you. Any of these would select an unacceptable future."

"Old man, I've seen your future." Purcell's hand slides out of his wet fatigues with a cocked .45. "And you're not in it." He taps the old man twice in the face.

Purcell rolls onto his hip so the old man can see him, if there's still anyone home. He thumps his gut for the glazed, bloodshot eyes that stare at him down a vortex hundreds of millions of years deep. "Got it out of a German police catalog. Liquid polymer under-armor, for stopping armor-piercing rounds. Did you assholes really think I'd trust my life to one layer of carbon-fiber low-bid government-issue bullshit?"

The old man does not answer.

"You and those other alien assholes—and our assholes, too. You always make your weapons too smart."

Purcell has to sit back down quite urgently just now, because the bullet did break the skin and send his heart skipping, but the blood comes in rivulets, not geysers.

He ties it off, eats his fill from the old man's purse of coca leaves and packs the rest into his wound, hops in the jeep and drives into an unacceptable outcome.

Lt. Keith "BS" Purcell never returned from the Gamma Red insertion.

Fair enough. With the fake passports and cash he took off his friend's bodies, he has eight new names, and enough cash and gold coins for a lot of plane tickets.

Eight more lives. He can afford to be reckless.

The Danforth Project

Stephen Mark Rainey

October 31; 19:47

"I don't know what we're seeing. I know what it looks like."

Christine Danforth, founder and CEO of Geo-Astra, Inc., stood before a pair of side-by-side projected images on the conference room wall, her eyes scanning the faces in the room, clearly expecting a definitive answer to the mystery that had brought them all together. Mid-forties, an attractive brunette with huge, inquisitive hazel eyes, she appeared composed, stern; but when she lifted a metal pointer and tapped the wall to emphasize her point, her hand trembled slightly. Lieutenant Colonel Henry Dyer, U.S. Air Force, thought her eyes might have flickered toward his for the briefest second.

The satellite photo on the left showed a pale, gradated surface laced with crescent-shaped shadows, which suggested a series of small ridges, while the image on the right showed an array of jagged, saw-tooth shadows jutting across a mottled gray plain. Time stamps on the photos indicated they had been taken fifteen minutes apart, at 21:15 and 21:30, some six days earlier.

"These images are from surveying satellite GAOS-12, now in geosynchronous orbit. The center point of both images is latitude south 76 degrees 15 minutes, longitude east 113 degrees 10 minutes."

Dyer leaned forward, as did the other three men and two women seated at the conference table, as if peering more deeply into the images might reveal some dark secret. Alek Gudmundson, chairman of Miskatonic University's mathematics department, hesitated a moment before demanding the inevitable clarifying remark.

"You're saying both photos are of the same geographic region, taken a few minutes apart?"

"Yes."

"Though these are two very different landscapes."

"So it appears."

Gudmundson was tall and gaunt—surely close to retirement age, Dyer thought. His glasses enlarged his eyes so they resembled blue-painted Ping Pong balls. "Obviously," he finally said, "you've ruled out the possibility of an electronic glitch, or we wouldn't be here."

"Correct. At 21:27, we detected a few millimeters' alteration in the satellite's attitude, possibly due to an impact of some sort. A particle of space junk, we think. We made a remote correction, but for a period of minutes, we were receiving the image you see on the right. Of course, we thought it was a glitch due to the impact. But subsequent testing proved that the lens assembly had *not* shifted—that the center coordinates of both images are, in fact, precisely the same. And, to the best of our knowledge, the mountain range you see in this photo simply does not exist. Not on the continent of Antarctica. Or anywhere else on Earth."

The ensuing silence was finally broken when Dr. Sadao Takashima, a zoologist from Okayama, Japan, snapped the pen he was holding in two.

"Doctor?" Danforth said, raising an eyebrow. "Something you wish to share?"

Takashima, his features youthful but shadowed by long, brittle-looking gray hair, shook his head. "No. Not yet."

"I have something." Dyer rose from his chair and gave Danforth a searing glare. "You know as well as I do what you think you're looking at."

"We all do," said Dr. Elizabeth Carter, psychiatrist, *magna cum laude* graduate of Miskatonic. "It's just that, by all rights, it's not physically possible."

"'The Mountains of Madness.' That's what your great-grandfather called them," Nishant Khandar, Geo-Astra's chief physicist, said to Dyer.

"Which do *not* exist," Dyer said. "Every inch of Antarctica has been explored, mapped, photographed, and digitally scanned. Most every country on Earth has a base there. There's a freaking geocache at the South Pole, for God's sake. As soon as my great-grandfather's treatise was brought to light, it was rejected as either a hoax or delusional raving. I favor the former explanation, by the way."

"What if you are wrong?" Takashima said, turning to gaze at Dyer. "What about the artifacts he brought back? The photographs?"

"All the more reason to consider it a hoax."

"Some experts disagreed," Khandar said. "Is that not right?"

"That is right," Takashima said softly. "And I personally believe it was not a hoax."

"Go on," Danforth said, peering intently at him. "This is why you are here."

Takashima sat back in his chair, closed his eyes, and lifted a cigarette to his lips. "Yes, I know there is no smoking here," he said, without opening his eyes. "I beg your indulgence." From his pocket, he produced an ancient butane lighter and a small metal ashtray, and then lit his cigarette with infuriating deliberation. Only after several long drags did he deign to speak again.

"Near the end of World War II, my grandfather was serving aboard an Imperial Japanese Navy destroyer. Japan was critically short of oil, and the military government believed there were great reserves to be found in Antarctica. In 1944, an expedition brought back promising results from the Ross Sea. So in early '45, they deployed two teams, one to build a derrick in McMurdo Sound and another to begin exploratory drilling farther inland, past the Transantarctic Mountains. My grandfather's destroyer was one of the escort ships, specially adapted to operate in the ice. The first expedition had discovered a channel near the original Scott base, which led through the mountains, and they went in for many miles without discovering its end. The experts believed it would lead them to the plains of Victoria Land. But they had seriously overestimated their ability to deal with the conditions there. One of the Japan Oil Company ships took serious damage. Both teams were forced to abandon their missions."

Dyer said dryly, "There is no such channel inland from the Ross Sea."

"Certainly not now," Takashima said. "Yet, at the time, it was painstakingly mapped. According to my grandfather, the inland expedition discovered a range of mountains that 'exceeded the height of the Himalayas,' where they should have come upon only a vast plain of ice. They never ventured as close to them as your great-grandfather, Colonel Dyer. But much like Ms. Danforth's own great-uncle, a number of the crew returned suffering from debilitating insanity. According to my grandfather, it was something they *heard* that drove them mad."

"Is this an official, documented account?" Dyer asked. "Or just a story your grandfather told you?"

"The military government suppressed many records that chronicled Japanese defeat. This venture certainly qualified."

"So again, there is only anecdotal evidence of such an anomaly."

"This photograph is not anecdotal," Carter quipped, pointing to the image on the wall. "How do you explain that?"

"I am not convinced it's anything other than a glitch." He glanced at Danforth. "Your satellite is the only one to pick up this image, is that not correct?"

"Yes, it is," she said. "We have done very thorough cross-checking."

"There you have it."

A long, uncomfortable silence followed, but Danforth gazed around the room like a school teacher preparing to discipline unruly children. Then her eyes bored straight into Dyer's. "You, Colonel, are in a unique position to help us make certain determinations about this phenomenon. Thanks to Geo-Astra's official military connections, we have received clearance to engage you for a special research mission."

"And that means what?"

"It means that, for the next thirty days or so, Colonel, you work for me."

NOVEMBER 24; 08:13

"Astra Tango, this is Orbweaver. Are you receiving?" Christine Danforth's sharp, distinctive voice.

It was distinctly unusual to be on supercruise at 30,000 feet, hearing the voice of a civilian on the radio. Particularly in an aircraft that did not officially exist.

"Five by five," Dyer responded.

"Stand by for nav update."

Dyer's TR-135 Aurora had departed from the top-secret Webb Island installation, some ninety miles southeast of New Zealand's Chatham Islands, and climbed to altitude on a preset course that even he didn't know; for the moment, his orders were simply to fly due south. Clearly, the images sent to Earth by Geo-Astra's errant satellite had rattled someone at the top—he didn't know who, but he wryly thought of them as the Men in Black. What he had not expected was for the group that Christine Danforth had assembled to be made virtual prisoners at Geo-Astra's headquarters in Boston while they analyzed, projected, formulated, and re-formulated the data desired by the powers-that-be. He had come to understand quickly that this project was not the brainchild of some half-assed government think tank, but a meticulously if hastily engineered response to a phenomenon no one yet fully understood.

Sending him in a secret spy plane rather than utilizing satellites or drones meant they required more than electronic data. They needed a measurable and immediate human response.

"Call me Ham," he said to himself.

"ETA to terminator three minutes," came Danforth's voice. "In the event of communications failure, you are to assume manual control using instructions in packet six-zero-one. Repeat to confirm."

"Roger, packet six-zero-one."

"Begin final checks of all onboard surveillance systems."

Superficially, the TR-135 Aurora resembled an F-35 Lightning fighter, but with an extended, wider fuselage and longer, more sharply angled wings. Its charcoal-hued body, designed for pure stealth, generated only a marble-sized radar signature, and with its powerful Pratt & Whitney F190 engines, the aircraft could cruise at supersonic speeds without afterburners at an altitude of 80,000 feet. Its operational range was almost 5,000 nautical miles. Only six of the planes existed, as manned, long-range surveillance missions had been virtually eliminated since the retirement of the Aurora's venerable predecessor, the SR-71 Blackbird. Dyer had been flying the Aurora for two years, mostly over North Korea, with numerous incursions into China's airspace. For this mission, the Aurora was the perfect option: fast, invisible, and capable of transmitting, recording, and analyzing every aspect of a location or event with absolute precision, in real time. The Aurora put him at a vantage point that the Geo-Astra "experts," based several thousand miles away, warranted to be "safe."

He still wasn't sure the Danforth Project's theory was anything more than hogwash. He had to admit, however, that the evidence the others had presented—the theories, the calculations, the projections—all had led him to the edge of doubting his long-held convictions about the nature of reality. Convictions that, until these past few weeks, he would have sworn could never be shaken.

Ahead, in the pale, hazy light of the Antarctic spring morning—which would vary little over the course of day—he could make out a series of angular shadows against the horizon, which meant he was approaching the Transantarctic Mountain range. Far to the left, he could see an expansive veil of swirling clouds, and in its midst, a huge gray mass that seemed to peer back at him like a curious giant. From this distance, he couldn't tell whether it was the face of Mt. Erebus itself or a lazy column of smoke creeping out of the lava lake in its cone. Almost a decade earlier, he had skirted the edge of Antarctica, during a training run in the Aurora prototype. No matter where one flew in this speeding, ultimately fragile manmade construct, so high above the earth, it was a lonely, risky endeavor; yet if he even briefly allowed his mind to dwell on the remoteness of the continent below, on its harsh, unforgiving nature, he became all the more aware of his own fragility, his mortality. Years of training and experience had more than conquered that natural inclination, yet now, inexplicably, he felt a profound sense of isolation, of *insignificance*, so intense that for a few moments he lost all recollection of his mission, even his identity.

He forced his attention back to his instruments, but then something off to his right pulled it away again. A blur, or vague shadow. Whatever it was, it was gone in an instant, and then he was back to himself, to his mission, and he heard Danforth's voice over the radio advising him that he was one minute from the terminator.

"Astra Tango, do you copy?"

"Roger," he replied, regaining his focus as quickly as he had lost it. "All systems check."

"Visibility?"

"Twenty miles. Low cloud cover, moderate to heavy. Cumulus stacked to three-five thousand beyond McMurdo Sound."

At the preflight briefing, Danforth had warned him of the strong possibility that, once he reached a specific point on his programmed course, he might lose all communications with the outside world. That moment was approaching at almost mach two, half a minute away; now twenty seconds. His rationality, his conditioning, assured him that nothing unusual would happen. The Aurora would blaze its way through the Antarctic sky, its instruments detecting not even the slightest anomaly. And a few minutes later, he would arrive at way-point Delta Echo Seven, where the plane would turn itself around and begin its long descent back to Webb Island. It would have been an expensive trip for naught, and Christine Danforth would have a lot to explain to the Men in Black.

As for him, it would be back to training nuggets, with only an occasional recon flight to interrupt the tedious routine.

The digital timer on his right-hand panel counted down the final seconds, which he watched from the corner of his eye. His main focus was on the panoramic expanse of snow, ice, and clouds that stretched to the pale gray horizon ahead and to either side. Nothing out there was going to change. Nothing out there *could* change.

A mellow chime sounded over his helmet speaker.

The terminator.

The clouds. The sky. The snow. The distant mountain range. All remained the same. All normal.

A sharp clanging pierced the warm layer of relief that he had allowed to close gently around him. The GPS had lost its signal. His attention now riveted on his clocks, he started to go through the checklist. Another electrical jolt when he realized he had also lost VOR navigation. Transponder was operational. All avionics checked nominal. Engine functions nominal.

"Astra Tango to Orbweaver, do you copy?"

Dead air.

"Astra Tango calling Orbweaver, do you copy?"

Outside, something beyond the nearest clouds began to take shape.

Something big. So big it couldn't exist on this earth.

No; not on *this* earth.

November 5; 23:11

"Your great-grandfather's manuscript indicates that this race occupied select regions of the globe for eons. They had amazing, vast intellects. On first examination, you'd think it unlikely they could ever adapt to our gravity and atmosphere, yet their physiology was complex and efficient. Professor Lake likened them to certain types of sea life."

Dr. Takashima handed the tablet to Dyer so he could better examine the displayed image. It was a scan of one of Professor Lake's drawings of a grotesque, barrel-shaped thing that did resemble some kind of sea creature sprouting tendrils and translucent wings. One end— presumably the "head"—resembled a starfish, but with large, eye-like orbs protruding from each tip. "If this thing were ever real, most likely it *was* some kind of sea life."

"That has never been definitively proven one way or the other," Takashima admitted. "But there's no fossil record of anything such as this. These specimens were unique."

"That's hardly convincing."

Out of the corner of his eye, he noticed Dr. Elizabeth Carter, the only other person in the room at the moment, staring at him with almost painful intensity. She was young, probably not yet thirty, but as stern and severe-looking as his long-deceased grandmother. He gave her a questioning glance.

"Colonel Dyer, I admit that I'm somewhat skeptical about this whole business. But purely for the sake of the project, I am prepared to accept certain premises at face value. I will tell you that I do have some background—both professional and personal—with events and individuals that lend credence to your great-grandfather's account."

"And?"

"I wonder if you could, at least temporarily, suppress your natural skepticism and take something of a leap of faith. Call it a tactical scenario. A professional exercise."

"In other words, you want me to follow your example and just play along."

"That's about the gist of it."

"For your sake."

"For the job."

Takashima chuckled, a little nervously. "Colonel Dyer, have you ever heard of Walter Gilman?"

"Don't think so."

"A brilliant young mathematician. A student at Miskatonic University, early twentieth century. He was studying non-Euclidean physics and geometry. Developed some intriguing theories about alterations in space and time—specifically, about the possibility of multiple, coterminous realities. He died under mysterious circumstances after completing his thesis. It's a revolutionary work. Not my area of expertise, of course, but I find it fascinating."

"And how does this concern us? Me?"

Carter interjected. "I want you to think back to your great-grandfather's account. Do you recollect any of the history of those creatures that he referred to as the 'elder race' or 'elder things'?"

"Only vaguely. I haven't had any reason to revisit his work since I was a teenager."

"Their stronghold was there, in those mountains in Antarctica. The Dyer expedition deciphered an amazing amount of that race's history from the ruins they discovered. Evidently, at some point in their history, those elder things were subjected to repeated assaults by some kind of hostile force—or forces. Clearly, they developed defensive measures we don't fully understand."

"Maybe they stood still and made like ugly shrubberies."

"I'm going to bet not. No, this is where we believe that Walter Gilman's work becomes relevant."

"You see," Takashima said, "Gilman's formulas involve juxtaposing certain angles into the natural curvature of space, which, in essence, open doors to *other* spaces. I'm certain you're familiar with the concept of parallel and alternate dimensions."

"I know of various theories, yes. My work involves more conventional uses of mathematics, of course."

"Of course. But Gilman's formulas closely correlate with certain of your great-grandfather's observations about the ruins in Antarctica. He claimed that many of the structures exhibited unique geometric properties—particularly that most were arrayed in patterns of five. Together, they may have formed some crucial geometric 'key' we haven't yet deciphered." Takashima's expression dared Dyer to challenge him. "Recall what I said about alternate dimensions. We are convinced, Colonel, that those mountains do exist in Antarctica. They exist precisely where William Dyer placed them in his report—but in a different plane of reality. A nearby but parallel dimension of space."

"By whatever process," Carter said, "the elder race altered three-dimensional space as a means of shielding themselves against their attackers. What we do know is that those angular structures are the key to passing from one space to another. But these parallel spaces are unstable—perhaps simply due to age and weathering of the interface components. Thus, from time to time, when we approach that region from certain, narrowly defined spatial coordinates, we are afforded an entry point to that other world. William Dyer's expedition happened to make its approach on a vector that led to what he called 'the Mountains of Madness.' Clearly, most of those that followed did not."

"But years later, my grandfather also entered that space," Takashima said. "The mission records that survived would suggest his route very nearly matched the Dyer expedition's."

"Our satellite just happened to track one of the corridors to that alternate world," came Christine Danforth's voice. She was striding through the conference room doors with Alek Gudmundson in tow. "No doubt due to the minute alteration of the scanner's calibration mechanism."

"But there are countless satellites up there," Dyer said. "Regular commerce to Antarctic bases. You're telling me only a handful of human beings have ever observed this . . . anomaly?"

"Colonel," Gudmundson said, "imagine a table with an umbrella over it. In the fabric of the umbrella, there is a small hole. Now, the umbrella is not completely stationary. Occasionally it shifts in the wind. And you. You're standing some distance away, throwing rocks at the umbrella, unaware of the hole. Occasionally, one of your rocks might pass through it—come in at the right angle, as it were—but I would hardly expect it to be a frequent occurrence. Would you?"

"Over time," Danforth added, "the hole begins to enlarge. Eventually, the fabric will shred, and the umbrella becomes useless."

"Is that what you think is happening?"

"Remember," Gudmundson said, "the elder race existed on the Antarctic continent millions of years ago. Our preliminary calculations tell us that, yes, over many millennia, the passages between worlds have been expanding. Or, more correctly, the ancient defenses have been disintegrating."

"For thousands of years, you say?" Dyer asked.

Gudmundson's eyes appeared huge and watery behind his thick glasses. "Millions, probably."

"Just for argument's sake. How long do you suppose we have before the whole business collapses?"

"I couldn't predict that any more than I could tell you when the super volcano beneath Yellowstone might erupt, or when the Sun might go supernova. It could be today. Or decades from now. Centuries, even."

"But it is inevitable," Takashima said, his voice barely above a whisper.

Carter broke in. "Dr. Gudmundson, what would be the end result of these defenses completely giving way?"

The older man shrugged. "Who can tell? Certainly, the alteration of space would be evident to us, here on Earth. And if I were to hazard a guess, also to whatever those defenses were erected against."

"After all this time? You think those forces could still exist?"

"The elder race referred to them as spaceless and timeless—to us, for all practical purposes, eternal. The more important question, I think, is there any reason that they would *not* exist?"

NOVEMBER 24; 08:23

The peaks resembled mammoth, crooked stalagmites silhouetted against the opalescent sky, so tall that they towered over a thick layer of cumulus clouds that crested around 25,000 feet. Dyer could see numerous angular outcroppings of black stone even from this far away—at least thirty miles, he estimated, though it was difficult to gauge distance by something so massive, so unfamiliar to his perceptions. He remembered seeing the skyscrapers of New York when he was a child and feeling dizzy, his youthful senses overwhelmed by their vertiginous heights. That same disconcerting sensation overtook him now, despite the extreme distance. From 30,000 feet, he should be looking *down* at any object anchored to the earth, yet the summits of these behemoths glared back at him from near his own eye level.

His discipline quickly reasserting itself, he entered his personal security code into the Aurora's computer interface and initiated the procedure to open Packet 601, per instructions for this contingency. He switched the aircraft off autopilot as a set of nav instructions appeared on the screen: set a heading of 188 degrees, climb to flight level 40,000, reduce airspeed to mach 0.67, and proceed to a designated waypoint still 20 miles distant. From there, he would navigate according to his best judgment, following the range of mountains as far as his fuel would allow. He started the automapping routine, which would record every minute detail of the topography, using an array of photographic processes, including radar and infrared. Per his instructions, he periodically keyed his radio transmitter, in the event there might be pockets from which signals could traverse the terminator. He recalled from his great-grandfather's journal that the expedition had been able to contact the outside world, at least sporadically.

As the Aurora sped toward the colossal mountain range, he began to notice curious angular structures amid the ice below, many of which, from the air, resembled five-pointed stars. Numerous arrays of blocks, cones, and cylinders formed complex structures that grew larger and more intricate the nearer they pressed to the mountains. Indeed, the preponderance of structures bearing five wings, or arms, reminded him of his great-grandfather's notes to the effect that, for reasons unknown, five appeared to be a significant number to the intelligence responsible for this wonder. How could something like this be hidden to virtually all mankind for . . . how long? Unimaginable eons, by any calculation.

All his doubts had been vanquished, vaporized by the dizzying sight of these unthinkable geometric constructs, which sprawled with ever-increasing density toward the monolithic towers coming up ahead. His altitude was now 35,000, the Aurora climbing steadily toward 40,000 at 5,000 feet per minute. He noted his accelerated heartbeat, his steady but rapid breathing. *This* was why they had sent him. None of his instruments could register the sheer awe of beholding the alien landscape laid out before him.

He heard a brief crackling sound, and he focused all his attention on his headset. It was something more than dead air, he was certain. He double-checked his frequency and called out, "Astra Tango to Orbweaver, do you copy?"

Nothing. But for a brief moment, he detected a very distant, shrill warble, almost like a bird call amid a rush of wind.

"Astra Tango to Orbweaver, do you copy?"

He reached 40,000, leveled off, and throttled back to maintain mach 0.67, angling his course to parallel the most prominent craggy ridge, which arced roughly toward the South Pole, its tallest, sharpest peaks reaching toward the speeding aircraft like gigantic talons. As he stared toward the thick curls of white mist in the distance, he thought he could make out a dark, shadowy mass, all but hidden by the wild, mad clouds.

For a second, he glimpsed it through a brief break in the cloud cover.

He had thought nothing the size of *these* mountains could exist on Earth. But this was an immense, conical silhouette, towering over the terrible range, still unimaginable miles away, its summit merging with the deepening blue above, climbing into outer space itself.

The gateway itself? The means those ancient ones used to pass from this reality to others?

On and on he flew, the penultimate range seemingly endless, never drawing closer to that unspeakable monster beyond the horizon. Amid the mountains, the inevitable five-pointed alien constructs still extended away as far as his eye could see in every direction. Surely, he had left the familiar confines of Earth; this was some alien planet, masquerading as the world he thought he knew. He realized his heart was pounding like a hellish jackhammer in his ears, while the onboard cameras and sensors silently, dispassionately recorded the landscape as if it were as prosaic as the McMurdo ice shelf.

A soft beep crept through the steel hammering of his pulse. He was reaching the limit of his fuel. Within 50 miles, he had to turn back to ensure he had enough fuel to reach Webb Island.

If that infinitely remote place even existed anymore.

Something ahead—out there beyond that distant, impossible peak—began to move. Tendrils of cloud parted, dissolved, and coalesced, affording him only a glimpse of something shapeless and pale, something worming its way through the gap in space through which that mountain passed.

Massive. Titanic. A living thing, bigger than even these towering monstrosities.

His eyes couldn't focus on it, as if its contours defied any semblance of terrestrial logic. Again, he heard a strange crackling in his earbuds.

Then the noise became a deafening, screeching, *shriek-chirp-buzz*: a million organic sounds blending in a diabolic symphony, crossing the ether, transforming electrons, infiltrating the dedicated frequency between the Aurora and the Webb Island base. An eerie, mournful wail, like the cry of a whippoorwill amplified a billion times, piercing his skull like an iron spike, driving into his brain with absolute, deliberate malice.

It knew he was there. *It* had detected his presence.

He throttled up and swung the Aurora into a tight 180-degree climbing turn, then kicked on the afterburners, knowing it was the wrong thing to do, that it would burn too much fuel too fast. Yet compelled, he pushed the nose over and dove to build speed, his brain screaming that it would be better to retreat and perish in the frigid ocean than to face *that*, the crawling chaos, the horror on the threshold of beyond . . . the thing surely at the heart of all madness.

The Aurora screamed past the sound barrier in a 9,000 foot-per-minute dive, the pressure of acceleration crushing Dyer into his cushioned seat, dimming his vision as if a charcoal-hued shroud had fallen over his eyes. He barely registered the crests of the mountain range sailing past on either side as his aircraft hurtled into the valleys between them. At some point, his earbuds had gone silent. Some remnant of rationality clawed its way through his blind panic, prompting him to shut down the afterburners, the Aurora's speed now so great that, under normal power, its momentum might well send it soaring out past the continent—assuming the alteration of geography hadn't transformed the entire Earth itself into an alien, unfamiliar world that bore no resemblance to the one he had left such a short time before.

"Teki . . . teki . . . teki . . . ."

The strange syllables came unbidden to his lips.

Something crackled in his ears, and he feared he would once again hear the horrific voice of the *thing* from beyond, the entity of which he had seen only the vaguest shadow, yet which had seared its presence indelibly into every cell of his brain. He realized he was not breathing.

"Orbweaver to Astra Tango. Do you copy?"

"Teki . . . teki . . . teki . . . ."

"Orbweaver to Astra Tango. We're reading you, with interference.

Say again please. Astra Tango, please say again."

Danforth's voice wove through the writhing, tangled threads of his mind, its effect almost calming. His training attempted to reassert itself, to cast all fear back into a safe compartment in the shadows of his consciousness.

It wouldn't go.

A new beeping sound, muted yet shocking in its suddenness, filled his ears. After a moment, he realized his nav systems were back online. He must have reached the terminator—surely, that was it—but something immediately struck him as wrong. It only took him a moment to realize he was not seeing a "normal" Antarctic landscape below, but the transformed, alien peaks, valleys, and clusters of insane, five-armed structures. His altimeter showed 18,000 feet. Dangerously low in this realm of towering nightmares.

"This is Orbweaver. Astra Tango, do you copy?"

This was more than a dimensional pocket from which he might communicate.

At last, his muscles began to obey his mental commands. His voice still barely made its way past his lips.

"Astra Tango to Orbweaver. Five by five."

There was a long silence, but he knew his transmission had gone through. Danforth was hesitating.

"We have your transponder. Sitrep, please."

"Nav and com systems back online. Fuel . . . minimal. All other systems . . . nominal."

"What do you see?"

He kept his eyes straight ahead and refused to look back. The alien formations below were thinning, giving way to the more familiar plains of Victoria Land. Ahead, still many miles distant, he saw a glint of silver amid a vast bank of cumulus clouds. "I believe I have visual on the coastline. I estimate twenty miles. Resuming programmed course to Orb One, reducing fuel burn for maximum cruise."

Danforth remained silent for several moments. Dyer knew she wanted to question him, to learn everything he had witnessed in the foreign world that had somehow invaded their own. Glancing down, he realized the Aurora was flying along a broad channel, virtually free of ice.

The channel Sadao Takashima's grandfather had discovered over a half a century before—hidden to all but a few, virtually since time began.

Finally, Danforth's voice came again. "The umbrella has collapsed."

He felt nothing, for he knew as surely as he had seen that pale thing, that *wyrm*, slithering into existence from some other place.

As surely as he had heard its *voice* filtering through his receiver.

"The umbrella." It was all he could manage.

"I say again, the umbrella has collapsed."

Teki-teki-teki . . . .

NOVEMBER 24; 23:44

Dyer was sitting in the debriefing room, the rest of the team gathered around him, all gazing in awestruck silence for the tenth time at crystal clear images of the five-armed structures that wound their way up one of the tilting peaks like living entities that had been frozen in place, captured by the questing eye of the speeding Aurora. And then, *it* was there: that infinitely remote tower silhouetted against the gunmetal sky, *something* even vaster, the essence of absolute madness, wriggling down from outer space, its contours—even in the video—impossible to register, as if its composition, its *color*, were too alien to be grasped by mere human senses.

Another series of monitors displayed live newscasts from all over the world as the human race began waking up to the reality of the new, ancient domain that had revealed itself at the South Pole. So far, there was no panic—not on any mass scale—but he knew it would come, as soon as the world's populace began to grasp the nature of this staggering, marvelous, life-altering event.

"Henry?"

It was Elizabeth Carter, concern clouding her wide, querying eyes. "You should get some down time. This is too much for one day."

His weary eyes were losing their focus, had been since his harrowing landing on the Webb Island runway, the Aurora's fuel spent, its landing gear touching down just at the edge of the tarmac after a long glide in from 10,000 feet. He had wrestled the aircraft, with no reverse thrusters, to a jolting stop at the farthest end of the runway, preventing any significant damage either to the plane or to the facility. Under normal circumstances, his actions might have been hailed as heroic.

At the moment, they had been completely forgotten.

"What's that?"

It was Dr. Takashima's voice. His eyes were on the monitor that was running the news from Japan. The announcer had been speaking in Japanese, his figure silhouetted against a large map of Antarctica, upon which numerous images of the elder race's structures had been superimposed. But now he was babbling excitedly, and the picture switched to an aerial view of the ocean; a non-descript scene, as near as Dyer could tell—at least until the camera's lens zoomed in on a long, churning wake, left by something barely visible in the upper right-hand corner of the screen. The helicopter carrying the camera crew began to descend, allowing the view of the thing in the water to expand until its half-hidden contours began to take form—unrecognizable, yet maddeningly familiar.

"Shoggoth," Takashima whispered.

"It is," Alek Gudmundson said. "It's a goddamn shoggoth."

"Heading for Japan. For Tokyo."

The images on the other monitor screens began to shift; some to the same shot of the massive entity in the ocean, others to scenes of people running in obvious terror. Different places. Australia. New Zealand. Africa. A disease of horror, he thought; of madness. Inexorably, the contagion would spread farther north.

No, they're not just running, Dyer thought. *They're fleeing. Stampeding.*

"They're coming down from the stars," Danforth said, her voice barely audible. "Coming from the stars."

"The portal is open."

"The umbrella has collapsed."

"It's worldwide," Nishant Khandar said. "They're everywhere."

"That which the elder race feared. It's been watching . . . waiting . . . for all these eons."

"And now it's coming."

Everything was becoming clear in his mind. All that would surely happen. All that was destined to happen. There could be no escaping it.

The umbrella had collapsed.

It was written in the stars. The stars were right. Yes, that was it.

Dyer rose from his seat and, without a word, left the debriefing room, bound for his quarters. Per his custom when on an official mission, he had brought his sidearm.

He had sufficient ammunition.

For all of them.

In the midst of all that was to come, the world—at least this small corner of it—so needed an angel of mercy.

Two heroic acts in one day. Yes. He *was* capable.

"Teki . . . teki . . . teki."

TEKELI-LI!

EDWARD MORRIS

"He was about to rest now, after a continuous day's work
of almost unparalleled speed, strenuousness, and results."
—Howard Phillips Lovecraft

FADE IN: INT, STUDIO SOUND STAGE, DAY

NARRATOR paces, smoking and looking pensive. NARRATOR is ROD SERLING.

ROD SERLING:

Tonight's hour-long special broadcast was originally written in Nineteen and Thirty-One, by a gentleman from New England whose imagination was too big for his time. It is brought to the CBS screen by a good friend of mine, another great writer, Charles Beaumont, and a star-studded cast.

I told Chuck no one else could do this like he could. Chuck says, 'No one's going to.'

Material may be strong for some viewers. Please use your discretion. And enjoy the show. Based on At The Mountains of Madness, the great novel of Cosmic Horror by Howard Phillips Lovecraft, we present "Tekeli-Li!"

DISSOLVE TO: STOCK OPENING "TWILIGHT ZONE" MONTAGE

CUE OPENING THEME:

ROD SERLING (Voice-Over)

You are about to leave the last hint of the known world behind, and enter a haunted, accursed realm where Life, Death, Space and Time, have made blasphemous pacts in the unknown aeons since Life first wriggled and flopped in the primal steaming waters as the continents slid across the planet like butter on a hot skillet. The stars overhead are not of this Earth . . . but of the Twilight Zone.

SLATE:

"TEKELI-LI!"

STARRING:

DARREN MC GAVIN as DR. DERLETH
PAUL PETERSEN as HOWIE
VINCENT PRICE as DR. PICKMAN
HENRY DANIELL as DR. WAITE
and SLIM PICKENS as GEDNEY

FADE DOWN OPENING THEME. FADE IN:
INT, BEAUMONT HOME; WOODLAND HILLS, CALIFORNIA, NIGHT
SLATE: AUGUST 13, 1963

Chuck leans back in his leather office chair, massaging his temples. Under his fingers, his chestnut hair is going gray there, nowhere else. Slowly. He catches sight of his reflection in the window-glass. Outside his window, two houses away, a transistor radio is playing the Drifters' "This Magic Moment", but he hears the song only as white noise.

Chuck's been preoccupied tonight. He doesn't want to have to admit the headache has returned. Not now. God damn it, not tonight.

Tonight feels like a dream, like everything is just that tiny bit off, down the rabbit hole, as clear as it is utterly unearthly. Perhaps the headache will keep him awake to finish. They almost invariably do. But magic moments come with them, and sometimes decide to stay.

When the headaches come, Chuck feels like a child with a nosebleed, or a case of the mumps. Like a child who had to go and get meningitis, and make his poor mother work so hard she had to get . . . mad, a little mad, sometimes mad enough to punish him. He never told Dad about those punishments. Dad must have known. He must have known something.

Mom called him a faker. Mom made him put on . . . those clothes, the wig. Made him go about in a dress until he said he was sorry, or she'd do for poor little Belshazzar with strychnine in the Alpo. A man didn't talk about those things with anyone, not when a parent went crazy like that.

All right, *parents*. And the creepy Aunts up in Washington wondered why he got so twitchy when they tried to tease their foundling, after he stopped living with Mom and Dad. He couldn't tell them, and Grandmother knew enough to keep quiet.

A man didn't talk about those things with other people. Only on the page. "Better this present than a past like that." Chuck mutters into the silence of his own studio. Lovecraft's father died of syphilis on a nut ward, he thinks for the thousandth time, staring at the typer and waiting for the red cloud to clear.

He'd seen a picture of the young writer in pigtails and a middy blouse, never explained, a half-forgotten plate in an old collection. The Providence Spook had crazy parents, too, and aunts who tried to clean up the mess.

As he thinks this, the thought gives rise to thoughts of several other kinds. He is so consumed, he barely has time to scribble them down, right on the typescript of his notes for the teleplay.

Chuck snickers. It's coming easier now. He can't believe how easy any of this is. This show, this new show of Rod's, is the greatest gift anyone ever dropped into Chuck's lap, or Dick Matheson's lap, or any of the boys in that gang.

Even Chuck's own kids get as ramped-up as he does when a new episode comes closer and closer to air-time. His wonderful, long-suffering wife Helen wept when she saw a younger version of him, played by an actor, suddenly popped out of his Walter Mitty job by a little wooden doll coming to life and playing a clavichord.

Everyone loved what he and his friends were doing, and the stick of female dynamite who was his best editor loved it best of all. And in workshop, Richard Matheson kept him honest, or he kept Dick honest, or somewhere in between.

One of the two of them was always going under the earth to mine raw ideas, while one stayed above to weigh them and clean them. Like sparring-partners. "Or like a drag race," Chuck grins tiredly. "Like a couple of goddamn J.D. kids drag-racing."

The teasing doesn't touch his heart. What does is the chance he has been given to take so many chances, the buffer that Rod Serling makes between the writers and the network execs as thick and strong as a mountain.

Like their writing workshop. Chuck thinks of the way everyone in that room looks at him sometimes. Like he was a real writer like Bradbury, or that young fireball Harlan Ellison. Like he, Chuck, was somehow responsible for anything the rest of them were doing. Like he was . . .

But he can't say it. Not even to himself.

BOOM. BOOM. The headache starts up again at the base of Chuck's skull, twisting red fibers down his spine.

Not now. God damn it, not tonight. The kids are doing homework or in bed. Helen just cut the label on a bottle of Scots whisky that was almost as old as he was.

The Leonid meteors were supposed to fall tonight, or the Perseids, or some -id or other. He was lucky he could remember she'd asked him to come watch them on the lanai, let alone what month it was for meteors. There were stories to get out, checks to collect . . .

But Poverty hasn't been Chuck's real motor for a little while. Chuck knows what his real motor is, and keeps it finely tuned and oiled. He learned that motor from the ground up.

It was never the money, the girl to impress, the mouths to feed. Chuck came to wind that motor out, to push the red, and if he went down in flames it would be at speeds no other human being was capable of the bare-wires courage to even attempt . . .

Chuck glances back at the beginning of the work. It's a kid like his son Chris he wanted to use for a protagonist, here. Lovecraft didn't, but Verne did, in *Voyage au Centre de la Terre*, which to him parts of this work almost resemble. If the Professor were entirely off his chump.

But a kid would work, for a TV audience. A canny, curious, fourteen-year-old bean-pole of a kid who can't keep his mouth shut, too smart for his own good and knows it. Funny, that. "Somebody who fights with their wits . . . But what happens when wits . . . Oh, bloody hell. . . ."

Chuck leans back toward the machine, fully engaged again. To him, Howard Lovecraft was unjustly forgotten and remarkably talented. He would help keep alive the name of this genius who never made any real money at his work, yet worked like a dog until he died . . .

"Because it was *there*!" Charles Beaumont snarls, and winds his engine out into the long last lap. Outside, Woodland Hills could be at the other end of the galaxy. . . .

**(ROUGH NOTES TOWARD:)
TWILIGHT ZONE, SEASON 4,
EPISODE [T.B.A.]**

"TEKELI-LI!"
BASED ON THE NOVEL AT THE MOUNTAINS OF MADNESS BY
H.P. LOVECRAFT
TELEPLAY BY CHARLES BEAUMONT

FADE IN: BLACK.

SOUNDS OF AUSTERE, EMPTY HALLWAYS. DOORS SHUT-
TING. PEOPLE MOVING TO AND FRO. AMBIANCE IS INSTITU-
TIONAL.

FADE UP: INT, PSYCHIATRIST'S OFFICE, DAY

OFFICE is stark, Spartan, only basic furnishings and a diploma on
the wall, etc. In center foreground is PSYCHIATRIST, whose desk
nameplate reads DR. PICKMAN.

DR. PICKMAN. has a crew cut, and looks plainclothes military, rather like a recruiting sergeant. DR. PICKMAN is sitting at a desk, looking calmly at a tow-headed young BOY of about fourteen. BOY lays
on PSYCHIATRIST's couch, wringing hands. This is young HOWIE
DERLETH.

HOWIE

> I want to think it's all a dream. That you scientists, you po-
> licemen, this whole orphanage... That none of you want to
> come in and ask, and ask, all your questions, again and again.
> I was supposed to get school credit for going with Dad to the
> South Pole. Ha. Ha.
>
> Who, but God, is there to tell, really? Who'd believe how it
> really is, but how can I . . . how can I not talk about what I saw?
> Dad . . . Dad always said to tell the truth. The truth . . . It's too
> big.
>
> But I still have to say it. Maybe saying it might do something.
> Somewhere. I still only sleep a little at a time. Sometimes, there
> are no dreams. Sometimes.
>
> A lot of people had radiotelephones, down there. Word gets
> out. There's so few people, everybody knows your business, it
> feels like, sometimes, when the whole world is a ship, a radio, a
> cold white sky coming down, down, down.
>
> Sometimes, there's just no glass thick enough to keep out the
> sky.

You can believe me, or not. I don't care any more. I gave you the film out of my camera, and all my diaries and sketchbooks, too. I wish I could give you my nightmares.

There were all those cables and cables they got off to Life magazine and the AP wire service, too, although after a while they kept saying there was "interference" whatever that meant. I don't know what got through. You all . . . still won't tell me.

I dream the way our ship the Miskatonic, the second-largest Arkham, and all the boats, made landfall near McMurdo Station, Antarctica. I remember the jagged horizon at the end of the Earth. I remember thinking that if we got smashed on the rocks, scientists might find our bodies a million years later and wonder what happened.

If I'd known then that when we finally returned to the ships, they'd be covered in foul black stuff and bashed full of holes . . . But it was all right. We still got rescued. Cap'n Saknussem built a fire in the hold, on stones. The few of us who were left all fought over candy and jerked beef until we got a radio working, then slept the best we could. . . .

DR. PICKMAN takes notes. As DR. PICKMAN and HOWIE communicate in this tableau, we see MONTAGE OF IMAGES interspersed with HOWIE'S tale.

HOWIE

I found the National Geographics, Doc. You know the ones. Here. The ones I wasn't supposed to see.

All those pictures of the long, low main part of Vostok Station like hamster cages made of brick, a hard road on the ice that was only tire track after tire track in years of snow, the big chimney rising into the sky.

I just read about every Rooskie in Vostok Station disappearing, back in 1960, when the TV news started talking about some of the ocean getting warmer. My Dad said that the National Science Foundation thought that the whole western ice shelf of Antarctica might melt, or the southern ice shelf might slide into the ocean, or maybe it was the other way around.

But people don't melt. Fifty-two Russian scientists, two of them even women, don't melt. The Russians said they had a nuclear power plant there to desalinate their water and generate their electricity, and it went kaput, melted down or blew up, I could never figure out which they meant. Everyone knew enough to be scared of that. We thought. I hoped we didn't get anywhere near Vostok Station. But my Dad, Dr. Clark Derleth,

Chief Geologist Of Miskatonic University Whoopty Ding Dong Do PhD, he said that when he sent his team (I wasn't actually going) up to the South Pole, up to Amundsen-Scott Station to check the ice and get slate samples and such from the Pole station, they... They'd skirt around Vostok Station to the southeast. No need to even get close to the "hot zone," Dad said.

But the hot zone was a lot worse than nukes. And it found us.

DISSOLVE MONTAGE DOWN TO: INT, DR. PICKMAN'S OFFICE, SAME PRESENT TIME

DR. PICKMAN

Are you still angry at him, even though he's dead?

HOWIE scowls.

HOWIE

Yeah... I mean, yes, I am.

PICKMAN smiles. Smile does not touch PICKMAN's eyes.

DR. PICKMAN

Why are you angry with your father, Howie?

HOWIE considers, looking upward. When HOWIE looks down, his face looks a little more at peace, but there are still tics, and he still looks like hell.

HOWIE

Because it was supposed to be safe. Because I was supposed to be safe, and he was supposed to keep me safe. The Chief Geologist at Miskatonic University. He wasn't there to 'revolutionize biology', or whatever it was he said. We were all there, Doc, we, we... to look for shale oil, take core samples everywhere he turned around, lead all those oil-field cavemen, those Kellogg, Brown and Root people, to run drilling-pipe into the glacier, all these other things.

The newspapers were all over it. That fellow Bob Sheckley at Life magazine, he said, "Finally, we're talking about something besides Space!"

I wonder if they'll be all over it now. My Dad, my own Dad, didn't care about me, Doc, all he wanted was more grant money and his picture in the paper. As soon as he started talking to the National Science Foundation, he wanted to come down there.

You have the pictures I took. You have my notebooks with

the sketches in them, and everyone else's, too. All right, not you. J. Edgar Hoover, or whoever it is that won't let me talk to anybody about this but you.

DR. PICKMAN smiles again; Once more, PICKMAN's eyes don't smile.

DR. PICKMAN

Howie. Oh, Howie, my dear boy. No one is your enemy here. I've told you, and many others have here, too, as soon as we get a hold of your aunts in Providence, you're going right back Stateside. You don't like Germany?

HOWIE looks at DR. PICKMAN with eyes like drilling-pipes to Hell.

HOWIE

I'm not crazy! You're the ones who are crazy, for not listening to me! My Dad died, and the men—

HOWIE removes a large asthma inhaler from his pocket, uses it. PICKMAN waits.

DR. PICKMAN

Howie, you understand that you've been very traumatized by what happened. It's like shell-shock. The whole experience bounced your brain around a little. I need you to . . . if you can, I need you to not think about it so much. I know you're a bright boy, and you're terrified, that whatever you saw down there would do it to anyone, but . . . We've been trying for weeks, and you don't want to be hypnotized. Stop being so careful. Tell me as much . . . as much as you can.

HOWIE swallows a lump in his throat, looks around, conquers some inner hesitation and twitches a bit. When he speaks, we begin to DISSOLVE to NEXT SCENE.

HOWIE

Miskatonic's not that big of a school. Dad just knew how to talk to the press, and make them pay attention. But we didn't have our own planes or anything. We had to charter a private flight for all the men and the gear out of Logan to San Francisco International Airport. From there, we landed at Christ Church, New Zealand. Cap'n Douglas and Cap'n Saknussem already had the boats waiting for us, the *Arkham* and the *Miskatonic*. Dad said they were both old salts, and they used to command fishing boats up in the Arctic Circle . . .

INT, LIVING QUARTERS, MISKATONIC, DAY

HOWIE sits on bed. HOWIE'S DAD sits at desk, other side of room. BUNKS dominate room, eight or ten. HOWIE is fiddling with BIG EXPENSIVE CAMERA, a Leica or similar. DR. CLARK DERLETH, HOWIE'S DAD is doing what looks like some sort of computation in a notebook with a pencil.

HOWIE

> Ever notice how the sun sets lower and lower on the horizon every night, since we started out, Dad?

DR. DERLETH is preoccupied, acts like he isn't.

DR. DERLETH

> Yes, yes. Hangs higher in the sky, too, at its zenith. Just means we're close to the pole, my boy. Close to the work. Good to be back to work. Good to have money coming in again, and be publishing. Admit it, kid, we needed a vacation.

HOWIE frowns, sighs, looks away and does not respond.

DR. DERLETH

> You see that iceberg this afternoon? Looked like a great big island, all by itself, but flat as a board across the top . . .

HOWIE

> I see icebergs every time they let me suit up and go out on the foredeck, Dad. Neat.

DR. DERLETH

> I thought you wanted to be an explorer, when you grew up. Like your old man.

HOWIE fixes DR. DERLETH with burning gaze.

HOWIE

> When do we get to the 'exploring' part, Pop? I'm bored.

DR. DERLETH

> Act your age. Plenty to explore in a few more days when we get there.

HOWIE and DAD turn away, back to their respective tinkerings.

As HOWIE speaks next in VO, we DISSOLVE INTO MONTAGE of

the PROGRESSIONS OF THE JOURNEY which HOWIE is describing. LARGER VOLCANO looms behind the one that HOWIE and DR. WAITE are looking at. WHITE EARTH and WHITE SKY keep blending into a void behind them (CAMERA can suggest this with slow RACK FOCUS or other effect.)

HOWIE VO

I remember when I saw the first little land-blink of Ross Island, and then the hut that Robert Scott built overlooking the harbor sixty years ago, just the same as new. Dr. Waite told me this was the southernmost safe harbor in the whole world.

In the world, Doc. I remember seeing the foot of the Trans-Antarctic Range. I never saw mountains that big in my life, and they kept going up, and up, like some giant's castle covered in snow. Here and there, there were volcanoes that Dad would name for me, or Dr. Waite . . . Marty, Dad's colleague. Marty told me that the whole Antarctic continent only gets a little more precipitation per year than the Sahara Desert in Africa. I remember the big ice cliffs to the east when we landed, and the way Mt. Erebus looked like Mt. Fuji in that painting that they had at my old school. Marty said there was lava on the slope—

DR. PICKMAN, VO

What happened when you got to McMurdo Station? When they brought you here, you said . . .

FOLEY: Shuffling of paper notes

PICKMAN VO

Well . . . you said an awful lot. Tell me about the people at the station.

HOWIE

People . . . (chuckles weakly, effect sounds nauseous rather than cheerful) Well, when we got there . . .

CUT TO: EXT, MCMURDO STATION, ANTARCTICA

DAY

SLATE: SOUTHERN TIP OF ROSS ISLAND, ANTARCTICA

MCMURDO SOUND

ROAR of wind. We are on a SHORE where the ground is as white as the ice, and both are as white as the sky. SMALL SUGGESTION

OF MIRAGE OR ODD MOUNTAIN FORMATION, FAR AWAY on JAGGED HORIZON. PENGUINS gambol and waddle on the shore, make DISTINCTIVE PIPING SOUND like "Tekeli-Li! Tekeli-Li!" with last syllable accented highest.

PAN DOWN: MISKATONIC UNIVERSITY EXPEDITION DIS-EMBARKING, loading various SNOW VEHICLES, HITCHING UP DOGSLEDS.

HOWIE, VO, PRESENT DAY

> We had five sleds, two ArctiCats, sixty dogs or so, four snow-mobiles . . .

In BACKGROUND, MCMURDO STATION is a small congeries of BUILDINGS & OUTBUILDINGS, with warm-looking incandescent lights beckoning them, SODIUM LAMPS illuminating outside pe-rimeter, badly.

ANTARCTIC HOWIE, VO

> Dad, how many people live here?

DR. DERLETH, preoccupied VO

> Oh, it varies. We could get about a hundred in here, but we're down to skeleton crew since the Vostok accident. My . . . ahem, esteemed patrons at the good old NSF don't want to say it, How-ie, but they're quaking in their boots, too. I was at Bikini Atoll taking core samples of the ooze when the bomb went off. I know why they're skittish. I don't know, Howie, we might have about a dozen souls here now, but that's a pretty liberal estimate. Guess we'll find out. They're . . . cagey.

We PAN THROUGH EXPEDITION CROWD, and hold on DR. DERLETH and HOWIE. DERLETH seems capable with a DOG-SLED; HOWIE helps a bit, mostly STANDS BY as DERLETH, LAKE, ROUSTIE#1 and ROUSTIE#2 hitch up sled, stabilize gear, talk to dogs, &c.

A few PEOPLE at MCMURDO STATION are out and about, all in heavy gear and goggles. HOWIE watches them.

HOWIE POV: PEOPLE look and move like giant BUGS or other IN-HUMAN THINGS.

END HOWIE POV

DR. DERLETH gestures at the station as they HITCH UP and SLED

TOWARD IT. SLED DRIVER looks like OIL FIELD ROUGHNECK in ARCTIC GEAR. CAMERA is stationary near BACK OF SLED.

DR. DERLETH

> Did Bill sound strange to you, when we telephoned? Or on the way here, all those radio calls? He kept cutting out. I told him to let Sasha handle the comm, but he said something I didn't catch. Kind of an edge in his voice. Been down here too long. Might be burning out.

DR. WAITE

> Search me, Clark. I've still got a head full of what might have crawled out of that underground lake the Russians were talking about at Vostok before they blew themselves off the map.

DR. DERLETH

> That's what I cherish about you, Marty. Your rugged optimism. Bill said the place is barely even hot. The Rooshians just don't want to commit to another facility so close to ours. They signed the Antarctic Treaty, too, but you know how Commies are about honoring agreements. Why, Khrushchev wants that lake they found under the ice so bad he'd probably come down here and supervise himself if there weren't any of us here. They still think we're all Navy, even though they know darn well none of us would ever pass muster!

DR. DERLETH AND DR. WAITE laugh perfunctorily.

DR. DERLETH

> Soviet Russia is, was, and always has been hurting for natural resources. They knew about that lake way back when, right, they just couldn't make a powerful enough drill to get down there without . . .

DR. DERLETH pauses in thought, slow to speak again. SLED DRIVER is steering them toward a swiftly-approaching OUTDOOR TENT VILLAGE of blocks of snow, tarps, &c. TENT VILLAGE features FREAKISHLY ACCURATE CORRAL with just enough space for all the vehicles. TENT VILLAGE is set up just outside what are clearly LIVING QUARTERS OF STATION.

DR. DERLETH

> Say, Marty, what if they tried to nuke their way down to that lake and it backfired? No wonder they don't want our help now.

We'd have them Red-handed, heh heh heh . . .

DR. WAITE

> If you don't mind me asking . . . what's the status of our nuke plant here, Clark?

DR. DERLETH (irritated)

> It's only a little over a year old. Bill said they save a lot of money on oil now. Seems to be running fine.
>
> They truck the waste to a cave up in the mountains, he said, and sink it ten or fifteen miles down. Perfectly safe . . . and even if the thing does go off its chump, there are ten diesels for back-up power. I wish you'd quit worrying, Marty. God rest her soul, you're worse than my Elizabeth ever got.

WIND picks up, HOWLING, faint echoes of what might be SAME PENGUIN SOUND AS BEFORE. WIND bowls around the side of MAIN BUILDING which DR. DERLETH & PARTY are advancing toward.

BEAT: WIND blowing snow around sides of MAIN BUILDING. As DERLETH & PARTY shield their eyes, THREE SHADOWS become visible in the WHITE-OUT.

BILL is in the lead. BILL wears a black watch cap and the lowered hood of a parka. BILL's face is dangerously flat, like a waxen mask. BILL is pale, ferret-like, small and lithe, with a crew cut and wide blue eyes behind round, rimless spectacles.

We HOLD. CAMERA pans 180 right-to-left to show the two other men standing with BILL.

MAN #1 is about a mile-wide brick wall of bearded ugly drunk. This is ZADOK. MAN #2 looks like he wants to hide from the light like a mole. There is something wrong with his hands. He keeps putting them in his pockets, then looking around guiltily. This is PEABODY.

DR. DERLETH

> Bill! Long time no—

BILL cuts him off.

BILL

> Welcome to McMurdo Station, Clark. This is my new assistant Zadok . . . Say hello, Zadok . . . Oh, never mind, he's from

the Maritime colonies. They're not very effusive. Peabody, there's, a . . . meteorologist. Among other things.

BILL glances at PEABODY. PEABODY speaks.

PEABODY

We'll . . . let's get you men inside, set up, alladat. I think we still got soup on. Got a name, kid?

HOWIE startles at the word 'Kid'. So does BILL. In mid-sentence, BILL does a slow burn. Once more, BILL's face registers none of it. BILL acts like he is smiling, growing more friendly. Slow burn fades in what looks like an amused sneer, disguised very well as deadpan.

BILL

And welcome, Marty, after lo these seven years. Lot's changed, and-—You brought your child to my station, Derleth? This . . . Heh. Well, this certainly puts the cat in with the pigeons, Clark. Why . . . why wasn't I briefed about this?

DR. DERLETH grows indignant.

DR. DERLETH

I only mentioned it in every third communique, Bill! You been hittin' the sauce again? Come on! I paid for his innoculations out of pocket, trained him for the voyage, all of that. You were briefed. You read too fast. Let's discuss this inside.

BILL eventually acquiesces. 1 and 2 follow them back through the low foyer that looks strangely like a ski lodge or an old gymnasium in parts.

BILL (now evasively deadpan)

I'm sure I was. Sorry, Clark. Slipped my mind. We've gone through one full turnover of crew, out here. (laughs) I'm lucky I can remember my name.

BILL glances at HOWIE, trying to look convivial as they MAKE THEIR WAY INSIDE. The MEN stomp off their boots, remove scarves, put boots back on with laces out, etc.

BILL

Young Howie, you're what, fifteen?

HOWIE

Fourteen, Mr. Marsh. My Dad talks about you all the time.

He says you're one of the greatest ... palaeontologists ... on planet Earth. He also says ...

HOWIE looks away, embarrassed that everyone's looking at him. BILL looks like he's trying to remember how to have a facial expression.

BILL

Well, if I recall ... your father said you tested on the Stanford-Binet at a hundred forty I.Q., kiddo. Not ... too ... shabby.

BILL glances at CLARK, who is busy removing layers. BILL glances back at HOWIE with flat, dead squid-eyes.

BILL

Your Pop gonna take you to see the South Pole?

CLARK answers for his son before HOWIE can get the words out.

CLARK

If he toughs it out down here long enough. We're dug in for a whole trimester of research, bought sold and paid for. If we work through Midsummer, we can be done by March and be out of your hair before the midnight sun. Not like you have too many extra hands down here anyway.

BILL

No, Doctor. We do not. A lot of old faces are ... gone. We ... we miss the Russians, too.

BILL incongruously, unaccountably giggles, then hides it like a belch. CREW of various denominations are milling all around them, stomping off boots, unloading various equipment, proceeding in to the inner sanctum. LOCAL CREW act strangely stiff, wooden, emotionless. LOCAL CREW look sick, their skins off-human hue.

DR. DERLETH

Who are the new people?

BILL

Like I said, we rotated out just after the nuke plant's one-year anniversary. After it had been running for a year, things ... changed. People ... took notice.

DR. DERLETH

What people?

BILL's dead eyes fall on HOWIE again.

BILL

> You'll . . . all . . . be briefed . . . soon enough.

BEAT: TIME LAPSE out of long UNLOADING, PROCEEDING TO LIVING QUARTERS. CAMERA follows VARIOUS CREW performing VARIOUS UNLOADS in-station. Everywhere in MCMURDO STATION, the walls are uniformly, classically muralled with GREEN MURALS IN PATTERNS OF FIVE, WITH GROUPS OF SWOOPS AND GROUPS OF DOTS.

LIVING QUARTERS ARE SINGLE MONASTIC CELLS, BARE ESSENTIAL FURNITURE. LOCAL CREW wear black, skitter and whisper and act oddly guarded. HOWIE looks around his CELL, making faces, unloading SUITCASE.

HOWIE VO

> They all put on a pleasing face for us, but everyone at that station was so cold to me. So distant. They were butted up to a glacier on the edge of the world, and their bodies just looked like hollow skins, doc. Like they were walking around hollow. Hiding things.

BEAT: CAMERA suddenly turns, BREAKS FOURTH WALL. NO DIALOGUE for a moment. CAMERA traverses MCMURDO STATION, and we pass several open doors.

HOWIE VO

> The radios were cutting out. We had to use these walkies that operated, like, on a lower frequency. And even they kept making that noise, that noise . . .

FOLEY SOUNDS: Wind howling, penguin/flute sounds

VO, CREEPY LOCAL VOICE (muffled behind wall)

> When they come. When they come, there's always got to be somebody. And there always is. Bill makes sure of it. He knows how to game those guys, back in the world. He says he could keep things going down here as long as it takes, as long as we all do what we're told . . . and give thanks and praise to the ones who let us live here. Hey, when it's my time, I might even volunteer. That way they don't come for me . . .

VO, CREEPY LOCAL #2

Yeah, but . . . we can't all be meat for the beast. Someone has to run the station. I don't . . . I don't mind, but . . .

CAMERA BREAKS FOURTH WALL again, EYELINE 180's to HOWIE, poking around in the HALL past DOOR #3. HOWIE is gasping like a fish out of water.

BEAT: HOWIE reaches for his INHALER. INHALER is DEAD.

HOWIE hits floor on his back, looking up. HOWIE begins to HALLUCINATE: DISSOLVE TO:

MONTAGE: HOWIE sees STONE MURALS on VAST WALL, similar to SQUIGGLE-DOT WALLS OF STATION. Scale is indeterminate. HOWIE beholds ANCIENT CITY on MCMURDO SOUND, reaching down into the waves and up into mountains of itself more vast than a shaman's eye could dream. We hear CREW in VO, getting HOWIE to his room. CREW #1 and CREW #2 sound suspiciously like CREEPY LOCAL #1 and CREEPY LOCAL #2.

CREW #1

Derleth said he wanted this poor kid to grow up to be an explorer.

CREW #2

He must not want him to grow up. Not very much. Let's get him to bed. You cap that needle you used on him? Dosage was just right. He's breathing fine, now. Doc says the kid has three more of those inhalers in his kit bag. . . .

CUT TO:
EXT, INLAND FROM MCMURDO STATION. FOLEY SOUNDS: Wind howling. Faint suggestion of a flute, "wild & half-sentient piping."

EXPEDITION HAS BEGUN. We PAN DOWN from ESTABLISHING SHOT:

BARREN, MYSTERIOUS MOUNTAINS loom in the west like teeth chewing the sun into varicolored sunset. MOUNTAINS are so vast that they hurt the eye. The mountains have suggestions of crystalline features toward the peaks, caves within these, and squarish bits further down that look like fitted stone walls made by sentient hands, but only on very close inspection.

HOWIE stands outside IN CAMP, wearing LAYERS OF GEAR, GOGGLES. HOWIE is aghast at the sight of the MOUNTAINS but can't look away. WIND carries faint, oddly distorted echoes of PEN-

GUIN SOUNDS.

SLOW DISSOLVE TO: EXT, ICE SHELF, DAY

BREATHTAKING, NONSTOP SLED RUN over the lofty shelf ice. JAGGED HORIZON DARK IN WEST. WHINE OF SNOWMOBILE ENGINES.

HOWIE, VO

> We crossed to the mainland to get rock samples in the foothills. We got lost pretty quick, no matter what Dad said. Bill . . . Bill never radioed once. Neither did anybody. Anybody . . .

SLOW DISSOLVE TO:
EXPEDITION calls HALT at GIANT SANDSTONE OUTCROPPING. DR. DERLETH is first off the sled with hammer and chisel, curious. DERLETH grows curiouser and curiouser, and so do a few SCIENTIST TYPES, WAITE among them looking sheepish but quickly swept up in what they see before them.

BEAT: WAITE, DERLETH et.al act in pantomime, directing HOWIE and the MEN in monosyllables, mostly with gestures. They begin chiseling away a SECTION OF ROCK full of ferns and trilobites and normal PRECAMBRIAN FOSSILS.

BEAT: DR. WAITE uncovers a FIVE-POINTED FOOTPRINT. WAITE et.al scratch their heads. FOOTPRINT is chiseled out. TWO MORE and part of a THIRD emerge. WAITE et. al are entirely at a loss.

DISSOLVE TO:
EXT. COLD, WINDSWEPT PLAIN where SNOW and STONE are the only recognizable features.

We follow HOWIE, DR. DERLETH AND PARTY on TWO DOG SLEDS. Far off on the horizon, Cyclopean aggregations of black stone loom further up than CAMERA shows, suggesting some perversion of geometric law by their scale.

HOWIE is beside DR. DERLETH; both have WALKIE-TALKIES. EXPEDITION appears to be using WALKIE-TALKIES for all communication.

When DR. DERLETH speaks, his voice is the voice of a West Point Lieutenant on his first day in combat: scared and trying to hide it behind the voice of Authority.

DR. DERLETH (Walkie-VO)

All right, who else thinks that what they are seeing is an actual city, off due west, and not some kind of strikingly vivid mirage? If we're going to do 'Mutiny On The Bounty' as a radio-play on walkies, my friends, let's at least put it to a vote. You all see a couple of fossils sticking out of the ground, and you turn into screaming little kids. Let me just put this to bed, once and for all. No matter what's melting down here, or where, there's been nothing living south of the northern edge for millions of years! We are men of Science . . .

INHALER sound. DR. DERLETH looks at HOWIE and sighs. Up ahead, SLED upsets on PRESSURE RIDGE in ICE. EXPEDITION HALTS; Everyone helps UPSET SLED. SOME OF THE MEN remark on fossils in the exposed rock that look like the same kind of footprints.

DISSOLVE TO: STOCK FOOTAGE, ANTARCTIC SNOWSTORM

DR. WAITE, RADIO VO

Yeah, we . . . we found some of those same kind of footprints, Clark, when we took a core sample and blasted down to take another one. There's . . . there's a sort of a cave. But . . .

WIND SOUNDS drown out WAITE'S next few words.

WAITE VO (cuts back on)

. . . but we have to keep going, don't you understand? This is an unknown species! If I don't get an answer outta you, it's Silence Gives Consent. And don't even get me started about the mountains we see off in the distance from my position. Bigger than the Himalayas, and I see volcanic activity at thirty thousand feet . . . Gotta bring this little plane of yours down, though. The snow's blowing down off the peaks. Some of that stuff looks like it was built . . .

FOLEY: RADIO INTERFERENCE. A FEW BEATS OF RADIO SILENCE, THEN:

WE PAN LEFT, SHOWING LONG VIEW OF MCMURDO HARBOR

CAPTAIN DOUGLAS, RADIO VO

Base camp outside McMurdo Station is secured, sir. We've built fires for youse, but if it's all the same . . . We'll stay on two weeks, and then we're away off. This place is turrible bad luck, nowadays . . .

FOLEY: RADIO INTERFERENCE. SUGGESTION OF A DIFFER-
ENT FREQUENCY.

CREEPY LOCAL #2

> Derleth wants to bring back some of that prehistoric water
> for Jack Kennedy and the U S of A. What if we sent him back
> with a shoggoth?

INHUMAN RADIO LAUGHTER.
CUT TO: INT, DR. PICKMAN'S OFFICE, DAY

HOWIE on the couch, reliving the event. SUGGEST THIS with
MONTAGE projected on CURTAIN in PICKMAN'S OFFICE or other EFFECT.

HOWIE

> It's the coldest place on Earth. They say Mars is that windy,
> too. That one day we'll go there, too, and . . . Doc, if we find
> things like what I saw down there, but on another planet . . .

DR. PICKMAN

> You're getting away from it. Did they find more fossils?

HOWIE

> Oh, sure. And fast. The fossils . . . (sick laugh) . . . started get-
> ting closer and closer to the surface. Too close, for me. Down in
> the cave . . .

CUT TO: INT, FOSSIL BED CAVE, NIGHT

TROUBLE LIGHTS flare, and TORCHES. DR. WAITE and a few of
the MEN labor with BRUSH and HAND AXE, sometimes SHOVELS.
DR. WAITE is chiseling in FOSSIL BED, in a section where BRA-
CHIOPODS, TRILOBITES, SHARKS, &c. teem.

DR. WAITE

> Hard to believe this area was temperate, even tropical. Teem-
> ing vegetable life. Nothing now but Skua, penguins, seals and
> such.

WAITE brandishes WALKIE-TALKIE. As he speaks next, we cut
back and forth between his position at the FOSSIL BED and FUR-
THER DOWN IN THE CAVE, where a rangy Texan with a mighty
tall hat is spluttering orders through his mustache and visibly trying
to restrain himself from whacking a few of his underlings with said

hat. This is GEDNEY, who answers WALKIE-TALKIE as we cut.

DR. WAITE

Gedney! How are you coming with that dynamite?

GEDNEY has a thick Texas accent.

GEDNEY (RADIO VO)

We're threw the hangin' wall, there, Doc. Boy, I never saw such a messed-up Cavalry charge as I have today. But we can see down in it, at least. Good thing, too. We already lost that hand-car. The cavern goes a long, long way back along the seam. It's limestone. Shallow, like.

DR. WAITE (musing)

Worn thirty million years' smooth by the groundwater of a lost tropical world, where a blind herdsman might lead mammoths down to lap at a sunless sea . . .

GEDNEY (RADIO VO)

Repeat last call, Doc? Couldn't get hide nor hair of that'n.

DR. WAITE

Nothing, nothing. I've got a sandwich of ten million years' worth of different fauna that all died of five-pointed wounds. The same kind of five-pointed wounds. Or they're sheared in half, like if an octopus did it. But . . . then why the groupings of the dots?

Above WAITE, several CAMP DOGS start to GO BERSERK and BARK into the FOSSIL BED.

DR. WAITE

And . . . again, the five-pointed footprints. Uniform, in every age. Appears to indicate, as I suspected, that Evolution may have flowered well before Homo Sapiens Sapiens. This is a well-developed upright-walking critter, not a dinosaur, but co-existed with dinosaurs . . .

BEAT: In WAITE's hand, RADIO squawks into life. Cut back and forth between WAITE and GEDNEY ON-RADIO at the scene GEDNEY is describing presently.

GEDNEY

Doc! Doc! Orrendorf and Watkins, they done found a . . . thing . . . I can't. . . . Aw, git down here and hang a name on this! I got nothin'!

CUT TO: INT, DARKER CAVE, FOSSIL BED, NIGHT

ORRENDORF stands before MONSTROUS, BARREL-SHAPED FOSSIL OF WHOLLY UNKNOWN NATURE. FOSSIL is shrouded in shadow, resembles ANEMONE/SEA URCHIN/SEA CUCUMBER. DOGS freaking out. WATKINS is trying to SUBDUE DOGS, eventually has to lead the two DOGS out of frame.

DR. WAITE bursts onto the scene, shines his light and GASPS. We see WAITE'S POV, but LIGHT BLINDS US to NATURE OF MONSTROUS FOSSIL. FOSSIL is surrounded by CHEWED BONES that look too new.

SLOW PAN IN TO: FIVE-POINTED FEET ON FOSSIL. We HOLD, then:

STOCK FOOTAGE, DESCENDING A CAVE

HOWIE, VO

Gedney and some of those roughnecks found the other thirteen like that. Fresher ones. Looked kind of like a . . . pineapple, with wings coming out of it on seven points, ugly bat wings the same color as the pineapple. And this flower thing on a stalk in the middle.

The stalk had gills, like a mushroom. They had sort of . . . tentacles, coming out in between the wings. Like a squid. Ugly. I thought they still smelled. Eyes on stalks n the middle of their heads, and mouth-tentacles in between. Arms between that, and the bottom tentacles that looked so odd no one would tell me what they were for . . .

CUT TO: STOCK FOOTAGE, SNOWSTORM

DR. WAITE, VO

Cannot yet assign positively to animal or vegetable kingdom, but odds now favor animal. Probably represents incredibly advanced evolution of radiata without loss of certain primitive features. Echinoderm resemblances unmistakable despite local contradictory evidences. Wing structure puzzles in view of probable marine habitat, but may have use in water navigation . . .

FOLEY: BURST OF STATIC INTERFERENCE

DR. WAITE, VO

... Fabulously early date of evolution, preceding even simplest Archaean protozoa hitherto known, baffles all conjecture as to origin. Vast field of study opened. Deposits probably of late Cretaceous, judging from associated specimens. State of preservation miraculous, evidently owing to limestone action. No more found so far, but will resume search later. Job now to get these things onto the Skiddoos. Or the trailers for the Skiddoos, rather. Gentlemen, we must now adopt radio silence with the outside world until we determine what we're looking at. Please. For my sanity. I don't want them mucking this up ...

CUT TO: EXT, CAMP , DAY

DR. DERLETH and OTHER SCIENTIST TYPE are arguing.

BEAT: HOWIE approaches, silent in Arctic gear, wide eyed in goggles and balaclava.

DR. DERLETH

Well, forget what we all voted on. There'll be a new vote. Don't you get it, Allan? This is going to turn evolutionary biology on its ear! I have never seen this organism before in my life, and I've forgotten more than most people know about fossils. There was not one critter in the whole pre-Cambrian Era that looked a thing like thi—

HOWIE butts in.

HOWIE

Pop! POP!!!

DR. DERLETH and OTHER SCIENTIST TYPE look over involuntarily. HOWIE is unsteady on his feet. The wideness of HOWIE's eyes looks a little off, almost glassy.(It is the ghost of the look he will wear in DR. PICKMAN'S OFFICE PRESENT DAY.)

HOWIE

You two gotta come see this. Come quick. Quick! They ... Oscar is pretty sure it's dead, but it sure ... doesn't ... look ...

HOWIE almost falls forward. MURPHY rushes to catch him; DR. DERLETH shoves in and takes HOWIE'S arm. HOWIE is breathing in short, ragged gasps, trying to get his breath.

DR. DERLETH

> You bet, you bet. Come on, son, show us where it is.

HOWIE reaches for INHALER, shakes it, takes SMALL PULL, looks at it, puts it back.

CUT TO: EXT, OTHER SIDE OF CAMP, DAY

On the ice in FOREGROUND, the ABOMINATION takes up most of our view. ABOMINATION is barrel-shaped, with a tough, plated hide like an Ankylosaur, but with ridges that give rise to stalk-like limbs. There is the suggestion that one is a head, with a sort of star-shaped face-organ. Some of the stalks have webbed wings between them. ABOMINATION looks battered. We PAN BACK, slowly, to get a sense of ABOMINATION's size, irrationality, relation to surroundings.

OTHER SCIENTIST TYPE and DR. DERLETH stand, clearly in shock.

DR. DERLETH

> Were you . . . just saying something about exercising caution?

CUT TO: INT, DR. PICKMAN'S OFFICE, DAY

SAME TABLEAU. HOWIE is still RELIVING these past events.

HOWIE

> We left Cap'n Douglas back at McMurdo main station with those . . . people. He was supposed to keep an eye on . . . things. I never saw him again. We took the specimens back to camp, and dug a trench to lay them out in the snow, then put tarps on them. All but . . . one . . .

SLOW DISSOLVE TO: INT, CAMP OPERATING THEATRE, NIGHT

**ROARING GAS STOVE. TROUBLE LIGHTS.
ABOMINATION ON TABLE, CRUSHED IN THORACIC AREA.
FOREGROUND: DR. WAITE, AUTOPSYING KIT WAITE
TAPE RECORDER is RUNNING ON TABLE CLOSE TO AUTOPSY TABLE.
VO suggests actions.**

DR. WAITE, VO

No blade will cut it. Perfect, perfect specimen . . . and it's . . . thawing? Foul odor.

WIPE TO: DR. WAITE, POV: WAITE is TIRED, HALLUCINAT-ING. OTHER VERSIONS OF SPECIMEN slither and pulse and move about at the corners of DR. WAITE's vision when he looks away.

WIPE TO: PREVIOUS POV. DR. WAITE is sweating profusely, large circles under his eyes. EYELINE SWINGS 180. We see HOWIE look-ing through HOLE IN TENT. WIND blows, WAITE keeps looking over. HOWIE has to HIDE, occasionally, and we FOLLOW HOWIE and WAITE intermittently, with suggestions of SPECIMEN in vari-ous stages of DISSECTION.

DR. WAITE, VO

> Thick, dark-green ichor sweating out uninjured side . . . Di-gestion . . . Hmmm . . . circulation, eliminated waste matter through the reddish tubes of . . . starfish-shaped base. Could respirate through mouths . . . gills . . . or . . . pores? Amphibious, long periods of biostasis. Lungs . . . some kind of larynx . . .

WAITE makes pressing motion. WIND blows TENT. HOWIE's view is obscured, but sound is not:

FOLEY SOUND: *Tekeli-Li! Tekeli-Li!*

DR. WAITE, VO

> . . . Five-lobed brain, with . . . external ganglia, like . . . an-tennae? Seems to reproduce with spores, and fertilizing cloacae, pre-animal . . . It's a vegetable with three quarters of the essen-tials for animal structure. Later . . . footprints . . . have degrad-ed, rather than evolved.
>
> Will call these "The Elder Ones," for want of a better . . .

OUTSIDE TENT, DOGS are going BERSERK. WAITE begins clean-ing up, WEIGHTS TENT against WIND which is GETTING LOUD-ER.

CUT TO: LIVING QUARTERS, NIGHT.

FULL DARK. Sounds of WIND OUTSIDE; HOWIE BREATHING INSIDE ROOM. HOWIE sounds like he has sat bolt-upright after a disturbing dream, but doesn't scream. BEAT: Loud THUD. Outside, WIND PICKS UP. Suggestion of PIPING FLUTE, repeating same single ##SOUND or three-note combination of sounds as earlier.

At this, HOWIE begins breathing harder, in terror. In VO or UNDER

BREATH, HOWIE begins to rattle off some Sunday-school attempt at a prayer. WIND picks up more. NOISES increase. NOISES draw closer. NOISES do not all sound like WIND.

CUT TO: EXT, CAMP, DAY. We slowly PAN BACK from SCENE OF DEVASTATION.

LIGHT PLANE is battered slightly and upended. Most of the SHELTERS are blasted apart. ARCTICATS are both still upright on their treads. TARP and ENCLOSURE full of "ELDER ONES" knocked to pieces. All "ELDER ONES" are gone. SEVEN MOUNDS OF EARTH are covered with CAIRNS OF GREEN SOAPSTONE, same soapstone as EARLIER SPECIMENS IN ROCK

BEAT: We HOLD on DEAD SLED DOGS lying in pools of blood in the snow, then SLOW PAN TO a man's boot, with a foot in it, lying just beyond the trail of blood. PAN BACK to MANGLED HUMAN BODIES ARCTIC GEAR. MORE DEAD DOGS. FIVE-POINTED HOLES AND SHEARED-OFF HEADS THE SAME AS THE FOSSILS.

HOWIE, PRESENT-DAY VO

> I can only dream in white, now. White, like snow. And sometimes pink, and red. I'm just a kid. A normal kid with a normal life that was stolen from me. Now I hear that horror everywhere. It's always too loud. Too loud. . . .

CUT TO: INT, OPERATING THEATRE TENT, DAY

DR. DERLETH & CO. break through TENT FLAP, RECOIL IN HORROR.
BEAT: DR. WAITE is on his OWN TABLE. So is SLED DOG. NEITHER HAVE HEADS.

HOWIE, PRESENT-DAY VO

> Can't go back there. Can't. There. Can't. Can't. People are always curious. People forget what that does to cats. I have to tell them. I have to tell all of you about those mountains of madness. About what happened when my Dad lost his mind. When he told everyone who was left that no one was going home yet . . . Not even then! And he took a snowmobile up in those mountains. No one even tried to get a hold of those . . . people . . . back at the station. We . . . me and Dr. Danforth, and some others, we all decided . . . Danforth and me took the plane.

CUT TO: INT, LIGHT PLANE, HELLISHLY BRIGHT DAY

DANFORTH is flying plane. DANFORTH is in his late thirties, receding hairline, horn-rimmed glasses. HOWIE goggles below.

BELOW: BACKDROP: Grotesquely weathered stones, fantastically symmetrical,wind-carved, almost endless labyrinth of colossal, regular stone masses that rear above a glacial sheet, thin in places. It is a blasphemous CITY, the same one as that of the mirage, merely a REFLECTION.

BEAT: HOWIE's CAMERA keeps going SNAP. SNAP. SNAP. CITY is monstrous, NON-EUCLIDEAN, IN RUINS, HALF-SUBMERGED IN GLACIAL ICE. DOT GROUPS AND SWIRL GROUPS SAME AS MURALS IN MCMURDO STATION.

HOWIE keeps exhibiting signs of SHOCK. HOWIE POV shows NOTICE OF FIVE-POINTED ARCHITECTURE.

BEAT: HOWIE's CAMERA keeps going SNAP. SNAP. SNAP. Formations of BLOCKS and CRYSTALS similar to EARLIER VIEWS of MOUNTAINS, SUGGESTIONS of ORDERED BUILDING.

DANFORTH

>   Mortarless masonry . . . What kinda . . . Who coulda . . . built
>   this stuff?

Far below, CITY WALL at edge is SHATTERED, shows HISTORICAL HIEROGLYPHS on SAME COASTLINE, CITY LARGER, GOING DOWN BENEATH THE WAVES. ELDER ONES and LARGE, MULTI-HEADED & -LEGGED, GELATINOUS BEASTS OF BURDEN BUILDING MORE.

HOWIE watches MURAL. HOWIE leans back in SEAT. HOWIE's eyes go back in his head.

DISSOLVE TO: HOWIE, DREAM.

DREAM MONTAGE OR ANIMATION SEQUENCE shows the OLD ONES coming to BROILING, BARE PLANET EARTH, down from the STARS.

Show OTHER ALIENS, FOUR-LEGGED FUNGI WITH WINGS etc. COMING AND GOING.

CITY extends UNDERSEA, BATTLES FOUGHT with ODD WEAPONS.

LIBRARIES OR SCHOOLS where OLD ONES live, and SLEEP UPSIDE DOWN.

SHOW CEPHALOPODS from SEA warring with OLD ONES. Then

SEVERAL CONTINENTS SINK. CEPHALOPODS LEAVE.

Then previous BEASTS OF BURDEN, the SHOGGOTHS, rise up and begin slaying OLD ONES.

OLD ONES keep SHOGGOTHS in their places with similar ODD WEAPONS.

SHOGGOTHS rise up with numbers, DRIVE OLD ONES BACK TO MAIN CITY IN ANTARCTICA.

FOLEY: AIRPLANE ENGINE, WIND, HELLISH PIPING from beyond the wall of sleep.

MAIN CITY grows old, dies, becomes SMALLER VERSION OF IT-SELF, the one HOWIE is flying through awake.

HOWIE VO PRESENT DAY

> You can't let them go back down there, Doc. It's lost. We should just let it be lost. No one will believe me. They'll say I'm a kookaboo, a nut. I guess I can't change the world, but if I hear about too much going on down there, I might . . . I don't know, Doc. It'd make any guy want to hang up his jock if he saw what went on down there, and might come up here. Probably every-where up here. Already. But don't let them go after that lake. Don't let them go poking around in the mountains. None of it.

DR. PICKMAN'S voice is as cold and final as the grave.

DR. PICKMAN

> What did you find, when you went out in the plane?

HOWIE

> Dad's snow-mobile. Wrecked. Outside a cave.

CUT TO: INT, CAVERN, HELLISH DAY

FAR BACK from CAVERN MOUTH, we see what may be WING OF PLANE, suggesting PLANE is parked JUST OUTSIDE. . . .

We follow HOWIE, DANFORTH, THREE extras dressed as NSF or ROUGHNECKS, through CAVERN full of HALF-CHOKED ARCHES, OLD ONE ARTIFACTS that keep looking newer and newer. We see that GROUP are FOLLOWING HUMAN DRAG MARKS.

BEAT: They find some sort of STAGING AREA, with HUMAN RELICS arranged in GROTESQUE FASHION. SQUIGGLE/DOT GROUPS in dust on FLOOR mark out MCMURDO STATION and OTHER CAMP. In middle of floor are DR. WAITE'S head, DOG'S HEAD and something that might be DR. DERLETH'S BUTCH-ERED BODY, but we don't see it long enough to tell.

GROUP bolts pell-mell, turns CORNER OF TUNNEL.

BEAT: WHEN CREW EMERGE AROUND CORNER, group find MANY OLD ONES with HEADS TORN OFF, COVERED WITH BLACK SLIME. MUSICAL PIPING SOUNDS EVERYWHERE. GROUP bolts pell-mell toward LIGHT at opposite end of TUNNEL, barely makes it out to FALL DOWN A HILLSIDE.

As GROUP tumbles through SNOW, we follow GROUP GAZE back up to MOUTH OF CAVE.

BEAT: From the cave, a great black front looms out of infinite subter-ranean distance, constellated with colored lights and filling the bur-row with a nightmare, plastic column of black iridescence that picks up unholy speed, vaster than any subway train, a shapeless congeries of protoplasmic bubbles, faintly self-luminous, with myriads of tem-porary eyes forming and un-forming as pustules of greenish light . . .

HOWIE, VO

> And then it just went under the mountain again.

HOWIE swallows hard.

HOWIE, VO

> Maybe it didn't like the cold.

CUT TO: INT, DR. PICKMAN'S OFFICE, PRESENT DAY

HOWIE'S eyes start to show some of the effects of the tale.

HOWIE

> That wasn't the worst, Doc. When we were coming back, I . . . I looked behind us. There were mountains that were even taller. Older. I could see them. I could . . .

DR. PICKMAN

> Howard, I see I've upset you. The nurse will be in with your shot. We'll . . . We'll try again tomorrow.

We PAN IN to EXTREME CLOSEUP of PICKMAN'S FACE. PICK-

MAN'S eyes go flat and squid-dead the same as BILL'S had done.

DR. PICKMAN

> More things to be seen than the eye of Man was meant to behold. ORDERLY!

ORDERLY #1 and ORDERLY #2 appear in DOORWAY. ORDERLY #1 is ZADOK, ORDERLY #2 PEABODY. HOWIE begins to scream.

CAMERA tracks in to DR. PICKMAN'S DESK. We see NEWSPAPER on DESK. HEADLINE reads:

MCMURDO STATION, ANTARCTICA OBLITERATED IN FREAK STORM

PRESIDENT PLEDGES TO SEND UNITED STATES NAVY

FADE OUT.

Chris Beaumont stands in the doorway, watching. He's proud of his Dad. He sees what book Pop has welded to his left hand, and keeps picking back up. The one with the lurid cover, the awful pictures and the hard words to sound out. The one he loves . . . *At The Mountains Of Madness, And Other Tales.*

"WHAT THE HELL ARE YOU DOING UP?" Chuck pretends to roar. Chris jumps half a foot, then settles down.

"You finished it."

His father turns, smiling a little sadly. "Yes, I did. And if you don't get your country butt to bed, I'm gonna finish y—"

But when the hug comes, he expects it. The clock on the wall says midnight. Chuck is surprised, as he kisses his son goodnight, tries to stand up . . . and creaks with the effort. Both his knees pop.

"G'night, kid. Thanks for checking on me."

Chris nods, and says nothing. The look in his eyes says it all, and his father is taken aback by the stars in Chris' eyes. As his son exits the room, Charles Beaumont looks back at the final page in the stack before him on the desk.

"Yes," he mumbles fuzzily. "I finished it. Good God, I finally did."

At that, he makes his trembling, careful way out of his writing studio, through the house and onto the lanai. In the dark, he can sense and see the Delphic silhouette of his Helen, in a caftan and bare feet, sitting on a chaise lounge under the stars, waiting for him. The whisky's still on the little table, and one spare shot glass.

Helen sips one of her own, like a hummingbird at a flower. As he draws close, she smiles up at him. Charles Beaumont sits down beside her, fills and raises his glass.

To Howie Lovecraft.

"To Charles Beaumont." When Helen kisses him full on the mouth, the stars begin to fall on Los Angeles.

PAN UP TO:
FULL STAR FIELD, FALLING PERSEIDS
CUE: CLOSING THEME MUSIC
WE HOLD, THEN:

FADE TO BLACK

For the men of the original Expedition,
Foremost, Captains Price, Pulver and Goodfellow.
And Edward Lipsett and Glynn Barrass,
who got us the hell out of there.

Static

Will Murray

With the steady retreating of the polar icecaps, diverse governments rushed in to stake claims to vast tracts that were formally forbidding moonscapes of uninhabitable ice.

New fishing zones were opened up. Fields of land, locked under thick glacial crusts for millennia, became exposed and their virgin mining and mineral potentials were avidly sought.

Minor skirmishes broke out between nations over areas previously too barren to warrant economic consideration. Battles were fought on land, on the high seas and in United Nations back rooms, as well as vocally over the airwaves.

All that constituted unimportant backdrop to the true threat to mankind.

Deep in Antarctica, the thinning ice exposed new continental quadrants holding subterranean vaults belonging to the race of star-headed beings called the Great Old Ones by their so-called discoverers, the infamous Miskatonic University Expedition of 1930–31.

The opening of these previously-unexplored preserves fell under the operational aegis of the Cryptic Events Evaluation Section of the National Reconnaissance Office. Low-orbit NRO satellites had initially detected the denuding of a portion of the megalithic proto-city that had flourished eons before the last pole shift.

I was called into the office of the Director in our Chantilly, Virginia headquarters and briefed.

"Banis, you're on a C-130 headed to the South Pole Station within an hour. It's waiting for you at Andrews Air Force Base."

I didn't blink an eye. I was used to moving fast in order to deal with External Threats—Crypticspeak for Extra-Solar menaces and other-dimensional incursions.

"I'll pack an extra sweater," I said dryly. No matter how I pitched my humor, the Director seemed impervious. But what can you expect from a guy who requires regular exorcisms the way you and I need to scan our home computers for viruses?

He didn't disappoint me this time. "Do that. Here's the drill: We have a team already on-site. They've encountered anomalous material they can't decipher with mundane methods. Maybe you can break through the block."

"What kind of team?" I asked.

"Exo-archeologists. That's all you need to know. They'll fill in the rest down under."

I didn't bother correcting his geography. I just said, "I'll bring an extra deck of Tarot cards."

I did bring an extra deck. A Rohrig. My war deck, I called it. But I just used it to pass the time as the C-130 blundered south to the pole, rattling all the way down to the Antarctic Circle.

I had started with CEES as a Cartomancer First Class, back when Special Powers was a pilot program. The Old Guard fought it tooth and nail. Time passed. After a decade or so of casualties and fatalities, the Old Guard fell by the wayside and the psychic operatives moved up in the ranks.

Now we were the normals. Not that we really were. But growing threats meant adapting to new challenges. Multisensory applications were the only ones that seemed to work any more.

We landed at the McMurdo Sound Station on the edge of Antarctica for final refueling and to be fitted with skiis. I was no fool. The C-130 was heated, so I stayed on board. I would have my taste of the true South Pole soon enough.

On the last leg, I slept in a netting hammock, waking up only when the great engines changed pitch for landing and the entire aircraft rumbled as it made contact with a skiway.

When the drop gate yawned open, I was blown back by a blast of cold air, and several mittened hands reached in to drag me out.

My beard and cheeks frosted over immediately. I had to shut my mouth to keep the tip of my tongue from freezing, too.

"Banis Power?"

I nodded.

"Come on. There's a Sea Stallion helicopter waiting for us. No time to lose."

I had been looking forward to the comparative warmth of the cluster of regulation buildings that constituted the South Pole Station since they tore down the big geodesic dome. But once they bundled me into the Sea Stallion, I was fine with that.

I shook hands with a bunch of frozen beards like myself. There was one woman. She introduced herself as team leader.

"Kim Greene. We're headed directly to the dig. Hope you don't mind."

"Have I a choice?"

The way she laughed said No. I took her for a Sagittarius, and since I needed to warm up, I put it to her for validation.

"Sag Sun?"

"No. Rising. Leo Sun."

I laughed it off. "Close enough for government work."

We both laughed. Then she grew serious.

"We discovered a fortress west of the great plateau. Dome shaped. Intact. One way in and one way out. Interior consists of a winding hall running to the center in a spiral."

Receiving a flash impression of a mollusk, I asked, "Like a sea snail shell?"

"You got it. Along the walls on either side are bas-reliefs of a kind we date from the later period of habitation, during the Jurassic era. We think they're important. But there appears to be some defacing of the carvings at critical points. We don't know what's missing, but we hope you can help visualize the absent designs."

I got it then. In dealing with essentially alien bas-reliefs, even experts couldn't deduce or adduce what was missing from the surviving work. That was my job.

"Can you do it?" Kim asked.

"I usually do. No brag. Just fact."

That was all the conversation for the remainder of the ride. We fortified ourselves with assorted coffees and hot chocolate beverages to prepare for the ordeal ahead.

The Sea Stallion set down amid a dust devil of whirling snow, and we piled out into almost unendurable cold. Or rather, they piled. I hesitated. So they yanked me from the warmth of the cockpit, and rushed me past a row of inflatable tents to the object of my long journey.

I had read the reports of the pre-human ruins first stumbled upon back in the 1930s. I knew that the five-pointed star motif predominated. So I was surprised when I saw nothing of the kind here.

Instead, a spiral black dome reared up some twelve stories, looking like a basalt vault dusted with snow. There was a bulge at the top, like a Christmas ornament atop a domed mosque.

Kim said, "We call it the Fun House. It's not."

We advanced to the sole entrance. It was an arched opening, easily twelve feet high, and obviously designed for barrel-shaped non-humans. A sign or sigil was carved into the lintel over this portal. It gave me a creepy feeling just looking at it.

"What is that?" I asked.

"We think it's a deformed starfish."

That was one interpretation, but my personal opinion was that she was reading into what could have been anything. If it was a starfish, it was curled up in death. Or warning.

Kim added, "Perhaps the way its arms are clenched conveys a specific meaning. But we haven't decoded it."

Under the protective layers of my various sweaters and Gortex parka, I felt a deep chill. It was not a chill produced by the steadily blowing wind, or the horrific temperature. I called it The Chill That Knows.

We passed within. It was not appreciably colder, but the absence of punishing wind carrying needles of clothing-penetrating cold was a kind of comfort. The icicles clinging to my beard began running, as if my body warmth actually meant anything.

Portable halogen lights and light sticks came on. I could see that the floor sloped upward at a recognizable pitch. By human standards, it was steep. But it was the carvings crawling with moving light that grabbed my attention.

Kim explained, "This frieze runs the entire spiral, around and around, always ascending, to the top. There it stops."

"Frieze?" I asked.

"A series of decorative panels. Think of it as a comic strip carved in the igneous rock. You follow along and it tells a story. Only we can't read the key action."

"It's well-named," I said dryly.

My humor didn't go over with her any more than it had my boss. But I let it pass. I was here to work.

"Let me follow it without any running commentary, okay?"

Kim looked dubious. I could tell what she was thinking. Without her expertise, I didn't have a context for the blank spots. But I wanted to test my divinatory skills without frontloading—or the risk that her team had made suppositions where they should have made discoveries. But I couldn't exactly tell her that.

The first panels depicted the classic star-headed Old Ones going about some business that I couldn't pretend to fathom by induction or adduction. As I moved upward, following the panels, I began to glean that they were making something. I hadn't even shifted to non-local focus, and I was getting associative impressions of medieval alchemists trying to transmute elements, one from another.

"Don't tell me what you think you know," I said to Kim. "Just confirm my first impression: They are creating or transforming something by scientific means."

"Yes, exactly. Very good."

I strode along, my breath seemingly leading the way.

"The first defacement lies just up ahead," she said.

When I came to it, I could see what she meant. At the critical stage of the process, the Great Old Ones produced . . . something. But what that something was, had been scoured from the stone. All that remained was a mass of striations, as if those monstrous cosmic beings had, after depicting them, decided that they were too horrible to allow to stand.

I touched the area of defacement. I got nothing. No surprise there. I was still downshifting into an Alpha brainwave state. The cold had me keyed up in survival mode. I needed to relax in order to become receptive. This was going to take a while.

I moved on. The next curving set of panels—I wanted to call them cartouches, but that was an Egyptian concept and I was fuzzy on what the word meant, anyway—contained several defacings. It was clear that these involved the first activities of the element or substance that their ancient alchemy had produced.

"Looks like things have got well out of hand," I said dryly. "I sense a hint a panic."

Kim said nothing. She was smart. And she had been around psychics. She knew the less she put forth, the clearer and cleaner the surrounding atmosphere. And the better I could pick up coherent vibrations.

The farther along I moved, the quicker I climbed—for this was like ascending a flat stair-less lighthouse. Until I heard the others struggling to catch up, I hadn't realized I picked up my pace.

The drama unfolding was picking up *its* pace. Whatever the Old Ones had created or transformed, it had gotten away from them. Desperate attempts were made to capture or control it. I recognized as instruments carven apparatus unknown to 21st century humans—and likely to remain so for millennia.

Body language is difficult to read even in stylized carvings. And when you're analyzing depictions of barrel-shaped beings with starfish heads and retractable wings, the concept of body language is a joke. Yet I was able to discern panic in the attitudes of the Great Old Ones as the tableau unfolded. Panic, and heroism, too. For near the summit of the winding maze, some of their efforts appeared to have made progress toward bringing their ultra-cosmic Frankenstein's monster under control.

Eagerly, my heart pounding, I raced to the final grouping.

—Only to discover that the final chapters had been obliterated. Scarred stone remained. That was all.

"What could have been so horrible that they elected to erase it from their records rather than let it stand?" I asked dully.

"Shame?" Kim suggested. "Embarrassment?"

"I am not sensing those emotions," I breathed.

"Would you recognize non-human emotions?" she countered.

"I have in the past," I said absently. Kim did not question me further.

I turned and retraced my steps, following the bas-reliefs backward. I tried vibing the striations. They told me no more than I had discerned coming up.

"Strange, . . ." I muttered.

"What?"

"I'm drawing blanks."

"Maybe you're blocked."

"One way to find out." I turned to her, closed my eyes, and let my third eye do the perceiving for me. A quick gestalt of images and impressions resulted. I opened my physical eyes. "You wanted to be an astronaut when you were little?"

She actually turned red. "No contest."

"I'm not drawing blanks," I decided.

I would have to take off my right mitten to touch the carvings. They were too cold for casual contact. I asked. "How long is it safe for flesh to touch a surface this cold?"

"About six seconds. When you take your hand away, the skin will be left behind."

"Psychometry is out, then. Too bad. I think I can break through if I have a few minutes of direct contact. Maybe I can access the minds of the ones who obliterated the carvings."

"But they're long dead," Kim pointed out.

I didn't bother to explain the theory of post-mortem contact to her. She struck me as a left-brainer, anyway.

I made my way back to the bottom of the spiral and chewed the inside of my right cheek in nervous frustration.

"I'm usually better than this," I said at last.

"Maybe you jumped into it too fast," Kim suggested. "Why don't we repair to the big tent, chow down, and brainstorm a fresh approach?"

"You read my frustrated mind," I said.

Kim laughed. "Or your frozen face!"

Exiting, my head shifted back, almost of its own volition, my eyes coming to rest on the curled-up starfish over the entrance. Again, that creepy sensation came over me. I'd swear my heart gulped for two beats.

I was definitely on. That image was trying to talk to me. But I couldn't hear what it was saying.

In the tent, dinner was chicken pot pie. Microwaved. Even though I knew better, I wanted to stick my hands in the microwave oven for warmth. That's how bone-chillingly cold it was.

As we shoveled forkfuls into our mouths before the cold got to the food, I asked, "What are the chances of detaching a panel for psychometrizing in a warm environment?"

"Slim. This site falls under the Alien Artifacts Act. Without knowing the consequences, we can't dismantle it."

"Figured as much."

I started to spit out my food. I was slow getting it to my mouth. It had frozen solid.

"Thirty below," one of the others pointed out.

I didn't need to hear that. I had deliberately refrained from asking the local temperature. Not knowing is sometimes better.

"Shall we sleep on it?" I suggested hopefully.

"It won't be any warmer tomorrow," I was reminded.

Someone blew their red nose into a linen handkerchief and then rolled it up in a plastic baggie before pocketing. It gave me an idea.

Minutes later, we were standing at the first bas-relief that had been defaced. My mitten off, I inserted my hand into a food freezer bag and then laid my palm against the scared surface.

Closing my eyes, I slowing my breathing. I was already in Alpha. I was trying for a Theta State now.

It took over a minute and I feared for my flesh. But something began to resolve in my mind's eye. Fuzzy, colorless, yet somehow noisy.

After I while, I muttered a disappointed "Damn."

"Nothing?"

"I saw static. And I felt a cold like in Outer Space."

Kim sighed. "Not much help, I'm afraid."

Hastily, I stuffed my hand back into my mitten. "I wonder if they possessed psi-blocking techniques?"

"The Old Ones? Wouldn't put it past them."

"It's the only possible explanation," I said. "I'm on. I know I'm on. But I can't penetrate this."

No one said anything. You didn't need to be psychic to read their expressions. The Government had dropped a dud in their midst.

We all turned in for the night.

I slept. But as I slept, I dreamt. I experienced the kind of too-vivid dreams that sometimes trouble my sleep. Every time I dreamed, I woke up. And each time I awakened, I couldn't recall what I had been dreaming about. Except for one thing: Static. I kept waking up to mental static. Anxiety dreams. I gave up on sleep. Snug in my multi-layer bedroll, I let my mind wander. I perceived static. Maybe my subconscious was trying to talk to me.

But if it was it took me nowhere. I recalled a demonstration of quantum mechanics that used the noisy static of an old analog TV screen as a visual model for underlying reality. On the quantum level, everything was an undifferentiated potential of sub-atomic particles. Concepts I hadn't thought of in years came back to me. The Implicate Order. That was the underlying reality—the so-called quantum realm. Our physical universe constituted the Explicate Order. The realm of surface appearances. It was difficult to fathom. But the most recent thinking postulated that the principle of quantum entanglement enabled psychic functions to operate. That part I got. It explained everything from synesthesia to common telepathy.

Giving up on sleep, I roused Kim.

I whispered. "Walk me through your best understanding of the frieze account."

She was too good an archeologist not to. Without getting out of her bedroll, she sat up.

"The Great Old Ones were always experimenting with new life forms," she began softly. "Never mind the specifics. Some are too horrible to contemplate. But whatever they created or whatever emerged from their transmutative experiments, it got away from them. They couldn't control it."

"Yes. But what was it? Animal? Vegetable? Energy?"

"Try other."

"Other?"

Kim looked me straight in the eye. "Did you notice the sequence where the octopi were dropping down from the sky?"

"Vaguely," I said. Actually, I had tasted calamari. No point in derailing the conversation with a lecture on gustatory synesthesia.

"Those were Cthulhu spawn. The Great Old Ones were forever battling them, and things allied with them. To that end, they devised counteragents or other lifeforms designed to be inimical to the Cthulhu spawn. The important thing to understand is that these opponents were not made of matter known to us. That's why they were so hard to defeat."

"I understand. They operated on a different vibrational level, or frequency."

"Exactly."

"You think they produced or attempted to produce a counterforce which operated in the same segment of reality as the Cthulhu spawn?"

Kim shrugged in her bedroll. "That's the best reading of the record."

"Doesn't make sense," I said.

"What doesn't?"

"If the Cthulhu spawn were their worst enemies, and the created energy or whatever it was they concocted was so terrible, why erase all records? Why not leave to posterity the ability to recreate the counteragent? In the event the spawn of Cthulhu returned."

"Why not indeed?"

We gnawed that bone far into the night. Our best supposition was that the experiment turned out so terribly that the star-headed creatures wanted to hide the result from future generations—even the outcome of the entire doomed endeavor.

As pat and logical as it was, that explanation failed to satisfy me.

We slept no more that night. After breakfast, Kim and I decided to go it alone. Out into the inhospitable elements we went.

I started with the so-called deformed starfish over the entrance.

"I feel that if we glean what it was supposed to represent, it would tell us a lot."

"The five-pointed star motif is as ubiquitous here as McDonalds arches in America," Kim reminded.

"But this is different. The arms seem to be recoiling. Ever see anything like it before?"

"No. But there are gobs of them scattered about the frieze. Didn't you notice?"

I shook my head. "Tunnel vision," I returned. "Show me."

Kim led me inside, and to the section where the Cthulhu spawn first oozed down from the stars. There were a few of the starfish things scattered about, arms twisted and contorted.

"What do you make of them?" I asked.

"Well, they're not heads, I don't think. They lack some of the features of the star-headed Old Ones' crania. And there are no headless Great Old Ones in any of these depictions. Our best guess is that they are lesser allies of the Cthulhu spawn, and more easily defeated."

"So they represent enemy corpses?"

"Without question."

It was logical. But that's all it was. I kept that opinion to myself.

Kim started to move on, but I lingered, staring at the freckling of dead starfish as depicted by an ancient artisan who used no known tool.

On a hunch, I doffed one mitten and resorted to the freezer bag. Touching my protected palm to several of the starfish carvings, I received instant and clear internal impressions. I saw skulls. Human skulls. Symbolic decodings, no doubt. Humans had not existed during this epoch. The Great Old Ones would not produce the first of mankind from their hellish vats for ages yet to come.

"I think you're right," I allowed. "These represent the dead."

Hurrying along, I touched a defaced section. Again, I drew a kind of a blank.

My impression was staticky, as if I was being blocked on some mental level from resolving whatever supersensory impressions were trying to come through.

"If these carvings are charged with some kind of vibrational-blocking technology," I said tightly, "it's so far advanced of anything I can imagine that using the term technology doesn't even fit the presumed mechanism."

"Nothing fits," Kim said. "Nothing at all."

Soon we were at the apex of the spiral once more, facing the last sequence of defaced panels. Nothing remained of them. It was frustrating. I palmed every frigid surface I could stand before I had to warm up my hands. Static. Only static. And a cold sensation as of interstellar space. A void beyond all voids.

Kim was directing her flashlight in all directions except up. Suddenly, I looked up. Dimly I saw something.

Raising my light, I transfixed it. Another starfish. Like the others, it was not splayed outward, its five triangular arms outflung. Rather, it was curled almost in a ball, as if protecting itself from something.

"That one is practically curled up in a fetal position," Kim breathed.

I reached up, but of course it was too far above my head to touch. It was carved on the ceiling under the bulbous tip of the structure, which appeared to be an enclosed void like an attic or crawl space.

"I wouldn't do that if I were you," she warned.

"You're right. But I have this overwhelming feeling that if I can touch it, this entire maddening mystery will unlock itself."

She looked at me speculatively. "Are you saying that psychically?"

"Intuitively anyway," I admitted.

Kim grinned "You're on." She got down on hands and knees and offered me her back at a step stool.

I clambered up, steadied myself and stretched ungloved fingers toward that curled carving. I grazed it. Tried again, and this time I touched it with four fingers.

The carving retreated from my touch. There came a distressing sound. A kind of click. A cold sensation settled into the pit of my stomach. Then it dropped. My stomach, that is.

"*What was that!*" Kim's voice sounded as scared as I felt. I jumped off her back, helped her find her feet.

"I don't know," I said. "But I don't like it. Not one bit."

"Any impressions?"

"Yes. To flee."

We fled. It was not a rout or a panic. But we made good time. It was all downhill. So that helped. I only half-fell once.

Reaching the early morning air, we looked back. Nothing had changed. The bulbous top was intact. That had been my first concern.

I was having trouble getting oxygen. I could see Kim's breathing was also labored, gasping. The air seemed unnaturally thin. But soon we were respirating normally.

"Maybe it was nothing," Kim said as her breath returned.

"Then why is my heart in my mouth and my stomach in my scrotum?"

"I know how you feel. But I think we overreacted."

We stood staring expectantly at the black dome for a long time. When nothing happened, we found our way back to the main tent, and tried to negotiate breakfast on stomachs that were spasming in sympathy to our pounding hearts.

When we told the others, they groaned.

"That means you'll have to fill out a Triple-A report," one reminded.

Kim rolled her eyes. That hardly seemed worth worrying about.

Before long, a storm seemed to come up. Storms were so common no one bothered to poke their inquisitive faces into the punishing wind. It passed with amazing suddenness.

A radio check with South Pole Station occupied the team's energies while we digested breakfast and considered our options.

The radioman was on routine voice contact when he suddenly yanked his headphones off, wincing.

Kim demanded, "What?"

"Listen."

We both took the headphones, pressing an ear to each receiver.

A horrific rush of disorganized sound came to our ears.

The radioman explained, "They were reporting an approaching storm when they started breaking up. All of a sudden, he got excited."

"What was he saying?" Kim asked.

"Sounded like he said he could see static approaching."

"You mean hear?" Kim countered.

"He said see."

"But you said he was breaking up."

"He was. But I know what he said. And he said he was looking out the window and could see static approaching."

"You don't *see* static," Kim returned impatiently. "You *hear* it."

"He said approaching. It was approaching. Sound doesn't approach. It only gets louder."

They started arguing. Nerves, obviously. We were all keyed up. I suggested they concentrate on raising the station.

After an hour of intense effort, all they could raise was an unceasing static.

"Getting to be a recurring theme of this operation," Kim complained. "Anyone hear anything about sunspot activity?"

"Sunspots wouldn't affect my abilities," I pointed out.

"Are you sure? What about the Spottiswoode Window?"

She was referring to the discovery that psychic functioning increased some 400-fold in a time window on either side of 1330 Local Sideral Time. It corresponded to the time of day when a particular spot on the globe was facing the Galactic Center. Since it retrograded four minutes each day, the window was always shifting, and difficult to work on a practical basis. There was a null on the other side of the window, 12 hours earlier or later. But in my case I never noticed any diminution of psi ability.

"Point taken," I admitted.

Two hours later, the impenetrable static ceased. But we couldn't raise the Station.

By that time our nerves were raw, so we decided to fly back and re-think the operation.

Stepping out to the horrendous cold, we got a shock. It was only the first of several to come.

The top of the black dome had separated into four quadrants, like an ebony tulip opening four equal petals. The exposed cavity was empty.

Somebody made a joke. "Now we'll all be filing out Triple-A's in trip-licate."

Kim turned and slapped him. "This is serious, you idiot!" Spittle flying out of her mouth froze and struck the man's face like sleet.

A quick search of the base camp area showed nothing strange. We climbed aboard the Sea Stallion and took off in a cloud of manmade flurries.

I looked down at the Fun House dome and suppressed an involuntary shudder. Then it dropped behind us.

The flight back to South Pole Station was emotionally frosty. No one spoke. The radio was left on. But only normal discordant crackling and carrier-wave hiss came over the loudspeaker.

"No radio bearing," the pilot reported. "No nothing."

Kim demanded, "Can you fly by compass?"

"What do you think I am doing?" he hurled back. "I said there was no radio bearing emanating out of SPS!"

We overflew the station without realizing it. The pilot consulted a handheld navigational device and said, "I think we overshot it."

"How can you miss an installation of that size?" Kim snapped. She looked more sick than angry now.

He jockeyed the helicopter back, but after 20 minutes of criss-cross-ing blank permafrost, gave up the search as too risky for our limited fuel supply.

Now everyone looked sick.

I spoke their unvoiced thoughts aloud, "It's not there any more..."

"Is that a psychic flash, Mr. No-Brag, Just-Fact?" Kim said bitterly.

"Something got out of the dome," I said evenly. "That sudden storm we heard back at base camp. That was it. It headed this way. We have to warn the world."

"First we have to return to base camp and contact McMurdo Sound," Kim said. "Tell them what happened. Get a C-130 up here to evacuate us."

The pilot set a new course and we all settled into our thoughts. I felt as useless as horns on a goose. None of my abilities had produced good data. And I may have pressed the damned doomsday button. Unwittingly, like any half-blind five-sensory normal.

We got our second shock on the way back. Flying a different heading, we saw in the cold mist a second black dome sticking up from the ice. It, too, was open at the top, exposing an empty cavity.

"What the hell!" the pilot growled.

"This isn't good," Kim said.

"It doesn't fit, either," I pointed out. "If the Fun House functioned as a container for whatever menace got out, why is there a second housing?"

No one offered any good opinion. We flew on in bitter silence.

The third dome became visible on the eastern horizon and Kim let out an audible groan. I started rethinking everything.

We dropped down at the camp and Kim rattled out orders. "Contact McMurdo. Scout for a skiway long enough for a C-130. Plan for being here another night."

"I have an idea," I said, once we were back in the main tent.

She fixed me with a glare. "Stay out of our way. You're just supercargo now. No brag. Just fact."

You didn't have to be psychic to see what was coming. She was going to file a report blaming me for the event, absolving herself of any involvement. I didn't bother vocalizing that impression. Instead, I asked to use a laptop.

"No e-mails!" she ordered.

"Not my plan."

I got online and found a website containing a working Local Sidereal Time clock, punched in our longitude and latitude, and got the local star time. It was 12:28 LST.

I looked at my watch. Almost twenty-four hours had passed since I'd arrived. I hadn't been far from the window when I first worked the frieze. Now we were coming up on it again.

While the others went about their frantic tasks, I continued rethinking things.

All along, I'd been blaming myself for the poor signal acquisition and decoding. Between the fatigue of the long journey, the harsh conditions, and the bizarre nature of the tasking, I hadn't been on my game. Or so I thought.

But what if I was? What if everything I had perceived had been valid—just outside of normal conceptual thinking?

It was the concept of static that got my thoughts moving in a new channel. I grabbed Kim.

"I want to check out the Fun House again. Alone."

"It's your funeral."

I took that as a yes, bundled up and braved the cold.

I went directly to the first defaced frieze. This time I didn't bother touching it. Maybe it had told me all that it could.

Cycling my breathing down into deep rhythmic respiration, I cooled down to an Alpha State, then pushed on into ultra-deep Theta. I set myself. This work was best done alone. Once I opened up to Spirit, I would be exposed to any person in the local consciousness field, specifically their thoughts and emotions. I didn't need panicky people around me when I was tuning in to one long-dead entity.

Long ago, someone had carved this. I didn't know his name, and probably couldn't pronounce it if I did. I decided to call him Carver.

All consciousness, human or otherwise, is an energy as indestructible as any other energy or matter. I learned this during my post-mortem communications training. Bodies could be extinguished, but not minds. I reached out to the Carver.

My first impressions were rough, inchoate. They resolved into a sensation like a thinking cucumber. I figured that meant I had contact.

I sent out an interrogative, trying not to use human words, but concepts.

"Purpose of structure?" I queried.

Back came a concept: DEFENSE.

"Not container?"

DEFENSE.

This was followed by the impression of octopoid things possessing an ethereal substance that decoded like vaporous jellyfish. This reminded me of the starfish curled in a fetal position.

"Meaning of image?"

Immediately I received the picture of a human skull, as before. But this time crossed arm bones lay beneath it, as on a Jolly Roger flag.

I think I got it. I moved on to the defaced sections.

"Why obliterated?"

I got back a very firm negative in the emotional language that often comes through in this form of communication.

"Are you saying this information is blocked?"

Another negative wave, more strong—even frustrated. I sensed that I was not grasping his meaning. I tried again.

"Why defaced?"

NOT DEFACED.

"Symbolic?"

NO, the Carver responded.

Then he sent me a series of images. I could see the big clumsy brute carving section after section, leaving some areas blank. I sensed that he had not figured out a way to depict the problem images. When the entire frieze was completed, he went back and attempted to depict the thing imprisoned above.

Finally, frustrated, the Carver wielded an instrument that abraded the blank areas until he got the effect he wanted to achieve.

I asked him, "It was literal?"

NO. REPRESENTATIVE.

And he sent me a burst of static. I "heard" it in my left temporal lobe. At the same time I saw the image of a TV screen tuned to an unused channel. The pixels danced and sizzled soundlessly, formless yet full of unrealized possibilities. Like quantum foam. I got it then. I thanked him and ran back to the tent.

Fighting the tied flap open, I gave it to them in one excited burst.

"I was wrong about being wrong. Those deformed starfish weren't dead enemy, but the Great Old Ones' pictorial equivalent to a skull. The one over the door meant enter at your own risk. The other was a control that activated all the defensive domes in Antarctica."

Kim looked angry and blank at the same time. "Defensive?"

"Getting ahead of myself. The Great Old Ones were experimenting with ways to fend off Cthulhu and his spawn in the event of a future incursion. They needed a non-physical counter-defense because the enemy vibrated at a higher frequency than local matter. They went looking for a non-local energy source. They found it on the quantum level of reality—the Implicate Order, you might say. I don't know if it constituted quantum foam or some undifferentiated potential, but whatever it was, it was worse than any shoggoth ever to emerge from a vat. A shoggoth was at least organic matter as they knew it."

"So why did they deface the images?"

"Don't interrupt!" I said hotly. "They didn't. They didn't know how to depict this new quantum matter in two dimensions, never mind three. It was utterly undimensioned, defying representation. But the Carver did his level best to represent what our senses and theirs might consider static."

That started to sink in.

"So what is it?" Kim asked thickly. "What have we loosed on the world?"

"Matter. Energy. Sentient weather. All three. Look, maybe we can't categorize it. The point is that several containers opened simultaneously and these things are out hunting Cthulhu spawn."

"But there are no Cthulhu spawn in this era."

"Exactly. So they are going after anything they come in contact with, the way an unleashed pit bull will attack everything in its path."

"We can't stop this," Kim said dully, her eyes going into shock. "We don't have the tools, the technology."

"We can warn the world," I pointed out.

Kim seemed to snap out of it momentarily. Her eyes refocused. She gave her golden curls a defiant toss.

"The C-130 is on the way. Get yourself organized."

"I have to file a report to my HQ. Washington needs to know ASAP."

"We go through channels here."

"I have my orders, too," I flung back.

She grabbed the only laptop and threw it to the ground. That settled that. It was probably the most thoughtlessly destructive act ever performed by a human being. But I didn't know that then.

The C-130 lumbered down and pancaked on the terrain. Doors were flung open and we piled aboard. The take-off was rougher, but the pilot was a solid professional. He got the big howling bird off the ice.

In the air, we settled into netting seats on either side of the cargo bay. Kim and I ignored one another. I itched to reach out to the Director. Time enough to do that at McMurdo Station.

Not an hour into our flight, I began getting a headache. I get them from doing my work, so I attributed it to one of those balloon-headed post-psychic pressure skullbusters.

Then I started tasting static. I don't know how I knew it was static, but I could taste it on my tongue. It tasted electronic. Don't ask me to explain that either.

I went to the pilot compartment door and asked, "Getting any static over the radio?"

"A little."

"Expect more." I don't know why I said that, but the words came out of my mouth of their own volition. I do that sometimes.

Back in my seat, I tried to meditate my headache away. It got worse instead. I kept getting right-temporal lobe images of static while the bitter taste on my tongue grew metallic.

I waited. Maybe the cold feeling in my stomach pit meant only danger. But it felt like death. I could only wait. I continued to receive mixed sensory impressions I couldn't process.

From up ahead, the pilot called back, "Prepare for landing!"

The big aircraft began its descent. I checked my cellphone. No reception. Of course. I felt an overwhelming urge to call HQ anyway. That wasn't good.

The pilot was talking to the tower and his voice grew excited. "Say again, McMurdo?"

But McMurdo Station did not respond.

The co-pilot gave a yell. "What in hell is that!"

I shot out of my seat to see. Kim was right behind me. She screamed.

Whatever it was, it had hit the station like a staticky snow squall. It was not invisible. It was not anything. There was no color to it. It impacted the human retina like a distortion, or vibrational anomaly. And I realized that the Carver had done an excellent job of depicting it.

It was a kind of swirl of semi-apprehendable energy, entirely foreign to the Earth. It coruscated over McMurdo Sound Station, and like an alien storm seemed to turn into a precipitate, suggesting snow or sleet. To call it unearthly was to minimize it.

The ground snow began melting. No! *Disintegrating.* Building roofs sublimed into nothingness. Side walls lost clarity, molecular coherence, atomic cohesion, became unglued. Tiny human figures popped out of existence like soap bubbles.

Oblivious to Kim's shrill chanting that it was all my fault, I watched as the fabric of reality that had been a sprawling scientific outpost dissolved back into the unitary quantum matrix from which it had arose.

Then we were hurtling into the leading edge of the storm that was beyond our comprehension and my skull filled with sensory impressions that overwhelmed my quailing brain. My vision clouded over with a screen of snarling *static.*

With an ugly sizzling hiss, the C-130 began to come apart in a way that suggested dissolution, not disintegration. I would have run, but where was there to run *to?* We were in the thick of the anomaly.

Under the roaring static filling my ears, I could hear the others' death screams. But I felt strange, detached and separate from it all. I would never place my call.

Suddenly all sound cut out. I couldn't breathe. My lungs felt like dead wings.

In my final flash of clairaudient knowledge, I understood: the hell-storm was devouring everything that was real and earthly—even oxygen....

There's a tradition among working mediums that human souls, facing imminent death, will eject from their bodies, leaving their mortal soon-to-be remains to face death unoccupied.

I had no such luck. The static devoured every atom, molecule and sub-atomic particle of my be—

Into the Black

William Meikle

I don't expect you to believe all of what I have to tell you—after all, I'm not even sure I believe it myself. But what follows here is as true and accurate an attempt at some kind of clarity as I can muster. Whether it is enough to deter you from the course of action you seem hell bent on following, only you can decide. Know this—I intend to be as distant from that dashed place as is humanly possible if and when you make a fresh expedition there.

You already know why we were there, so I shall gloss over the basics and get to the pertinent part. Our problems began a month after drilling started. Hodgson's new screw bit worked superbly, and we were growing increasingly confident that the latest British Expedition was going to go down in history as the one which finally pierced the secrets which lay hidden under the ice on the Antarctic Shelf. We passed the four hundred yards depth and kept going straight on, setting a new drilling depth record in the process. But there was no time for celebration just then. We were men on a mission—a mission of discovery.

Indeed, that morning brought a breakthrough we had not foreseen, for we thought that our drilling might come to an abrupt end when we hit bedrock, so I was most surprised when I stood over the drill head and heard a distinct gurgling in the shaft, coming up from the depths. The drill's fixtures rattled and shook, and I urged the others to retreat a safe distance, but in the end it was all rather anti-climactic as there was merely a small burp leaving a puddle of water, already starting to freeze, for six feet around the shaft.

We hurried to collect what samples we could before the cold could take its toll, but I was dismayed to find on getting them back inside to the lab that much of it was just so much crushed ice and slushy water. My dismay was fortunately short lived, and a quick look under the microscope soon had me excited again—for there was clearly life on the slide I had prepared, life brought up from the depths where it had lain for ages too long to comprehend. I saw diatoms and algae, amoebae and hydra, a veritable profusion of microscopic life, such things as had never been thought possible in such a harsh environment. And as the water heated up under the light stage of the microscope, so things began to get more frantic under the slide. Frenzy and fights for survival replaced the torpor of the deeps; a long awaited spring was sprung.

And that was when I caught my first glimpse of the thing.

It was so tiny at first that I took it for a mere speck of mineral brought up with the water, too small to allow me to make out any features even under the scope's highest magnification. But it quickly became apparent that, although it was small, it was moving under its own volition—it was, in some sense, alive. Even as I watched it the mote made its way swiftly across my field of view, moving with what seemed like singular intent, embedding itself deep inside a spinning Volvox colony. The result was startling and immediate. The colony went from green to black in an instant, the individual cells subsumed into a smooth-surfaced oily globe that spun slowly and glistened in the faintest rainbow aura.

I had to look twice to make sure it was still there, for I could not quite bring myself to believe what I had just witnessed. But there was one fact of which I was certain—I currently had something completely unknown to modern science under my microscope, and much as I could hardly take my eyes off it, I had to tell someone—anyone. I left the lab and went out into the corridor. Hodgson was there, stowing his outside gear in his locker.

"Quick, man—you have to see this—you won't believe what we've found."

I was gone for less than thirty seconds, barely enough time for Hodgson to close his locker and follow me back into the lab. The black stuff had been busy in my absence. The slide, the light stage and an area some six inches in diameter around the base of the microscope was now coated, black and oily and glistening, giving off the same faint shimmering rainbow aura I had seen through the lens. I instinctively started to back away but Hodgson wasn't quite so quick—perhaps it was because he was unused to laboratory procedures, perhaps it was no more than simple curiosity—or perhaps the glazed look I thought I saw in his eyes had a more disturbing cause. The last was something I only thought about much later, but whatever the case, Hodgson had stepped over to the microscope before I had time to stop him. He put a hand on the counter some ten inches to one side of the scope as he bent over to have a closer look. The black stuff flowed, smoothly, like Mercury across glass, and engulfed the hand before he had a chance to pull it away. Hodgson turned towards me—the glazed look had gone, if it had indeed ever been there, to be replaced by confusion.

"What in blazes is this?" he said. Those were his last words—the black stuff surged up his body—I can describe it no other way, and was over his mouth and nose before he took another breath. Hodgson made a grab for the counter, missed and pulled the microscope with him as he fell to the floor, his heels drumming twice on the linoleum then going still. Black stuff foamed and bubbled in his mouth for a long second—then vanished down his throat.

It was only then I remembered my training, and instinct took over. I backed out the door, slammed and locked it, and hit the emergency alarm by my left hand. John Greer arrived twenty seconds later. He was just in time to see what the black did to poor Hodgson.

It was almost like watching a speeded up film of a body turning to corruption—his chest caved in under his clothing, and his skin, what we could see of it, writhed and swelled as if infested by a small army of burrowing insects. Then the black came out, oozing like diseased sweat, small beads at first, then rivulets that tore at flesh, rendering it into so much mincemeat before running to the linoleum. It spread tendrils, moving faster than if it had been a mere spillage of liquid—moving purposefully, as if looking for something else on which to feed. What had mere seconds ago been a pinprick was now pints—perhaps even a gallon—of oozing, pitch black, fluidity.

"Freeze it. Do it now," Greer said softly.

"But Hodgson…"

"Is gone and you know it. Freeze it, before it's too late."

Our purge procedure was a simple one. I pushed the button, and heard a hiss as the liquid nitrogen was released. The viewing window in the door fogged up for a second, and I had a moment of panic, stepping back quickly and checking at my feet, for I was sure that the black had made its way under the door. But there was only an increasing blast of cold, and when the window cleared it showed a dark mass of mangled flesh and frozen tissue.

It had been my best friend mere minutes before.

Carruthers called for an immediate meeting in the mess, and spent the first five minutes trying to apportion blame before Greer marched him back through to the window in the laboratory door. After he'd had a long look through the window Carruthers was less worried about any possible scandal and more focussed on the more immediate problem at hand. His first question inadvertently echoed Hodgson's own last words.

"What in blazes is it?"

It was directed at me—indeed, as resident biologist, it was my job to know. But I was completely at a loss to explain either what I had seen under the scope, or what had happened to Hodgson. My ignorance only served to irritate Carruthers further.

"I suppose we'll have to stop drilling," he said, as if that was some kind of disaster in and of itself.

"Only if you want to stay alive," Greer piped up sardonically. "And I'd suggest closing off the shaft too, just to be on the safe side."

"But that will lose us days—weeks," Carruthers blustered.

"Would you rather lose another man?" I said softly, and he had the good grace to blush, and back down.

Matters went more smoothly after that. Greer and I closed and capped the shaft, taking care to watch out for any trace of blackness in the crushed ice underfoot. When we went back inside it was to find the remaining three geologists—Williams, Jackson and Boyle—crowded at the laboratory window to see for themselves what the fuss was about.

"Where's Carruthers?" Greer asked.

"On the blower, calling it in," Williams replied, not taking his gaze from the scene on the other side of the door. "Will we be recalled do you think?"

"Most likely," Greer replied. "A cock up of this magnitude is going to take some explaining."

"And what about Hodgson?" Boyle asked. "We can't leave him lying in there like that. It ain't Christian."

"I don't think that stuff gives a shit," Greer replied, and without another word headed off towards the mess.

I followed, and found him breaking open a bottle of J&B. It seemed like a bloody good idea to join him. We had a drink for Hodgson, one thing led to another, and by the time the evening darkness came round I was feeling little pain and was more than a bit drunk. Carruthers popped his head in at one point, but obviously realized we were not in the mood to be chastised and left us to it.

After the whisky was gone, Greer suggested making a start on the vodka, but by then I was more than ready to slip into oblivion and forget that the day had ever happened. I left Greer there in the mess—he'd already started with two fingers of the Russian falling down water—and made a careful way back to my bunk. I didn't bother taking off my clothes—the effort was beyond me by that point in any case. I put my head down, closed my eyes to stop my head spinning, and made a dive for the darkness.

But oblivion would not have me. Almost as soon as I fell asleep I dreamed.

My head swam, and it seemed as if the walls of my room melted and ran. The light bulb above me receded into a great distance until it was little more than a pinpoint in a blanket of darkness, and I was alone, in a vast cathedral of emptiness where nothing existed save the dark and a pounding beat from below.

I danced.

Shapes moved beside me in the dark, black shadows with no substance, shadows that capered and whirled as the dance grew ever more frenetic and we joined, two, four, eight, sixteen, ever growing, ever doubling.

We grew. And we built, there in the dark, built in time with the dance.

There was stone, and ice, then there was just stone again, a vast plain of blocks given form and purpose by the rhythm. And still we danced, and still we built.

There was light.

Then there was dark—long dark, long and cold, and we forgot how to dance. We slept. We slept for a long, dark time.

And then there was light.

And the dancing started again.

I came to my senses slowly. I was upright, which in itself seemed unusual. And I was not in my bunk, but was instead standing outside the locked door of the laboratory. More worrying still, I had a hand on the lock, as if I was ready to push the door open and go inside.

The rhythm beat in my head again, and I felt the dance well up inside me, despite the fact that I was now most definitely awake. Something drew me forward, and I looked through the small window. The remains were still there on the floor—but they were no longer quite so frozen— the blackness bubbled and seethed, throwing up thin, snake-like tendrils to taste the air and thrash, as if in anticipation of a meal.

The beat grew stronger, more insistent, and my hand crept toward the lock again.

There was only one thing that stopped me—and even now I am not sure if it was but another part of my fever dream. The black tissue split and opened up a small fissure and a single, lidless eye, pale green and milky, stared out from the new fold in the protoplasm.

Once again my self-preservation instinct saved me—I hit the purge button before I even thought to do anything else, and the loud hiss as the nitrogen flooded the room did much to break whatever spell was laid on me. The door window misted and clouded and when it cleared I stared in at a frozen mess of tissue on the floor, and the beat, the dance, had stopped, for now at least.

I am not prone to sleepwalking—in fact I do not think I have ever done it—but then again, I had never seen my best friend die in front of my eyes either. I put my experience down to the stress of the day and the cumulative effect of the Scotch on top of that. I had to—it was the only way I knew to remain sane. I took myself back to bed, and this time, when my head hit the pillow it was to fall down into the blessed, dreamless, darkness I had sought earlier.

There was no dancing.

I woke at some point later, bleary eyed, in darkness, with the sound of the alarm ringing and heavy footsteps in the corridor outside the dorm. I roused myself—not as fast as I might have done, for I was sour in the stomach and slow in the head—and went to see what was going on.

The cause of the commotion was not hard to guess. The three geologists and Carruthers stood in the corridor. The laboratory door was open. There was no sign of any frozen tissue on the floor, no black fluid—and no Greer. We quickly ascertained that he wasn't anywhere on the base—and one of the powered sleds was gone.

When Carruthers asked for a volunteer to accompany him and go after Greer, I put my hand up right away. I am not making any claim to bravery or honor; I felt responsible, somehow—guilty even. There was the drink, and the dream and the invitation to dance, all jumbled up in my mind. And if I was jumbled, what defense could Greer have made, what with having taken the same amount of Scotch, and then some vodka on top? He had answered a call that was meant for me.

At least that's how I rationalized it to myself, there in the mess. By the time I got suited up and went to meet Carruthers in the sled bay I wasn't feeling quite so bold, but the decision had been made, there was no backing out now—and Greer was getting further away by the minute.

If he was even still Greer.

I put that thought away. Had I let it take root, and paused to think what might have happened to the black, and what manner of thing was out there riding the sled, I might not have been able to leave at all. I might have instead returned to the mess in search of what was left of the vodka and some real oblivion.

Instead I focussed on the task at hand. Boyle handed me a rucksack as I made sure the sled had plenty of fuel for what might turn out to be a long trek.

"Soup, coffee and sandwiches. You'll need them. And make sure you come back. It's starting to feel bloody lonely around here."

I put on my goggles, pulled the parka hood over my face, and kicked the sled into gear, following Carruthers out onto the plain.

Greer's sled was not hard to follow. The twin track led in a straight line away from the base. I had thought the black might have made a run for the coast, but it was clear that whoever—or whatever—was driving had only one goal in mind; they were headed straight for the tall mountain range some twenty miles to the south. As far as I knew the terrain in that direction was *terra-incognito*—no one had surveyed there, no one had mapped; the mountains were considered too harsh an environment and too barren to yield much of scientific value.

So why would Greer—or even the black—want to go there?

It was a question I had plenty of time to ponder for the chase was going to be a long one—I tried to peer into the distance, tried to catch any glimpse of our quarry, but the summer glare on the ice was too strong, even through the goggles.

At least the journey was not arduous in itself—the plain swept up in a gentle incline toward the mountain foothills, and the ice was crisp and even over soft snow. Our sleds navigated it with little difficulty, and Carruthers, in the lead, kept up a good pace as if determined to hunt Greer down.

There was only one other item to note during that long morning out on the ice. Just as we arrived at the spot where the climb became steeper and the tracks we followed led higher toward a mountain pass, we found something half-embedded in the snow, discarded in the black's flight.

I stopped beside Carruthers's sled as he tore the find, already frozen, from the ground and held it up for me to see. It was a pair of long johns, the kind we all wore under everything else, the kind we kept on, even when sleeping. The ones Carruthers held up were torn and tattered— and bloodied, the red mixed with streaks of something darker, something black.

"Be careful, Carruthers," I said, but he didn't need to be told twice. He dropped the torn undergarments to the ice—but not before showing me the nametag stitched into the lining at the waist. They had belonged to Greer—and he was now out on the open ice, headed into the mountains, without their protection.

It was harder going after that—both because of the increasing incline and accompanying frigidity, and the growing feeling of doom that threatened to overwhelm me entirely. I was more than ever convinced that what we were chasing had little or nothing of Greer left in it, for what man would voluntary speed so readily toward a certain death in these precipitous canyons?

The walls of rock—so sheer that no snow would cling to them, climbed high around us, and fell away below us in places. We crossed up and through a series of narrow valleys, many of which could not have seen even a hint of the sun for many a long year, as we traveled single file for long stretches along narrow ledges above drops that fell away, down into stygian depths.

Carruthers stopped at a long, curved corner, forcing me to do the same. He got off his sled and waved me forward.

"Have we caught him?" I asked.

"Not yet," Carruthers replied, and there was something in his voice and manner that gave me pause. Then I followed his gaze and saw why we had stopped.

The cliffs that surrounded us might once have been natural formations, but they had obviously been worked extensively into a series of caves that ran like honeycomb across, down and up the rock faces in intricate, bewildering patterns. I saw spirals and ellipses, funnels and cones, and other geometries too strange to be understood let alone described. Each cave was taller than a man, and wider by far, smoothly hewn by some machinery I could not begin to fathom. The workings stretched off down into the gloom as far as we could see, an unimaginable number.

"What the blazes have we here?" Carruthers whispered. "Who could have done something like this? Is it something the Egyptians might have managed do you think?"

I wasn't thinking of *who*—I was thinking of *what*, and remembering my febrile dreams of the night before.

Two, four, eight, sixteen, ever growing, ever doubling.
We grew. And we built, there in the dark, built in time with the dance.
There was stone, and ice, then there was just stone again.

I believed I knew the answer to Carruthers's question—but there was little sense in telling him then, for although he was a man of great strengths, none of them came from his imagination or willingness to embrace things beyond his ken.

"Whoever built this marvel, they are long gone," I replied. "We must press on—the day is getting away from us. If we don't catch Greer soon, we will have to turn back."

On that matter at least Carruthers did agree with me, and after a rapid lunch of some soup and a sandwich we remounted the sleds, following Greer's tracks ever deeper into the mountain fastness.

We were almost at the point of no return as far as our fuel tanks were concerned when we rose up through one final pass and came to the entrance of a cave far larger than any we had seen previously. Greer's sled lay on one side, discarded at the entrance. There was no sign of the man—but footprints in the frost on the rock showed that he had got off the sled and, without pausing, headed into the cavern.

I was loath to follow. I was having a tough enough time as it was keeping the fear at bay while travelling in what passed for sunlight here in the mountains, and the thought of delving in the dark held no appeal whatsoever. Carruthers was made of sterner stuff—in this situation his lack of imagination was serving him well. Another of his strengths was forward planning—he took two head-mounted flashlights from his pack and passed one to me without a word.

"The batteries will last an hour if we're lucky. We go in, and if we don't find him in twenty minutes, we come out and head back—that gives us some margin for error. Agreed?"

I was more than willing to go along with that. I did however have a question—one that I had been pondering on the journey.

"And what do we do when we find him?"

"Persuade him to return with us, of course. He is clearly not himself."

I almost laughed aloud at that—my nerves were shot to pieces, and mania was not far from the surface. But when Carruthers headed toward the cavern mouth, I followed behind—I owed it to Greer to see this though—whatever the outcome might be.

It was even darker inside than my worst fears had imagined—colder too, a biting cold that settled quickly into every fiber of my being. We walked quickly, our lights picking out marks on the floor of the cavern that were sometimes footprints—and sometimes something else entirely. Five minutes after entering the cavern I noticed that this place, like the ones we had seen on the cliff path, had most definitely been manufactured—the walls were too smooth, too regular. And then there was the carved relief that seemed to cover every surface—pictorial representations of cities and war, natural disasters and calamity—millennia of history that we had to hurry past, leaving it unread, for the gait of the footprints on the floor had changed again. Whatever we followed now seemed to be going on all fours.

After another five minutes the path took a downward turn, and got markedly steeper such that we had to take great care not to go tumbling headlong into black depths.

"This is madness," Carruthers said after a stumble nearly sent us both flying. "We should turn back—if Greer wants to kill himself this badly, I suggest we leave him to it."

I was almost tempted to agree, and might even have done so—but then I felt it—a warmer breeze on my face. And accompanying it, somewhere not too far below us, the clear and unmistakable sound of feet slapping on rock.

Carruthers did not wait for me—he headed off in rapid pursuit, his headlamp bobbing away from me in the darkness. I knew that if I did not follow, I would forever after feel like a coward, but it took every ounce of bravery I could muster to make the first step downward.

The hot air on my face grew hotter still the further down we went, and a minute later I noticed that I did not need the headlamp—the cavern was filled with an all too familiar shimmering rainbow aurora that lit our passage down into ever warmer depths.

And so, finally, we came to it.

The passageway leveled off after a particularly steep final section, leading us out onto a vast cathedral-like space of vaulted rock, crystal stalactites and a long, wide expanse of what I at first took to be water, lying flat and black under a shimmering aura of dancing color.

Greer was already there, on the edge of the lakeshore—or at least, the thing that Greer had been. It was slumped and hunched, round-shouldered and more simian than man. It turned at the sound of our approach—and I saw that the man I knew was not completely gone, for his haunted eyes stared back at me from a strangely flattened face.

"Come on back, Greer," Carruthers said, although I noticed he had not taken any steps closer toward that black lake. "There are doctors who can take a look at you—chaps who can find a cure."

I wasn't so sure of that myself, but held my peace. Greer looked from one to the other of us. His mouth opened, as if he might speak, but all that came out was a rush of black fluid. Without another word he turned, took two steps, and fell face first toward the lake—which rose up to meet him as he fell, and swallowed him whole. It was not a lake as such—it was not water at all.

The whole vastness of the floor of the cavern was little more than a seething, roiling sheet of the black.

As Greer's body sank into it, a beat began, faint at first but growing ever stronger. I felt it tug at me, calling me to the dance.

I pulled Carruthers away.

"We need to leave. Now."

The rainbow colors swirled and danced in time to the rhythm.

I danced with them.

I can see it even now—all I have to do is close my eyes. I can see the pattern and design. They were made as builders you see, and they did indeed build. But they also danced, living and breathing, in their own way, dancing in time to a beat only they could hear. The rhythm from which they were born also gave them purpose, a beat that defined the dance from its very beginnings in the dark caverns under the mountains—and would ultimately, inexorably, lead the dance to its end.

I was lost to it, filled with it, awestruck by it.

And I might be there yet, dancing in that cavern with what was left of poor Greer, had Carruthers not slapped me, hard, on the face. I believe it was that singular lack of imagination of his that saved me in the end—might well have saved us both.

I followed, he led, and we raced up and away out of the depths, back up into the twilight through which we sped back to the base, reaching home just as the last of our fuel gave in.

The dance followed me all the way.

So there it is—my tale, for you to make of what you will. I only ask that you consider it carefully before you go back to those mountain passes. I know Carruthers has spoken to you of the workings, of the long history in the relief work, and of the wonders that lie there waiting to be explored. But that same lack of imagination that saved us is also the thing that might doom everyone.

For I still dance—it is in me even now, all these months and miles distant. And I have seen the pattern, the inexorable result of our building, our dancing. With each passing year the black creeps further in the deep cavern, and the dance strengthens and grows. We have danced since before life walked on land, and we will dance long after there is nothing else but the black and the rock. We will dance in the black as the moon falls into our arms, and when the sun dims and goes dark we will dance on, into the stars, black on black, until the very end, when all is black, all is the dance.

We will dance.

In Amundsen's Tent

John Martin Leahy

"Inside the tent, in a little bag, I left a letter, addressed to H.M the King, giving information of what he (sic) had accomplished . . . Besides this letter, I wrote a short epistle to Captain Scott, who, I assumed, would be the first to find the tent."
> Captain Amundsen:
> *The South Pole.*

"We have just arrived at this tent, 2 miles from our camp, therefore about 1–1½ miles from the pole. In the tent we find a record of five Norwegians having been here, as follows:
> Roald Amundsen
> Olav Olavson Bjaaland
> Hilmer Hanssen
> Sverre H. Hassel
> Oscar Wisting
> 10 Dec. 1911.

"Left a note to say I had visited the tent with companions."
Captain Scott: His Last Journal

"Travelers," says Richard A. Proctor, "are sometimes said to tell marvelous stories; but it is a noteworthy fact that, in nine cases out of ten, the marvelous stories of travelers have been confirmed."

Certainly no traveler ever set down a more marvelous story than that of Robert Drumgold. This record I am at last giving to the world in 192-, with my humble apologies to the spirit of the hapless explorer for withholding it so long. But the truth is that Eastman, Dahlstrom, and

I thought it the work of a mind deranged; little wonder, forsooth, if his mind had given way, what with the fearful sufferings which he had gone through and the horror of that fate which was closing in upon him.

What was it, that *thing* (if thing it was) which came to him, the sole survivor of the party which had reached the Southern Pole?

Yes, we thought that the mind of poor Robert Drumgold had given way, that the horror in Amundsen's tent and that thing which came to Drumgold there in his own—we thought all was madness only. Hence our suppression of this part of the Drumgold manuscript. We feared that the publication of so extraordinary a record might cast a cloud of doubt upon the real achievements of the Sutherland expedition.

But of late our ideas and beliefs have undergone a change that is nothing less than a metamorphosis. This metamorphosis, it is scarcely necessary to say, was due to the startling discoveries made in the region of the Southern Pole by the late Captain Stanley Livingstone, as confirmed and extended by the expedition conducted by Darwin Frontenac. Captain Livingstone we now learn, kept his real discovery, what with the doubts and derision which met him on his return to the world, a secret from every living soul but two—Darwin Frontenac and Bond McQuestion. It is but now, on the return of Frontenac, that we learn how truly wonderful and amazing were those discoveries made by the ill-starred captain. And yet, despite the success of the Frontenac expedition, it must be admitted that the mystery down there in the Antarctic is enhanced rather than dissipated. Darwin Fontenac and his companions saw much; but we know that there are things and beings down there that they did not see. The Antarctic—or, rather, part of it—has thus suddenly become the most interesting and certainly the most fearful place upon this interesting and fearful globe of ours.

So another marvelous story told—or, rather, only partly told—by a traveler has been confirmed. And here are Eastman and I preparing to go once more to the Antarctic to confirm, as we hope, another story— one eery and fearful as any ever conceived by any romanticist.

And to think that it was ourselves; Eastman, Dahlstrom, and I, who made the discovery.

How vividly it all rises before me again—the white expanse, glaring, blinding in the untampered light of the Antarctic sun; the dogs straining in the harness, the cases on the sleds long and black like coffins; our sudden halt as Eastman fetched up in his tracks, pointed and said, "Hello! What's that?"

A half-mile or so off to the left, some object broke the blinding white of the plain.

"*Nunatak*, I suppose," was my answer.

"Looks to me like a cairn or a tent," Dahlstrom said.

"How on Earth," I queried, "could a tent have got down here in 87°30' south? We are far from the route of either Amundsen or Scott."

"H'm," said Eastman, shoving his amber-colored glasses up onto his forehead that he might get a better look, "I wonder. Jupiter Ammon, Nels," he added, glancing at Dahlstrom, "I believe that you are right."

"It certainly," Dahlstrom nodded, "looks like a cairn or a tent to me. I don't think it's a *nunatak*."

"Well," said I, "it would not be difficult to put it to the proof."

"And that my hearties," exclaimed Eastman, "is just what we'll do! We'll soon see what it is—whether it is a cairn, a tent, or only a *nunatak*."

The next moment we were in motion, heading straight for that mysterious object there in the midst of the eternal desolation of snow and ice.

"Look there!" Eastman, who was leading the way, suddenly shouted. "See that? It *is* a tent!"

A few moments, and I saw that it was indeed so. But who had pitched it there? What were we to find within it?

I could never describe those thoughts and feelings which were ours as we approached that spot. The snow lay piled about the tent to a depth of four feet or more. Nearby a splintered ski protruded from the surface—and that was all.

And the stillness! The air, at the moment, was without the slightest movement. No sound but those made by our movements, and those of the dogs, and our own breathing, broke that awful silence of death.

"Poor devils!" said Eastman at last. "One thing, they certainly pitched their tent well."

The tent was supported by a single pole, set in the middle. To this pole three guy-lines were fastened, one of them as taut as the day its stake had been driven into the surface. But this was not all; a half-dozen lines, or more, were attached to the sides of the tent. There it stood, and had stood for we knew not how long, bidding defiance to the fierce winds of that terrible region.

Dahlstrom and I got each a spade and began to remove the snow. The entrance we found unfastened but completely blocked by a couple of provision-cases (empty) and a piece of canvas.

"How on Earth," I exclaimed, "did those things get into that position?"

"The wind," said Dahlstrom. "And, if the entrance had not been blocked, there wouldn't have been any tent here now; the wind would have split and destroyed it long ago."

"H'm," mused Eastman. "The wind did it, Nels—blocked the place like that? I wonder."

The next moment we had cleared the entrance. I thrust my head through the opening. Strangely enough, very little snow had drifted in. The tent was of a dark green color, a circumstance which rendered the light within somewhat weird and ghastly—or perhaps my imagination contributed not a little to that effect.

"What do you see, Bill?" asked Eastman. "What's inside?"

My answer was a cry, and the next instant I had sprung back from the entrance.

"What is it, Bill?" Eastman exclaimed. "Great heaven, what is it, man?"

"A head!" I told him.

"A head?"

"A human head!"

He and Dahlstrom stooped and peered in.

"What is the meaning of this?" Eastman cried. "A severed human head!"

Dahlstrom dashed a mittened hand across his eyes.

"Are we dreaming?" he exclaimed.

"'Tis no dream, Nels," returned our leader. "I wish to heaven it was. A head! A human head!"

"Is there nothing more?" I asked.

"Nothing. No body, not even a stripped bone—only that severed head. Could the dogs . . . ?"

"Yes?" queried Dahlstrom.

"Could the dogs have done this?"

"Dogs!" Dahlstrom said. "This is not the work of dogs."

We entered and stood looking down upon that grisly remnant of mortality.

"It wasn't dogs," said Dahlstrom.

"Not dogs?" Eastman queried. "What other explanation is there? Except—cannibalism."

Cannibalism! A shudder went through my heart. I may as well say at once, however, that our discovery of a good supply of pemmican and biscuit on the sled, at that moment completely hidden by the snow, was to show us that that fearful explanation was not the true one. The dogs! That was it, that was the explanation—even though what the victim himself had set down told us a very different story. Yes, the explorer had been set upon by his dogs and devoured. But there were things that militated against that theory. Why had the animals left that head—in the frozen eyes (they were blue eyes) and upon the frozen features of which was a look of horror that sends a shudder through my very soul even now? Why, the head did not have even the mark of a single fang, though it appeared to have been *chewed* from the trunk. Dahlstrom, however, was of the opinion that it had been *hacked* off.

And there, in the man's story, in the story of Robert Drumgold, we found another mystery—a mystery as insoluble (if it was true) as the presence here of his severed head. There the story was, scrawled in lead pencil across the pages of his journal. But what were we to make of a record—the concluding pages of it, that is—so strange and so dreadful?

But enough of this, of what we thought and of what we wondered. The journal itself lies before me, and I now proceed to set down the story of Robert Drumgold in his own words. Not a word, not a comma shall be deleted, inserted or changed.

Let it begin with his entry for January the 3rd, at the end of which day the little party was only fifteen miles (geographical) from the Pole.

Here it is:

JAN. 3.—Lat. of our camp 89°45'10". Only fifteen miles more, and the Pole is ours—unless Amundsen or Scott has beaten us to it, or both. But it will be ours just the same, even though the glory of discovery is found to be another's. What shall we find there?

All are in fine spirits. Even the dogs seem to know that this is the consummation of some great achievement. And a thing that is a mystery to us is the interest they have shown this day in the region before us. Did we halt, there they were gazing and gazing straight south and sometimes sniffing and sniffing. What does it mean?

Yes, in fine spirits all—dogs as well as we three men. Everything is auspicious. The weather for the last three days has been simply glorious. Not once, in this time, has the temperature been below minus 5. As I write this, the thermometer shows one degree above. The blue of the sky is like that of which painters dream, and, in that blue, tower cloud-formations, violet-tinged in the shadows, that are beautiful beyond all description. If it were possible to forget the fact that nothing stands between ourselves and a horrible death save the meager supply of food on the sleds, one could think he was in some fairyland—a glorious fairyland of white and blue and violet.

A fairyland? Why has that thought so often occurred to me? Why have I so often likened this desolate, terrible region to fairyland? Terrible? Yes, to human beings it is terrible—frightful beyond all words. But, though so unutterably terrible to men, it may not be so in reality. After all, are all things, even of this Earth of ours, to say nothing of the universe, made for man—this being (a godlike spirit in the body of a quasi-ape) who, set in the midst of wonders, leers and slavers in madness and hate and wallows in the muck of a thousand lusts? May there not be other beings—yes, even on this very Earth of ours—more wonderful—yes, and more terrible too—than he?

Heaven knows, more than once, in this desolation of snow and ice, have I seemed to feel their presence in the air about us—nameless entities, disembodied, *watching* things.

Little wonder, forsooth, that I have again and again thought of these strange words of one of America's greatest scientists, Alexander Winchell:

"*Nor is incorporated rational existence conditioned on warm blood, nor on any temperature which does not change the forms of matter of which the organism may be composed. There may be intelligences corporealized after some concept not involving the processes of ingestion, assimilation and reproduction. Such bodies would not require daily food and warmth. They might be lost in the abysses of the ocean, or laid upon a stormy cliff through the tempests of an arctic winter, or plunged in a volcano for a hundred years, and yet retain consciousness and thought.*"

All this Winchell tells us is conceivable, and he adds:

"*Bodies are merely the local fitting of intelligence to particular modification of universal matter and force.*"

And these entities, nameless things whose presence I seem to feel at times—are they benignant beings or things more fearful than even the madness of the human brain ever has fashioned?

But, then, I must stop this. If Sutherland or Travers were to read what I have set down here, he, *they* would think that I was losing my senses or would declare me already insane. And yet, as there is a heaven above us, it seems that I do actually believe that this frightful place knows the presence of beings other than ourselves and our dogs—things which we can not see but which are watching us.

Enough of this.

Only fifteen miles from the Pole. Now for a sleep and on to our goal in the morning. Morning! There is no morning here, but day unending. The sun now rides as high at midnight as he does at midday. Of course, there is a change in his altitude, but it is so slight as to be imperceptible without an instrument.

But the Pole! Tomorrow the Pole! What will we find there? Only an unbroken expanse of White, or . . . ?

JAN. 4.—The mystery and horror of this day—oh, how could I ever set that down? Sometimes, so fearful were those hours through which we have just passed, I even find myself wondering if it wasn't all only a dream. A dream! I would to heaven that it had been a dream! As for the end—there, there. I must keep such thoughts out of my head.

Got under way at an early hour. Weather more wondrous than ever. Sky an azure that would have sent a painter into ecstasies. Cloud-formations indescribably beautiful and grand. The going, however, was pretty difficult. The place a great plain stretching away with a monotonous uniformity of surface as far as the eye could reach. A plain never trod by human foot before? At length, when our dead reckoning showed that we were drawing near to the Pole, we had the answer to that. Then it was that the keen eyes of Travers detected some object rising above the blinding white of the snow.

On the instant Sutherland had thrust his amber glasses up onto his forehead and had his binoculars to his eyes.

"Cairn!" he exclaimed, and his voice sounded hollow and very strange. "A cairn or a—*tent*. Boys, they have beaten us to the Pole!"

He handed the glasses to Travers and leaned, as though a sudden weariness had settled upon him, against the provision-cases on his sled.

"Forestalled!" said he. "Forestalled!"

I felt very sorry for our leader in those, his moments of terrible disappointment, but for the life of me I did not know what to say. And so I said nothing.

At that moment a cloud concealed the sun; and the place where we stood was suddenly involved in a gloom that was deep and awful. So sudden and pronounced, indeed, was the change that we gazed about us with curious and wondering looks. Far off to the right and to the left, the plain blazed white and blinding. Soon, however, the last gleam of sunshine had vanished from off it. I raised my look up to the heavens. Here and there edges of cloud were touched as though with the light of wrathful golden fire. Even then, however, that light was fading. A few minutes, and the last angry gleam of the sun had vanished. The gloom seemed to deepen about us every moment. A curious haze was concealing the blue expanse of the sky overhead. There was not the slightest movement in the gloomy and weird atmosphere. The silence was heavy, awful, the silence of the abode of utter desolation and of death.

"What on Earth are we in for now?" said Travers.

Sutherland moved from his sled and stood gazing about into the eery gloom.

"Queer change, this!" said he. "It would have delighted the heart of Dore."

"It means a blizzard, most likely," I observed. "Hadn't we better make camp before it strikes us? No telling what a blizzard may be like in this awful spot."

"Blizzard?" said Sutherland. "I don't think it means a blizzard, Bob. No telling, though. Mighty queer change, certainly. And how different the place looks now, in this strange gloom! It is surely weird and terrible—that is, it certainly *looks* weird and terrible."

He turned his look to Travers.

"Well, Bill," he asked, "what did you make of it?"

He waved a hand in the direction of that mysterious object the sight of which had so suddenly brought us to a halt. I say in the direction of the object, for the thing itself was no longer to be seen.

"I believe it is a tent," Travers told him.

"Well," said our leader, "we can soon find out what it is—cairn or tent, for one or the other it must certainly be."

The next instant the heavy, awful silence was broken by the sharp crack of his whip. "Mush on, you poor brutes!" he cried. "On we go to see what is over there. Here we are at the South Pole. Let us see who has beaten us to it."

But the dogs didn't want to go on, which did not surprise me at all, because, for some time now, they had been showing signs of some strange, inexplicable uneasiness. What had got into the creatures, anyway? For a time we puzzled over it; then we knew, though the explanation was still an utter mystery to us. They were afraid. Afraid? An inadequate word, indeed. It was fear, stark, terrible, that had entered the poor brutes. But whence had come this inexplicable fear? That also we soon knew. The thing they feared, whatever it was, was in that very direction in which we were headed!

A cairn, a tent? What did this thing mean?

"What on Earth is the matter with the critters?" exclaimed Travers. "Can it be that . . . ?"

"It's for us to find out what it means," said Sutherland.

Again we got in motion. The place was still involved in that strange, weird gloom. The silence was still that awful-silence of desolation and of death.

Slowly but steadily we moved forward, urging on the reluctant, fearful animals with our whips.

At last Sutherland, who was leading, cried out that he saw it. He halted, peering forward into the gloom, and we urged our teams up alongside his.

"It must be a tent," he said.

And a tent we found it to be—a small one supported by a single bamboo and well guyed in all directions. Made of drab-colored gabardine. To the top of the tentpole another had been lashed. From this, motionless in the still air, hung the remains of a small Norwegian flag and, underneath it, a pennant with the word "Fram" upon it. Amundsen's tent!

What should we find inside it? And what was the meaning of that—*the strange way it bulged out on one side?*

The entrance was securely laced. The tent, it was certain, had been here for a year, all through the long Antarctic night; and yet, to our astonishment, but little snow was piled up about it, and most of this was drift. The explanation of this must, I suppose, be that, before the air currents have reached the Pole, almost all the snow has been deposited from them.

For some minutes we just stood there, and many, and some of them dreadful enough, were the thoughts that came and went. Through the long Antarctic night! What strange things this tent could tell us had it been vouchsafed the power of words! But strange things it might tell us, nevertheless. For what was that inside, making the tent bulge out in so unaccountable a manner? I moved forward to feel of it there with my mittened hand, but, for some reason that I can not explain, I of a sudden drew back. At that instant one of the dogs whined—the sound so strange and the terror of the animal so unmistakable that I shuddered and felt a chill pass through my heart. Others of the dogs began to whine in that mysterious manner, and all shrank back cowering from the tent.

"What does it mean?" said Travers, his voice sunk almost to a whisper. "Look at them. It is as though they are imploring us to *keep away*."

"To keep away," echoed Sutherland, his look leaving the dogs and fixing itself once more on the tent.

"Their senses," said Travers, "are keener than ours. They already know what we can't know until we see it."

"See it!" Sutherland exclaimed. "I wonder. Boys, what are we going to see when we look into that tent? Poor fellows! They reached the Pole. But did they ever leave it? Are we going to find them in there dead?"

"Dead?" said Travers with a sudden start. "The dogs would never act that way if 'twas only a corpse inside. And, besides, if that theory was true, wouldn't the sleds be here to tell the story? Yet look around. The level uniformity of the place shows that no sled lies buried here."

"That is true," said our leader. "What *can* it mean? What *could* make the tent bulge out like that? Well, here is the mystery before us, and all we have to do is unlace the entrance and look inside to solve it."

He stepped to the entrance, followed by Travers and me, and began to unlace it. At that instant an icy current of air struck the place and the pennant above our heads flapped with a dull and ominous sound. One of the dogs, too, thrust his muzzle skyward, and a deep and long-drawn howl, sad, terrible as that of a lost soul, arose. And whilst the mournful, savage sound yet filled the air, a strange thing happened:

Through a sudden rent in that gloomy curtain of cloud, the sun sent a golden, awful light down upon the spot where we stood. It was but a shaft of light, only three or four hundred feet wide, though miles in length, and there we stood in the very middle of it, the plain on each side involved in that weird gloom, now denser and more eery than ever in contrast to that sword of golden fire which thus so suddenly had been flung down across the snow.

"Queer place this!" said Travers. "Just like a beam lying across a stage in a theater."

Travers' simile was a most apposite one, more so than he perhaps ever dreamed himself. That place was a stage, our light the wrathful fire of the Antarctic sun, ourselves the actors in a scene stranger than any ever beheld in the mimic world.

For some moments, so strange was it all, we stood there looking about us in wonder and perhaps each one of us in not a little secret awe.

"Queer place, all right!" said Sutherland. "But . . ."

He laughed a hollow, sardonic laugh. Up above, the pennant flapped and flapped again, the sound of it hollow and ghostly. Again rose the long-drawn, mournful, fiercely sad howl of the wolf-dog.

"But," added our leader, "we don't want to be imagining things, you know."

"Of course not," said Travers.

"Of course not," I echoed.

A little space, and the entrance was open and Sutherland had thrust head and shoulders through it.

I don't know how long it was that he stood there like that. Perhaps it was only a few seconds, but to Travers and me it seemed rather long.

"What is it?" Travers exclaimed at last. "What do you see?"

The answer was a scream—oh, the horror of that sound I can never forget!—and Sutherland came staggering back and, I believe, would have fallen had we not sprung and caught him.

"What is it?" cried Travers. "In God's name, Sutherland, what did you see?"

Sutherland beat the side of his head with his hand, and his look was wild and horrible·.

"What is it?" I exclaimed. "*What* did you see in there?"

"I can't tell you—I can't! Oh, oh, I wish that I had never seen it! Don't look! Boys, don't look into that tent—unless you are prepared to welcome madness, or worse."

"What gibberish is this?" Travers demanded, gazing at our leader in utter astonishment. "Come, come, man! Buck up. Get a grip on yourself. Let's have an end to this nonsense. Why should the sight of a dead man, or dead men, affect you in this mad fashion?"

"*Dead* men?"

Sutherland laughed, the sound wild, maniacal.

"Dead men? If 'twas only that! Is this the South Pole? Is this Earth, or are we in a nightmare on some other planet?"

"For heaven's sake," cried Travers, "come out of it! What's got into you? Don't let your nerves go like this."

"A dead man?" queried our leader, peering into the face of Travers. "You think I saw a dead man? I wish it was only a dead man. Thank God, you two didn't look!"

On the instant Travers had turned.

"Well," said he, "I *am going* to look!"

But Sutherland cried out, screamed, sprang after him and tried to drag him back.

"It would mean horror and perhaps madness!" cried Sutherland. "Look at me. Do you want to be like me?"

"No!" Travers returned. "But I am going to see what is in that tent."

He struggled to break free, but Sutherland clung to him in a frenzy of madness.

"Help me, Bob!" Sutherland cried. "Hold him back, or we'll all go insane."

But I did not help him to hold Travers back, for, of course, 'twas my belief that Sutherland himself was insane. Nor did Sutherland hold Travers. With a sudden wrench, Travers was free. The next instant he had thrust head and shoulders through the entrance of the tent.

Sutherland groaned and watched him with eyes full of unutterable horror.

I moved toward the entrance, but Sutherland flung himself at me with such violence that I was sent over into the snow. I sprang to my feet full of anger and amazement.

"What the hell," I cried, "is the matter with you, anyway? Have you gone crazy?"

The answer was a groan, horrible beyond all words of man, but that sound did not come from Sutherland. I turned. Travers was staggering away from the entrance, a hand pressed over his face, sounds that I could never describe breaking from deep in his throat. Sutherland, as the man came staggering up to him, thrust forth an arm and touched Travers lightly on the shoulder. The effect was instantaneous and frightful. Travers sprang aside as though a serpent had struck at him, screamed and screamed yet again.

"There, there!" said Sutherland gently. "I told you not to do it. I tried to make you understand, but—but you thought that I was mad."

"It can't belong to Earth!" moaned Travers.

"No," said Sutherland. "That horror was never born on this planet of ours. And the inhabitants of Earth, though they do not know it, can thank God Almighty for that."

"But it is *here!*" Travers exclaimed. "How did it come to this awful place? And where did it come from?"

"Well," consoled Sutherland, "it is dead—it must be dead."

"Dead? How do we know that it is dead? And don't forget this: it didn't come here alone!"

Sutherland started. At that moment the sunlight vanished, and everything was once more involved in gloom.

"What do you mean?" Sutherland asked. "Not alone? How do you know that it did not come alone?"

"Why, it is there *inside* the tent; but the entrance was laced—from the *outside!*"

"Fool, fool that I am!" cried Sutherland a little fiercely. "Why didn't I think of that? Not alone! Of course it was not alone!"

He gazed about into the gloom, and I knew the nameless fear and horror that chilled him to the very heart, for they chilled me to my own.

Of a sudden arose again that mournful, savage howl of the wolf-dog. We three men started as though 'twas the voice of some ghoul from hell's most dreadful corner.

"Shut up, you brute!" gritted Travers. "Shut up, or I'll brain you!"

Whether it was Travers' threat or not, I do not know; but that howl sank, ceased almost on the instant. Again the silence of desolation of death lay upon the spot. But above the tent the pennant stirred and rustled, the sound of it, I thought, like the slithering of some repulsive serpent.

"What did you see in there?" I asked them.

"Bob—Bob," said Sutherland, "don't ask us that."

"The thing itself," said I, turning, "can't be any worse that this mystery and nightmare of imagination."

But the two of them threw themselves before me and barred my way. "No!" said Sutherland firmly. "You must not look into that tent, Bob. You must not see that—that—I don't know what to call it. Trust us; believe us, Bob! 'Tis for your sake that we say that you must not do it. We, Travers and I, can never be the same men again—the brains, the *souls* of us can never be what they were before *we saw that!*"

"Very well," I acquiesced. "I can't help saying, though, that the whole thing seems to me like the dream of a madman."

"That," said Sutherland, "is a small matter indeed. Insane? Believe that it is the dream of a madman. Believe that we are insane. Believe that you are insane yourself. Believe anything that you like. Only *don't look!*"

"Very well," I told them. "I won't look. I give in. You two have made a coward of me."

"A coward?" said Sutherland. "Don't talk nonsense, Bob. There are some things that a man should never know; there are some things that a man should never see; that horror there in Amundsen's tent is—*both!*"

"But you said that it is dead."

Travers groaned. Sutherland laughed a little wildly.

"Trust us," said the latter; "believe us, Bob. 'Tis for your sake, not for our own. For that is too late now. We have seen it, and you have not."

For some minutes we stood there by that tent; in that weird gloom, then turned to leave the cursed spot. I said that undoubtedly Amundsen had left some records inside, that possibly Scott, too, had reached the Pole and visited the tent, and that we ought to secure any such mementos. Sutherland and Travers nodded, but each declared that he would not put his head through that entrance again for all the wealth of Ormus and of Ind—or words to that effect. We must, they said, get away from the awful place—get back to the world of men with our fearful message.

"You won't tell me what you saw," I said, "and yet you want to get back so that you can tell it to the world."

"We aren't going to tell the world what we *saw*," answered Sutherland. "In the first place, we couldn't and in the second place, if we could, not a living soul would believe us. But we can *warn* people, for that thing in there did not come alone. Where is the other one—or the others?"

"Dead, too, let us hope!" I exclaimed.

"Amen!" said Sutherland. "But maybe, as Bill says, it isn't dead. Probably . . ."

Sutherland paused and a wild indescribable look came into his eyes. "Maybe it—*can't die!*"

"Probably," said I nonchalantly, yet with secret disgust and with poignant sorrow.

What was the use? What good would it do to try to reason with a couple of madmen? Yes, we must get away from this spot, or they would have me insane, too. And the long road back? Could we ever make it now? And what *had* they seen? What unimaginable horror was there behind that thin wall of gabardine? Well, whatever it was, it was real. Of that I could not entertain the slightest doubt. Real? Real enough to wreck, virtually instantaneously, the strong brains of two strong men. But—but were my poor companions really mad, after all?

"Or maybe," Sutherland was saying, "the other one, or the others, went back to Venus or Mars or Sirius or Algol, or hell itself, or wherever they came from, to get more of their kind. If that is so, heaven have pity' on poor humanity! *And*, if it or they are still here on Earth, then sooner or later—it may be a dozen years, it may be a century—but sooner or later the world will know it, know it to its wo and to its horror. For they, if living, or if gone for others, will come again."

"I was thinking . . ." began Travers, his eyes fixed on the tent.

"Yes?" Sutherland queried.

"That," Travers told him, "it might be a good plan to empty the rifle into that thing. Maybe it isn't dead; maybe it can't die—maybe it only *changes*. Probably it is just hibernating, so, to speak."

"If so," I laughed, "it will probably hibernate till doomsday."

But neither one of my companions laughed.

"Or," said Travers, "it may be a demon, a ghost *materialized*. I can't say incarnated."

"A ghost materialized!" I exclaimed. "Well, may not every man or woman be just that? Heaven knows, many a one acts like a demon or a fiend incarnate."

"They may be," nodded Sutherland. "But that hypothesis doesn't help us any here."

"I may help things some," said Travers, starting toward his sled.

A moment or two, and he had got out the rifle.

"I thought," said he, "that nothing could ever take me back to that entrance. But the hope that I may . . ."

Sutherland groaned.

"It isn't Earthly, Bill," he said hoarsely. "It's a nightmare. I think we had better go now."

Travers was going—straight toward the tent.

"Come back, Bill!" groaned Sutherland. "Come back! Let us go while we can."

But Travers did not come back.

Slowly he moved forward, rifle thrust out before him, finger on the trigger. He reached the tent, hesitated a moment, then thrust the rifle-barrel through. As fast as he could work trigger and lever, he emptied the weapon into the tent into that horror inside it.

He whirled and came back as though in fear the tent was about to spew forth behind him all the legions of foulest hell.

What was that? The blood seemed to freeze in my veins and heart as there arose from out the tent a sound—a sound low and throbbing—a sound that no man ever had heard on Earth—one that I hope no man will ever hear again.

A panic, a madness seized upon us, upon men and dogs alike, and away we fled from that cursed place.

The sound ceased. But again we heard it. It was more fearful, more unearthly, soul-maddening, hellish than before.

"Look!" cried Sutherland. "Oh, my God, *look at that!*"

The tent was barely visible now. A moment or two, and the curtain of gloom would conceal it. At first I could not imagine what had made Sutherland cry out like that. Then I saw it, in that very moment before the gloom hid it from view. The tent was *moving!* It swayed, jerked like some shapeless monster in the throes of death, like some nameless thing seen in the horror of nightmare or limned on the brain of utter madness itself.

And that is what happened there; that is what we saw. I have set it down at some length and to the best of my ability under the truly awful circumstances in which I am placed. In these hastily scrawled pages is recorded an experience that, I believe, is not surpassed by the wildest to be found in the pages of the most imaginative romanticist. Whether the record is destined ever to reach the world, ever to be scanned by the eye of another—only the future can answer that.

I will try to hope for the best. I can not blink the fact, however, that things are pretty bad for us. It is not only this sinister, nameless mystery from which we are fleeing—though heaven knows that is horrible enough—but it is the minds of my companions. And, added to that, is the fear for my own. But there, I must get myself in hand. After all, as Sutherland said, I didn't see it. I must not give way. We must somehow get our story to the world, though we may have for our reward only the mockery of the world's unbelief, its scoffing—the world, against which is now moving, gathering, a menace more dreadful than any that ever moved in the fevered brain of any prophet of wo and blood and disaster.

We are a dozen miles or so from the Pole now. In that mad dash away from that tent of horror, lost our bearings and for a time, I fear, went panicky. The strange, eery gloom denser than ever. Then came a fall of fine snow-crystals, which rendered things worse than ever. Just when about to give up in despair, chanced upon one of our beacons. This gave us our bearings, and we pressed on to this spot.

Travers has just thrust his head into the tent to tell us that he is sure he saw something moving! This must be looked into.

(If Robert Drumgold could only have left as full a record of those days which followed as he had of that fearful 4th of January! No man can ever know what the three explorers went through in their struggle to escape that doom from which there was no escape, a doom the mystery and horror of which perhaps surpass in gruesomeness what the most dreadful Gothic imagination ever conceived in its utterest abandonment to delirium and madness.)

JAN. 5—Travers had seen something, for we, the three of us, saw it again today. Was it that horror, that thing not of Earth, which they saw in Amundsen's tent? We don't know what it is. All we know is that it is something that *moves*. God have pity on us all—and on every man and woman and child on Earth if this thing is what we fear! ·

6th.—Made 25 mi. today. But that must have been imagination. Effect on dogs most terrible. Poor brutes! It is as horrible to them as it is to us. Sometimes I think even more. Why is it following us?

7th.—Two of dogs gone this morning. One or another of us on guard all "night." Nothing seen, not a sound heard, but the animals have vanished. Did they desert us? We say that is what happened, but each man of us knows that none of us believes it. Made 18 mi. Fear that Travers is going mad.

8th.—Travers gone! He took the watch last night at 12, relieving Sutherland. That was the last seen of Travers—the last that we shall ever see. No tracks—not a sign in the snow. Travers, poor Travers, gone! Who will be the next?

JAN. 9.—*Saw it again!* Why does it let us see it like this—sometimes? Is it that horror in Amundsen's tent? Sutherland declares that it is not—that it is something even more hellish. But then S. is mad now—mad—mad—mad. If I wasn't sane, I could think that it all was only imagination. *But I saw it!*

JAN. 11.—Think it is the 11th but not sure. I can no longer be sure of anything—save that I am alone and that it is watching me. It is always watching. And some time it will come and get me—as it got Travers and Sutherland and half of the dogs.

Yes, today must be the 11th. For it was yesterday—surely it was only yesterday—that it took Sutherland. I didn't see it take him, for a fog had come up, and Sutherland—he would go on in the fog—was so slow in following that the vapor hid him from view. At last when he didn't come, I went back. But S. was gone—man, dogs, sled, everything was gone. Poor Sutherland! But then he was mad. Probably that was why it took him. Has it spared me because I am yet sane? S. had the rifle. Always he clung to that rifle—as though a bullet could save him from what we saw! My only weapon is an ax. But what good is an ax?

Jan. 13.—Maybe it is the 14th. I don't know. What does it matter? Saw it *three* times today. Each time it was closer. Dogs still now. That sound again. But I dare not look out. The ax.

Hours later. Can't write any more.

Silence. Voices—I seem to hear voices. But that sound again.

Coming nearer. At entrance now—now . . .

<h1 style="text-align:center">CONTRIBUTORS</h1>

Ken Asamatsu was born in 1956 in Sapporo, Hokkaido, graduating Toyo University to work at Kokusho Kankōkai, famous in Japan as the publisher of Lovecraft and many other works of horror and fantasy. Debut work as an author was *Makyo no gen'ei* (Echoes of Ancient Cults), in 1986. He continues to be active in a wide range of activities, including writing extensively in the weird historical and horror genres. While remaining extremely interested in the Cthulhu Mythos, lately he has been concentrating on weird historicals set in the Muromachi period (1333–1573). In 2005 was a candidate for the annual award of the Mystery Writers of Japan, Inc. in the short story genre, for his *Higashiyamadono oniwa* (Higashiyamadono Villa Garden). He has also made considerable contribution to Japanese fiction as an anthologist, proposing a number of collections successfully published in Japan. *The Lairs of the Hidden Gods*, which won high praise in the original Japanese, is now available from Kurodahan Press. His website is http://homepage3.nifty.com/uncle-dagon/

Glynn Owen Barrass lives in the North East of England and has been writing since late 2006. He has written over a hundred short stories, most of which have been published in the UK, USA, France, and Japan. He also edits anthologies for Chaosium's Call of Cthulhu fiction line, also writing material for their flagship roleplaying game. To date he has edited the collections *Eldritch Chrome*, *Steampunk Cthulhu*, and *Atomic Age Cthulhu*, for Chaosium, and *World War Cthulhu* for Dark Regions Press.

Pierre V. Comtois is a newspaper reporter writing from Lowell, MA who has been editing and publishing Fungi, the Magazine of Fantasy and Weird Fiction intermittently since 1984. Comtois' latest book, *Marvel Comics in the 1980s: An Issue by Issue Field Guide to a Pop Culture Phenomenon*, was published in 2015 by Twomorrows Pubs. Two earlier volumes, *Marvel Comics in the 1960s* and *1970s*, appeared in 2009 and 2011. In addition, Comtois has contributed fiction to many small press magazines over the years including *Haunts, The Horror Show, Thrilling Tales*, various magazines for Cryptic Publications and Rainfall Books, and e magazines *Planetary Stories* and *Liberty Island Magazine* and currently is a regular columnist for PJMedia.com. Comtois' fiction has also appeared in such collections as *Lin Carter's Anton Zarnak: Supernatural Sleuth, Eldritch Blue*, and Chaosium Books anthologies. The author has also written a number of books including novels such as *Strange Company* and *Sometimes a Warm Rain Falls*; non-fiction such as *Our Lives, Our Fortunes, Our Sacred Honor*; and short story collections such as *The Way the Future Was, The Portable Pierre V. Comtois*, and the forthcoming *Goat Mother and Others* from Mythos Books. For more information about the author, visit www.pierrev-comtois.com

Laurence J. Cornford is an Englishman who works in IT for the University of Sheffield, UK. A long time fan of Howard, Lovecraft and Smith, he started contributing illustrations to legendary fanzine *Dagon* in the 1980s. His short stories have been published in various fanzines and books, including: *Perfect Timing* (1998); *The Sorcerer's Apprentices* (1998); *Cthulhu Codex* (1998); and *The Book Of Eibon* (2002); *Lost Worlds Of Space and Time* (both volumes, 2004, 2005). He has also written essays, RPG material and the occassional poem.

Steven Gilberts has been producing fine art since 1981. In 1995 he began displaying his work at science fiction and fantasy conventions. In 2003 Steven made the jump into professional horror illustration starting with *Space and Time Magazine*. Steven and his lovely wife Becky live in a spooky Queen Ann cottage in a small Dunwich-esk village in Indiana. While hiding from the townsfolk, he concocts odd covers and interiors for the small press industry. His work can be seen on the world wide web at StevenGilberts.com

Cody Goodfellow has written five novels—his latest is Repo Shark (Broken River Books)—and co-written three more with New York Times bestselling author John Skipp. He received the Wonderland Book Award twice for his short fiction collections, *Silent Weapons*

For Quiet Wars and *All-Monster Action* (both Swallowdown Press). His third collection, *Strategies Against Nature* (King Shot Press), is out now. He wrote, co-produced and scored the short Lovecraftian hygiene film *Stay At Home Dad*, which can be viewed on YouTube. He is also a managing director of the H.P. Lovecraft Film Festival–Los Angeles and cofounder and editor at Perilous Press, a micro-publisher of modern cosmic horror.

CJ Henderson created both the Jack Hagee hardboiled PI series and the Teddy London supernatural detective series. He also authored *The Encyclopedia of Science Fiction Movies*, several score novels, hundreds of short stories, and thousands of non-fiction pieces. In the wonderful world of comics he wrote everything from Batman and the Punisher to Archie and Cherry Poptart.

John Martin Leahy (1886–1967) was an American author apparently active only during the 1920s. He has three known longer works: *The Living Death*, a serialized sf novel that appeared in Science and Invention, and two serialized novels published in *Weird Tales*: *Draconda* and *Drome*. He published only four short stories, all in Weird Tales, of which this is justly the most famous.

Edward Lipsett is an American-born immigrant to Japan who has made his living as a translator there since some time in the prior century. He hopes some day to make his living translating interesting books and stories instead of commercial material.

William Meikle is a Scottish writer, now living in Canada, with twenty novels published in the genre press and over 300 short story credits in thirteen countries. He has recent novels and novellas published by the likes of Dark Regions Press, DarkFuse and Dark Renaissance. He lives in Newfoundland with whales, bald eagles and icebergs for company. When he's not writing he plays guitar, drinks beer, and dreams of fortune and glory. He can be reached via his website at http://www.williammeikle.com/

Edward Morris Edward Morris is a 2011 nominee for the Pushcart Prize in Literature, also nominated for the 2009 Rhysling Award and the 2005 British Science Fiction Association Award. He has over 120 short stories under his belt, including works sold to the *Lovecraft Ezine*, the *Starry Wisdom Library*, Scott R. Jones' *Resonators* (Martian Migraine Press) and Celaeno Press' *In the Court of* *the Yellow King*. He lives and works in Portland, Oregon as a writer, bouncer and soon-to-be Graduate English student.

Will Murray is a lifelong New Englander who has contributed to numerous fanzines devoted to HPL, as well as a growing number of Cthulhu Mythos prose anthologies. As one of the three founding members of the fundraising group that placed the memorial plaque dedicated to H. P. Lovecraft on the grounds of the John Hay Library on the occasion of the Providence author's centennial in 1990, Murray is both pleased and proud to be working in HPL's fictitious milieu. The author of over sixty novels, he currently writes the Wild Adventures of Doc Savage for Altus Press, which will also publish his first Tarzan novel later in 2015. He created the legendary mutant superhero, Squirrel Girl, with the equally legendary Steve Ditko, for Marvel Comics.

Robert M. Price, a fan of H.P. Lovecraft since the Lancer paperback collections of 1967 appeared, began writing scholarly articles and humorous pieces on HPL and the Cthulhu Mythos in 1981. His celebrated semi-pro zine *Crypt of Cthulhu* began as a quarterly fanzine for the Esoteric Order of Dagon Amateur Press Association in 1981 and made it to 109 issues. In 1990 he began editing Mythos anthologies for Fedogan & Bremer and Chaosium, Inc. and still does! His fiction has been collected in *Blasphemies and Revelations*.

Joseph S. Pulver, Sr., is the author of the novels *The Orphan Palace* and *Nightmare's Disciple*, and he has written many short stories that have appeared in magazines and anthologies, including *Weird Fiction Review, Lovecraft eZine*, Ellen Datlow's *Best Horror of the Year*, S. T. Joshi's *Black Wings* (I and III), *Book of Cthulhu, The Children of Old Leech*, and *Year's Best Weird Fiction*. His highly–acclaimed short story collections, *Blood Will Have Its Season, SIN & ashes*, and *Portraits of Ruin*, were published by Hippocampus Press. He edited *A Season in Carcosa* and the Bram Stoker nominated and Shirley Jackson Award winning *The Grimscribe's Puppets*. He has two new collections of weird fiction upcoming, *A House of Hollow Wounds*, and *The Protocols of Ugliness*, both edited by Jeffrey Thomas. Joe is currently editing several new anthologies, including *Cassilda's Song, The Leaves of a Necronomicon*, and *Born Under A Bad Sign*.

Stephen Mark Rainey is author of the novels *Balak, The Lebo Coven*,

Dark Shadows: Dreams of the Dark (with Elizabeth Massie), *Blue Devil Island*, *The Nightmare Frontier*, and *The Monarchs*; five short story collections; over 100 published works of short fiction; and several Dark Shadows audio productions, which feature members of the original ABC-TV series cast. For ten years, Mark edited the award-winning *Deathrealm* magazine and has edited several anthologies, including *Deathrealms*, *Son of Cthulhu*, and *Evermore*. He is an avid geocacher, which frequently takes him to fascinating places – many of them quite creepy. Mark lives in Greensboro, NC. Visit him on the web at www.stephenmarkrainey.com

Pete Rawlik has been collecting Lovecraftian fiction for forty years. In 2011 he decided to take his hobby of writing more seriously. He has since published more than twenty-five Lovecraftian stories and the novel *Reanimators*, a labor of love about life, death and the un-dead in Arkham during the early twentieth century. A sequel, *The Weird Company* was released in the fall of 2014. He lives in Royal Palm Beach, Florida, with his wife and three children. Despite the rumors he is not now and never has been a resident of Kingsport.

Brian M. Sammons is an author, editor, critic, and Managing Editor of Dark Regions Press' Weird Fiction line. His stories have appeared in the books: *Horrors Beyond, Dead but Dreaming 2, and Horror for the Holidays* and in the magazines: *Dark Discoveries, Nightland*, and *Bare Bone*. To date he has edited 10 anthologies including *Undead & Unbound, Dark Rites of Cthulhu, Eldritch Chrome, Edge of Sundown*, and *World War Cthulhu*. He has also written extensively for the Call of Cthulhu role-playing game and has been a reviewer/critic for twenty years. You can follow Brian on Twitter @BrianMSammons

In the Court of the Yellow King

Winner of two 2014 Occult Detective Awards:

Best Short Story

Best Short Story–Swords and Sorceries

Featuring stories by:

Glynn Owen Barrass
Tim Curran
Cody Goodfellow
T.E. Grau
Laurel Halbany
C.J. Henderson
Gary McMahon
William Meikle
Christine Morgan
Edward Morris
Robert M. Price
W.H. Pugmire
Stephen Mark Rainey
Pete Rawlik
Brian M. Sammons
Lucy Snyder
Greg Stolze
Jeffrey Thomas

Edited by Glynn Owen Barrass

CelaenoPress.com

AVAILABLE FROM PETE RAWLIK AND NIGHT SHADE BOOKS

Lovecraft enthusiast Pete Rawlik reveals a dark side of Herbert West, a story that's never been told.

Dr. Stuart Hartwell, a colleague, contemporary, and the greatest rival of West, sets out to destroy him by uncovering the secrets of his terrible experiments, only to become what he initially despised: a reanimator of the dead. From the grisly battlefields of the Great War to the haunted coasts of Dunwich and Innsmouth, from the halls of fabled Miskatonic University to the sinking of the Titanic, their unholy quests leave their mark upon the world — and create monsters of them both.

$14.99 trade paperback
978-1-59780-478-3

Rawlik returns, crafting a superteam of Lovecraftian proportions… monsters to fight monsters.

Dr. Hartwell teams up with a witch, a changeling, a mad scientist, and a poet trapped in the form of a beast. Their adventures rage across the globe, from the mountains and long-forgotten caves of Antarctica to the dimly lit backstreets of Innsmouth that still hold terrifying secrets. Unholy creatures released upon the world must be stopped. And only the weird company stands in their way. Lovecraft expert Pete Rawlik takes some of the most well-known H.P. Lovecraft creations to tell a true Frankenstein's monster of a story.

$15.99 trade paperback
978-1-59780-232-1

AVAILABLE FROM
NIGHT SHADE BOOKS

**Nearly thirty tales of tentacles, te
ror, and madness paying tribute
Lovecraft's Cthulhu mythos.**

Anthologist Ross E. Lockhart h
delved deep into the Cthulhu cano
selecting twenty-seven sanity-shatterin
stories of cosmic terror. Featuring fi
tion by many of today's masters of tl
menacing, macabre, and monstrous, i
cluding Laird Barron, Caitlín R. Kierna
Cherie Priest, and Thomas Ligotti, *T
Book of Cthulhu* goes where no colle
tion of Cthulhu mythos tales has go
before: to the very edge of madness.
and beyond!

$15.99 trade paperback
978-1-59780-232-1

**Over twenty more mind-shatterin
tales set within the Cthulu mythos.**
Anthologist Ross E. Lockhart div
back into the Cthulhu canon, combi
through moldering tomes to bring y
The Book of Cthulhu II, with even mo
tales of tentacles, terror, and madne
Featuring stories by many of weird fi
tion's brightest lights including: N
Gaiman, Laird Barron, Cody Goodf
low, Michael Chabon, and many other

$15.99 trade paperback
978-1-59780-435-6

www.ingramcontent.com/pod-product-compliance
Lightning Source LLC
Chambersburg PA
CBHW020129310726

48970CB00006B/1791